The Tortured Detective

PIRATE IRWIN

© Pirate Irwin 2014

Pirate Irwin has asserted his rights under the Copyright, Design and Patents Act, 1988, to be identified as the author of this work.

First published by Endeavour Press Ltd in 2014.

Second edition published by Sharpe Books in 2018.

This edition published by Pirate Irwin in 2019.

Dedicated to a vibrant and elegant French lady Florence, an inspiration for so many things

"There is no such thing as white or black there is just grey;"
Francois Mitterrand

PROLOGUE

I am dying. There is no point anyone coming to my aid for I feel the life ebbing out of me, the bullet is lodged inside me and I can feel the bile and blood rising to my mouth.

I'm done for and I want to use these few moments remaining to express myself, regrets and joy at the life I have lived. Sadly though not to an age that I would have liked to have lived to. But hell, at some point or other, we all end up in the same sodding ground, just another name on a headstone and good business for all those undertakers and others who profit from death.

However, if you are thinking that amidst these final thoughts of mine that I will reveal who shot me, then you will be disappointed.

That, readers, is for the police, the Gestapo or others to discover, for I have other matters to deal with. Such as how did it come to this that I, one of France's finest up and coming acting talents, should end up lying dying on a sofa and without having achieved the superstar status that was due to be met? The country – nay the world of cinema – has been robbed of my star quality and my legacy aged just 31 will be but a dozen films.

It's so unfair. But then there will be those who will rejoice that I, Marguerite Suchet, has been murdered, the tart that spread her legs for a German enemy and profited by immortalizing herself on screen.

That they cannot destroy.

For my enemies may have this small victory but it is they who are losing the war and by taking the life of an unarmed and harmless actress they do nothing to enhance their claims of righting the wrong done to them by an invader.

They fight for some previously unknown unremarkable General, de Gaulle! A man who like many of his rank betrayed his country, his people and either deserted their troops or fled to our other accursed neighbour across the water, England.

There he hides behind the petticoats of those fine ladies of England and every so often spouts rubbish on the radio exhorting those he left behind to their fate to rise up and return France to its former glory!

Fine words indeed, but I believe that mine uttered on screen have had a bigger effect on raising the morale of ordinary French men and women even if they have come in films produced by Germans under the Continental Films mantle.

So what, we are actors and actresses and our job is to entertain, to give life to words, to give people an exit from the mundane lives they live even if it is just for an hour or so. And yet here I am, having given so much pleasure to those of my compatriots who live in fear and occupied by a largely humourless nation, lying on my sofa gasping for breath, one of which will be my last, although I will not know it till it arrives, and having to explain myself for my actions.

For behind every crime, they say, there is a reason or a motive, and the detectives will be looking for that to make it easier to solve this latest murder.

Not the brightest of sparks detectives these days, those who were more intelligent were also too independent for the new regime and thus have been advised to seek employment elsewhere.

A nice euphemism for your career is at an end and unless there is a remarkable turnaround in the war, you might as well kill yourselves.

Oh well, I might as well prepare for a rather long and drawn out process of determining who my killer is but that is what they are paid for, and no doubt if they find themselves stuck for a culprit there are always plenty of Jews or other such *Untermenschen* – as the Germans charmingly refer to those they despise – to pin it on.

Anyway, I digress and with so little time left to me I must hurry and relate as to why or how I came to such a violent end.

The bullet has thankfully not touched my spine for I can turn my neck and I have feeling in my legs so I can look at the photographs displayed on my mantelpiece and on the tables beside the sofa.

They are a mix of better times and some ultimately unhappy liaisons, but I have always been one not to hide the bad from the good and in every affair there are happy moments to be recalled and not to be discarded like an old handkerchief.

But there is one photograph that for me reflects the unhappy circumstances I find myself in now. There is me of course, slightly off center – which is rather annoying – dining at Maxim's after the première of my finest performance in 'Les Femmes qui chassent les Hommes'.

No, not a tale of nymphomaniac women but a group of responsible ladies, who have no time for the men of their village lying around doing nothing after the defeat and through a mixture

THE TORTURED DETECTIVE

of cajoling and calling on their last vestiges of pride get them to offer their services to the Nazis to go and work in Germany so that German men can be liberated to fight for their country.

It got rave reviews as you can imagine from both inside the Reich and here in France. 'Suchet is without doubt the Arletty of the next generation' wrote Robert Brasillach in his outstanding publication 'Je suis partout'.

No less a figure than Pierre Drieu la Rochelle wrote a personal letter to me declaring his admiration for my ability to transfer the message to the slothful French male worker and also cheekily asked me out for dinner. I took him up on that offer but more of that later if I have the chance.

So there I am, off center as I said in the photo, but then understandably so because also in the shot are Otto Abetz, the German Ambassador, and his French wife, as well as the Count and Countess de Chambrun, parents of Vichy Prime Minister Pierre Laval's son–in–law, and my beau, my dearest, dearest love, Colonel Karl von Dirlinger.

Oh so handsome, so cultured and so much the antithesis of the Nazi brute that is portrayed outside of France and the Reich!

Indeed I look more Aryan than he does, me with my blonde hair, in braids that evening, my green blue eyes and my firm jaw and he with his rather louche look, dark hair, brown eyes and slightly feminine mouth. But so capable and able to turn his hand to anything. A former actor and Grand Prix driver turned spy for the Abwehr, the least indoctrinated of all of Hitler's military services and run by the sphinx–like Admiral Canaris.

"Quite some performance Marguerite, one that will be revered and talked about for generations to come," I recall Abetz saying.

"Why thank you Ambassador, it was a most exhausting but rewarding experience and I certainly hope notwithstanding personal rewards that it will have the desired impact on my compatriots to get off their bums and do the right thing," I replied.

"Quite, quite," interjected Countess de Chambrun, an imposing lady with a deep voice and not easy to understand with her American accent. But she was well worth getting along with, not only because of her link to Laval but also because she was related to Theodore Roosevelt and the present American president Franklin.

"You must call on us at the American Hospital too and visit with the wounded French soldiers. It would give them a huge fillip to see someone of your stature caring for their welfare," piped up the Count, who was descended from one of the great French heroes the Marquis de La Fayette, who had helped the Americans free themselves from British tyranny.

"Thank you Count, I would be honoured to perform such a service for you and for those Frenchmen who, through no fault of their own, were conned into defending their country against Germany and whilst their officers fled, they suffered appallingly."

All nodded at my wise words, Karl patting my knee tenderly.

I remember Karl being uncommonly silent that night at dinner, preoccupied by something that he obviously felt better about keeping to himself, or at least in front of the others, and not spoiling my moment of glory.

However, it was when he took me home and we had a nightcap in my drawing room, my last resting place as it turns out, that he unburdened himself to me.

"Margot," he said addressing me by the affectionate first name he preferred using when alone with me, "there is something terrible I have learnt which directly affects you and which I feel compelled to tell you."

I was rather taken aback, my life seemed so uncomplicated and my career such a roaring success that I couldn't think of anything that could possibly impinge on the happiness I was feeling.

"It's regarding a piece of intelligence I received a day ago about Pierre," he said in rather a severe tone.

Christ Pierre or rather Pierre–Yves de Chastelain, known as Pierre to his intimates, my former lover – or rather fiancé, one of Paris's most flamboyant and successful young lawyers. He had been generously allowed to continue his career despite becoming progressively more and more radical in his views on the Nazis and the Vichy Government in the two years since they came to power.

He had certainly become too radical for my comfort and realizing what damage this could do to my career and not being one for lost causes, I abruptly broke off our engagement and discarded him.

Hence my enthusiasm for acting in such films as 'Les Femmes qui chassent les Hommes', such projects served to enhance my fervent belief in the powers that be. Pierre had let it be known in no uncertain terms his disgust and disdain for my behaviour, but then what could he do about it? He was powerless.

I wasn't one of his clients in the dock, I was protected from up high and with Karl as my lover doubly so.

"Pierre? What about him? I have no contact with him, indeed not for a long time now," I said, though I was lying as I had had a discreet lunch with him in his apartment only two days before, after he implored me to.

Needless to say it hadn't gone very well, he had tried to persuade me to boycott the premiere and to return to him. As you can tell, I rejected him on both fronts, but now I was nervous that Karl had been apprised of this by a spy covertly observing Pierre's apartment which was in Rue Monsieur Le Prince in the 6th arrondissement, near the Sorbonne, on the left bank.

"Listen Margot, I know you had lunch with him, he told me himself and told me what it was about, so the fact you have lied to me I will let slide," Karl said smiling.

"He told you? How on earth did you manage to persuade him to talk to you, the enemy?" I asked in a steady tone.

"Let's just say we share some common ground, and it isn't just with regard to you!" he replied laughing – rather nervously I thought.

"Anyway, it's not what he said that is of interest but what I have since learnt with regard to his own safety. Karl Oberg, the brutish head of the SS in Paris and its equally thuggish affiliates, wants him badly, and up to now he has been thwarted by me and by several influential French people, who shall remain nameless, as well as to a certain degree by Abetz, for reasons I do not know.

"However, Oberg believes he has enough information – true or not it won't matter if he gets hold of him – to arrest him. A sympathetic soul at the French police headquarters supplied me with this nugget because Oberg doesn't trust me.

"Anyway, that goon and his buffoons have instructed René Bousquet to entrust his arrest to his most trusted lieutenants as it has to look like he has been plotting against Vichy. Keep it all nicely in house if you will. Bousquet, being the parvenu and puffed up peacock that he is, is only too willing to acquiesce.

"So Pierre is due to be picked up tomorrow when he arrives to defend Arnaud Lescarboura, your friend the jewel thief, at the Palais de Justice. Of course, all those noble members of the 'independent' press corps will be there to catch on camera his moment of humiliation."

Oh my God! I gasp, not then but now, my breathing is getting shorter and I can hear the rattle in my chest, it is heaving and I can all but feel myself suffocating.

No, God, please! not quite yet, let me have my say, for if there is to be a prosecution, I will not be present to give my version of events, for they are pertinent to this story. Good, thank you, the pain has eased ever so slightly and I can still, though my memory too appears to be shutting down, just remember enough.

"Christ Karl! This is awful. I mean I don't have any romantic attachment for him anymore, I love you, the person, not because you wear the uniform of the victor, but I still don't want any harm to come to him. Can't you intercede?" I pleaded.

He shook his head and replied: "No darling Margot, I have no power in the matter, I cannot let Oberg and Bousquet become aware I have a mole inside the French police department, for he is a card I need to hold back for the future. It is pointless phoning him because it will be tapped so there is only one solution and that is for you to warn him."

It was my turn to shake my head, it was impossible for me also and I didn't want to endanger myself just when everything had come right for me. The simple girl from the Lot region, who had fought for everything she had achieved. Well alright, a one night stand with Marcel Carné had helped get my foot on the ladder, but hell, everything else was my doing.

"How the hell do you expect me to warn him when there is a curfew in place and I have no transport or any way of getting to him? Besides how do you know he would even let me in as I have rejected him?"

He sighed and gave me a knowing look.

"Margot, you may lack sound political judgement and not be the brightest of girls but you are blessed with resourcefulness.

"Besides, thanks to Abetz, you have an Ausweis which allows you to travel even after the curfew. That is that out of the way. Now how you get there, well, taxi is the only option, and I am sure by chance you will find one when you exit your door," he smiled and winked at me conspiratorially.

I nodded and thought, well, there is enough on my conscience, and still having some feeling for Pierre, at least for his safety, I acquiesced. I was a little surprised at this turn of events but not being the most reflective of types, I didn't dwell on why Karl was so eager for Pierre to be forewarned, although I had a pretty good idea.

Thus it was that yes, there was a taxi miraculously waiting outside with a gruff looking driver, who turned out to be monosyllabic as I gabbled on in my nervous state.

He did manage one sentence lasting longer than two words to reassure me that he would wait for me, but I should not dally.

In that I was in full agreement, so I ran up the three flights of stairs to Pierre's beautiful apartment that he would have to leave behind him, come what may. He answered after the first ring of the bell, was genuinely surprised at me being there, looked furtively around and ushered me in.

His drawing room was tidy for him, though there were some dossiers flung over his sofa, so he directed me to one of the leather armchairs that were placed either side of his fireplace.

"I can't stay Pierre, I have just come to warn you that you need to go somewhere else, you are in danger," I said my voice trembling.

He stared at me, his blue eyes searching my face for any hint of betrayal, and then scratched his brow. I proceeded at great speed to relay to him the information I had gleaned from a conversation with a French admirer, preferring to keep Karl's name out of the story in case Pierre was to be picked up.

He smiled but his eyes did not.

"Thank you for this Marguerite. Now you can go," he said.

I was rather offended by his lack of gratitude, but not wishing to overstay my welcome and keen to return home to the comfort of Karl's embrace in my well–appointed apartment on Avenue Foch, I pecked him on the cheek, wished him well and left.

That was five days ago and the very least that can be said is that he took my warning seriously and went to ground. It wasn't just me who was relieved, Karl was as well, whilst poor old Lescarboura, my old friend the jewel thief, was left in abject despair as his great advocate failed to turn up and he received 10 years hard labour for his latest misdemeanor.

It was nothing compared to the fury of the Vichy authorities, who wanted to further ingratiate themselves with the Nazis. Their bird had flown, leaving Bousquet seething with arriviste rage and his German paymaster Oberg having to explain himself to his boss, the former chicken farmer and now head of the SS Heinrich Himmler – a man with little humour at the best of times. Well, I didn't cry for them.

Ah… so melodramatic I am, my parents always said that of me. They said me milking a cow was a theatrical performance in itself. Though they exaggerated somewhat in saying the geese and the ducks and the pigs wandered into the barn to watch me do it. Funny that, I wonder what would have befallen me had I just stayed on the farm in the dreary but safe environs of the Lot... Too late now old girl.

Ah, is that a siren I hear? I can hear steps on the stairs, is this help at hand? If it is, thanks, but no thanks, the flip of the coin has been delivered. I called tails and it came up heads, and I enter the unknown unwillingly but having at least been able to divest myself of my final thoughts. Of course, they are just for you, the reader. It is for the rather somber looking detective – another face from my past – standing over me to work it out for himself, and you are as incapable as me of helping him.

THE TORTURED DETECTIVE

CHAPTER ONE

Gaston Lafarge looked down at the stunning corpse lying tidily on the sofa and harrumphed several times in what for him was his way of taking in the scene and assessing what lay before his eyes.

He had been surprised to be called to the crime scene, as he never usually worked such chic areas as this, but his superior, Pierre Moreton, had that tone in his voice that signified he had been a special request for this particular murder.

Lafarge had survived the cull of the police force when the Germans had marched in, more owing to the fact he was idling his time away in a prisoner of war camp after being swept up in the remorseless march of the Nazis through France.

Thus he had reclaimed his previous job without too much trouble once he had been part of a release engineered by the Vichy Government in 1941, in exchange for sending several thousand of his compatriots to Germany to help their war effort.

Eighty POW's released for several thousand workers, it didn't take an intelligent man to work out who got the better end of the deal, but Lafarge was just grateful to have a job.

Still, Lafarge regretted that many of his old colleagues were no longer around. Most appeared to have vanished, probably, he mused, into the open arms of the resistance, who would be delighted to have recruits who already knew how to handle a gun.

Instead, in their place he had come across several who had been former colleagues and been reinstated after having been drummed out by the previous regime for a range of reasons, from petty crime to more serious offences.

Their interest in solving crimes, even when given a second chance, was to say the least, minimal. No, they were back doing what they knew best and that was shaking down anyone, from businesses to Jews, who remained and who thought a bribe here or there would ensure their safety. *Hah* to that, thought Lafarge, once their money runs out so will their insurance.

Thus with so little enthusiasm and honesty around it was no wonder that he had been called upon to this particular address and asked to solve the murder of Marguerite Suchet, actress by profession, athough for him, that was pushing it somewhat as a job description.

He had seen several of her films but really the idea she could be the future Arletty was so ludicrous that he had decided to boycott buying 'Je suis partout', which was edited by the brilliant homosexual cinema critic Brasillach.

While Lafarge had for a while put up with Brasillach's outrageous pro–Nazi and anti–Semitic views for the sake of the film reviews, now that they were losing their bite, he had decided they could afford to do without his subscription. Rumour had it that the Germans financed the publication in any case.

Anyway, that debate over her being the next Arletty was now over, for he was looking down at a very dead Suchet.

She was certainly beautiful, and whoever had killed her had taken great care to leave her looking at her best, thoughtful of him or her Lafarge reflected. She lay on the sofa, with her shoes off but tidily placed below her, with one leg hanging off the edge. She had, it looked like, been shot just the once in the chest, below her right breast, but that would be for the pathologist to decide on.

Lafarge bent down so he could take a closer look to see if there were any markings round her neck, but there were none, even when he lifted the silk scarf that covered it.

The victim herself had a peaceful look on her face, a slight smile almost on the edge of her lips. Her head was propped against the end of the sofa and her eyes were directed towards the table that was situated at the opposite end of the sofa.

The table had on it several photographs, a lamp, with oriental design going up the body of it, and an ashtray which had several butts in it.

Lafarge stroked his clean shaven jaw and walked over to the table, glanced at the photographs and poked around in the ashtray. There were six cigarettes, some with lipstick on them, others of a different brand with no lipstick.

The murderer? Perhaps thought Lafarge but let's not be hasty. The rest of the large drawing room was tidy, no signs of a struggle and there were two wine glasses on the mantelpiece. Strange, not on the respective tables by the sofa, he thought, and once again harrumphed and stroked his chin.

THE TORTURED DETECTIVE

Time for a cigarette, he thought, that will help me think it through as it used to in the old days and in the camp whenever I could scrounge one from the guards. Thinking and smoking at the same time, hmm two things that makes me unique from the morons I work with, he thought sourly.

That was why in general he preferred to work alone, though, Moreton objected but was more often than not slapped down by his superiors.

Fortunately they still believed that even though there was a war on, crime still flourished and needed to be solved from time to time. However, the fact that over 50 percent of crime was perpetrated by their own detectives didn't seem to concern them and those were certainly not the crimes that they wanted solved.

As for concerns that on his own Lafarge would not be able to handle suspects if they were reluctant to accompany him to the station, they were dispelled by the very size of the man.

He wasn't a giant but at six foot and a fit 13stone he had more than enough strength to cope with the nastiest and meanest on the streets. Something told him that whoever was responsible for this crime would not be one of those, more brain than brawn and evidently had at one point strong feelings or still did for the victim.

Crime of passion? Possibly. Political motive? Possibly too as she was well known for her relationship with the Abwehr officer but she would be the first such victim of the resistance for conducting such a 'treasonable' adventure with the enemy.

As for the crime of passion, well, he would have to talk to the present lover von Dirlinger obviously and then look at her past lovers. Easier for them if they were found guilty of a crime passionnel because even now, and despite the Nazis' lust for the death penalty, French courts still treated such crimes with a certain sympathy.

Thankfully we haven't surrendered everything to them, Lafarge thought. We're still standing there naked being fucked and laughed at by them but there are every so often moments of sanity.

"Can we take the corpse now?" asked the medic with a resigned and impatient tone which reminded Lafarge that Suchet's last deathbed scene had not just had him as the lone spectator. Lafarge grinned at the tired looking medic, who was probably working a 24 hour shift, and nodded his assent.

"Yes you can take her, not much I can do until I see her naked later," he replied dryly.

The medic summoned up somehow a tired laugh and motioned forward his helper, the ambulance driver, who looked as if he could also be dropped off at the morgue, and they lifted her as decorously and gently as they could onto the stretcher and carried her for the last time out of her apartment.

Lafarge eyed the large bloodstain that marked where she had bled out onto the silk covered sofa, the dark blue cloth on one of the cushions now like the last cry of a sunset as the dark embraced or ate up the red of the sun. Where, though, had she been shot for she had surely not been shot lying down?

Lafarge walked through the rest of the large apartment, having bagged the cigarette stubs just in case they were relevant, and having also done the same with the glasses to give to the fingerprint boys.

He had found little else of interest in the well–furnished drawingroom, which had no less than three sofas and six art deco style chairs with beside each one a delightful (if inappropriately named) mahogany shabby nightstand table, for they had only been on the market since 1940. He grimaced at the several nudes and pastoral scenes – a bit of a culture clash for Lafarge's taste – that adorned the pale blue wallpapered walls...

Avenue Foch was so wide that there was little chance that those living opposite would have been able to see anything going on in the apartment and in any case the pink curtains with a rose imprint were drawn.

The sparsely decorated kitchen – that is in terms of cooking utensils – looked like it hadn't been used apart from for fetching the ice and a bottle opener, though, in the fridge there was a can or two of foie gras, expensive stuff too and a tin of caviar, largely untouched.

Two bottles of champagne and a bottle of vodka were the only other inhabitants of the fridge, but reflected the expensive tastes of the victim.

Lafarge looked around him and seeing that the two uniforms from the neighbourhood were idling outside the front door availed himself of a glass of vodka. He puffed on another cigarette,

THE TORTURED DETECTIVE

downed a second glass of vodka, which was indeed high quality stuff, and proceeded to visit the other rooms.

The bathroom, was in contrast to the kitchen, well stocked with everything a beautiful youngish lady would want but yielded nothing of interest save that her lover liked to put pomade in his hair.

The huge bedroom, though, was full of intriguing clues. For her clothes were strewn all over the floor, polished wood surface covered by expensive looking rugs, and not in a manner that Lafarge thought had been done by her as she mulled over what to wear, for the attire she had been wearing was more daytime than night time.

No, this looked like either she, under pressure, or her murderer had rifled through the cupboards that were set against one wall, which was egg white in colour, and her drawers by her dressing table had been thrown onto the floor.

There was no suitcase on the double bed as if to suggest she had been preparing to pack for a trip, so that too discounted a desperate rummage through her clothes to pick what she required. No, this was definitely a search for something.

Then he noticed her several jewellery boxes, beautiful Chinese former opium containers, were also open with their contents spread over her dressing table. Difficult to tell if anything had been taken but he would ask her maid, for he imagined she had one given her status, and her lover too for he must have given her some jewels to keep her sweet.

It was only when he looked up from the jewels that he noticed it, taking a deep breath as he did so. There was blood on the mirror, splashed in several droplets.

The room was dimly light, hence his tardiness in noticing it. Lafarge got down on his hands and knees to look for any other clue of a struggle or a blood trail that would lead him back to the drawing room. However, apart from some blood on the carpet beneath the dressing table there was no trail.

He looked too to see if there was any sign of where the bullet had ended up, but again there was none and he surmised it must still be in the victim.

With a weary sigh he retraced the route back to the drawing room, and perused the photographs on the tables.

As her final position had been sitting upright staring at the table at the opposite end of the sofa where some photographs stood he had the wit to think that she, and not the murderer, had made the effort even in her weakened state to pull herself up so she could perhaps give a clue as to the identity of the killer.

Of course that was a long shot but Lafarge was willing to embrace any scenario if it could take him a step further down the line. He studied the photos, there was one of her with Otto Abetz, his wife, a couple he didn't recognize and another man.

There was one taken in the country with an elderly couple and there was one of her with a man he did recognize the celebrated lawyer Pierre–Yves de Chastelain.

He and Lafarge had crossed swords on more than one occasion before the war.

De Chastelain had this fault of some aristocrats that they felt guilty for their being born better off than most and the advantages that came with it like schooling, name, title and of course money.

Thus he had taken to defending those accused by the State and its apparatus, the police for example, of crimes. No matter the severity of the crime or the wealth of evidence assembled against the suspect, you could count on de Chastelain to be up for a fight, to allege brutality or that his client had been fitted up for the murder, robbery or rape.

Time and time again Lafarge, who rarely if ever bent the rules, had faced him in court and done his utmost to keep his temper as the advocate sought to needle him and to try and expose any weakness in his evidence.

He liked to think that it had never been personal between them, that he was just one in a long line of police officers who had been targeted by this bleeding heart liberal aristocrat. However, because he had got the better of de Chastelain on several occasions he sensed an increasing antagonism from him.

None more so than in a serial rape case where the defendant Jean Cartignon, a seemingly respectable 35–year–old accountant, had alleged that Lafarge had tried beating a confession out of him and when that failed had slept with one of the victims so as to coerce her into testifying that the guilty man was the man in the dock.

THE TORTURED DETECTIVE

All of it was sheer nonsense of course, although a bit of physical encouragement was not unusual and was generally permitted so long as the object of the attention didn't end up in hospital.

That he had slept with one of the victims was just risible. He liked women every bit as much as any fellow did but the thought that he was so desperate or so depraved as to strong arm a rape victim into bed was downright slander.

Needless to say de Chastelain had made good use of this in court playing to the gallery, and while the judge did not appreciate such theatrics, the spectators had, as had the press. With de Chastelain having drawn out his cross examination of Lafarge to the end of the day it allowed the press to feed off it.

'Defendant's lawyer puts dubious police methods under spotlight' read the headline in the right wing leaning 'Le Figaro'.

The left leaning L'Humanité – which had made so much out of the Dreyfus scandal at the turn of the century – reveled in the establishment's discomfit running a banner headline 'Rape case defendant's lawyer puts police on trial'.

Another a trashy far–right journal, normally a defender of the police, used it for its own political ends against the government at the time to say in an editorial: 'This disgraceful display of investigative ardour is reflective of the malaise at the heart of the Third Republic and is yet another reason why a full scale revolution is needed to infuse France with National Socialist principles and laws,' it trumpeted to no avail at the time.

De Chastelain, though, lost the case, for the other victims had held steady under examination whilst the woman accused of sleeping with Lafarge had not been permitted to testify.

That itself left Lafarge bitter against the lawyer, for he felt as if he too had emerged guilty from the case and now all three parties were reunited again several years later. Although Marguerite would not be able to have her day in court again, this time through no fault of her own.

Lafarge smiled grimly, pocketed the photos of the group out celebrating plus the one of de Chastelain and Marguerite, took a last sweep of the apartment, a final slug of the excellent vodka and bid a gruff goodnight to the two gendarmes positioned either side of the front door.

The thrill he had had of being handed his first murder case since returning from the camp had quickly died away. Instead it had been replaced by a deep anxiety that he was being set up and he would have to tread very carefully if he were not to end up in the same state as Marguerite.

CHAPTER TWO

Lafarge returned to Quai des Orfèvres, the solemn grey stone building which housed his department the Brigade Criminelle, and which adjoined the Palais de Justice where the major cases were heard.

For those who faced the possibility of the guillotine it was rather appropriate, he mused, that the building also housed the Conciergerie where Marie Antoinette among others had awaited the arrival of the tumbrel and their final journey.

Lafarge, though, had many other thoughts running through his mind, such as who had arranged for him to be the detective to handle the Suchet case, for unless the person was completely gaga or naïve they must have been aware of his connection to her, albeit events that had taken place seven years ago.

Like with her murder, he could envisage several different possibilities for his being called to the scene.

He tried to dismiss them from his mind as he settled down at his desk and started typing out his initial thoughts and concrete facts, of which there were not many, while awaiting the call from the pathologist to summon him for the autopsy.

On another piece of paper he jotted down in his elegant clear handwriting names of people he would wish to talk to.

The maid, whose name Mathilde Langlois had been furnished to him by one of the gendarmes who had done a canvas of the apartment block. The neighbours would have to be spoken to at greater length, though all professed ignorance at either hearing anything or having made the call alerting the police to a disturbance, as would the German lover of course and de Chastelain.

De Chastelain, though, would be a bit problematic for he had disappeared suddenly a few nights back, for reasons that were not altogether clear or at least whatever they were had not filtered down to Lafarge.

He had been rather pleased to hear the news but now, his pleasure was lessened by the fact the crusading lawyer was at the very least a person of interest to his case.

He hoped Moreton could enlighten him about the disappearing act and also aid him in having access to the Abwehr officer, for the Germans were especially touchy about French detectives interrogating one of their own.

He wasn't too sure that Moreton would have the balls to help him on the latter request but he would push him as hard as he could. Moreton was a decent bloke but he was no Horatio at the bridge when it came to fighting causes that could harm his rise up the ladder.

In the meantime, Lafarge was impatient to go home to his small but charming apartment on rue de la Roquette, near Père Lachaise, best known for its huge historic cemetery. Why not live near death when you deal with it almost every day, had been Lafarge's reasoning behind the decision to move there.

It was also not far from two great symbols of the France he had grown up to admire, revolutionary symbols in Place de la Bastille and Place de la République, but there was little in present day France of the equality, fraternity and liberty as espoused by the imperfect but idealistic heroes of a bygone age.

Lafarge sighed at that thought and calmed himself by lighting up another cigarette, breathed in deeply holding the delicious smoke inside his lungs for as long as he could and then exhaled. France might have lost and been occupied but for him, French tobacco retained its superiority over any other.

That thought cheered him up, and prompted him to spring into action and phone the pathologist to see if there would be an autopsy anytime soon because if not, he was going to go home.

"Frédéric? Lafarge here. Good, good, thank you and you? Excellent, how you remain in such good spirits with your daily routine leaves me with nothing but astonishment and respect.

"Quite, quite. Anyway Frédéric, I was just ringing to check whether the corpse that was brought in from Avenue Foch would be dealt with soon?"

Frédéric Durand, the pathologist, was a man who did not like to be hurried, tending to his subjects with almost adoring tenderness despite the intrusive nature of his work.

It was borne out of 25 years on the job, inspired by – perversely – his experiences on the World War I battlefields as a soldier. Seeing too many of his friends die, and their replacements too, had

THE TORTURED DETECTIVE

sparked in him a sentiment he preferred to be with the dead than the living for with them, there was no chance of feeling a sense of loss.

Regardless of his reason for becoming a pathologist, he had become a well–respected one and some people like Lafarge also appreciated his intense but respectful approach to the victims.

Many of Durand's colleagues were no better than butchers and as a result often missed crucial clues that could have yielded quicker resolution of the cases. Durand too had respect for Lafarge, he had also joined up for the latest military folly and been wounded for his pains. However, he was now back in charge of his area of expertise and as enthusiastic as ever.

"Ah yes, Marguerite Suchet. She is as beautiful in death as she was on the screen. Pity she never got to play Ophelia for she makes a convincing corpse," Durand joked darkly. "Well Lafarge it is what, 3 in the morning and I still have a few before her. But if you wish, for you I can push her to the head of the queue."

"Yes, she'd be ideal for a silent movie now," replied Lafarge, grinning at his riposte to Durand's remark.

"No, don't bother Frédéric. She isn't going anywhere whereas I still have a bed to go to and I need some sleep because I think come the dawn, there will be pressure on all sides to solve it as quickly as possible," replied Lafarge, relieved that he could go home with an easy conscience.

It was as he picked up his fedora that he saw the hand written note which confirmed his suspicions that this was a case the top brass wished to be kept abreast of and also if necessary to lean on him, should they feel the investigation was either going too slowly or he thought more likely in a direction they rather it didn't.

"Inspector Lafarge, please could you be at my office at 7 tomorrow morning. We need to discuss the murder of Marguerite Suchet. Regards. Commissaire Massu."

Lafarge sighed. He had been summoned for a face to face with the head of the Brigade Criminelle Georges–Victor Massu, which meant he would already have to have some answers for his boss when he turned up in a few hours.

He reached for the phone and dialed Durand again.

"Sorry Frédéric, better make Marguerite Suchet a priority, just received a summons from up high and it is as I suspected, they are

19

all over this one and I better be on my game if I am not to be their scapegoat."

Lafarge replaced the receiver, breathed in deeply and said: "Another sleepless night in paradise!"

CHAPTER THREE

"Ah! Lafarge. Good to see you, right on time too! Come in, come in!" said a smiling Massu as a rather weary and unshaven Lafarge appeared at the doorway to his sparsely–furnished office.

Lafarge grinned at his superior and took his seat opposite Massu, who had risen from his leather chair and indicated he should sit.

Massu, who was an impressive fit looking man of average height with an intelligent face and darting brown eyes – suitable, Lafarge thought, for a detective as if he was always looking and searching for the decisive clue – sat himself back down again, fidgeted with a folder in front of him, having poured Lafarge a large cup of black coffee and settled back all the time observing his subordinate.

Massu was not one for idle chit chat and with Lafarge he would say they had a businesslike relationship and a mutual respect for each other.

He was, to be honest, the best – well certainly the one with the most integrity – in his division. These days, though, integrity was not easy to judge, given the political circumstances, and all he asked was that his detectives conducted themselves with that quality, with respect to their police work.

He did not care to hear any political talk, either for or against the regime, be it the Nazis or Vichy, because for him his job was still, whether it be for a democratically–elected government or a dictatorship, to conduct oneself professionally as a policeman.

He knew Lafarge had been a prisoner of war but beyond that, he did not wish to know whether he harboured any political feelings that ran counter to those in power today. For him, Lafarge was a results man and for a case such as this he was ideal. However, he wanted to be straight with him, because while he had no doubts about his ability to carry out a thorough investigation, there were areas he could see that would be sensitive to their German confreres.

"So Lafarge, sorry for giving you a sleepless night, but I imagine you are as keen as I am to resolve this matter as quickly as possible," said Massu.

Lafarge nodded his assent but didn't profer any further comment.

"Thus I thought it would be useful to have a chat before you get going fully on the case, define the borders if you will," said Massu.

"That would be useful, sir," said Lafarge, unwilling to add any more until Massu had outlined the parameters of what was in play and what was out of bounds.

Massu absent mindedly swept his right hand through his slicked back black hair, and eyed Lafarge with a friendly grin on his face.

"This is as you know a delicate case, as it involves the Germans. As you are aware, Mademoiselle Suchet was having an affair with an Abwehr officer. Hence and for your own sake, Lafarge, you must tread carefully. I try and keep this department as independent as I can under the present circumstances, which is not easy, but it is something that I value. Thus if you are to formally question the officer in question, then I would ask you to inform me first so I can be present.

"I know this is not the norm in murder investigations but I feel that in this case it would be better for you and for the service that I am there. For if there were to be a misunderstanding, then at least I could support you and secondly, any protests would have to be addressed to me. Is that ok with you?"

Lafarge puffed out his cheeks, felt in his pocket for a cigarette and having withdrawn one, lit it. He waited until he had exhaled the first toke before speaking.

"Am I to understand from this, sir, that I am to be babysat throughout the investigation? For if that is the case then I would rather hand it to somebody more pliable.

"I can see your point about it being a delicate matter, but I would have thought that having been specifically chosen for it, this had already been taken into consideration. Especially as it is well known that the victim played a significant role in a previous case of mine which also involved one of the people I wish to speak to, Pierre–Yves de Chastelain.

"Thus I am surprised that already you are first of all speaking with me directly, as you normally observe from a distance, and that you are laying out the do's and don'ts of my investigation. I acknowledge that you should be interested in the case.

"Compared to some of your fellow commissairs, you are an enthusiast of our profession and that is welcome. But I wouldn't want it to become an obsession of yours to the point that I feel I am merely Sancho Panza to your Don Quixote, for that would serve neither of us well."

Massu fiddled with his cup, ran his finger round the lip of it and rubbed his chin.

"I take your point Lafarge and good heavens no, I have no intention of babysitting you through the investigation, and no, we won't be sitting outside the Moulin Rouge!" he said laughing at his own rather heavy joke in reference to the Don Quixote remark.

Lafarge smiled.

"Well, that's a relief then, I'm glad you clarified that. I admit that the German will have to be handled with care, but I believe I am capable of that, even if I have been a guest of theirs for some time."

"Yes, yes, quite regrettable, not something I would have wanted to experience," nodded Massu, who had been too old to enlist.

"Right, you have carte blanche with regard to everyone that you wish to speak to apart from the German, is that understood?" he said and shot a look at Lafarge that brooked no argument.

Lafarge nodded and said: "Here is the list of the other people of immediate interest: the maid, though she wasn't there as she lives on the top floor, de Chastelain, and I think for the moment that's it. Not a long list so hopefully, either one of them is the murderer or they give us a lead to someone else."

Massu nodded but Lafarge sensed it wasn't the end of the matter as his boss poured him and himself another cup of coffee, without asking him mind you, but he was grateful for it as he was dog tired. Massu took off his glasses, rubbed the bridge of his nose and pulled at his bottom lip. Lafarge could sense that whatever Massu had to say it wasn't going to be good news.

"There are two further tricky things I have to discuss with you, Lafarge. Firstly, de Chastelain may prove harder to interview than you think, for as you may be aware, he disappeared from view a few days ago.

"It was rather timely on his part, for he was due to be arrested the following day over some of his 'patriotic activities' apparently.

"It left René Bousquet hopping mad as you can imagine. He had wanted to prove that his boys were capable of arresting someone who has actually perpetrated crimes against the present government rather than just carrying out routine reprisals against the Jews which he has enforced with such ardour and unbridled enthusiasm," said Massu with a note of disgust in his voice.

"Ah and no sightings of de Chastelain since?" asked Lafarge.

Massu shook his head and added: "I have a feeling that his disappearance wasn't coincidental, indeed we know that he received a visit from your victim the eve of his date with Bousquet."

Lafarge sighed and thought how convenient and even more so that his ex–lover dies a few days later, perhaps there is a link there too.

He kept it to himself for the moment, preferring that his discussion with his superior come to a quick end so he could get on with his investigation.

"I am sure I will be able to get a lead on where he is sir, I know several of his friends personally and one of them should be able to help. I have found no–one is especially loyal when a friend of theirs is implicated in the murder of a woman."

"I am reassured by your confidence in people's morals these days," said Massu smiling sadly.

"Anyway I will let you get on with that, but just the second and final thing and it is something I touched on earlier.

"I have fought hard to try and keep as I said this department as independent of interference from both Bousquet and our foreign overlords, and I have to say with a fair amount of success," he said with pride in his voice.

"Thus I cannot emphasize more that you play this one very carefully Lafarge, there is no really by the book these days, that I acknowledge, but play it tough but fair and with the utmost delicacy. There is no light at the end of the present dark tunnel politically speaking, so for the moment we play the masters tune, or at least on the outside we do.

"I need not say more than to let you know that Bousquet himself is paying close attention to this case, not just because the victim was a favourite of the Germans but because he wants to take charge of it if there are any complaints or serious errors in our enquiry.

"He wishes to ingratiate himself even further with the Nazis. It is said he harbours ambitions to replace either Laval or even the Marshal.

"So no foul–ups and I speak with regard not only to my own goal in keeping ourselves free of his dark influence but also with regard to your long term health. The stakes for all of us are extremely high, inspector, if one of us falls, we all fall."

Lafarge wandered back to his office in a thoughtful mood.

Nothing he had experienced during the German invasion had posed quite so many problems as what he now faced.

Admittedly, the fight hadn't lasted very long and the Germans, for the most part, had acted in a chivalrous fashion towards their defeated opponents. But now he felt very alone and if it wasn't bad enough having one key potential player in the story missing, he also had the weight of his service and its future weighing on his shoulders.

It was times like this that he regretted not having a partner, not just to share the burden of the investigation but also to give him some sound advice.

Having a younger version of Massu alongside him would have been ideal but there was nobody, so it would have to be him, his gut instinct and his limited diplomatic skills, that ploughed on and would probably dig up more skeletons than lay fertile seeds.

Sure, he had family and friends. But the former were scattered around France, his parents were in Vichy where his father was Marshal Petain's most trusted advisor, his wife Isabella was in Nice with the two children, so it was only the latter he could fall back on.

Fortunately, several of his friends like his father were high up in Vichy circles or were much valued by the Nazis, although Bousquet was not one of them.

Indeed there was personal animosity between them dating back to before the War, when Bousquet took great pleasure at ridiculing Lafarge and his choice of profession. But it was more due to the fact that the detective he so despised had won the hand of Isabella Contreras, daughter of an Argentine diplomat, when he had been keen to marry her.

Lafarge mused on the irony that now Bousquet was in charge of a force he claimed to despise and also that the other reason for their discord, Isabella, was no longer in Paris.

He would not surrender to the thought that she was gone forever, but her coolness on departing once he had returned from the POW camp hadn't encouraged him to join her in Nice. That had been a year ago, and contact since had been limited to a phone call a month and mainly involved talking about how the children were: Philippe their five–year–old son and daughter Isadora, who was three. Well at least she had yet to say she wanted a divorce, but she never enquired into whether he was seeing anyone else and likewise he preferred not to know if she was.

He still missed her, not just for her blonde hair, brown eyes and petite physique, but for her solid common sense which was most unlike Latin Americans, and her ability to make him laugh.

And Lafarge had to admit there were not many of the opposite sex who achieved that. Marguerite Suchet had at one time, despite her ordeal at the hands of the rapist, but her association with de Chastelain had brought the curtain down on that possibility.

Lafarge tore himself away from such maudlin thoughts and looked on the upside which was that with Isabella not in Paris he at least had no distraction and could devote himself wholeheartedly to the case.

Christ, the case! What bloody case, or at least where the hell do I start? He stroked his unshaven jaw – which despite his full head of sandy blond hair and only being 38 was salt and pepper colour – and took one more look at the autopsy findings so as to clarify those details and to buy himself some time in deciding on his next step.

They made relatively pleasant reading, well compared to many other murders he had investigated where the corpses had been mutilated or dismembered.

This certainly reeked of a crime of passion. For Marguerite had been shot once, just below the right lung, and had enjoyed a bout of lovemaking prior to the fatal shot, though when was difficult to ascertain.

The sex had definitely been consensual according to Durand, who had added the time of death would have occurred around midnight.

Judging by the careful manner in which the corpse had been laid out on the sofa, there was no way that this was a burglary despite the disarray in her bedroom. His general experience with burglars was that murder was the last thing on their minds and if it led to

THE TORTURED DETECTIVE

that they left the scene in a hurry and not after looking after the corpse.

With the sex having been pleasurable, well obviously he didn't know if she had derived ultimate pleasure from it but it hadn't been forced, the most obvious candidate for the man in the act was Colonel von Dirlinger, but he didn't want to interview him straight away, for Lafarge wanted to be fresher than he felt now.

Massu would also probably prefer he had shaved as well so as to give a good impression of his service, and he wanted to at least have some deeper background to play with when they met. For that reason he decided to pay a visit to Marguerite's maid first.

CHAPTER FOUR

Mathilde Langlois was an attractive woman, somewhere in her forties guessed Lafarge, with well brushed short black hair, a shapely figure with large breasts its most marked feature, and also somewhat surprisingly for a maid her hands were well manicured and didn't appear to have endured too much manual labour.

Obviously someone who looks after themselves and perhaps not the most ardent of workers, Lafarge surmised.

He prayed that she was rather better at noticing things. She had preferred to meet with him in her former employer's apartment, explaining that her small flat was not ideal for conducting the interview.

Lafarge had agreed, though, he half–regretted doing so as he would have liked to have seen her place if only to confirm that she lived alone and had no one of interest, de Chastelain for example, hiding there.

But he dismissed that as unlikely and hence they were now sitting in the kitchen, her with a coffee and him with more of the vodka he had taken such a liking to on his first visit.

"So Mathilde, when was the last time you saw Madamoiselle Suchet?"

"Around nine o'clock last night, Inspector."

"Anything you noticed in particular about her that seemed different?" asked Lafarge.

Langlois eyed him carefully for a moment before replying.

"She appeared to be her usual self, sir" she answered, though her eyes betrayed the fact she was thinking the opposite.

Lafarge decided to play along for the moment, thinking in his most charitable fashion that perhaps he had misread her eye gesture.

"And what would that be, Mathilde? What was her usual manner?"

Lafarge's tactic worked because thinking she had got away with the lie, if indeed it was one, she relaxed, sitting back in the wooden chair and loosening one of the buttons on her red coat.

"Well, Madame was usually gay, rather carefree, always courteous but not in a high handed manner, and very funny," she replied with a smile to add impact to the veracity of the statement.

"Hm! Sounds like the employer made in heaven. One we all dream of having!" Lafarge said with a smile of his own, which he hoped was a winning one.

Langlois nodded her assent, but didn't feel it necessary to add any more to her comments. Lafarge took a deep breath and thought to himself, this is going to be more difficult than I thought, she is a wall. Indeed the very essence of what an employer looking for a ladies maid would desire, discreet and loyal.

But with her employer dead, there was no point her remaining loyal, so was there somebody else that she was protecting?

Why jump to that conclusion so early, thought Lafarge, the interview has been but ten minutes and is three questions old and already you are thinking that she is stonewalling you?

Not everyone is a liar for God's sake, and loyalty is still a quality that exists even in France, he reminded himself.

Trouble is, as in the case of Langlois, there are two parties vying for loyalty, and choosing one over the other could be very bad for one's health depending on the outcome of the war.

"Right Mathilde, last night, was Ms Suchet expecting anyone? Did she ask you to prepare anything for a guest?" asked Lafarge as if he was going through the motions.

He hoped by doing that, she would slip–up or at the very least let her guard down.

"Yes, she was expecting someone, a gentleman. Colonel von Dirlinger. But then you probably know that already, don't you, sir?"

"Her lover. Why, yes of course that would be normal. Did you see him? Did you wait to let him in and serve them dinner?" he asked quickly, to try and hurry her along, let her lose her train of thought.

"Erm. No. Madame told me that would not be necessary, that they would just be having a light dinner and retiring to bed early. Therefore I said goodnight and went to my room upstairs," she replied.

"Ah yes of course, a light dinner of caviar and vodka. Nice to see how the term light carries different meanings these days," said Lafarge caustically.

"I don't know what you mean sir. Madame deserved everything that she got as reward for her success in the cinema, so I find your remark out of place and disrespectful.

"Quite apart from the fact you appear to be profiting from the vodka yourself," remarked Langlois giving him a look of disapproval.

Lafarge thought more of her type in the frontline in 1940 and the Germans would have had a far tougher time, the sort to seduce by her good looks and then plunge a dagger between the ribs just as you lay there expecting a pleasurable moment with her.

He shuddered at the thought. He didn't usually place people in pigeonholes, but this woman did not fit the image of a ladies maid. Either she had fallen like many on hard times and had taken a job that suited her in terms of lodging and a certain standing, or she had been placed there deliberately to keep an eye more on her employer than to serve her.

"How long have you been in the employ of Ms Suchet, Mathilde?"

"A year, sir."

"And would you say that having worked for her for a year, you would have gained enough trust that she could feel confident in confiding in you if she was worried by something?

"Obviously not a trivial matter, but something grave? I mean that if you have been with someone for a year, regardless of the nature of the relationship whether it be man and wife or employer and employee there has to be a measure of trust. Being a personal maid places you in a very specific category.

"So I imagine there were moments when she felt impelled to talk to you like perhaps she wouldn't to her make–up artist or dresser at the film company. No? " he asked putting on one of his more reassuring smiles.

"Yes, she did confide in me from time to time. But I am not of the mind to tell you what these confidences were," she replied sternly.

"I would remind you Ms Langlois, that you are part of a murder enquiry, in fact you are a key part of it. Your employer being the

THE TORTURED DETECTIVE

victim, firstly any confidence she shared with you would be of interest to the investigation and secondly there will be serious consequences for you if I discover later that you have withheld information pertinent to it.

"Do you understand me?" he said in an exasperated tone, deciding to dispense with the softly softly approach and adopt a more aggressive style.

She looked annoyed by the change in tack, raised her eyes to the ceiling, swallowed deeply, got up and picked up a tumbler, filling it halfway with vodka. Lafarge waited patiently to see if the tactic was her trying to buy time, think of something she could give him and hope that it was enough.

"Madame was despite her public appearance, a private person," said Langlois.

"I don't think she shared her inner thoughts easily. I'm not saying she was a simple person, not given to thinking too deeply about the consequences of her actions, but she was a little too carefree sometimes, and I am not referring to her relationship with the Colonel.

"However, if she confided in you then she believed she had that person's loyalty and trust forever.

"She did allude to me that something recently had shaken her faith in one of the few people she trusted.

"Whether it was Colonel von Dirlinger, I do not know, but something happened a few days ago, something she was asked to do that provoked this unease in her. That much she did tell me, without telling me names or anything that could be of material interest to you," she replied, before taking a gulp of the vodka.

Lafarge was not satisfied. She may feel she has given me something to think about, a lead of some sort to take to the next stage, but it was too general and frankly didn't wash that Marguerite had been so vague in her unburdening herself to her maid.

"Did it revolve around her late night visit to the lawyer, de Chastelain?"

Her eyes widened at that question, obviously not expecting the police to be privy to such information.

"You know about that then?" she asked in a rhetorical fashion, her tone not as sure as it had been.

Lafarge nodded and by implication encouraged her to go on. She sipped some more vodka, Lafarge without being invited to filled both their glasses, offered her a cigarette, which she took and lit them both. She inhaled and as she exhaled, she appeared to have experienced a Damascene conversion.

"Yes, it was from that moment she appeared to be concerned about something. Not so much about being called in by the French authorities, for she said she had been asked by a higher one, the Colonel I imagine, to warn M. de Chastelain, but from something else that was affected by his disappearance.

"She was agitated too that while she risked nothing from the Germans, she was afraid that should her part in it come to light, she could have problems with M. Bousquet."

Ah and so René Bousquet's name comes up again, mused Lafarge, only her fear was understandable, given she had interfered with and prevented a high profile arrest by the preening master of police and, judging from what Massu had said, impeded his chances of replacing Laval or Pétain at the very top of the Vichy Government.

Not a very wise move, Marguerite.

"Did M. Bousquet ever visit Ms Suchet? asked Lafarge.

"Yes, he came here on several occasions," replied Langlois, visibly more relaxed and, with the aid of the vodka, more willing to reveal these confidences.

"Alone?"

"Yes."

"Would he stay long?"

Here Langlois hesitated before replying. Lafarge tried to encourage her by saying soothingly: "It's alright Mathilde, no–one need know apart from us. I don't think I need bring your name up should I have to talk to M. Bousquet, it could always have come from her diary."

He cursed himself for giving such an assurance as he had yet to find a diary, but hey how was Bousquet to know she didn't keep one.

"He stayed the night on a couple of occasions, but that was a while ago. I mean I think it was when I first started here and before the Colonel and Madame became romantically involved."

THE TORTURED DETECTIVE

"Don't worry Mathilde, infidelity is far from being a crime, even more so these days. Besides one can only perhaps question her choice of man, but then that would be disloyal of me given I work for him!" he said laughing bitterly.

She smiled for the first time, it lit up her face and transformed it from a cold and wary look to one of great warmth and rather sexy and alluring.

"Some employers are more enjoyable company than others!" she said jokingly.

Lafarge didn't respond, for he was very much on his guard with this lady, lord knows where she had come from or by whose influence she had been placed with Marguerite. He would have to probe deeper into her background, for there was much more behind her story than was possible to ascertain now.

However, more of concern to him was that aside from Colonel von Dirlinger and having Massu backing him up on the interview, was the thought he might have to convince his superior that their overall chief was a person of interest in the case.

He could not, for the life of him, imagine Massu allowing such an interview given his already nervous disposition that Bousquet wanted to take complete control of the service and the case.

Of course, to Lafarge it was logical why Bousquet should be so keen, but without Massu's co–operation there was no way he could dig any deeper.

He could go behind Massu's back, and, albeit reluctantly, seek his father's help. However, he did not wish to go down that road, but if he deemed it necessary he would do so. It was not his dislike of Bousquet, he tried to convince himself, but his consummate professionalism that egged him on.

"We're nearly finished Mathilde. Not just the bottle but also the interview," he said smiling.

"Did you see M; de Chastelain in the past few days, and secondly is there anything else you can recall that could be of help to the investigation?"

She shook her head.

"M. de Chastelain would have been a fool to show his face here. Madame may have saved him from arrest, but her feelings for him were more of a nostalgic nature. She would do anything to prevent him being harmed but for her, the romantic side of their relationship was over.

"I don't think he would have come here anyway because hopefully, he knew that it would endanger her more.

"Also being a wanted man, her place might be the one of those the police would search first, especially given as you told me, they knew she had visited him on the eve of his disappearance.

"However, sir, there is one other thing that may interest you, and which you appear to have forgotten, with your sudden interest in M. Bousquet.

"When I said she was more worried about something that was directly affected by the disappearance of M. de Chastelain, it was not to do with any damage it might have done to Bousquet's reputation with the Germans. It was more what happened to Arnaud Lescarboura."

Lafarge was stunned by this last piece of information. Lescarboura, the gentleman's jewel thief, which despite the complimentary adjective did not really make him any different to the run of the mill thief, and Marguerite?

"Why would she be worried about his welfare? I find it hard to believe them being associated. Forgive my skepticism, Mathilde. Perhaps you can enlighten me?"

With that he poured the remnants of the vodka in equal measures into their respective glasses, while waiting for her clarification on her previous response.

"She and Arnaud were old friends from the Lot, he was like an older brother to her and remained so. M. de Chastelain met him through her when they were together, and I think that is how he came to be his lawyer at the trial because they too had remained on good terms.

"Arnaud would often come round here, and no, he would not stay the night, or if he did, he would be in the spare bedroom. If Madame had a real confidant then it was him.

"Thus you can imagine her anxiety when she realized that by saving her former lover she was also condemning her closest friend to a prison term of greater magnitude than he would have got if he had been ably defended. If one could use the term, perhaps it is inappropriate but Madame and René were as thick as thieves together, chief inspector".

THE TORTURED DETECTIVE

And with that astonishing revelation Mathilde [
and enigmatic maid to Lafarge's mind, smiled k
and downed her vodka.

"That is an interesting turn of phrase Mathild
have paid for their link with de Chastelain. One is dead, shortly after warning de Chastelain of his imminent arrest, and the other got 10 years for stealing Countess de Marchand's jewels after his lawyer failed to turn up. What are we to make of that?" sighed Lafarge.

Mathilde looked at him with a quizzical look on her face.

"Oh don't worry Mathilde, I have a habit of thinking to myself out loud. That will be all then, and thank you for being ultimately so helpful," he said with a smile. Mathilde held him in a steady gaze, not returning the smile.

"Well Chief Inspector, as that is all I will take my leave of you. If you could, erm, let me know when it is possible for me to restore order to the apartment, or at least Madame's bedroom, I would appreciate that," she said.

Lafarge nodded and rose to say goodbye, extending his hand which she took in a firm grip. As she departed the kitchen, she said over her shoulder: "You needn't give me the usual garbage of don't leave town etc Chief Inspector. I'm not going anywhere, and you know where to find me. I'm sure we will see each other again. It's been a pleasure."

Lafarge nodded, looked at his empty glass, regretted the vodka bottle was as dead as Marguerite and stared vacantly into space.

Lafarge sat in the kitchen for a while, the day was turning to night by the time he rose from the chair, as he had tried to piece together the various bits of information that Mathilde had furnished him with.

Marguerite and Lescarboura, Lescarboura and de Chastelain, where, apart from being the victim's lover did Colonel von Dirlinger fit into the puzzle. Could he have warned Marguerite about de Chastelain's arrest or had he unwittingly imparted it to her.

Then there was Bousquet and his connection, but Lafarge groaned inwardly he was virtually untouchable and he didn't even want to think of Massu's reaction were he to hint at questioning him.

her than just being a maid to a film star.

...en there was Mathilde, the witness to all these comings and
_oings, a person definitely of interest and also perhaps in danger
herself. Lafarge also was quietly happy that he would have the
chance of seeing her again, digging deeper into her background
would be a fascinating exercise he thought, because there was more
to her than just being a maid to a film star.

He reproached himself immediately at even thinking of a
romantic liaison with her, for Isabella remained not only his wife
but despite her glacial attitude to him since their enforced
separation, he still loved her very much.

Lafarge, who was by now through a mix of no sleep and the
vodka feeling exhausted and light–headed, decided to give the
apartment one more sweep before heading home. He looked in at
the drawing room and searched under the sofa, and looked in the
fireplace, though, it was clear it had not been used for a long time,
and came up with nothing.

He padded down the elegant chairs either side of the sofa where
Marguerite had been laid out, and there he did discover something,
a silver cigarette case, embossed with the initials, the ones he really
didn't want to find, of RB.

Christ! He opened the case gingerly and saw that the brand of
cigarette was the same as the ones he had found in the ashtray.

Now there was no option but to cross paths again with René
Bousquet. For quite apart from the fact he was probably missing
his cigarette case, which he saw had also the dedication of 'To
René, a man of Teutonic ideals and values, with great affection.
Otto A,' Otto Abetz, no doubt, thought Lafarge, he was now placed
squarely at the scene of the crime.

What fun I'm going to have, he said to himself darkly. The thing
was, could he just keep it to himself? Or could he approach
Bousquet on his own, show him the cigarette case and thereby let
him know that he knew the victim and had been there in the
apartment? That was a dangerous risk to run as Bousquet could do
him much harm without having recourse to due process.

Or he could go to Massu, tell him the facts and then hopefully
both of them would deal with their overall superior. None of the
options appealed to Lafarge.

Feeling heavy–footed and weighed down with this extra burden,
Lafarge dragged himself into the main bedroom, the spare one

THE TORTURED DETECTIVE

having yielded nothing of interest. Indeed, the bed had not been slept in, and the cupboards and drawers were filled simply with the overflow of Marguerite's clothes and hats.

He searched under her bed, and her bed linen, and checked the drawers of the bedside tables, again nothing of note. Final stop was the table where she had met her end, with the jewels strewn all over it and indeed some were on the floor.

It certainly was a fine collection, fortunate for her she was a friend of Lescarboura, because otherwise, she would have been a lucrative target for his twitchy hands. He lifted up the splendidly decorated box and felt under it to see if there was a hidden compartment, or a key, and chastised himself for beginning to act like Charlie Chan. He performed a similar exercise with the table, and there he did retrieve something.

It was a piece of paper, which had been slotted into the join of a corner of the table and the back right leg. He unraveled it and saw that something had been written on it. The lighting being so dull in the bedroom – she was evidently not much of a reader of books, he surmised – he took it out into the corridor and read what was scrawled on the note.

There were a series of to do's on it: '1 – Invite the Countess for dinner, 2 – René hides in spare bedroom. 3 – Once she arrives, he leaves. 4 – Keep her here till he returns. 5 – Guard them till safe to go to middleman.

Lafarge was stunned not for the first time that day.

Just to double check, he compared the handwriting to that on a piece of paper he had seen in the drawing room, and it matched.

Bloody hell, he thought, Mathilde couldn't have put it better, for Marguerite Suchet and René Lescarboura, childhood friends, had indeed been as thick as thieves, only for real. Next stop Lescarboura, and at least he knew he wasn't going anywhere as he was tucked up in Fresnes prison awaiting his transfer to where he would serve out his sentence.

CHAPTER FIVE

Lafarge woke early after a disturbed night's sleep. Despite his state of exhaustion there had been no sweet dreams for him, the size of the task facing him and the political minefields he would have to traverse intervened to disrupt any hope he had of recharging his batteries.

He stumbled into his small bathroom, and one look in the mirror confirmed how he felt, deep bags lay under his deep blue eyes, his tousled hair required more than just a brush to make it neat and tidy, but he was out of priceless shampoo, and only a sad cheap block of soap was at hand to remedy that problem.

Well make do with what you have, Lafarge mumbled. He was interrupted in his train of thought over his toilette by the phone ringing in his equally small drawingroom. He sighed and decided he'd postpone his ablutions for the moment.

"Hello, is that you Lafarge?" asked the person at the other end of the phone.

"Yes, it is. Good morning to you too," Lafarge replied grumpily down the phone to Pierre Drieu La Rochelle, whose crisp tones he had recognized immediately.

"Hope you are keeping well Lafarge. I was just wondering whether we could meet?" asked Drieu, his tone agitated.

"Well Drieu, I don't really know whether I have the time right now to see you, much as it would give me pleasure to," replied Lafarge with as much enthusiasm as he could muster for he was talking to one of his friends who had embraced the German occupation with unbridled joy.

"That is a shame, Lafarge. You must be a very busy man, is it an interesting case you are working on?" Drieu asked, though his tone suggested to Lafarge that he knew very well what his case was.

"I think you know exactly what I'm working on. So let's cut to the chase, shall we, of what interest is it to you?" asked Lafarge, who was desperate to end the conversation as he had better things to be doing.

"Well, let's just say that I could be of help in relation to one of the persons involved," said Drieu in his most mellifluous tone.

THE TORTURED DETECTIVE

Lafarge knew that his phone was tapped – all members of the Vichy administration and important members of the security forces were subject to this eavesdropping – and Drieu would also be aware of this hence his reticence to expand on what he had rung him about.

"Okay. Let's meet at the Café de Flore, say at seven o'clock this evening?" said Lafarge conceding that Drieu may have something useful to tell him.

"Perfect. It will be good to catch up with you. See you at seven."

*

Lafarge strolled into Quai des Orfèvres, feeling somewhat refreshed after his rigorous toilette, though, he acknowledged washing his hair with the soap had left it looking most unruly.

He put in a call to Massu's secretary asking to see his superior, and was told he could see him in 20 minutes. Prior to that, Lafarge drew up a plan of attack: He would ask to see Lescarboura first for he held perhaps the key to the murder, although, of course he was not the perpetrator, as he had a cast iron alibi, for he had been behind bars.

However, he could tell him, if he proved amenable, how far Marguerite's involvement went and if the plan he had come across taped onto her dressing table had been the one put into action.

The German, he would keep waiting. For not only did it give him some pleasure that a man used to giving orders to him and his compatriots should be at his behest, but also perhaps Lescarboura would be able to provide him with some information concerning his relationship with the victim.

After that, he would broach the subject of Bousquet, for he had not decided yet whether to tell Massu of his discovery at Marguerite's apartment. A trip to the imposing Fresnes prison and then on for drinks with Drieu La Rochelle at the fashionable Café de Flore, a stark contrast indeed, he mused. From a place where brutality is the daily routine to a literary master in a café frequented by the literati, what a varied life being a policeman is, he reflected dryly.

He thought of Drieu La Rochelle and their friendship, forged at university and which had survived through the political turbulence that had marked France and indeed mainland Europe since the end of the Great War. Drieu had indeed travelled a long way from the left to the far right, a journey taken by many of their generation and a route which Lafarge had taken to a certain degree, but one which he had refused to go as far as his father had done.

For his father's closeness to Pétain was a blessing and a curse to Lafarge at the same time. A blessing because it probably earned him the official stamp of approval to return to the force, but a curse because it had sparked some of the trouble between him and Isabella, who despite being the daughter of a diplomat loyal to the far right dictator of Argentina, Juan Peron, repudiated such politics.

She had been delighted that Lafarge had enlisted for his second dose of a continental war, which had not been the case for many of his contemporaries who had decided one was quite enough thank you.

However, she had expressed horror when he had announced on his return from the camp that he was to rejoin the force. They had had a blazing row, which had also brought out her disgust at his father's craven decision to devote himself to Pétain and the reprehensible policies of Vichy, which had a few weeks later prompted her to depart with the children for the South of France.

He admitted his father's behaviour decision to follow the Marshal while his eldest son languished in a POW camp had been beyond explanation, but given the divisions that had developed within families all over France since the humiliation of the defeat, their family was not any different.

His two brothers exemplified this. One, Patrick was an officer in the Vichy Army in Lebanon, the other, Albert, was a pilot with the Free French Air Force based as far as he knew in England.

His sister Vanessa was the mistress, to his horror, of one Pierre Bonny, a disgraced former detective who had done time in prison and was now with a crook called Henri Lafont, one of the two heads of the French Gestapo as they were known in the chic Rue Lauriston. Ironic, Lafarge mused, that Bonny should be having an adulterous relationship when after being released from prison he had made money out of exposing errant husbands.

Lafarge arrived on time for his rendez–vous with Drieu and he was in a foul humour because having made the trip out to Fresnes Prison, he had been told by a distinctly unapologetic prison

THE TORTURED DETECTIVE

governor that Lescarboura was not there at all and was in fact at the Cherche–Midi prison.

It was even more infuriating as geographically it fell nicely with meeting Drieu at the Café de Flore as both were in walking distance of each other.

Still, the governor in charge of Cherche–Midi, which housed those political prisoners or criminals who the present authorities had the most interest in keeping a close eye on and interrogating, had been more compliant when Lafarge had rung him. He said that so long as the chief inspector was at the prison by nine thirty that evening, he could see the prisoner.

Lafarge just prayed that Drieu would not be late. It being a warm late summer evening, he sat himself down outside on the terrace and ordered a glass of chilled white wine, light a cigarette and thought back over his meeting with Massu earlier in the day.

Massu hadn't been in a particularly good mood, seemingly pre–occupied by something else. Lafarge had decided that the Bousquet discovery could wait till after he had seen both Drieu and Lescarboura, so he could at least hopefully give him some good news on how the case was progressing.

Massu had agreed with his stratagem of seeing Lescarboura first and then going together to see von Dirlinger, hopefully armed with some information they could use to get something out of him.

Lafarge didn't bother to tell Massu about his meeting with Drieu because he was not sure whether it would be pertinent to the enquiry or not, and also if his friend wished to be publicly involved.

If he was not directly involved, then there was no point in implicating him in it. Lafarge was not in the habit of involving his friends in investigations if he could help it and Drieu was also one who was highly esteemed by the Nazis, not just for his writing, which Lafarge thought was too flowery for his own taste, but for his devotion to their credo.

"Deep in thought as ever, Lafarge," said Drieu, causing Lafarge to jump. "Mind if I sit down? What's that you're drinking?" he enquired.

When Lafarge responded, Drieu's lips curled up in dissatisfaction and he ordered a brandy when the waiter came to take his order. Lafarge noticed that as ever, Drieu was impeccably turned out, indeed he looked extremely well, healthily bronzed, looking fit and had a rather self–contented air about him.

Well, why shouldn't he be, his heroes were winning the war even if with the entry of the United States it tilted the odds towards an eventual Allied victory, but the Soviet Union looked beat which meant mainland Europe at the very least would remain under their governance.

Anyway that wasn't Lafarge's concern, he had more mundane matters to deal with like the murder of a famous actress which could involve at least two members of the present establishment. Light fare indeed! It would be hard enough to probe under a democratically elected government, but under a dictatorship and an occupying force, almost impossible.

"You're looking well, Drieu. You have obviously been prospering," remarked Lafarge. Drieu smiled, raised his glass to his friend and downed the brandy in one.

"I have indeed been making hay while the sun shines Lafarge," he replied, while trying to attract the waiter's attention, who was involved in an animated discussion with a Wehrmacht officer and his well–decorated female companion.

Drieu rose to intervene but then thought better of it and continued his conversation with his friend.

"I have been writing furiously since I returned emboldened from the First European Writer's Congress in Weimar last year. I gained so much from that trip, to see Germany as it is today, the all–conquering democracy that it is, only served to strengthen my belief that we have done well to integrate ourselves fully into their system. Of course we French also taught our German writing contemporaries some things too, but it has spurred me on in my own writing.

"Aside from obviously my diary, which will serve to be perhaps the reference book of this era, I am presently writing a novel.

"It isn't pretentious and distant like Céline, but something that ordinary French people can read and relate to. I have already received a generous payment for it so these drinks will be on me. Judging by a detective's salary, you would be hard–pressed to pay for drinks here anyway," he smiled and swept his finely–manicured hand through his receding curly hair.

THE TORTURED DETECTIVE

Lafarge was pleased for his friend, although he worried about his almost manic devotion to the Germans, for if the fortunes of war did turn there would be little reward for him other than the guillotine.

"Well, I'm pleased for you Drieu. Now, perhaps you could tell me exactly what you thought would be of help to me regarding my case."

"Ah yes, that. Let's order some more drinks, shall we, and then I will tell you".

Again, Drieu smiled, this one though had seen the smug look return to his face. Lafarge nodded, looked at his battered watch and saw that he still had a good 90 minutes before he had to be at the Cherche–Midi prison, and waited till the grumpy waiter, who had obviously come off second best in his argument with the officer, had taken their order and returned with the drinks.

Drieu La Rochelle took a sip of his brandy this time. He lit a cigarette, having taken it from what Lafarge noticed was a similar cigarette case to the one of Bousquet's he had found, obviously a job lot from Ambassador Abetz's cellar he reflected, and prepared to tell his old friend his tale.

"That tart, Marguerite Suchet, who was murdered, I had dinner with her the other night. I just thought I ought to tell you that before I go on," said Drieu La Rochelle.

"There's nothing really more to our relationship than that. I didn't sleep with her, she refused my advances, though, heaven knows why as she has slept with pretty much anyone since Germany came to our rescue."

Lafarge sighed loudly to indicate he wasn't for the moment interested in Drieu's social activities and indicated he preferred he moved on.

"Anyway Lafarge, much to my surprise the other night I was at home, having returned from a most pleasant evening at Guitry's house when my bell rang. It was around midnight. Being after curfew, I thought it must be my rather attractive neightbour, who I have serviced from time to time, and so I opened my door.

"Well I can tell you my smile quickly disappeared when I saw that it was not her but the much sought after fugitive Pierre–Yves de Chastelain," and there, Drieu La Rochelle, ever the dramatic tenor, stopped waiting for Lafarge's reaction. He was to be disappointed for all Lafarge said was "Go on."

Drieu didn't bat an eyelid even if he was disappointed and moved on.

"Well I was stunned. I hadn't seen him for a few months, perhaps just after I had returned from Weimar and we had had a lively discussion about what he termed collaborating with the enemy. So he was the last person I expected to come to me for help."

"Help, what sort of help?" asked Lafarge, intrigued as much as Drieu was by de Chastelain's behaviour which seemed very out of character even if he was on the run.

"I'll come to that in a moment," replied Drieu La Rochelle, enjoying the fact he had a captive audience.

"He was, I must say, looking the worse for wear, his hair was unkempt and his clothes smelt. Far from being the neat, dapper lawyer we grew accustomed to seeing in court. Anyway I let him in, for as you know, Lafarge, I am loyal even to those who have contrary views to mine. I gave him a drink and he took his time to gather himself before he asked me for a huge favour."

"And that was?" asked Lafarge somewhat impatiently.

"He said he needed to get out of Paris immediately and that with my contacts I could facilitate that. He wanted me to get him an Ausweis! An Ausweis for God's sake! I retorted that it was quite impossible, that I would need a photograph and other papers which even if it were possible would take a long time.

"So then he said, well you have a car, you can drive me to Limoges. Well really, the man had lost all sense! I told him as such but he was insistent. He called on all our links going back two decades, including the fact we are second cousins, though our families rarely saw each other.

"I said I was tired and would need to think it over. He then asked whether he could stay the night, to which I gave in."

"And was he there in the morning?" asked Lafarge.

"Oh, yes, and you know what I did my friend? I like the stupid cavalier fool that I am, I drove him to Limoges." Drieu La Rochelle smiled weakly and signalled to the waiter to bring them another round of drinks.

THE TORTURED DETECTIVE

"You drove him to Limoges! How did you manage that? Even with papers he would have been arrested as his name was listed as top priority. I don't believe you, Drieu," said Lafarge.

"Well, it was really rather simple Lafarge. I put him in the back seat, covered in books and blankets, and with my Ausweis and my relaxed manner with the guards at various checkpoints, of which there were not many, I succeeded in getting him to Limoges."

"Christ, Drieu. You know that I should arrest you for this. You have aided a wanted man to escape.

"Imagine what Bousquet would say. His prize catch snatched from him, humiliating him in the process, and then one of his fellow travelers makes it even more difficult to make up for that episode by driving him several hundred kilometers out of Paris. It's barely credible," said Lafarge angrily.

"Well Lafarge, loyalist as I am to the Germans, I am not so well disposed to people such as Bousquet and their overweening desire for personal aggrandizement," sneered Drieu.

"Much as his enthusiastic work in resolving the Jewish problem pleases me, I do not care for the man. Any embarrassment I can inflict on him or barricade I can place in his way gives me great pleasure.

"To be quite honest Lafarge, it can only be a matter of time before de Chastelain is caught, for all his friends and colleagues are here in Paris. Why you could do with some time outside Paris, couldn't you? Get away from the loneliness of the apartment," said Drieu.

"Kindly leave that out of the equation," replied Lafarge acidly.

He was furious, not because of the last comment which was hurtful, but because his friend had willingly aided a fugitive to escape, someone who he desperately needed to talk to in his present investigation.

Would he report Drieu to Massu? He was torn between that and just using the information and calling in a huge favour from his friend later, when he might need it.

"When was this?" he asked.

"Two nights ago. He didn't say very much about where he had been hiding out, but the weird thing was that I noticed when he washed the morning of our escapade, that he had dried blood on his shirt, quite a lot of it in fact. That made me wonder, as he didn't seem to be hurt or wounded himself," said Drieu teasingly.

Lafarge thought to himself, if it was two nights ago, that was when Marguerite was murdered. Her body had been dragged through the apartment and if the murderer had come into contact with the entry wound then he would have been covered in her blood. This made it even worse that Drieu had aided de Chastelain.

"Christ, Drieu, that was the night Marguerite Suchet was murdered. You may well have helped her killer escape. What's more, you say that he will be caught soon, that he has no friends down there, but you are forgetting something."

"What's that old chap?" asked Drieu in an insouciant tone.

"It's bandit country down there. Limoges is renowned for being a hub of Résistance recruitment and activity, or at least the countryside around it is," replied Lafarge shaking his head in bemusement at his friend's apparent naiveté.

For the first time that evening, Drieu La Rochelle looked unsure of himself, and Lafarge shook his head again as if to rub in his stupidity, a characteristic he was shocked to see he possessed. He hoped it was stupidity and not Drieu trying to make a fool of him.

"Well, in one way, I guess I should thank you. It is the first piece of hard evidence I have regarding the whereabouts of de Chastelain, his movements and perhaps an indication of where he might have been prior to turning up at your place," said Lafarge with a note of appreciation in his voice.

"Also, you didn't have to volunteer this information, so I am grateful. On the other hand you have willfully broken the law, such as it is these days. But given that we all have something to hide, even more so now, I will use the information but will for as long as I can keep your name out of it.

"On the understanding that if further down the line I am in trouble or I need a big favour, you reciprocate. That is clear, yes?" and while he posed it as a question his tone made it crystal clear that it was a rhetorical one.

Drieu nodded with visible relief.

"I am very grateful for your understanding, Lafarge. I am sorry, but if I have a failing it is that unless someone has really crossed me, no matter that we may disagree on political beliefs, I am fiercely loyal," he smiled thinly, almost apologetically.

THE TORTURED DETECTIVE

"Good. Right I have to get off now, I have someone else to see and under circumstances less welcoming and charming than these ones. I will see you soon, Drieu. Thank you for the drinks," Lafarge said curtly, patted his old friend on the shoulder and strode off in the direction of the Cherche–Midi Prison and what was sure to be a captive audience there.

CHAPTER SIX

Arnaud Lescarboura shuffled into what passed for a visitor's room at Cherche–Midi, looking none too pleased at being awoken, even if it gave him a rare chance to leave his miserable little cell which not even the hardiest of monks would have put up with.

To Lafarge's eyes Lescarboura was not a good bet for surviving 10 years inside, as just a few days of relative comfort prior to his departure for an unknown destination and hard labour had already left its mark.

Physically he looked as if he could handle the work that lay ahead of him for he was stocky and muscular. However, the way he dragged himself to his chair in the sparsely furnished stonewalled room either indicated an unwillingness to accept his abject circumstances, or someone who was already prepared to give up on life itself.

The trouble was Lafarge could not offer him much in the way of hope. A reduction in sentence perhaps if he could get his full co–operation and if his information led to uncovering the truth, but even then he would have to pressure Massu, who would then have to probably go to Bousquet and so on and so forth.

So from that point of view, Lafarge also started from a disadvantageous point, for without too much to offer Lescarboura, there was not much point in him being co–operative. Perhaps the only thing that might keep Lescarboura going through his years of hell would be the thought that one day, he might prosper from the jewels wherever they might be hidden.

However, given the comportment of Lescarboura it appeared that even the hope of that had disappeared.

Lafarge offered something that at least was in his powers and that was a cigarette, indeed he left the pack on the table, just in front of him so that Lescarboura could reach for them but not without having to ask him if he could.

Lescarboura eagerly accepted the cigarette, and Lafarge lit it for him. He noticed that whilst there were no visible marks on the prisoner's rather handsome if slightly effeminate face, or indeed on his hands, he was shaking and it wasn't because of the cold bare floor or walls. Lafarge waited while Lescarboura smoked his

THE TORTURED DETECTIVE

cigarette, which he did with sparing puffs, so as he could enjoy it to its utmost.

"Looking after you alright in here Lescarboura?" asked Lafarge in as warm and concerned a manner as he could muster, though, years of similar discussions had eroded any real sentiment of caring for people who had known the risks they were running by committing crimes.

"I suppose so. In as much that I get some sleep, I eat three times a day, slops that they are, and haven't been beaten yet. Better than I expected. But it's not the Hôtel Meurice!" he replied laughing bitterly.

A heck of a lot better than wherever you are going, thought Lafarge.

"Right. You may be surprised that a policeman is still interested enough in you to want to ask you further questions, but there have been developments since you were sent here, and which I am certain you are not aware of," said Lafarge.

Lescarboura stroked his stubbled chin and looked at Lafarge suspiciously but didn't say anything, allowing his inquisitor to carry on and inform him of these developments.

"You must prepare yourself for a shock, another unpleasant one I am afraid. Marguerite Suchet was murdered two nights ago," said Lafarge gently.

Lescarboura reacted as Lafarge had anticipated, tears welled in his brown eyes, his shoulders sagged, and he rose from the chair and paced the room with his hands covering his eyes.

Lafarge kept his counsel for a while, allowing the wretched Lescarboura his moment of grief. After his sobs had subsided and he had wiped the tears from his eyes and cheeks and returned to the table, Lafarge resumed his discourse.

"I am sorry for your loss, Arnaud, for I have learnt that you and Marguerite were friends since childhood and this blow cannot have come at a worse time for you," he said his tone sympathetic.

Lescarboura nodded in appreciation at Lafarge's remark, but remained silent, only opening his mouth to place another cigarette in it.

"Now, also knowing that you had remained very much in contact with her, and indeed spent some nights at her place, staying in the spare room I might add, I was wondering whether you could throw any light on her private life.

"Whether there had been anything especially worrying her, or if anyone had been threatening her?" asked Lafarge, preferring to take a roundabout route to the interrogation.

Lafarge waited patiently while Lescarboura collected himself and was able to think more clearly, for after the shock he had received it might take some time.

Lescarboura had screwed up his face into a contorted shape. Lafarge didn't know whether this was how the most notorious jewel thief in France always looked when he had to think, and if it was, then no wonder, thought Lafarge, he had never moved from the spare room to Marguerite's bedroom.

He looked like a badly disfigured gargoyle. Lescarboura also tugged at his long black hair, twisting it round and round until he came away with a few strands in his hand.

"I'm afraid I can't say much mister policeman, unless I know what you can offer me. You see I am already in a system where life is not valued very much, indeed it barely has a value to it at all in the present regime," said Lescarboura miserably.

"The information I have would place me at risk of not even seeing the light of day, which of course could prove to be a blessing as I am not eager to see the place I am being sent to to serve my time," he added with a grim smile.

"I am not empowered to strike any deal with you for the moment. I have to be straight with you, because in the present situation while I still have power to investigate cases I am no longer allowed to barter for information, much as I would like to in your case," said Lafarge smiling apologetically.

Lescarboura swallowed deeply, he cast his eyes down to the wooden table surface and his shoulders sagged again. He stayed like that for several minutes, his sorry figure illuminated solely by the naked light bulb that hung over the table.

Lafarge kept silent considering his options and as far as he could work out there were none.

His attitude to criminals may have hardened over the years but he was not totally immune to sentiment towards some of them and frankly to his mind it was ridiculous, especially now when so many

THE TORTURED DETECTIVE

people were subject to arbitrary justice, that a jewel thief should be set to serve 10 years hard labour.

In that moment, though, Lafarge grabbed onto an idea, a crazy one, but it was worth a shot in the dark. However, given the unbelievable avenues that had already opened up since he started the investigation, he decided it would be worth a try and perhaps at the same time give Lescarboura some reason to hope his present perilous position could be reversed.

"How well did you know Pierre–Yves de Chastelain?" Lafarge asked.

"Pretty well, why?" mumbled Lescarboura.

"You met him through Marguerite, I take it?"

"Yes, when they were together as a couple. I stayed in contact with him afterwards too. Well a man of my profession never knows when he will need a good advocate," smiled Lescarboura.

"Quite. None better than de Chastelain to fight the criminal, sorry, the accused's corner. So I imagine you ran to him straight away when you were arrested for this theft?"

"Yes. Well, no, he came to see me and said he would defend me. I didn't exactly get the chance to phone him," he replied sourly.

"Thus I imagine you were devastated when he failed to turn up to defend you at your trial?"

"Well of course I was pissed off. Wouldn't you have been! I had a great chance of not exactly getting off but at the very least of not receiving too heavy a sentence. Instead I was allocated a jobsworth lawyer, who had to read up on the case in half an hour, and here I am," replied Lescarboura bitterly.

"Most inconvenient timing, I admit. Then soon afterwards Marguerite is murdered..." Lafarge let his voice trail off hoping Lescarboura would bite.

"Yes. So what? What are you inferring, copper?" asked Lescarboura.

"Well, let's say that in both cases, de Chastelain is a person of interest. Obviously he is a fugitive from whatever charge Bousquet wished to bring against him. I am also pursuing him not just as a potential witness to the murder, but very possibly given evidence that I have received this evening of potentially being the murderer himself?

"That is what, as you put it, I am inferring," said Lafarge.

What Lafarge had gambled on proved to be a winner. For Lescarboura's whole demeanour changed in that instant. From being downcast and cynical he was transformed, anger flashed in his eyes, his mouth quivered whether in grief or fury Lafarge could not discern, but he was an animated human being now, not the limpid beaten one he had been minutes before.

"The son of a bitch! The son of a bitch!" yelled Lescarboura.

"Who, Arnaud? Who are you talking about?" enquired Lafarge, knowing full well who the target was of his venomous outburst but wanting to encourage him to say his name, and more to the point why.

"De Chastelain, of course! He had this obsession with Marguerite, he would try any ruse to get back with her, any chance he had of seeing her he would manufacture a way of doing so.

"That all failed, so he came to us with this failproof plan, like he thought he could impress Marguerite with it, make her rich beyond her wildest imagination and then all but blackmail her into returning to him!" sniped Lescarboura, who looked ready to be sick.

"What? You're saying de Chastelain was behind the jewelry theft? It sounds a bit convoluted and fantastical that he would risk a prison term just to win back Marguerite," said Lafarge with the appropriate amount of skepticism in his tone.

"You must be living in another world, copper. Think of de Chastelain and you get arrogance, greed and lust all in one smooth package. He couldn't lose Marguerite to some German colonel, he wanted to be rich enough to be able to not care about the poor people he defended, and his lust for Marguerite was what drove him on.

"I swear to you that he was the man who proposed the theft. He was a former lover of the Countess and had remained friends with her.

"He knew everything, the layout of the apartment, where the jewels were kept, and he even encouraged Marguerite to invite the Countess for dinner, hoping he too would be asked to dine with them.

"He wasn't of course. Marguerite wasn't going to have him fawning over two of his former mistresses, and all the time winking at her at their collaboration over stripping the other lady of her

THE TORTURED DETECTIVE

jewels. No, in that at least Marguerite proved smart," said Lescarboura with a mildly satisfied look on his face.

"So, what happened when he came to see you in jail? He must have lost some of his cockiness, fearful you would try and buy yourself a lighter sentence in exchange for revealing his role in it," said Lafarge.

Lescarboura shook his head sadly and answered, "I couldn't because to do so would be to implicate Marguerite, and even with her having a German colonel as her lover, she would have had to be punished. No, the only hope I was left with was that de Chastelain would call on all his oratorical powers and see me right in court."

"So what did you talk about, other than your defence, which obviously wouldn't have taken up too much of his time as he was already au fait with the case," said Lafarge dryly.

"Ah, all he wanted to know, the great man, was where the jewels were. Were they safely in Marguerite's apartment, or somewhere else? I told him nothing of course, because I knew if I did I would not have any leverage over him, and he would disappear. Little did I realize how right I would be!" he said shaking his head ruefully.

"Quite. However, there is one thing that doesn't seem right. Why would Marguerite allow herself to go along with such a plan, devised by a man she clearly didn't want anything more to do with? Seems a bit weird to me," said Lafarge, raising his eyebrows to accentuate his skepticism.

"I have to take the blame for that. I persuaded her that the price I would be able to get for the jewels would be enough even split between ourselves to make her rich for the rest of her life. Sadly she will never enjoy that feeling," replied Lescarboura.

"I see. That makes sense, given I found the plan for the burglary taped to one of the legs of her makeup table," said Lafarge, enjoying the exasperated look that crossed Lescarboura's face.

"Yet, she still obviously entertained feelings strong enough for him to go to his apartment and warn him of his imminent arrest. They evidently had a very complicated relationship.

"This German colonel, appears to have provided her with the information about de Chastelain's impending misfortune. Again it doesn't sound right, why would her present lover help her former one, who is obsessive about her? One would have thought he would prefer him safely out of the way."

Again, Lafarge hoped Lescarboura would fill in the blanks but he was to be disappointed this time as all he received in reply was a shrug of the shoulders. Undeterred, Lafarge tried one last time, though he expected a similar response.

"Our head of Police also appears to be involved, at least through his friendship with Marguerite and also being responsible for wanting to arrest de Chastelain. Would you happen to know the reasons why?" Lafarge asked, flashing his most charming smile at Lescarboura.

"I know nothing about René Bousquet's involvement, either with regard to Marguerite or with wanting de Chastelain arrested," replied Lescarboura.

Lafarge smiled, pushed the packet of cigarettes towards Lescarboura and proferred his hand. Lescarboura took it, but as he did so, Lafarge held it tightly and pulled him towards him.

"Bousquet falls in the category of not up for discussion unless you get a deal, right?" whispered Lafarge, hoping that if the room was bugged it would not pick up either the question or the answer.

Lescarboura simply nodded, and Lafarge noted too that there was genuine fear in his eyes when he did so. It reflected too how he felt.

CHAPTER SEVEN

Lafarge returned home not in the best of moods, for while the investigation was making progress, his main suspect was now miles away and perhaps already safely in neutral Portugal. For Limoges was usually the first stepping-stone for those wishing to take the risky option of fleeing France.

Tracking de Chastelain down could prove impossible, but he relished that challenge far more than the likelihood of his having to interview formally Bousquet. Quite apart from their personal animosity, it was not in his interests, personally or professionally, to even suggest that the Prefect of Police was linked to a murder enquiry.

He slipped off his suit jacket and flung it onto a chair, and contemplated easing his anxiety by opening one of his fine bottles of red wine. He had a well–stocked cellar, courtesy of a wedding present from his parents and also having built it up himself in happier times.

Having opted to open one, he settled down into his comfortable reading chair. The arms were showing wear and tear with the brown leather torn, but no springs had sprung yet so he didn't have to shift around continually to get a more comfortable position.

He sipped from the glass, swirled the liquid round his mouth and swallowed it appreciatively. He lit a cigarette and with his head back exhaled, making smoke rings like a little child would do when blowing leaves off a dandelion.

He sighed and wondered whether he was drinking too much.

However, he pushed that thought aside and shrugged, thinking 'so what?'. That's what most people who could afford it are doing every night, just to get through these times, whether they are collaborating or just going along with their ordinary lives and trying to ignore the beastly, inhuman acts going on around them every day.

Acts, he smiled bitterly, that he was powerless to do anything about because their Teutonic conquerors were perpetrating them brazenly and according to the laws they had imposed on first their citizens and now people all over the continent.

His thoughts returned to Bousquet. For it was people like him who were willingly acquiescing in the Germans determination to eradicate any opposition, and stamp down on those they considered beneath them.

Well, Bousquet would perhaps have to answer for that later but it bemused Lafarge that intelligent and able people such as the head of the Police should fall under the spell of the Nazis. Bousquet, for example, was no coward, for aged just 21 he had along with a friend, who died in the process, using just a canoe, saved countless lives when floods devastated the area he lived in near Montauban, in the south west of France.

He had deservedly been awarded the Légion d'Honneur for that selfless act. But now here he was on the flip side of the coin, enthusiastically aiding and abetting the Germans in their remorseless pursuit of the Jews – by all accounts even their defenseless children would not be safe.

Lafarge conceded that by performing his duties as a policeman under Vichy did not allow him to be too much of a moral judge. However, he at least had donned the French Army uniform, though that had not brought honour on the country with its abject defeat and surrender.

However, he was far from an enthusiastic supporter of Vichy.

He reasoned with his usual dark humour that better to be pre–occupied than to be occupied by the moral vicissitudes of daily life.

To this extent he would set aside the danger posed by Bousquet and he would pursue him over the death of Marguerite, for he had questions to answer and this murder as far as he could see was not state–condoned. He swallowed a healthy measure of his glass of wine and smiled at the thought of for once having the whip hand over Bousquet, whether Massu liked it or not.

*

"I could ask some delicate questions, sir, which may not be to your liking."

"I don't doubt that, Lafarge, you would disappoint me if you didn't. I am only coming along as a courtesy to our German friends."

Massu and Lafarge were seated in the back of the former's large black sedan on their way to pay a call on Colonel von Dirlinger, who had generously spared some time in what he termed was his incredibly busy schedule.

What that probably meant was in between breakfast and lunch and probably separated by a pre–lunch drinks party. What intelligence gathering needed to be done now that France was firmly under German control, and the parts that weren't were ruled by their puppets in Vichy, wasn't evident to Lafarge.

From what Lafarge had been able to learn about von Dirlinger it was clear that he preferred the uniform to the work he had to carry out.

A moderate actor turned top class skier before the War, and who had also competed in several Grand Prix, von Dirlinger had declined the invitation of Heinrich Himmler to join his Aryan elite of the SS – much to the pince–nez wearing puritan's annoyance.

Instead he had joined, by comparison, the more gentlemanly Abwehr, which was run by Admiral Wilhelm Canaris, and appeared to be more like an aristocrats club, whose members were keen to continue their pursuits of hunting, polo or shooting.

Nevertheless, Lafarge was determined not to underestimate von Dirlinger, for while he had the appearance of a daredevil playboy, the Abwehr did have a reputation for also only hiring people with agile and intelligent minds.

He also gave him a few marks out of ten for having rejected Himmler's courting call. Von Dirlinger while not head of the Paris section of the Ast as the Abwehr were known when they were based abroad, was in charge of their counter espionage and security department.

He would therefore possess a huge fount of information regarding the Résistance and most importantly what their strength or bases were around Limoges, commonly known as the 'Red Town' for its tradition of producing left wing politicians.

That could at least give him a lead as to where de Chastelain might be hiding, or give an indication as to the route he might be taking to leave the country.

However, he was not certain how helpful the Colonel would be, given that he might have been the leak for the information that had precipitated Marguerite's dash across the city to warn de Chastelain of his impending arrest.

The Ast headquarters certainly didn't disappoint in terms of the reputation of the Abwehr being an up market intelligence agency, as it was based out of the magnificent Hotel Lutetia, on the Boulevard Raspail in the heart of the chic sixth arrondissement on the left bank.

Both Lafarge and Massu cast an admiring eye over the luxurious world they entered as they climbed the steps and entered the lobby.

Certainly the orderlies were giving the impression of a busy day, walking backwards and forwards across the well–polished floor, knocking and entering at various doors and then exiting with businesslike expressions on their faces.

Massu and Lafarge presented their credentials to a shapely female receptionist, though unlike most hotel receptionists, she was dressed in the field grey uniform of the Wehrmacht.

She looked at their identification cards, then raised her eyes to meet theirs, holding them both in a steady gaze while she ran the rule over them, probably to make her feel more important than she really was. She then flashed her grey eyes at them and with a haughty wave of her well–manicured right hand, pointed them in the direction of the hotel bar.

Massu and Lafarge looked questioningly at her, but she shrugged her shoulders dismissively and they wandered off in the direction of the bar like two naughty little schoolboys who had just been admonished by their beautiful school mistress.

The bar was half full, even though it was only 11 in the morning.

Various officers were sitting at tables, chatting to each other, with bottles of champagne beside them in their ice buckets, while others had beers in front of them.

Massu raised his eyebrows at Lafarge and suggested they both stand at the bar, the former ordering a coffee, for real coffee was difficult to come by even in Paris, while Lafarge opted for a cognac, to steady his nerves, he told himself somewhat unconvincingly.

However, instead of reproaching him, Massu accompanied him by also ordering a cognac, along with his coffee, and they chatted away amiably while they waited for von Dirlinger to come and greet them.

About fifteen minutes later, the almost impossibly good looking Colonel sauntered in. He flashed them a film star type smile,

THE TORTURED DETECTIVE

showing off his perfect white teeth, and joined them in having a cognac, provoking the two detectives to have a second one to keep him company.

Von Dirlinger chatted about inane matters. He recounted a tale of how he had had a puncture the other day on returning from Longchamp racecourse, having lost a pretty penny. However, thankfully he had enough experience from his days as a racing driver to be able to fix it too quickly for the local résistants to get organised and claim the scalp of an Abwehr colonel.

Both Massu and Lafarge smiled at his weak joke, the latter commenting that perhaps the jockeys on his horses had been the résistants in depriving a German of his money. Von Dirlinger laughed heartily at the remark, though the timbre did not reflect any great sincerity.

"So Colonel, now we have got the small talk and the common courtesies out of the way, I was wondering whether we could go somewhere a bit more private?" asked Massu.

"Yes of course gentlemen, we can go to my office, though, I must apologise as it is in a bit of a state of disorder. Not very German is it? But I have some extremely important matters going on at the moment, and with all the information I am receiving, the papers are strewn everywhere.

"I would of course request of you not to cast a glance at them," he said flashing what seemed to be a trademark film star smile again.

Von Dirlinger led them through the lobby, taking the time to give a warm greeting to the receptionist, who flashed a look that suggested they were more intimate than just colleagues. He ushered them into a large room which was indeed dominated by mounds of papers covering the floor.

He pointed to two elegant Louis XV chairs that were positioned on the side of a magnificent antique desk while he brought over a bottle of cognac and three glasses.

They all took a sip of the excellent quality cognac, markedly superior to the one they had drunk at the bar, and settled back in their seats.

Lafarge felt completely at ease, the drink had not had an effect on him, and for that he was mightily thankful, for there might only be one chance to ask von Dirlinger questions.

"So, Colonel, can you start by telling us the nature of your relationship with Marguerite Suchet and what happened at your last meeting with her?"

Von Dirlinger smiled warmly, took a cigarette from his gold cigarette case, Lafarge noting that it was not one from the stockpile of Ambassador Abetz's collection, and thought for a moment.

"Well I think you are well aware of the nature of our relationship, Inspector. Thus there is no need to go into the details," he replied in a neutral tone.

"For the record colonel, it would be good to have it written down. It's chief inspector by the way," said Lafarge brusquely, not willing to let von Dirlinger set the tone for the interview.

Von Dirlinger eyed Lafarge carefully, assessing whether it merited pushing the point of what was worth noting down and what wasn't but in the end he decided he would concede on this point.

"Very well Chief Inspector. We were lovers, we had been for some time and I hoped it would continue. Unfortunately someone has intervened to make that impossible," he said sadly.

Both Lafarge and Massu remained silent, prompting von Dirlinger to answer the more pertinent part of the question.

"As for when I last saw Marguerite, well it was on the night she died. I went round to her apartment and spent around an hour there. It wasn't a very pleasant hour I might add," he said bitterly.

"Ah. How so?" asked Lafarge.

"Well, she didn't seem… how do you French say it? Ah yes, she didn't seem to be "bien dans sa peau". She was ill at ease and seemed very keen for me to make my visit a short one."

"Did she hint at all at why she was not her usual self with you?" asked Lafarge, sensing von Dirlinger was not being totally open with them.

Von Dirlinger looked Lafarge straight in the eye as he reflected on his answer.

"She, erm, said that she was expecting someone else, that he was not someone she could cancel or make excuses about not being able to see him, not even a colonel in the Abwehr was important enough to gain precedence over this gentleman," he replied with a mirthless laugh.

THE TORTURED DETECTIVE

Lafarge could sense his excitement rising, and thought, was it the moment to bring Bousquet's name into the game, but he decided to err on the side of caution, play dumb for as long as possible.

"Did she say who this important gentleman was, colonel?" he asked in a flat tone.

Von Dirlinger must have been expecting the question as only the stupidest detective would not have asked it, but he nevertheless didn't look comfortable at having to answer it.

He fiddled with his lighter, deliberated over smoking another cigarette before closing his case without taking one, and instead poured himself and the two policemen another glass of cognac.

"I have, as you can tell throughout my pre–war life, been attracted to sports that carry a lot of risk and a lot of danger to them, gentlemen.

"So you might think that I treat my professional life in the same manner. However, I am sorry to disappoint you but that is not the case.

"War is rather good at waking one up and teaching one what risks are worth taking, rather like receiving a piece of intelligence, you weigh it up with the utmost caution and do not react impulsively. For this reason I would prefer not to have to answer that question," he replied firmly.

Massu shifted uncomfortably in his seat at the reply and waited for his subordinate to come back at the colonel. However, Lafarge simply sighed and surprised his superior and von Dirlinger by moving on.

"I can vouch for that, spending time as a guest of yours taught me not to take any unnecessary risks, if one wished to return to some form of normal life," Lafarge commented in a suitably sarcastic tone which, he was delighted to see, made von Dirlinger bristle.

Without waiting for the German to get a riposte in, Lafarge continued with his questioning.

"What exactly did you say to the victim the night of her premiere when you returned to her apartment?" asked Lafarge, keeping his tone civil.

"I don't really see the relevance of that question, Chief Inspector," replied von Dirlinger, whose earlier air of bonhomie had disappeared.

"Well, colonel you being an intelligence officer, I would have thought that you would realize that whilst we may be more restricted in our duties these days, we still have informants and indeed eyes and ears of our own so that we can keep ordinary crime down," said Lafarge.

"So I would suggest colonel that you reflect on what you are going to say with regard to my question," he added in a firm manner.

Von Dirlinger puffed out his cheeks to register his annoyance at the persistence of the detective, looked somewhat despairingly for help from Massu, who did not provide any, simply shrugging his shoulders.

"Very well, Chief Inspector. I was somewhat indiscreet, maybe it was the excellent champagne we had had at Maxim's, or perhaps it was an offering of one lover to another, but I imparted some top secret information to Marguerite," he said.

"This information pertained to her former lover de Chastelain, the lawyer, I take it?" asked Lafarge, leading him on.

Von Dirlinger nodded vigorously.

"It was foolish of me, but in the greater scheme of things, hardly damaging to my country's interests, as there is little or no evidence to suggest de Chastelain is in any way involved in terrorist activities.

"I considered it a purely French matter, a personal argument between two adult men and about what, I have no idea," he said with a resigned look on his face.

"Two adult men, perhaps, but one of them wields a lot of power, and was going to use it to arrest the other.

"It was rather gallant of you to divulge this information, and also to provide the driver for Marguerite's voyage across Paris to deliver the message you were too afraid of doing yourself," said Lafarge acidly.

Von Dirlinger looked furious at this remark, but refrained from making an ill judged response, preferring to take a sip from his glass.

"You appear to have all the answers, Chief Inspector. I really don't see why you bother to even ask me the questions!" said von Dirlinger with a bitter laugh.

"Not necessarily colonel. For instance I would like to know why you wanted de Chastelain out of the way. I mean, you say he posed no threat to German interests, so why would you make such an effort to help a man, one who was also a former lover of your mistress, to escape from his nemesis? You must see that it is a bit confusing for us," said Lafarge.

"I can see that. But I can also see that you are entering into a discussion about something that doesn't appear to be related to the murder of Marguerite, so therefore it is a moot point why I helped de Chastelain," said von Dirlinger, looking smug.

"Let me take that look off your face, colonel, by saying it has everything to do with the murder of Marguerite, because de Chastelain has disappeared, but not before turning up at a friend's apartment covered in blood on the night of her murder," Lafarge said and noting that the smug look had disappeared as quick as it had appeared, he pressed home the point.

"Thus I don't think it looks terribly good for you, colonel, in that the man who you aided in escaping René Bousquet's clutches is wanted in connection with the murder of your mistress, the person you sent to give him the message. Now perhaps you see what a deep hole you are in?" Lafarge said trying to keep the satisfaction he felt out of his voice.

Von Dirlinger did indeed look as if he was starting to appreciate the seriousness of the situation he was in. He quickly lit himself another cigarette, cast his eyes around the room and waited for the heavy silence that had settled in his office to be broken.

Lafarge was in no mood to let the smooth German regain his equilibrium, and decided to press on while he had him under pressure. For it appeared to the detective that the good living in Paris had taken the edge off the sharpness and nervelessness that von Dirlinger had displayed in the sports he competed in before the war.

"I don't believe your reason for warning de Chastelain had anything to do with not being a danger to your country, why should you be so concerned about his welfare?

"I am sure there are countless people like him who have been arrested without you batting an eyelid and questioning whether they really merit it or not," said Lafarge acidly.

"Thus I am searching for the real reason, and I believe I have it. It wasn't to frustrate Bousquet either, though you evidently did, and it wouldn't be very good, for you were the big chiefs in Berlin, to learn of your role in it.

"At best, you would be sent to the Eastern Front and well the worst I am sure you are more than aware of what that would be, as you have consigned many to that fate. While I would find your outsmarting Bousquet a foolish act, I believe your motives were rather more venal. Do you know a man by the name of Arnaud Lescarboura?"

Von Dirlinger flashed a look of panic at the mention of the jewel thief's name. Massu too noted it, making any denial totally lacking in credibility.

"I've heard of him. Who hasn't, he was the poor beggar who was due to be defended by de Chastelain the day he disappeared," replied von Dirlinger, trying to shrug off the question.

"Yes, I believe that you may not have met him personally, even though he did spend some nights at Marguerite's, but we will leave that aside for the moment. However, my theory is that you used de Chastelain to get Lescarboura to steal from the Baroness, and then you were all to share the profits from the theft," said Lafarge calmly.

"That's an interesting allegation, Chief Inspector. I would hope you have the necessary proof before you take that any further. It would not do you any good at all to make such serious claims against a German officer," interjected von Dirlinger, but in a tone lacking any great assurance.

"Physical proof I have none, but I have enough circumstantial evidence to make your life extremely difficult, without making it into a public scandal. I realize my chances of bringing you to trial are non–existent, but de Chastelain is a different proposition.

"I believe that Marguerite, who I acknowledge was not an innocent party in the theft but was maybe unaware of your role, was murdered because she did not either keep the jewels or found a way to sell them.

"I think this was de Chastelain's motivation. He had not only lost her, for she was in love with you, but also the consolation prize of the money. One of those is motive enough, both together are pretty much conclusive."

THE TORTURED DETECTIVE

Von Dirlinger surprised Lafarge and Massu in applauding the Chief Inspector, poured what remained of the bottle of cognac into their glasses and having taken a sip and swirled it around his mouth before swallowing it, addressed his audience.

"I congratulate you on your theory, which I take it to be, and which certainly would be one I would myself have proposed if our roles were reversed. Without admitting to anything I would say that I did have a different motive to the one I claimed I had earlier in having de Chastelain removed from the scene, and Marguerite was the ideal instrument for that.

"I swear that I did not see de Chastelain from the moment he disappeared, I do not know what happened with the jewels, but you know all too well both of you that hackneyed phrase; honour among thieves wears thin quickly should there be a discrepancy in the figures!" he said smiling one of his smooth smiles.

Lafarge was on the point of opening his mouth, but was quickly silenced as the colonel held up one of his hands.

"You will not find my fingerprints on these jewels, Chief Inspector, and if you insist on intimating that again, I will take action. Having said that, it is obviously in both our best interests you find de Chastelain.

"I can help you with that by issuing you with that most prized of things, an Ausweis. Obviously, I would wish that my co–operation would be signalled should there be a problem further down the line with the secretary–general of the French police," he said, adding yet another of his maddening smiles.

Lafarge felt like hitting him with something harder than words, but preferring to keep Massu on side, he nodded his assent, without going so far as to say yes. However, he had one further weapon to use before this interview came to its conclusion and he wasn't going to let it slip.

"I will not make any comment on what you have said about your role, sorry, non–role in the jewelry theft for that will be resolved by my investigation.

"I will gladly accept your offer of the Ausweis as the investigation may well require me to travel outside of Paris, given the information I have been furnished with about the whereabouts of de Chastelain.

"I would also like from you any non–sensitive intelligence you may have about résistance cells around the Limoges area, as it is likely the fugitive is either holed up with one of them or has used one of them to pass him on down to another one."

Von Dirlinger nodded his head vigorously to his requests, and made to rise from his desk judging that the torrid two hours were over. However, it was Lafarge's turn to raise his hand to tell him not to be so hasty.

"I have of course suggested in my theory and in an earlier part of the meeting that I suspect de Chastelain of being the murderer," he said evenly.

"Yes, you have. However, by your tone you appear to have something to add to that," said von Dirlinger warily.

Lafarge smiled, enjoying the sudden return of uncertainty to the Abwehr colonel's features.

"Well as I said earlier, much earlier in fact and received a far from satisfactory response, aside from de Chastelain and yourself, Marguerite was meeting with someone else.

"You said that it wasn't worth your while revealing who this was. However, I may have lulled you into a false sense of security by letting you away with the answer at the time, for I know very well who this very important visitor was," said Lafarge.

Von Dirlinger looked flustered by this, intertwining his fingers so hard that the two policemen could hear his knuckles cracking, and instead of trying to block Lafarge by some obfuscation, he wearily allowed him to continue.

"I know who it is because, when I did a more thorough search of Marguerite's apartment, notably her drawing room, I came across a silver cigarette case, down the side of one of her armchairs.

"Now of course it may have been there for a while, it could even, I imagine, have been planted there, but it is not the type of object that its owner would simply shrug his shoulders at losing and move on.

"The case had a very personal inscription in it. It was a personal dedication from Ambassador Abetz to none other than your good friend René Bousquet."

Lafarge could hear the spluttering of surprise from Massu to his right, while he watched as beads of sweat broke out on von Dirlinger's temple.

He himself felt a sense of contentment, although he accepted that Bousquet was a far more difficult target to bring down, but for the moment, he would enjoy having got the better of von Dirlinger and taking a huge step forward in the investigation.

Whether he would be allowed to see it through was another matter entirely.

"I would like to thank you colonel for your time, your fine cognac and ultimately your co–operation. If you could be so kind to organize the Ausweis as soon as possible that would be of benefit to both of us. Good day," said Lafarge affably, leaving a confused Massu to follow him out of the room and a dumbfounded von Dirlinger staring into space.

CHAPTER EIGHT

On exiting the splendor of the Lutetia, Lafarge felt an extra spring in his step at not only deflating the large ego of von Dirlinger but also having had his suspicions about Bousquet re–enforced. However, his brief moment of joy was swiftly brought to a close as Massu gripped his shoulder tightly from behind.

"Let's take a stroll Lafarge," he said in a clipped tone.

The two of them walked in silence down Boulevard Raspail, with the sedan following them, Lafarge holding his tongue and awaiting his superior's lecture, for he felt sure that Massu, having recovered his senses and realizing the consequences of what von Dirlinger had told them, would not be best happy with him.

Massu maintained his silence until they came to a non–descript café further down the Boulevard, where he gestured Lafarge to sit at one of the outside tables, as if he was dealing with a school truant. Lafarge obeyed his boss, who surveyed the other people sitting outside, all of whom were sitting sufficiently far away for them to be able to hold a relatively discreet discussion.

A middle–aged puffy–faced waiter came and took their order, Massu opting for another cognac, Lafarge for a glass of white wine, and the two of them said nothing until their drinks had been served.

"Lafarge, I like you, I respect you and I appreciate your work. In the present circumstances that places both of us in a minority. You for getting results and me for liking you," said Massu with a weary sigh.

"However, I am disappointed that you did not feel it worthy of informing me, your superior no less, of your finding the secretary–general's cigarette case at the murder scene and of other facts surrounding M. Bousquet's potential involvement in the case," he added, giving Lafarge a disapproving look.

"Now it puts me in a seriously compromised position. I am duty bound to call Bousquet and either inform him of the findings so far, which he has already asked for, and to which I will have to add the evidence inculpating him or I will as I would normally in such cases have to call him in for formal questioning.

THE TORTURED DETECTIVE

"Obviously I do not wish to do either. It isn't worth my while to do so and I may add, Lafarge, it certainly is not going to be very pleasant for you if I were to go down the suicidal route."

Massu smiled thinly at Lafarge, who puffed out his cheeks and took a deep breath in order not to reply in too brutal a fashion and ruin his relationship with one of his few allies in the department.

"I appreciate that sir. I understand that I have placed you in an invidious position but you must comprehend that I had little option once von Dirlinger started playing his clever games with us in the interview," said Lafarge in a measured tone.

"It is the very reason I did not share any of the information regarding Bousquet with you because I wanted to keep you as far from him as possible and believe me, I was not happy when I realized that I would have to confront him at some point.

"However, we are where we are now and there is nothing we can do to go back on what we heard, which, allied to the physical evidence, makes it imperative I at least get to speak to Bousquet. That way, I can either rule him in or out of the enquiry.

"God knows I would rather not have to, but I can do it without you and prevent you being destroyed.

"Besides, while he may not respect me, he would be a fool to do me any harm as I can call upon my father, albeit reluctantly, to coo into the Marshal's ear and have Bousquet's wings clipped.

"Given that he is gunning to replace at the very least Laval in the German's affections, it would not do him much good to be publicly humiliated by the head of state, even if it is a tin pot regime," said Lafarge with a rueful smile.

Massu stroked his chin, twiddled briefly with his moustache, and ordered another round of drinks, which was not going to do either of them many favours as it was touching one in the afternoon and with no food inside them, their liquor consumption for the morning would start to take hold.

"I admire your confidence, Lafarge. I hope it is not the drink talking, because Pétain may be head of Vichy but it is Paris where the power is, that is to say where the Germans are, and who is pretty much the senior Frenchman in Paris, or at least the most powerful?

"Why, Bousquet of course! What's more, they love him, especially after his enthusiastic support for resolving the Jewish problem. So an attack on him, or indeed any hint of scandal, and I can guarantee you that no sweet words from your father would save you from a most uncomfortable time.

"I suggest that you steer away from Bousquet, you press von Dirlinger for the Ausweis and you get yourself on a train to Limoges and find de Chastelain. That way everyone will be happy, or at least those of us who want to stay healthy and prosper till the war comes to an end.

"There is no point fighting battles that you cannot possibly win, you above all should know that after your experience in 1940. I can guarantee you that the camp you find yourself in, should you not take my advice, will be a lot worse than the POW one. And this time, there will be no early release," said Massu patting Lafarge on the shoulder.

Lafarge nodded, for he knew Massu was right, but he was boiling over inside. For once again, those who had usurped power, through no democratic process, would get away with possibly murder, and in a case that ordinarily he and his colleagues were still allowed the necessary powers to solve.

It made him sick, and not a little bitter, that here was a chance to tackle Bousquet, the man who had sneered at him for becoming a cop, and he was being warned off even before he had a chance to at the very minimum give him a fright.

"I know, Lafarge, that you are a man of great integrity, and there aren't too many of those these days, but if one felt that there was political pressure before the war in delicate cases, it is nothing compared to what it is now.

"For there is not only the threat of being shunted into some broom cupboard for pushing too hard, but now there is a physical menace too. Some people I knew before these dark days walk to the other side of the street when they see me now, because they say I am a collaborator. My own family, well some of them, treat me with an air of disgust," he said sadly.

"Well yes, I might keep my head down and I might not raise my voice, but it is only because I love the work of a detective that I have stayed.

"I don't go around denouncing people, like some do, lord knows I wouldn't live with myself if I did, but at the same time I accept the limits of the job and what I can do. I just wish that those I like would follow that example," he said smiling kindly at Lafarge.

THE TORTURED DETECTIVE

Lafarge looked at the big bearlike figure, dapperly dressed as always and with his hair immaculately swept back off his forehead, and felt genuine tenderness for him. It was a feeling he did not hold towards many these days.

He knew Massu was right, there was little sense in pursuing such a futile course of action, but it was gnawing away at him.

His sense of justice was too strong to just let it ride. Also it was a case of putting behind him the feeble fight that the army had put up when the Germans invaded and regaining some pride in taking on one of those who had benefited from the collapse in French prestige.

He at least knew what the consequences would be, and he wouldn't bring Massu down with him.

"Sir I appreciate immensely your advice and I know it is well meant and also the right course of action to follow.

"However, let me have one shot at Bousquet. He may not respect me but there are old ties there, which I hope might count for something," said Lafarge, though he wondered how many newly termed enemies of the state thought their old ties with Bousquet counted for something and would probably see their hopes brutally dashed by his overweening ambition.

"Let me be the one to present the initial report on the investigation to him personally.

"You can say that you are involved in another enquiry and you have not been able to pay as much attention as you would have liked to this one, and there would be no better replacement to relate the details than the man Bousquet personally requested be placed in charge of it," he said with a conspiratorial wink.

Massu didn't return the wink, it wasn't his style anyway, and remained impassive and silent for several minutes.

Lafarge took the opportunity to order one final round of drinks, and went to the bar to pay the bill while Massu thought his proposition over.

While at the bar and waiting for his change from the owner, a big burly man with a distinct Auvergnat accent which Lafarge surmised was ones passport into owning cafes these days as all of them seemed to be from the Auvergne region, he appraised the rest of the clientele.

Even though it was lunchtime there were not many, some workmen dressed in their blue overalls munching on hard boiled eggs and drinking pastis at the zinc covered bar.

Two couples of elderly appearance sat in the corner, treasuring their small glasses of wine, and younger couples dotted at the tables on the terrace, smartly dressed, though, their clothes were not new by any means, perhaps parents hand me downs, but the one thing that impressed him was that there was no laughter.

That was it, these days, the majority of the Parisians went about their business, more earnest than ever, just living their lives day to day, hoping to get through to evening and avoid any trouble.

However, the gaiety that used to ring out from terraces all around the city had disappeared, even when people like those here were relaxing.

The humiliation of the defeat and the dark oppressive forces in charge now, German and French, and no sight to the end of them or the ever deepening rationing, had left most people without the reason or ability to laugh.

Lafarge wandered back to the table despondently, thinking for the first time since he had been released whether it would be a better idea to join the family in the south and try through Isadora's diplomatic connections to get a boat to Argentina or at the very least to Spain. His defeatist thoughts were interrupted by Massu.

"Well my boy. I have given it what thought is needed and whilst I think you are courting unnecessary danger, I will arrange for you to go and see our esteemed secretary–general. Whether you end up leaving by the door you enter through, I will leave up to your powers of diplomacy," said Massu gruffly.

"Thank you. I will tread cautiously of course, you never know where the trapdoor is these days, but at least, I can then feel that I have done all I can to honour the memory of the victim, even if there are many out there who view her as little more than a whore for the Germans," said Lafarge.

Lafarge's tone may have been bitter but inside, he was elated, for now the way had opened up for him to have a confrontation with Bousquet. With that knowledge, he all but skipped to the sedan, whose driver had been patiently waiting for the two men. It was just as well Lafarge did not see Massu's doleful look as he ambled to the car, and as he did so, muttered under his breath 'Dead man walking.'

CHAPTER NINE

Lafarge returned to the Hotel Lutetia faster than he imagined he would, for von Dirlinger had left a message for him at the office to be on hand to collect the Ausweis by 7 that evening from him personally.

The message added that if he were not able to make it, then he would have to wait for at least a week as the colonel would be away on official business. Lafarge was delighted that von Dirlinger had been hasty in organizing the much sought after Ausweis.

He hoped that von Dirlinger's trip was not a premise for one of his suspects to seek an alternative posting, well out of the limited reach of the French police.

The same decorative receptionist was at her post. A thought flitted through his mind at what she got up to in her leisure time and he half felt like asking her, then shooed it out of his head and proceeded to von Dirlinger's office.

The colonel was on the phone when he entered, but waved him to one of the chairs he and Massu had occupied earlier in the day. Von Dirlinger smiled warmly at him and indicated the bottle of cognac – freshly opened he noted – on the desk with two glasses as yet to be filled. Lafarge took the hint and poured for them both.

Von Dirlinger then wrapped up his conversation, though Lafarge, skeptical as ever, pondered whether he was really talking to anybody or if it was a show.

"Good to see you again, Chief Inspector," said von Dirlinger before he sipped at his cognac.

Lafarge replied in similar fashion and waited for von Dirlinger to hand over the document.

"Let me see, where have I put the damned thing. Ah yes, here it is! Sorry, I have so much bloody paperwork, half of which I never get round to reading," he said, delivering another of his film star smiles while handing the Ausweis to a grateful Lafarge.

"Careful colonel, one of the documents you neglect to read may tell you when the invasion is going to be," said Lafarge, half–in jest.

"Ah, yes quite! Very funny Lafarge," laughed von Dirlinger.

THE TORTURED DETECTIVE

"Anyway, thank you colonel, for both the drink and the Ausweis. It means I can get cracking in tracking down our fugitive and I should hope solving Marguerite's murder. Although before I go, I would like to ask you what you might be able to tell me on résistance activity in the area round Limoges," said Lafarge.

Von Dirlinger shook his head vigorously and wagged his finger at Lafarge.

"Not résistance, Chief Inspector, terrorist activity. Of course, that depends on one's point of view, but we Germans, and those of you in the forces of law and order, can only call their activities by one term and that is terrorist," said von Dirlinger and without his trademark smile, it meant he was being serious.

Lafarge shrugged apologetically and made to get up and leave, but was directed to remain in his seat.

"No matter Lafarge, don't worry about it. I am Abwehr, not a goon from the SS or Gestapo, though, lord knows Reichsführer Himmler tried hard enough to recruit me for his 'Aryan brotherhood'," said von Dirlinger raising his eyes to the ceiling.

"I prefer to belong to a gentleman's club, albeit one that is inhabited by intellectual snobs," he added with the smile having returned to the corners of his mouth.

Lafarge thought it best to not comment, indeed, he remained impassive in his chair and allowed von Dirlinger free rein to carry on.

"Anyway, enough of that.

"I was rather running away with myself. Yes, of course I can provide you with some information on the vipers operating in that area. You should yourself know from your colleagues in the Brigade specially designed to combat such operations what the situation is," said von Dirlinger crisply.

Lafarge shook his head.

"I am afraid they don't feel the need to share such information with us, ordinary criminal police. They don't regard us as being their equal, to them we are suspects as we lack their zeal for the cause," said Lafarge dryly.

Von Dirlinger laughed heartily at Lafarge's remark, and poured them another glass.

"Yes indeed, I see what you mean. Us Germans have certainly perfected the term "rule and divide". When one's collaborationist police force isn't even united then it is indeed true.

"Very well Lafarge, I will give you as much detail as I am allowed to, without divulging any operational details from our side, just in case you fall into the wrong hands," said von Dirlinger.

"However, I prefer not to do that here. Let's go and have dinner, then perhaps we might pursue a night of genuine leisure suitable for two gentlemen," he said amiably, winking at Lafarge.

Gretchen, for that was the receptionist's name, did not join them much to Lafarge's disappointment, though he reflected afterwards it was probably just as well. For as much as he missed having someone lying naked beside him in bed, a German mistress could prove complicated.

Nevertheless, he had to admit he had an enjoyable time with von Dirlinger, who was both cultured and amusing as well as extremely courteous to the waiters, who served them in Brasserie Lipp, on the Boulevard St Germain, just opposite the Café de Flore.

Von Dirlinger told Lafarge that he preferred to dine there than Maxims which was the favoured restaurant for most of the German high brass, as Lipp was more relaxed and was associated with French intellectuals, writers and artists.

It gave him a sense of being away from the war for a few hours, even if he went there most of the time, as he did that evening, dressed in his uniform.

Lafarge allowed his dining companion to dominate the conversation – well, he was from the conquering army he mused – and learnt that he was one of four children born to a minor catholic aristocratic line.

His father had a small estate in Bavaria, but had also enjoyed a career as a successful private banker, bucking the trend of so many who had gone bankrupt over unpaid loans and the market crashing in the late 20's and 30's.

He was unmarried and it shone through to Lafarge that while he may have had a fling with Gretchen, he had been in love with Marguerite.

However, that still did not explain why he had sent her on the risky trip across Paris to warn de Chastelain about his impending arrest. There maybe von Dirlinger's weakness lay, greed over love,

THE TORTURED DETECTIVE

for Lafarge still suspected he was involved in the theft of the jewels.

Lafarge didn't divulge much about his background when it came to be his turn to talk about his past. He guessed that von Dirlinger being in intelligence gathering would have already done his homework, so there was not much more worth adding to what he already knew.

"With a father as influential as yours, I am surprised you chose to return to being an ordinary criminal detective," said von Dirlinger after the pudding had been cleared away and they had ordered their by now seemingly mandatory cognacs with their espressos.

Lafarge was a bit taken aback by the sudden directness of von Dirlinger's conversation.

He certainly did not wish to start discussing his complex relationship with his father or indeed his mother. While he was fond of his father, he certainly did not see eye to eye with him on his politics or his devotion to the senile old Marshal in Vichy.

Lord knows what his father would have said about his impending meeting with Bousquet who, even if he was after Pétain and Laval's jobs, was still much admired by his father.

"I preferred not to trouble him with such mundane matters as my career," replied Lafarge tartly, hoping that would put an end to that topic of conversation.

"Yes, quite. I understand. There's enough nepotism going around as it is within your government. Still there are not many who show quite so much enthusiasm and tenacity as you. Even if it could be damaging to your future," said von Dirlinger.

"Ah, I see colonel, now dinner is over and you have me in a relaxed frame of mind, you feel it is time to return to veiled threats in the guise of compliments.

"Very well, but perhaps rather like yourself, I chose to work in an environment I felt more at ease in, which is less associated with the forces of repression imposed by an unelected government on its own people," said Lafarge more loudly than he wished and the anger he felt brought the colour to his cheeks.

Von Dirlinger appeared totally unruffled by his French guest's remarks and smiled sympathetically back at him.

"Yes, well I work for a democratically elected government, albeit one that hasn't bothered to call a session of parliament for several years now.

"But then it would be rather difficult to assemble all the members, as most of the dissident voices are housed in camps now, their upkeep paid for most generously by the state.

"Not much for them to complain about, bed and board paid for, no need to spend money on secretaries, or typewriters for their endless speeches.

"No extra cost to the taxpayer. Yes Germany is a splendid example of a democracy operating at zero cost in terms of the taxpayer paying for our representatives!" von Dirlinger said, laughing bitterly.

Lafarge smiled and signalled his appreciation of his host for his openness and honesty with him by raising his glass and downing it in one large gulp. Von Dirlinger looked at his watch and indicated there was still time for a refill, which was welcomed by Lafarge.

"The rate we drink cognac, they will need two harvests per year," joked Lafarge, who had rediscovered a rare sense of comfort and relaxation that had been largely missing from his life ever since he returned from the camp.

"I'll drink to that," laughed von Dirlinger, unbuttoning one of his jacket buttons.

"So colonel, just to be serious for a moment before we become insane with drink, is there anything I should be aware of in terms of terrorist activity in the Limoges area? I think after all this was meant to be the purpose of the dinner," Lafarge said.

"Ah yes of course Chief Inspector. Now it is you putting your official hat on. I understand, though, for the last thing any of us suspects in this dreadful case would wish for would be for something nasty to happen to the detective in charge of the investigation," said von Dirlinger humourously.

"Well my dear Lafarge, there are two groups based round there, hiding out in the undergrowth. Let's be kind, they are not quite vermin, but they are the type of animal who you would do well to avoid crossing paths with.

"One is the Kakarian band, run by an Armenian immigrant who worked on a farm down there and is an avowed communist. The other, which is more likely to have welcomed de Chastelain, is the larger 'Beau Temps va revenir' group. They are, as the name suggests of course, a bunch of misguided romantic idealists but have proved to be a major pain in the ass of the Vichy security forces down there.

"Why do I think de Chastelain will be with them? Simply because it is easier to hide among a group which is larger and made up of a vast cross section of society. I believe there are poets, painters, doctors, lawyers, the majority are Jews of course, so another legal eagle such as de Chastelain would fit in nicely," said von Dirlinger gruffly.

"God you make them sound more like a talking shop not a fighting force. Are they really that dangerous? Sounds to me you are more likely to be overcome by the weight of their verbosity and debating skills than by bullets and grenades," said Lafarge dryly.

Von Dirlinger shook his head and wagged his finger at his French companion.

"Lawyers and doctors are never more ferocious than when they want their bills paid, and these are men with nothing to lose.

"This is perhaps the largest bill they have ever countenanced and they want it to be paid in full, the sooner the better, and what is more the only signature they wish as confirmation of payment is the signed death certificate.

"A high–profile detective from Paris, whose father is senior counsellor to the leader of what they perceive as their bastard state, would go some way towards paying that bill," said von Dirlinger, a grim look clouding his handsome face.

"Point taken, colonel. However, I am in an unenviable position as I have no option but to go there and to find de Chastelain, otherwise this case will never be resolved to either mine or your satisfaction. We owe it at the very least to Marguerite," said Lafarge.

"Yes, that we do Lafarge. I am most impressed by your professional engagement. I have to say that I have found it rather lacking in your colleagues in general.

"That is apart from the Brigade Spéciales so keenly led by your chief René Bousquet, whose enthusiasm reflects the passionate fight against enemies of the state that is of course primarily the Jews and the Communists," said von Dirlinger, his voice dripping with sarcasm.

"Yes, well Bousquet certainly possesses leadership skills, whether they are being channelled in the right direction is a matter for some debate," said Lafarge evenly.

Von Dirlinger's expression remained impassive, Lafarge noted that the Abwehr colonel might give off the impression of being a playboy who used the uniform as an aid to such pursuits. However, he also acknowledged that behind the façade was a highly intelligent man, who he did not doubt had a ruthless streak running through him.

He would have to be watched, and Lafarge would choose his words carefully in front of him for any loose talk could be used by von Dirlinger against him, especially were the investigation to lead back to him.

Von Dirlinger suddenly rose from his seat and attracted the waiter's attention indicating he wanted the bill, which was duly brought to the table and despite Lafarge's protests paid for by the colonel.

"Tonight is for me, Lafarge. In any case, it is far from over. I am taking you to a real hotspot of Parisian nightlife, or what remains of it," he said with a convivial smile.

"Brothels aren't really my type of enjoyment," interjected Lafarge rather brusquely.

Von Dirlinger laughed uproariously, slapping Lafarge on the back.

"You fool Lafarge! Do you really think that I need to go to a brothel to enjoy myself! No, man I'm taking you to a cabaret owned by one of those French artistes that appeal to Goebbels, Suzy Solidor's place on Rue St Anne. Of course there are women there but generally speaking they prefer their own sex," said von Dirlinger.

Lafarge felt quite honoured to be taken to Suzy Solidor's famous cabaret 'La Vie Parisienne', which might geographically have been quite close to the Opéra Garnier but was worlds apart in terms of the music and entertainment offered.

Solidor herself was quite a personality, born of modest origins, though she claimed to be the bastard daughter of a politician from St Malo in Brittany, who had become a popular singer and also the subject of many famous artists, who adored her striking looks.

THE TORTURED DETECTIVE

However, for many French people she was tarred with the same brush as Marguerite had been and others such as the great actress Arletty and the actor Robert Le Vigan in that she openly consorted with the Germans and benefited from their favours.

She had indeed enshrined herself in their affections and in Vichy's by recording a version of the song that so warmed the hearts of the German soldiers 'Lili Marleen' and which she never wasted an opportunity in singing, not least at her own cabaret.

Whilst the Germans took a rather dim view of homosexuality, Lafarge noted that if you pleased them enough, they would compromise, and so it was with Solidor. She was openly bi–sexual and her cabaret certainly didn't hide the fact that it was open to all people with whatever sexual tastes they preferred.

Von Dirlinger was greeted with great warmth by the elegantly–attired doorman whilst the cloakroom girl, who was far from dowdily dressed herself and made up in the style of the roaring 20's in the United States, gave the colonel an affectionate kiss on the lips.

Lafarge received the more traditional kiss on both cheeks, though he did notice that the girl gave him an almost x–ray like examination. He wouldn't have minded giving her a similar examination, but he was taken away by his companion and they proceeded into the main room.

It was not very large, but Lafarge couldn't see that clearly as not only was it dimly–lit with the tasseled lampshades clouding out most of the light given off by the light bulbs, but also clouds of thick cigarette and cigar smoke filled the room.

A professional and serious looking head waiter – not the type Lafarge mused to embrace even the most regular of customers – showed them to a small table in the center of the room and didn't take their order.

Lafarge soon realised why as another waiter – this one dressed in the usual white shirt and black waistcoat but not so usually sporting mascara and lipstick – brought two champagne glasses as well as two brandy glasses with a bottle of each and served them a glass of champagne.

"Those poor sods who have to observe the curfew don't know what they are missing!" grinned von Dirlinger.

Lafarge could only agree, this was certainly a sanctuary for only those blessed with either having special passes to be out after midnight or because their jobs entitled them to be.

Most Parisians had to be back at home by midnight when curfew fell or else have a very good reason to be still out.

Not that there was much reason for Parisians to stay out.

The cinema served up largely propaganda–fuelled films, although during winter time it at least guaranteed warmth.

The opera, theatre and concerts, while of good quality, were priced out of most peoples reach. Also, they were heavily censored, no Jewish composer, playwright or film director living or dead, were to have their works performed under German and indeed Vichy laws.

Lafarge regretted this enormously for it left the choice rather limited.

There was only so much one man shows by the supreme egotist Sacha Guitry that one could put up with at the theatre, so he was extremely content to be able to relax and drink to his heart's content in a relative den of iniquity, even if it was alongside some of Paris's most despicable collaborators.

At least thanks to the smoke, he could barely see what terrible company he was keeping. That was until von Dirlinger nudged him.

"Ah Gaston. I may call you that? It just sounds so formal calling you Lafarge. And this is a place where formality is non–existent as you can plainly see. You obviously can call me Karl," smiled von Dirlinger.

Lafarge nodded his assent and paid some attention to the show being performed on the stage, which was mildly diverting with two women entwined in each other's arms singing a popular love song of the time.

"Darling, how are you? So wonderful to see you here," boomed a husky voice somewhere to the left of Lafarge's chair.

He looked up to see von Dirlinger being kissed passionately on the lips by not the cloakroom girl but someone rather more important, Suzy Solidor herself.

She was indeed striking looking. Her blonde hair was slicked across her forehead, not much in the way of breasts, but she had a pair of, what looked like in the darkness to Lafarge, hypnotic

THE TORTURED DETECTIVE

brown eyes, a prominent nose and full lips, highlighted by bright lipstick, some of which Lafarge could feel had been left on his cheek when she kissed him.

She sat with them, chatting amiably about nothing but making Lafarge feel that he had her undivided attention. He could feel that he was being appraised, whether it was as to what use he could be to her or just simply interest on her part he could not work out.

"We don't get too many criminal police in here, Gaston," said Solidor, trying to maintain the conversation and provoke Lafarge into talking about his work.

"Do you mean police who investigate criminals or police that are criminals," joked Lafarge, which Solidor politely laughed at, though even he admitted it was pretty weak and sadly the latter part of the statement was factually correct about most of his colleagues these days.

"No, we get more Germans, like Karl. More so now that his divine mistress has gone upstairs, and also lots of our compatriots who have interests in Germany find it useful to stop by," she said with pride in her voice.

"Why we even attract the post Opera crowd, including this evening by royal appointment Paris's favourite Ukrainian, and indeed there aren't too many of those welcome in Germany or here nowadays, the great ballet dancer himself Serge Lifar," she added pointing in the direction of a large round table situated at the right hand corner of the room.

Lafarge followed her elegant hand round and clocked Lifar immediately. His sharp but oddly attractive features stood out amongst the group at his table which was largely filled by Wehrmacht officers and their floosies and where Karl had drifted off to, leaving him and the hostess to chat.

Lafarge resumed his conversation with Solidor, who he found mildly interesting, though he detected clearly her sense of self–importance was of the equal of Guitry.

Name dropping was her main source of conversation, most of the names meant something to Lafarge, but he was starting to get a sore neck from shaking it when she asked whether he knew this or that general or baron, before thankfully another presence at the table distracted her.

"Ah Mathilde. I am delighted you have come! I have missed you so terribly since the awful murder of Marguerite," cooed Solidor, who rose and embraced the new arrival warmly on the lips.

Lafarge glanced up just to make sure that he hadn't misheard and sure enough to his huge surprise standing there was Mathilde, the enigmatic maid of Marguerite's. She glanced down to see who Solidor had been talking to and recoiled in shock, before pulling herself together and smiling thinly.

"We've met," she said coolly to Solidor when she started to introduce them.

Mathilde, who looked stunning and had dressed in a black silk dress, with slits up the sides, revealing her slender legs topped by rounded thighs which were revealed by the suspenders she was sporting, whispered something into Solidor's ear. Solidor nodded and then offered her the chair left vacant by von Dirlinger.

"Champagne will make a difference from the vodka I usually drink with the Inspector," commented Mathilde dryly, eying Lafarge in what he could only describe as a predatory manner surprising him given the coolness of her initial greeting.

Solidor laughed lightly and the three of them consumed the champagne with great gusto, leading to another quickly replacing it, Solidor tut tutting when Lafarge offered to pay for it.

"This, Gaston, is on the house. Let's say this is for Marguerite, a wake for her, after all, this is where she met both Karl and Mathilde," said Solidor airily.

Lafarge's interest level moved up a couple of gears at this revelation. Not even the copious amounts of alcohol he had consumed could dull the impact of this information. He could see Mathilde was not pleased by this indiscretion on Solidor's part, but it was too late to retract it.

"Really, that is interesting. I wasn't aware this is how Marguerite and Mathilde met or indeed that Karl had met her here either. You really are a go to person for connections, aren't you Susy?" said Lafarge teasingly.

Solidor smiled and her ego suitably boosted she reacted just how Lafarge had wished her to.

"Oh yes, Karl came to me and asked whether I could arrange for Marguerite to be introduced to him as he was a great fan of her

THE TORTURED DETECTIVE

acting. I told him not to be a little boy hiding behind such a thin excuse as that and told him I would arrange it," she said proudly.

"It seems you are a woman of your word. It certainly worked out well for everyone, especially Marguerite," said Lafarge dryly.

Solidor gave him a quizzical look and then laughed.

"Gaston you possess a very sharp wit. No wonder Karl likes you. Yes everyone did really well out of my networking skills, even Marguerite poor soul," she said wistfully.

"I'm done talking about this rather maudlin episode. You are off duty Gaston after all. No talking shop in my place unless you book an appointment and I've got a pretty full schedule in the next few weeks.

Lafarge acknowledged the rebuke, poured them another glass of champagne and took a look at Mathilde, who he found even more attractive than he had done when they were sipping vodka in Marguerite's kitchen.

He wondered if she was Solidor's lover or just close friend. If the latter, he wished to make himself one of those as well and not just to have her to use the euphemism he thought was so delightful 'helping with enquiries'.

No, Lafarge was determined to make their relationship a more intimate one. Isabella would never find out and once hostilities were over, he could once again resume his role as husband and father.

However, he needed Solidor to remove herself, Karl appeared to be ensconced in conversation with a woman at Lifar's table, and then he could have Mathilde all to himself.

As good fortune would have it, the two women who had been entwined on stage had come to the end of their session and it was time for Solidor to re–impose herself on her clientele.

"Do excuse me, I have my professional duties to perform. It's been a pleasure Gaston and please, feel free to call here anytime you wish.

"I hope that it will only entail private pleasure and it won't be for professional reasons," she smiled warmly at Lafarge and gave him a kiss on the cheek before embracing Mathilde in an intimate fashion that left little room for doubt in the policeman's mind what their relationship was.

There followed a rather embarrassed and long silence, Lafarge tried to ease it by grinning at Mathilde, who turned her head away. Undeterred and indeed spurred on by the extra challenge posed by Mathilde's evident sexual preference Lafarge then moved to the chair beside hers. One good sign was that she didn't get up to leave, though, she steadfastly refused to look at him.

"So Mathilde, do you and Suzy go back a long way?" Lafarge asked.

Mathilde turned towards him at last, and he saw there were tears in her eyes, whether it was the smoke or she was genuinely upset he couldn't tell, for his eyes were close to watering and he felt like going outside to get some fresh air.

"I thought you were off duty, Chief Inspector," she said coldly while accepting one of his cigarettes, which he lit whilst taking a closer look to see whether she was upset or just irritated by the smoke.

He laughed and told her yes, he was off duty and she could relax.

I'm sorry. I don't mean to be so offhand, but I didn't expect to see you here and I certainly didn't wish you to be privy to my private life," she said trying to wipe away the tears. "It's not exactly very decorous or indeed behaviour deemed acceptable in the present circumstances."

Lafarge shrugged and proffered his kerchief in his top pocket so she could address her make–up and dry her tears. She thanked him and, for the first time that night, smiled, which once again, like when they first met, did wonders for her looks and only encouraged Lafarge more to make his move.

"It's just that our kind have to live such a secret life, just as many others have to, and Suzy and I are only accepted for the moment because she curries favour with the Nazis. Vichy certainly wouldn't countenance allowing such decadence as they would put it to go on," she said sadly.

"Suzy is my first love, that is my first lesbian experience, and I cannot change the way I feel about her even if the risks are so grave. She provoked such passionate feelings in me, physically and emotionally, and I am incapable of thinking about anyone else.

"It's funny, you know, had my husband not been killed on the retreat to Dunkirk, I would never have unearthed this other side of myself. War can indeed be a liberating experience," she said dryly.

THE TORTURED DETECTIVE

Lafarge smiled appreciatively at her openness, groaning inwardly that there was little chance of getting to know her intimately, but gave himself one more chance of whisking her away for at least one night of passionate frolicking.

Solidor herself had strode on to the stage, dressed in an outrageous low cut gold dress, her hair now slicked back over her head, and was launching into her first number.

Whatever one could say about the size of her ego she was, Lafarge admitted, a commanding presence and everyone, even Lifar's table, had stopped their conversation and were rapt by her.

Lafarge observed that a male couple had arrived and been welcomed with a shriek of delight from the stage by Solidor. He could understand why as it was the celebrated poet and artist Jean Cocteau, for whom she had posed and was a muse of his, and his lover the actor Jean Marais.

Lafarge was suitably impressed. Not by Marais, who he considered a ham actor of the worst type, but by Cocteau, who he admired enormously and who trod the fine line between open collaboration and passive resistance expertly so much so that no–one could tell where his sympathies lay.

The excitement having died down once they took their seats, Lafarge thought it might be an inappropriate moment to suggest an alternative night's entertainment to Solidor's lover. Then he thought, hell, Mathilde said war was a liberator so why shouldn't he try his own form of it?

"Yes, I guess war can indeed be a liberating experience, mine came only a few months ago but it does leave you with the feeling that having been given a second chance one should make full use of it," said Lafarge in his most philosophical tone.

Mathilde turned her face towards him, having been solely focused on her lover on stage, and smiled at him. At the same moment, the rather formal head waiter approached their table and handed Mathilde a note.

She opened it and turned her eyes back to the stage where Lafarge noticed she got a kiss blown at her followed by a wink from Solidor, who was just preparing to sing the second song of her repertoire. Mathilde read the note and turned her attention back to Lafarge, her face emotionless.

"Chief Inspector, or rather Gaston, what would you say to escorting me home? Suzy says that we can't be together tonight as she has business to attend to after the club closes. She suggests that you are the ideal companion to ensure that I return home safely," she said evenly.

Lafarge couldn't believe his luck; here was his target being delivered into his lap by her unsuspecting lover. Things were certainly looking up for him, he thought as he bid farewell to von Dirlinger, who tore himself away from Lifar's table to bid them good night, slapping the Frenchman on the back, and then having helped Mathilde on with her splendid sable coat, stepped out into the coldish air of early morning Paris.

CHAPTER TEN

Lafarge awoke beside Mathilde alright but to his huge disappointment, even in his now sober state, fully–clothed.

Her tone had been firm enough to dissuade him from pushing the issue too hard but the offer of at least curling up beside her given his fatigue and being fairly drunk was too good to turn down. He raised himself on one elbow and searched for his watch.

He found it lying on the parquet floor, beside his shoes and socks, and glanced at it. It had just gone seven, which meant he had barely slept.

He groaned, feeling his head weighing down on him, and went searching in the tiny apartment – it was just a little bigger than the traditional maid's room, with a small kitchenette and a tiny bathroom – for, he hoped, some bottled water.

Tap water was out of the question as it was untreated and likely to give you stomach problems, if not worse afflictions, should one risk drinking it.

Lafarge reflected for a moment and then thought of course, I can go down to Marguerite's apartment and pilfer some from there.

There was bound to be some. He slipped on his shoes, left Mathilde's door ajar and took the flight of stairs down to the flat. He had keys to it but there was no need to unlock the door for someone had already done that.

He took off his shoes and stepped inside quietly just in case the person who had entered the flat had not left yet. He stood there, holding his breath for a minute, trying to discern whether there was another presence in the apartment, but didn't hear a sound.

Hesitantly, he crept along the wall of the hallway towards the kitchen, having looked into the drawing room and seen nobody, although there were signs that someone had been there and searched for something.

Halfway down the passage, he did hear something, somebody noisily rifling through drawers in what he thought was the spare room.

That was immediately to his left and then he cursed himself, for he had left his gun and his identification papers in his jacket up in Mathilde's apartment.

Terrific, he thought to himself, what the hell am I going to do if this intruder has a weapon? It was too late to withdraw for the person might leave while he went back upstairs so he had no option but to bluff it out.

First light was only just coming up, so to a certain extent he was aided by it being fairly dark and if he pointed something towards the intruder, it might be enough to convince them to surrender meekly.

It was a big if, but Lafarge thought one worth pursuing. Thus as nimbly as he could, he swung round into the doorway and said in as authoritative a manner as he could summon up: "Stop that immediately, police!"

His words did have an impact for the person who had his back to him, as the chest of drawers was against the opposite wall to the door, froze and slowly rose from his kneeling position. That's good, thought Lafarge I can dupe him even more.

"Right, turn round very slowly. I'm armed," he said trying to sound as confident as possible, though his heart was pulsating.

The man did as he asked and to Lafarge's astonishment he recognised him for he had worked with him once upon a time.

It was Pierre Bonny, weasel face and wiry body, and a totally unpleasant piece of work who had been thrown off the force and even done time for corruption.

Ordinarily, he would have been looking at some more unwanted holidays in prison for breaking in. However, the only problem was he now worked with Lafont, or Henri 'The Boss' as he liked to style himself, in the much-feared French Gestapo and operated from their elegant headquarters in Rue Lauriston in the exclusive 16th arrondissement, the same area of Paris where Bousquet lived.

Quite apart from that was the unpleasant fact Bonny was his sister's lover, something which had distanced brother and sister from each other despite having been close in their childhood.

However, that was not Lafarge's major pre–occupation right at this moment, for he had no idea how he would handle this.

He didn't even know if he had the authority to throw Bonny out, given that he and his odious gang of thugs, for they were little more than a gang of crooks who extorted money from rich Jews and businesses, were protected by the Germans.

Lafarge, nevertheless, because he despised the man and Lafont, despite the latter's outward charm and bonhomie, was going to chance it.

"What the hell are you doing Bonny?" he said firmly.

Bonny stared at Lafarge, saw he had no gun, and gave him a withering look.

Lafarge moved towards him, not caring whether Bonny drew on him or not, for he loathed the man and wanted to have an excuse to punch him.

Bonny, never one of the bravest on the force, tried to back away, while searching in his overcoat pocket for something.

Lafarge rushed him before he could find the item, probably a sap, and knocked him against the chest of drawers. That knocked the wind out of Bonny, who Lafarge then released and allowed to slide down the piece of furniture. Bonny was wheezing and coughing and flashed a look of hatred at his former colleague, who just smiled patronizingly back at him.

"You son of a bitch, Lafarge!" snarled Bonny, who removed his glasses to reposition them back on his nose which bore all the signs of a heavy drinker, red blotches covering it.

"You are not dealing with a run of the mill criminal here. I have protection and they don't take kindly to their boys being beaten up by anyone, not even one of Paris' finest," sneered Bonny.

"Ah yes of course, your German buddies. Dear me. I will be in trouble, although I have to say they may want to know why you were pilfering a murdered woman's apartment.

"Even they may find that a little low," said Lafarge, although he was far from sure that would be the case, the Gestapo not being known for their sensitivity in any case involving human misery.

Bonny smiled one of his weasel–like smiles, and it was certainly not in new found affection for Lafarge.

"You always were a holier than thou supercilious bastard Lafarge. You have certainly not changed," said Bonny venomously.

"If you think that I am here solely on my own behest, you are mistaken. I didn't even know the tart. I have enough fun with your sister as it is, and my how she despises you and your sanctimonious ways."

For that remark Bonny earned himself a brutal kick in the ribs from Lafarge, which to the detective's satisfaction had Bonny writhing on the smart Persian rug, the only shame being he started spitting out bile and blood onto it.

"No, you didn't know Marguerite, Bonny. Women of her quality wouldn't deign to associate themselves with you and Lafont and your gang of lice.

"Maybe that's why you have your headquarters in the 16th so you can breathe the air they breathe, but my God, that's about the only thing you have in common with them, you piece of shit!" said Lafarge and gave him another kick, this time in the stomach, for good measure.

Bonny crawled back as best he could to the relative sanctuary of the chest of drawers as Lafarge moved in on him again.

"Come on Bonny, tell me why you are here and how you got access to the victim's keys," snarled Lafarge, raising his right fist over Bonny's face.

Bonny instinctively raised his arms to protect himself, and then nodded vigorously at Lafarge that he wanted to talk. Lafarge withdrew his fist and waited for the loathsome human being to speak.

"I can't tell you who supplied me with the keys nor the orders, as they came from Henri," said Bonny, his voice trembling, with fear or anger Lafarge couldn't tell.

"All I know is that Henri called me at around five this morning and said he had an urgent matter for me to deal with. He said he was indisposed, he was with some German lady, but that on his desk were a set of keys and I was to come round here and search the place."

"That's all? What were you to search for? Surely he told you that", asked Lafarge in an exasperated tone.

"He said that he had been told on good information that there were diamonds here and that they were worth a pretty fortune if we could get hold of them. He said that they had been stolen from some French countess and that the victim had been murdered because of them," replied Bonny, who was slowly inching himself back up to a more comfortable sitting position.

Lafarge nodded, thinking to himself who had prompted Lafont, or rather where had all this information come from.

THE TORTURED DETECTIVE

The picture was becoming even more complicated, and drawing in all sorts of unwanted and dangerous forces, for he might have Bonny at his mercy for the moment but this type of incident would have ramifications for him.

Bonny and Lafont were not the types to take such a challenge to their authority by forgetting about it. It made it even more urgent for Lafarge to see Bousquet, have another go at Lescarboura, and then take a train down to Limoges as a car would be too risky, especially as he was acting alone.

Massu had some influence but he couldn't save him from thugs like Lafont and Bonny.

"Lafont is very well informed," said Lafarge drily.

Bonny afforded himself one of his unbecoming smiles.

"Yes, we are. You may not think very much of me Lafarge, but I still have contacts and friends inside the force. Indeed, I would say I have more friends than you have. One phone call from me and you could trip down the stairs in an unfortunate accident," he grinned.

"Yes, I could. But you are forgetting one thing, Bonny. Why do you think you are leaving this apartment alive?" said Lafarge coolly.

Bonny looked up at Lafarge, and gratifyingly for the detective, he could see the flash off fear cross his face.

"You wouldn't dare, Lafarge. How would you explain another corpse in the apartment to your superior?" said Bonny, his voice quavering.

"Very easily Bonny. I came upon an intruder at a crime scene and the person in question not being willing to give up quietly, I took the necessary measures to subdue him and in the course of that action, I unfortunately strangled him," said Lafarge.

"Except you won't Lafarge. You know why? Because you have an eye witness," said Bonny, gesturing to Lafarge to look behind him.

Lafarge thought Bonny was bluffing, desperate to extricate himself from the situation he found himself in. He smiled grimly at Bonny and went to search in the man's pockets hoping to find whatever weapon he had hoped to use on him. However, he was halted in his tracks by a voice from behind him.

"Gaston stop! You can't stoop so low as to murder someone in cold blood," pleaded Mathilde.

Lafarge stepped back and turned towards Mathilde, who was standing in the doorway, dressed just in a flowery dressing gown, her un–brushed dark hair falling all round her shoulders.

My, she was quite a sight even when she wasn't made up, thought Lafarge. He shrugged his shoulders as if to say, what else can I do, but then thought better of it and quick as a flash returned his gaze onto Bonny, who wisely hadn't tried to take advantage of his momentary distraction to rush him.

"Okay Bonny, you can get up. You are one lucky son of a bitch, and you of all people don't deserve any luck whatsoever," said Lafarge coldly.

Bonny rose unsteadily to his feet, Lafarge had the brief pleasure of patting him down, and removed as he guessed a sap from his pocket and waved it in front of his face in a moment of triumph.

"This I will keep as a little trophy from our unscheduled meeting," said Lafarge gloating, though in reality, he regretted that Mathilde had descended and interrupted him.

"She your squeeze then Lafarge? Not content on your own, and cheating on your gorgeous wife. Boy, those Latin Americans are fiery and I bet if she were to find out you wouldn't have much to show off afterwards. I should know as I often had to deal with unfaithful husbands and their furious wronged wives," grinned Bonny.

Lafarge slapped him on both cheeks, grabbed him by the lapels of his navy blue coat and dragged him as roughly as he could to the doorway and then along the passage to the front door. Mathilde didn't intervene this time, she just stood to one side and watched.

"Right Bonny, off you go. Slink back to your master and tell him that his information was incorrect, there are no diamonds here and to stay away from the case and more importantly me.

"If I get one inkling you or he or your thugs are sniffing around or following me, I will not be so generous next time. Understood, asshole?" And with that Lafarge kicked him in the backside and made to slam the door on him.

Bonny, though, whirled round and put his foot in between the door and the entrance.

THE TORTURED DETECTIVE

"Lafarge, you can make as many threats as you want. But you are powerless and almost friendless and therefore your words carry little weight.

"We on the other hand have both power and friends and no doubt the person who demanded that we search the apartment is an even more powerful man. We will come after you and we will destroy you, of that you can be certain.

"If we get the diamonds at the same time that will merely be a bonus. You have overstepped the mark, Lafarge, and there is no going back with us" hissed Bonny, who turned on his heel and descended the stairs whistling, his good humour fully restored.

CHAPTER ELEVEN

Lafarge could have adopted the wisest route and taken the train down to Limoges armed with his Ausweis, but he was intent on seeing Bousquet before he left.

Having earned the eternal hatred of Bonny and therefore the French Gestapo, he thought what the hell, why not round it off by confirming Bousquet's own dislike for him.

Neither was good for his career. But Lafarge was already weary of playing the obedient servant of a government, which only flexed its limited muscles when called upon by their masters the Nazis to round up the weak, mentally sick, Jews and largely invented enemies from within and shipped them off to god knows what fate in the East.

He had given up on his future prospects. If the Allies won the War, he would be all but washed up having volunteered to return to the police under Vichy. If they did not succeed, then at least he could take comfort that he had had the courage to confront the worst types who had profited from the defeat into becoming figures of authority.

Lafarge grinned grimly at the thought that he was in a no–win situation, but at least for the moment, his family were well away and relatively safe.

Whether Mathilde was, was another matter, but he couldn't very well send her to his apartment as it was likely to receive a visit from Bonny and his gang under some cobbled together pretext. So all he could do was give her some reassurance that she wasn't in their sights, but if she felt in danger, she was best advised to go and stay at Solidor's apartment for there, she would be protected by higher forces than even the Lauriston crew.

His pursuit of de Chastelain had become virtually superfluous because he now felt that he was the target, but professional pride being one of his qualities, he was going to get his man and then take the consequences from his political faux pas during the investigation.

Rather than go to the office, he returned quickly to his flat, washed and phoned Massu to see if the audience with Bousquet was arranged.

THE TORTURED DETECTIVE

Knowing the phone would be tapped by some service or other, he avoided relating the incident with Bonny and, in as relaxed a tone as possible, asked Massu in general terms about the meeting. Fortunately, Massu realized why he was talking in such a roundabout fashion and curtly replied that yes, he was to come round to the office at midday and that it shouldn't take more than an hour.

Lafarge at least afforded the secretary general of the French police the honour of dressing in his least tired looking suit – a sharp looking chalk pin stripe double breasted affair – and put on the tie that Isabella had given him as a farewell present. He hoped Bousquet would not read too much into the design, which was of an armoured St George killing the dragon, but if he did take offence so be it.

Lafarge arrived promptly at Bousquet's building on rue de Lutèce, which was only round the corner from his own on Quai des Orfèvres, and a middle aged, well presented secretary ushered him into his chief's office.

Lafarge was impressed by the opulence of the room in comparison to Massu's rather shabby and dowdy office, the latter more like the one in the Maigret films starring the collaborator Albert Préjean, a Great War hero turned yellow in Lafarge's mind and another stain on the police's image having him portray the great detective.

Bousquet's office was decorated more like a hotel room, without the bed.

Gold leaf covered the ceiling and encircled the walls, two or three sculptures of middling size and distinctly mediocre taste – at least to Lafarge's eye – were placed in three of the four corners of the room, while the fourth corner hosted a well–stocked drinks cabinet.

That was definitely to the detective's taste, and he was hoping, not least for his nerves, to be offered a drink from it.

In front of the large window, which looked out onto the street, was Bousquet's desk, overflowing with files, none of them opened, which Lafarge thought was more caginess on his host's part than laziness, for that was one characteristic not to be associated with Bousquet.

His enthusiasm for his job was well known and why he was regarded so highly by the Nazis and with great suspicion by the slothful lot in Vichy.

Bousquet, though, was not sitting in his splendid chair behind his equally ornate desk, but sitting with his legs crossed on an extremely comfortable looking sofa which faced a fireplace. Bousquet rose and crossed the room to shake Lafarge's hand, which rather surprised the detective as he had expected a formal greeting given their respective positions.

Bousquet, while considered stiff, cold and aloof, did at least know how to behave correctly, again rather a contrast to some of the Vichy high appointees.

Whilst Lafarge was justifiably satisfied with his clothes, he had to admit Bousquet was dressed even more smartly than he was. The secretary–general cut a fine figure in his navy blue single breasted suit, white shirt and black tie rounded off with shiny black laced up shoes.

Physically too, he was impressive, not dissimilar to de Gaulle minus the moustache, though Lafarge thought that was best left unsaid, being of similar height and carrying themselves with their head always held high in a proud manner reminiscent of those haughty Austrian show horses in Vienna.

Both of them, too, had a rather large nose, but while Lafarge could not vouch for de Gaulle's eyes, he could for Bousquet's and there was no warmth in those brown eyes even when he laughed. They were cold and wary and a warning to those in his presence not to offend the great man.

"Drink, Lafarge? Help yourself if you want one," said Bousquet, pointing to the drinks cabinet.

Lafarge needed no second prompting and strode briskly to the cabinet and helped himself to what appeared to be becoming his usual tipple these days, a cognac.

He returned to the fireplace and lit a cigarette before settling himself into one of the comfortably furnished armchairs while Bousquet remained on the sofa, though now sitting upright.

Bousquet had what looked like a large whisky in front of him, and aping Lafarge, he helped himself to a cigarette, Lafarge noting drily that it was from a large cigarette box on the coffee table as his lost cigarette case was lying in his desk drawer at headquarters.

THE TORTURED DETECTIVE

"I gather Massu is too busy to come and present the report on the investigation, which I find regrettable. So if you can keep it as brief as possible that would be terrific as I have a lunch date at the Ritz with Foreign Minister Fernand de Brinon, Sacha Guitry, Ambassador Abetz and some other guests," said Bousquet brusquely.

Lafarge nodded, but nevertheless he was going to take all the time he needed and wasn't going to be intimidated into going any faster by the list of Bousquet's lunch guests. He took Bousquet through the outline of the investigation without divulging too many details, for as he regarded him as a suspect, giving away too much would only help him conjure up his own answers.

"Well I know I told you to be brief, Lafarge, but really all that you have told me is that you are going down to Limoges armed with an Ausweis to try and apprehend de Chastelain, who may or may not be in the vicinity," remarked Bousquet sounding far from satisfied.

"While I am cheered that this damned lawyer may still end up in jail, and I would be delighted to know how he came to escape, I feel that we are a little light on detail here.

"For instance, how do you know he is down there and not still in Paris? Who warned him about his impending arrest and what sort of evidence have you turned up at the victim's address?

"The details you have given me now are so vague as to prompt me to question why risk your life by going to bandit country to apprehend somebody against whom you appear to possess little evidence," added Bousquet sharply.

Lafarge smiled and, having nursed his brandy through the first part of the meeting, thought it a good moment to down it and help himself to a second one, buying himself some time before broaching the touchy subject of Bousquet's involvement with the victim.

Having retaken his seat, Lafarge looked at Bousquet squarely in the face, assessing whether his boss was also playing games with him, all the time knowing the detective was holding back because of what he had discovered at the apartment, and this was his way of prising it out of him.

Lafarge rubbed his chin and closed the folder, then leaned forward to address Bousquet.

"The reason I have been sparse in details about the investigation, sir, is that I find myself in the uncomfortable position of a conflict of interests, in this case involving you. Indeed, my real purpose in coming here today to present the update on the investigation was to have an opportunity to put some of these questions to you. I hope that in doing so, it will clear up any doubts I may have over being totally frank with you the next time you require an update," said Lafarge coolly.

Bousquet's expression remained impassive, he didn't move an inch and just stared back at Lafarge, allowing the silence to drag on. Eventually, he patted at his slicked back, neatly parted black hair, stroked his nose and steepled his fingers together as if he was about to enter into a moment of deep meditation.

"Lafarge, Lafarge, I really don't think it is a very good idea for you to start probing around in such areas," said Bousquet finally.

"I have no choice, sir. The evidence that I have gathered so far indicate you were in the apartment the night of the murder.

"My remit when I was appointed, at your suggestion I may add, was to leave no stone unturned in solving the case. I am afraid that in doing just that, I have uncovered a piece of evidence that implicates you and therefore I have to ask you what may be uncomfortable questions for both of us," said Lafarge almost apologetically.

Bousquet sighed and glanced at his watch, no doubt mulling over whether he could just avoid the interrogation and use his lunch as an excuse for doing so, employing that battered old term of urgent state business as a reason.

However, he could ill justify that, as he had mentioned that the actor and self–proclaimed genius Guitry was going to be present, and whilst the showman never missed the chance to be present at the new elite's social gatherings, he would not be allowed if there were matters of political import to be discussed.

Bousquet rose and walked steadily over to the drinks cabinet, poured himself a generous helping of whisky out of a glass decanter. On his way back he dallied by his desk before picking up the phone, and told his secretary to ring the Ritz and let them know he would be delayed, but not for long, he emphasized, unwilling to give Lafarge too much cause for joy.

THE TORTURED DETECTIVE

"I will answer what I feel is relevant, Lafarge, but there must be no notes taken. I don't want this discussed outside of this room, not even with Massu. Although by allowing you to replace him today I take it he is aware I am somehow involved," he said resignedly.

"He is aware, yes. Furthermore, sir, I will take notes, as I would if I were interrogating anyone else in an investigation. However, they will not be used unless there is reason to at the trial," said Lafarge.

Bousquet laughed, not especially warmly and holding out his hands said: "What, you've come here to arrest me too, that is amusing Lafarge!"

Lafarge bit his lip, refusing to rise to the bait, and simply shook his head.

"You know Lafarge, I think you are taking the personal animosity between us which dates back a while now too far. Why oh why if I had anything to do with the murder would I want you involved, because doubts about you on a personal front apart, I know full well you are one of the few detectives capable of doing a thorough job.

"I don't think you are seeing things clearly, Lafarge, one hint of my involvement and you turn your full attention onto me meanwhile allowing de Chastelain to escape," said Bousquet.

"Excuse me sir but it wasn't me who let him slip through our fingers the first time," said Lafarge boldly.

"I don't like that tone detective, and as for your blaming me, well I think you should look at who told him I was after him. I was powerless to stop that happening," said Bousquet.

"Alright, we are getting away from the subject here. I will also make clear that I have not allowed my judgement to be clouded by our mutual dislike for each other, but I will concede that it doesn't seem logical you asking for me if you had something to hide. However, in the times we live in, logic and actions don't seem to gel," said Lafarge.

"In order that you can get to your lunch before it goes cold and so as I can return home and pack before leaving tomorrow morning, it would be best that you tell your secretary not to put anyone through to you on the phone," said Lafarge.

Bousquet nodded and did as he had been asked.

"Before you start, Lafarge, I want to say that you should be very careful in what you ask. Your father may be close to Pétain, but that is not a guarantee you are protected. Compare his protection with the protectors I have and you will see how uneven the sides are already.

"I mean I could just have you sacked, lord knows I wouldn't want to be directly implicated. For the moment, we will go on with our little game but should I believe you are deliberately going after me as part of some machinations being orchestrated down in Vichy, then you will suffer for it.

"I may not be able to touch them, yet, but you will do nicely as the first course," Bousquet said, his glacial tone leaving no room for imagining he meant otherwise.

Lafarge shrugged the threat aside, for he was certainly part of no plot against Bousquet. However, he would allow him his paranoid delusions of being targeted if that opened the way for him to be as honest as he could be in his answers to his questions about a real victim and a real crime.

"So tell me what you were doing in the victim's apartment the night she was murdered," said Lafarge.

Bousquet had somewhat surprisingly, given the tense atmosphere between the two men, got up and served them drinks and was returning to take his seat when Lafarge asked the question.

"I was there because Marguerite wanted my help. I was only too delighted to be asked to perform such a service, so I walked round to her apartment to aid her," said Bousquet.

"Why did she require your help? She had plenty of influential friends including her lover, that Abwehr colonel von Dirlinger," said Lafarge with an air of disbelief.

"Ah, here you are being disingenuous Lafarge. I am glad that it is not just me being equivocal. I know for a fact you spent most of yesterday with the good colonel. You really shouldn't take me for being a fool Lafarge, I believe that, rare among my fellow Vichy officials and ministers, I am there on merit," said Bousquet smugly.

"Yes indeed, I did. He asked me for dinner and I felt it rude to decline his offer. We had a most enjoyable time. It does not mean that I have ruled him out of my enquiry. As for taking you for a fool, sir, I would not allow myself such a misjudgement," said Lafarge.

THE TORTURED DETECTIVE

"Very well Lafarge, let's move on. Time is pressing," Bousquet said impatiently, again glancing at his watch.

"I already asked you a question which you have yet to answer," said Lafarge.

Bousquet shot him a glance, which conveyed the message clearly warning him to watch his tone.

"She wanted my help because she was not keen to pursue her relationship with von Dirlinger, and thought that with my position, I could weigh in should he react badly to her terminating the affair," said Bousquet.

"Weigh in, how so? I mean, you hold a high position of state but I don't think that runs into telling people who to have relationships with, or to tell a spurned lover how to conduct themselves. You are the father of our state security but a moral guide, I think not!" said Lafarge.

"Lafarge, that is enough! I think you are getting way above yourself here! How dare you come in here and treat me as if I was one of your usual weasels that you interrogate. I don't think you are taking my warning seriously enough. I am granting you some leeway, but you are going far further in your remarks and your sarcasm than I will allow," said Bousquet now visibly furious.

Lafarge moved to reply, but Bousquet waved him aside.

"You know who I had a personal audience with the other day? Reinhard Heydrich, who came to Paris to personally see me and congratulate me on my efforts in trying to resolve the problem of foreign Jews in France.

"Yes, Lafarge, Heydrich. He didn't seek out de Brinon or summon Laval from Vichy, it was me he came to see. That is the indication of the power I wield, and perhaps why Marguerite sought me out for protection. That of course can be turned on its head should I feel threatened," said Bousquet menacingly.

Lafarge thought about asking him if he had been presented with a cigarette case by Heydrich, but thought better of it. Funny, Lafarge thought to himself, that here was a highly intelligent and capable man who knew the difference between right and wrong but who had allowed ambition to override his moral judgement.

He didn't have the slightest moral scruple when it came to bathing in the congratulations and praise of a sociopath like Heydrich. He had fallen so completely under Heydrich's spell that he had promised his French police would resolve the problem of foreign Jews in France, whatever that meant though Lafarge had a pretty good idea what measures would be implemented.

How ironic that the foreign Jews had sought refuge in France believing they had found sanctuary. Even those in the so called Free Zone could not feel too safe now that Bousquet had sworn to devote his forces to ridding France of them.

Did Bousquet see himself as Heydrich reincarnated in France, assuming the totally inappropriate title of 'Protector of France' like the German's present role as 'Protector of Bohemia and Moravia'?

Protector of what exactly? Of prejudice and brutality and imposing laws that no normal human being could possibly believe were just and which simply were weapons to punish those that the regime felt were races or creeds or deviants that did not deserve to be part of the new ruling order?

However, Lafarge while revolted by the smugness and arrogance of the man in front of him realized that he was his boss. Nevertheless, he didn't accept his reason for being round at Marguerite's apartment, but he knew he didn't have much more time to probe as Bousquet's patience was running out.

"So what was your answer to her request? I trust you gave her one," asked Lafarge.

"Well I of course told her that I would do anything I could to help her should von Dirlinger, your friend," Bousquet said with a sly smile before adding "persist in annoying her once she had told him the bad news.".

Lafarge noted this down and made to gather up the rest of his papers, before sitting back in his chair, hoping he would catch Bousquet off his guard.

"Sorry, I won't detain you for much longer. However, I was wondering whether anything else was discussed that night. I found quite a few cigarette butts in the ashtray which suggests that your stay was rather long. Are you free to discuss what else you talked about?" asked Lafarge.

Bousquet nodded his head, Lafarge thought for one minute it might be to salute his remark over the length of time he had spent there, but then he rather doubted that, given the animosity between them.

THE TORTURED DETECTIVE

"Not much of interest to you I would say. Pleasantries and idle gossip, her latest film, her future projects with Albert Greven, that sort of thing. Who was the next innocent virgin Guitry had his eyes on... The sort of relaxed conversation that I rarely get to have these days," he sighed with what seemed to be genuine regret.

Lafarge, though, felt no pity for him on that score, he had assumed his high rank knowing very well that it was perhaps the most onerous and the one where the Germans would come calling more often as they prized security above anything else.

"On that note regarding gossip and Guitry's sexual adventures, not to mention the victim wanting your protection were it needed with von Dirlinger, I would have thought you might have asked whether she had seen your missing prey de Chastelain," asked Lafarge, delighted to have had this line of questioning opened up for him by Bousquet.

Bousquet bit his bottom lip, a reproach to himself, Lafarge reckoned, but he had no choice but to answer the question.

"Oh I think I touched on the subject with her. She seemed so concerned about the possible fallout from ending her affair with von Dirlinger that I thought it unnecessary to pursue it too earnestly with her," replied Bousquet smoothly.

That is a load of bullshit, Lafarge thought. Regardless of the tension between the two, he wasn't going to let that answer suffice. Bousquet himself would not have been satisfied with him if he had let that one ride in an interrogation of another suspect.

"I am afraid I don't believe that, sir. It is well known how furious you were after he failed to show up in court and vowed to hunt down not only him but also those who helped him avoid his arrest.

"You can accuse me of being many things, but I am not stupid and indeed one of the reasons why you may have asked for me to be appointed to this case is because of that, for you think I can lead you to those who did help him.

"I have already learnt from an authoritative source that Marguerite was the person who warned him. So if I know that, I am sure you also being an intelligent man would have asked yourself the same question too and helpfully being in her apartment taken the time to ask her," said Lafarge.

"You certainly are well informed, detective," said Bousquet, Lafarge noting that he had not used his title, probably deliberately.

105

"You are certainly better informed than me, or smarter at prising information out of others. All I will say further on the matter is that she denied it outright and I left there not much the wiser over who the mole had been," he added with a pained expression clouding his handsome features.

"My information tells me otherwise, as does my instinct. I do not believe that you would have been satisfied with her response, I also do not believe that the reason you were in her apartment was because she invited you to ask about protection.

"It may have cropped up to distract you, but I believe you got yourself invited there on the pretext of some invented excuse and then interrogated her, politely of course, on de Chastelain.

"You are also the last person known to have been in her apartment while she was alive. All in all secretary–general, the evidence is stacking up against you," said Lafarge coldly.

Bousquet looked at Lafarge with first disbelief and then rose from his chair, walked to one of the large windows and started laughing.

"You do want to stay in the police force, don't you Lafarge?

"I mean, I could always find you a role as a comic in a one man show, a clown at the circus, or perhaps a lion tamer, where hopefully the lions would devour you. From what you have just said you are all but accusing me of murder," he spluttered incredulously.

"I wouldn't go that far. I think, and so do you, that de Chastelain committed the murder, but I am simply laying out the facts that could be presented as an alternative case. One that, whispered into the right ears, could cause you problems you wouldn't care for," said Lafarge crisply.

Bousquet whirled round, his eyes narrow slits, and shot a look of venom at Lafarge.

"You have powerful friends, sir, but so do I, and loathe that I am to use them, I will do in this case. Not for my own self–preservation, but because I believe that the victim and her family deserve the truth. At a time when there is little of it around, it would be nice to say that at least it still exists," Lafarge said forcefully.

Bousquet sighed deeply, looked at his finely–manicured fingernails, and took his time to speak.

THE TORTURED DETECTIVE

"I repeat Lafarge that I asked her, I got a denial and I left. She was very much alive, she was I think expecting someone else and I have no idea who that was. Maybe it was that prick de Chastelain, or von Dirlinger," said Bousquet glacially.

"Either of them would be more suitable targets for your investigation, rather than trying to settle a score with me.

"On the subject of de Chastelain I believe you have to prepare your things for your train early tomorrow morning. I suggest on your lengthy journey you reflect on our meeting today.

"And when you return, if you do, and I would recommend only do so if you have de Chastelain with you, I hope it is with a different perspective on my role that night. It would be better for both of us that it is the case," he added sternly.

Lafarge breathed in deeply and let out a steady sigh before rising from the chair.

"I take it that is another warning," ventured Lafarge.

"You are the detective, I think you can work that out for yourself," replied Bousquet sarcastically.

"However, all will be good if you, as I say, return with de Chastelain. Then not only will it put an end to your wild accusations but also perhaps it will provoke me into forgetting about this meeting.

"Unlike von Dirlinger I do not try and win over the investigating officer's goodwill with dinners and taking them to a cabaret, but then that is the difference between the two of us.

"I am not going to play a role and take you for lunch because you and I are not friends, and I would not try to persuade you otherwise. You would immediately suspect something was not right.

"I am what I am, Lafarge, you may not appreciate it but I am telling the truth when I say that Marguerite, while maybe evasive, denied any knowledge of seeing de Chastelain since their relationship ended.

"Now I must join my guests at the Ritz for at the very least a proper espresso and a cognac, perhaps the equal of the one you shared so copiously with von Dirlinger last night," said Bousquet in a firm tone that ended any further discussion apart from going through the formality of a cold farewell.

Lafarge departed a troubled man. It wasn't so much Bousquet's unsubtle warnings, that he had expected and in fact he was pleased overall with the outcome of the meeting, first it was over and secondly he had emerged unscathed for the moment and more importantly still in charge of the investigation.

No, what troubled Lafarge was that if Bousquet was indeed telling the truth about his conversation with Marguerite and she had intended on ending her relationship with von Dirlinger, then there was a clear motive, aside from the missing jewels, for the good colonel to have been the murderer.

Now he was goodness knows where, because Lafarge had believed his version of events and allowed him to leave Paris, thinking he was innocent.

The irony was not lost on Lafarge that the one person who was a suspect in the case and who he had liked, Mathilde aside, could very well be the man he should have arrested. If indeed that was the case, he had fallen for the old trick of keep your friends close and your enemies even closer. He had been royally played by von Dirlinger.

CHAPTER TWELVE

The train was rattling along under its own steam, that is gently passing through the outskirts of Paris and Lafarge was settled in a first class compartment. It had just two other occupants, a rather severe looking gentleman, bedecked in old style stiff winged collar and tailcoat, though by his facial expression, he was not off to a wedding but perhaps a banker's meeting.

The other passenger in his compartment was a youngish looking woman, well dressed in a tweed suit and a dark brown felt hat. She took the window seat opposite Lafarge but apart from a brief smile and a muttered good morning, that was all the social intercourse between them, as she then averted her gaze and somewhat wistfully stared out of the window.

Lafarge was happy that neither she – nor the severe looking technocrat – were keen on conversation. He had a lot to read and even more to think about on what would be at best a seven hour trip, provided of course there was no disruption to the trip by either resistance activity or an air raid.

He had packed a large suitcase because he realized that his pursuit of de Chastelain might take some time. He knew the elusive lawyer would not just drop into his lap and that he was going to an area of France that he knew little of and had never visited. However, he could not afford to fail as Bousquet had made it quite clear what the consequences would be were he to return without de Chastelain.

While the compartment was relatively well heated – late summer mornings could be chilly – he kept his jacket on, for he did not wish to unduly concern his fellow passengers nor draw unwanted attention on himself as underneath he had his M1935A standard issue pistol strapped in a shoulder holster.

Lafarge had also armed himself with a hip flask, cognac of course, and had fitted in three bottles into his suitcase as emergency supplies. He took a swig of the cognac and settled down to flick through the case dossier as well as some new information on the forensics of the bullet that had killed Marguerite.

It wasn't very conclusive in narrowing down his list of suspects as the type of gun used was the same one he was carrying.

While it had ostensibly been originally solely for French use, the Germans had been so impressed that they had continued producing it in its factory in Alsace – at least there's something apart from our women, drink, food and art that the Germans find useful, mused Lafarge sourly.

There was no record of Marguerite possessing a gun, so the murderer must have brought it with him, and while de Chastelain remained number one suspect, it similarly didn't rule out either von Dirlinger nor Bousquet.

Nor at a push, Mathilde, though he really couldn't envisage a scenario where she killed her mistress and how did she get hold of a service pistol? Mistress being the operative word smiled Lafarge. No, he didn't see Marguerite embarking on a sordid affair with her maid, there was certainly no indication from her past that she liked sex with both sexes.

However, there was definitely a link to Marguerite between von Dirlinger and Mathilde, for he had engineered the rendezvous with the victim and then procured the job for Mathilde.

Circumstantial evidence, but still a thread worth keeping in mind, although whether Marguerite really was going to end their relationship, he only had Bousquet's word for and that was self–serving at best.

Maybe they were all embroiled in it, and de Chastelain was their convenient scapegoat.

Had von Dirlinger purposefully set up Marguerite to forewarn de Chastelain of his impending arrest, thereby conveniently releasing into the ether a bitter former lover, also implicated in the jewel theft, who frustrated at not being able to win back his former mistress and with the jewels missing decided to kill her?

Both arguments had weight. And then there was Bousquet.

He would not have been pleased at all had he learnt of Marguerite's involvement in the incident that humiliated him in front of his adored German masters. Coming just days after he had received a personal visit from Heydrich, whose star was rising so fast that he seemed likely to replace Hitler should the Fuhrer be indisposed, had been a severe blow to his prestige.

God help humanity because should Heydrich replace Hitler, an already brutal regime would become even more vicious in its bid

THE TORTURED DETECTIVE

to subjugate those they felt were not worthy of sharing the same living space as they.

Thus Lafarge could imagine Bousquet's fury and desire to seek out those who had made a mockery of his plan.

While he did not see him as being one who delighted in killing by his own hand, Lafarge wondered whether Marguerite, with her sometimes naïve belief that her charm and beauty could win anyone over, had perhaps driven France's wannabe Heydrich to do just that.

Thus if there was one thing that drew them all together and made Lafarge indispensable for the moment was that he had to get de Chastelain. Lafarge too wanted de Chastelain, not from any personal vengeful point of view but because he knew he held the key to the whole scenario.

However, Lafarge also acknowledged that were he to bring him back to Paris, the case would be stamped solved and no matter who the killer was, both von Dirlinger and Bousquet had interests in the lawyer taking the blame.

There would be no argument, Lafarge would have to hand him over, he would be tried and he would be found guilty.

Probably alongside the unfortunate Lescarboura, as an accessory even if he had been banged up already, and then executed together. Both von Dirlinger and Bousquet had greater ambitions and were damned that they would be implicated in such a crime, what is more they had protection and scandal was not something either the Nazis or Vichy cared to have associated with themselves.

Then of course they would deal with Lafarge, and that he did not care to think about at the moment. He was entering the territory where having put both Bousquet and von Dirlinger on their guard, they had in their own way warned him that there was only one solution and that was catch de Chastelain, bring him back and all will be good between us.

Von Dirlinger may have been a delightful and generous host that night but as Bousquet said, each person has his own way of playing the game.

For instance, was it coincidence that Bonny had turned up that morning at Marguerite's, supposedly on a tip off from his partner Lafont? Who had given them the information? And furthermore why choose a time and a day when the detective in charge of the case is sleeping one floor above, or perhaps that was part of the game, von Dirlinger's way of having a little fun.

However, whilst Lafont and Bonny were well known for their close relations with the SS and the Gestapo, ties with the Abwehr were less obvious. If that had been von Dirlinger's warning, then it made Lafarge concerned as Bonny and Lafont played by no rules save self–aggrandizement, enriching themselves and their goons, and brutality especially against people that they disliked.

The trouble was, Lafarge was increasingly becoming sick of such political games, and never one to accept authority and its rules especially when it came to playing with the lives of others, he had not yet made up his mind what he would do if he did catch de Chastelain.

It depended of course on whether de Chastelain was innocent, and given the animosity between him and the lawyer, it would not be easy if he did find him to convince him to talk and subsequently return to Paris.

He sighed at the size of the task that confronted him and took a swig from his hip flask, lit a cigarette and swung his legs to the far side of the female passenger so he could stretch them out. She gave him a nod of appreciation and a faint smile.

"You seem very preoccupied," she said, with an accent that Lafarge defined as coming from central France.

Lafarge smiled back at her.

"I think it would be a rare person who isn't these days, madam."

"Quite. Are you travelling far? Most people tend to when they get their hands on an Ausweis," she asked in a friendly tone.

"Limoges is the extent of my trip. And you?" asked Lafarge.

"Same destination as yourself. I have family there," she said.

"You are fortunate. I have family too but sadly, they are further away than Limoges," he said.

"So it is business that is taking you to Limoges?" she asked in a manner that suggested little interest but was asking out of politeness.

"Yes, business. Will you be staying long in Limoges, madam?" asked Lafarge, wishing not to enter into too much detail of what his business was.

"Oh, I would think a month. I was working in the theatre, but the play has finished and we are yet to hear if our next production

THE TORTURED DETECTIVE

meets with the censor's approval. So I decided to take the opportunity to visit my family and should the censor approve the play the theatre will send word to me," she said her tone somewhat lighter.

"Theatre, that's interesting. Actress, dressmaker, director..." Lafarge said slipping in the last role as a dry joke.

She laughed, politely Lafarge thought at his lame effort.

"Actress, I have been appearing at the Théâtre de la Madeleine with Guitry. Normally, there is no problem with his plays as he is in favour with the censors, so I am confident I will be back treading the boards soon," she said smiling.

"What is your name, perhaps I have heard of you? Although I admit I am more prone to going to the cinema when time allows than the theatre," asked Lafarge, the name Guitry having exercised his interest given the French showman's closeness to Bousquet.

"Aimée de Florentin, but I doubt you have heard of me. My name is not lit up on the front of the theatre, mind you, wherever Guitry is playing it is hard to get space beside his name as it is written in such large letters!" she said laughing.

Lafarge too laughed for it was well known that Guitry's ego walked way ahead of him, indeed he appeared to have hijacked Oscar Wilde's famous phrase 'I have nothing to declare but my genius!'

She was correct too, because he hadn't heard of her, but he wouldn't mind getting to know her better as she was proving to be excellent company. Aside from apparently possessing a good sense of humour, self–deprecatory as well, she was also extremely becoming to the eye.

Long blonde hair curled round her thin face, while she also had striking hazel brown eyes and full lips.

Limoges is starting to take on a more fun hue, thought Lafarge, although, he reprimanded himself, just platonic dinners of course when he had the time. That depended too on her accepting his invitation in the first place.

"You are right, I am ashamed to confess I have not heard of you. However, we are equals in that matter as you will never have heard of me. I am Gaston Lafarge," he said extending his hand.

She smiled warmly, her eyes twinkled, he noted with some surprise, and took his hand briefly in hers.

"There you are wrong, Inspector. I do read things apart from plays you know! I saw your name in the newspaper the other day, with regard to investigating the murder of my fellow Thespian Marguerite Suchet. So sad," she said sighing regretfully.

Lafarge nodded, quietly happy that his work did not go unnoticed, though with the caveat that the reputation of the French police force never very high was probably at its lowest with the silent majority of French people that it had ever been.

"It's always good to put a face to a name," she said cordially.

"Quite. I always like it when I can put a face to a criminal," he said humourously.

She laughed, this time Lafarge was happy to see for longer and more genuinely than at his first lame attempt at humour.

"Did you know the victim?" he asked, more out of instinct which he cursed himself for as it threatened to ruin the atmosphere in the compartment.

"Sorry. I shouldn't have asked that, I never seem to be able to put my job aside," he said apologetically.

"Don't worry, I'm not offended. It's not as if I am a suspect! Yes I knew her, not well for the worlds of theatre and film are pretty separate apart from a few of the big stars who transcend both. However, I had met her on several occasions at social events. She seemed very charming, and fun too," she said.

"It would be very sad if she had been killed just because she was sleeping with a German. I mean, God, if that were to become a habit, there would be a whole spate of them. Mind you, it would help my career, a few of them falling by the wayside!" she said, giving out a deep rasping laugh.

Lafarge too laughed, then stopped and looked nervously to his right where the stern looking passenger had been sitting but saw thankfully that he was not there.

"The undertaker got out at Vierzon, while you were deep in thought, we are now in what remains of independent France" she said laughing again.

"Yes, he was rather serious looking, wasn't he? So I must have been locked up in my little world for rather a long time then, not even aware we had crossed into Vichy," he said apologetically, whilst firing a warning shot across her bows with a reminder to her

THE TORTURED DETECTIVE

he was part of the Vichy apparatus lest de Florentin start revealing facts about herself he would feel uncomfortable with.

"Yes, I think we must only be 30 minutes from Limoges, though with trains these days you never know," she said.

"Don't worry, though, inspector, I won't spread it around that you are in Limoges. Your secret is safe with me!" she added teasingly.

He grinned and shook his head.

"I don't think you need worry about that. I would think I will be met by a mixture of police and resistants when I arrive. Information such as my movements have a tendency to travel ahead of one, these days," he said.

"Yes, that is true. Where are you staying in Limoges, if that's not a state secret?" she inquired.

"I honestly don't know. I imagine a hotel, where I will be taken when I arrive. What about yourself? Does your family live in Limoges itself or are they in some farmhouse or chateau in the countryside?" asked Lafarge.

"Chateau? Hardly! But yes, in a farm house about five kilometers outside Limoges, near a village called Oradour–sur–Glane. It's very pretty. If you have a free afternoon you should come out and visit it," she said with a gleam in her eyes.

Lafarge could feel himself getting rather excited at this invitation.

"I would be delighted to, though I have no idea how long I will be kept here. Similarly I would very much like to invite you for dinner one night in Limoges, if there is such a thing as a proper restaurant," he said.

"I would love to accept your invitation inspector. Don't be too down on Limoges for there are two or three relatively good restaurants, though, like everything these days if you want something of quality you pay above average," she said.

Lafarge thought to himself that he was more than willing to pay above average to have dinner with Aimée de Florentin. Anyway, he was on expenses down here and he could write it off as dinner with a person of interest to the case. Well, she had met Marguerite at least, that was more than anyone else, apart from de Chastelain, will have done in Limoges.

115

She wrote out in neat handwriting, having removed her black velvet glove, revealing elegant thin fingered hands, her phone number and told him to ring anytime and leave his contact details.

He said he would do so as soon as they were to hand.

He wasn't doing anything against regulations he insisted, it was true that once he was settled in his hotel that word would leak out anyway, so there was no point guarding his whereabouts and Aimée didn't appear to be anything but genuine.

He had been a policeman for so long now, and met enough people down the years, that he could tell more often than not when people were being genuine.

The conductor passed by at this point to tell them they were five minutes from Limoges, so they gathered their baggage together and walked down the corridor to the carriage door. Lafarge dutifully helped her down onto the platform with her two suitcases and carried one to the end where they were met by their respective reception committees.

De Florentin introduced him briefly to a middle–aged couple, Bernard her brother and Lisette her sister–in–law, both good looking and certainly not, to Lafarge's eye, typical farming stock, and then bade them farewell so he could introduce himself to his colleagues.

There were two of them, one stocky with a friendly face, the other leaner with an intelligent face, and a humourous glint in his eyes.

"Welcome Inspector Lafarge, I'm chief inspector Paul Broglie from the Police Judiciaire and this is our colleague Inspector Bertrand Guillermot of the Bureau of Anti–National Activities (BMA)," said the squat one, taking his suitcase from him.

"Delighted and thank you for being here to meet me. BMA? Any particular reason?" asked Lafarge, wondering why it was necessary to bring along a member of the internal intelligence services.

"Well, down here, in what remains of France and where there is, shall we say, much more terrorist activity, we liaise together as it is impossible to work properly without mutual co–operation, there is no point competing against each other," said Guillermot amiably.

Lafarge nodded in agreement at that, for in Paris, it was a nightmare where different services all but hijacked some cases and

THE TORTURED DETECTIVE

in others openly sabotaged them if they felt that the suspect was useful to their own investigation.

"It is particularly the case now. For we are on a higher than usual alert after the news we received today from Paris," said Broglie in a hushed tone as they walked towards the exit of the station.

"News, what news?" asked Lafarge.

"Reinhard Heydrich has been wounded in an assassination attempt in Prague and we have been told to reinforce all our barracks and offices in case the terrorists take heart from this and launch widespread attacks," said Broglie.

Lafarge was stunned by this news, for it struck at the very heart of the Nazi hierarchy, their golden boy targeted in his 'hometown' of Prague.

That would shake not only the rulers in Berlin but also it would surely destabilize the paladins of Vichy and most notably Bousquet, who had been so proud of the person to person meeting with Heydrich. He may well recover but it would have rattled the overweening confidence of Bousquet and that, for Lafarge, was a decided plus, both personally and professionally.

CHAPTER THIRTEEN

Lafarge declined the offer of sleeping in the austere–looking barracks, preferring to take up residence in a hotel in the town.

They took him to the Hôtel des Faisans, where he was greeted by a friendly, rather overweight middle aged lady, who gave him a simple room, decorated with brightly coloured floral wallpaper, though with the bonus of a tiny en suite bathroom, overlooking the street.

Broglie and Guillemot then escorted him to the police headquarters, a typical non–descript greystone building in the centre of town – Limoges itself could be best described as an ordinary run of the mill medium sized town largely made up of two storey houses on small streets – where it became apparent that his two colleagues had not been exaggerating about the state of alert.

There was a massive group of civilians in the hall, sitting looking miserable and confused on the wooden benches guarded by uniformed gendarmes awaiting their turn to be registered and then taken to be interrogated.

When Lafarge asked who they were, Broglie replied that they were people of interest with links to the terrorists or were communists and some were Jews, who had not observed the law brought in in May that they were obliged to wear yellow stars on their clothing.

France is all but Germany in name, mused Lafarge. It made a mockery of the term Free Zone, for Vichy had cut a deal where effectively just for being able to hold onto some land they had surrendered themselves to imposing every law and wish of the Germans.

"I hope we have a good reserve of yellow cloth," said Lafarge sharply.

Broglie and Guillemot eyed him warily but then burst out laughing along with Lafarge, who felt it best to turn it into a sick joke so as not to arouse suspicion from his companions.

"Well, we supply and they pay for it, it's beautiful isn't it?" grinned Broglie, revealing chipped dark stained teeth.

Lafarge nodded, though he felt more like removing some of the disgusting teeth from Broglie's mouth.

THE TORTURED DETECTIVE

The trio moved on past the wretched crowd and through the doors where the noise level was no less as mostly men in plain clothes scurried around looking busy and shouting orders at, it appeared to Lafarge, nobody in particular.

They were a mix of Guillemot's BMA, his and Broglie's Police Judiciaire and the odious Brigades Spéciales, the latter being split into two sections, one to hunt down Jews and the second one to chase communists.

What made them effective and was repugnant to Lafarge was that all of them had volunteered for the service, which guaranteed no compassion wherever a Jew or communist was concerned.

Lafarge had had cause to come across the two leaders of the sections in Paris, David and Henocques, both of them highly effective but devoid of any human feeling towards their quarry. Needless to say brutality was never far from the surface. For them, torture rather than reason produced the results to please their commander Bousquet.

They finally arrived at the end of the corridor and Broglie indicated to Lafarge to enter. He walked into a largish office populated by around 10 plainclothes officers, all of them busy at their desks, either on the phone or typing away.

Lafarge wondered where on earth he was going to find space to work from until Broglie took him by the arm and ushered him to the end of the room and into an office where there were two desks, shutting the door behind them which thankfully crowded out the noise.

"This is my desk, which you can see needs tending to like my roses in my garden. A good pruning is required!" grinned Broglie gesturing at the mass of files on his desk.

The only other items adorning it were an overflowing ashtray, a half bottle of cheap looking red wine, a standard green–topped reading lamp – obviously not over–used given the amount of unread dossiers, thought Lafarge – and a framed photograph whose subject Lafarge could not see as its back was turned to him.

"This then I take to be my desk. Nice and clean for the moment, Inspector," smiled Lafarge gesturing towards one that was bare of any such detritus.

"Yes it is. We will soon remedy that problem. You have a phone, a typewriter and a lamp which should be all that you require," replied Broglie.

"Good. Well I might as well get started then. Our chief is extremely keen that this matter is resolved as soon as possible as it is of great personal interest to him," said Lafarge.

Broglie laughed and took out two empty glasses and filled them with the wine left over in the bottle, offering one to a reluctant Lafarge.

"Ah Inspector Lafarge, first we shall drink our pre aperitif and then us being a little different in our habits to the ever busy lot in Paris, because they have the Germans looking over their shoulders the whole time, we shall treat you to hospitality Free Zone style!" chortled Broglie, downing his well filled glass in one gulp.

Lafarge took a deep breath and did the same, deciding that although he wished to fulfill Bousquet's orders, he would accept their invitation on this occasion as it was best not to antagonize his hosts from the outset.

Besides, he needed their insight if there was any into the possible whereabouts of de Chastelain, he was tired after the long journey, and a relaxed dinner with them would be a nice way to end the day and allow him to be fresh for the chase in the morning.

*

Lafarge awoke early the next morning after sleeping soundly, having consumed an inordinate amount of wine and alcohol and eaten lavishly at no doubt great expense to the state.

It had proved to be not as painful as he had feared, a gathering of policemen never having been his preferred choice of social companions, and Broglie despite his earlier joke and rotten teeth a very pleasant host.

Guillemot too, whom they had picked up from his office, was sharp, witty and intelligent, making Lafarge wonder why he had opted for Limoges and not Paris, while several of the others also were amiable company.

Alas, in terms of information there was little to be had, although pleasantly that was more because Broglie imposed a rule that talking shop was largely off limits at such occasions.

Guillemot told him to drop by his office in the morning and they would talk the matter over, which pleased Lafarge and absolved him from chatting about work for the remainder of the evening.

The mood only darkened when a group of about five members of the Brigades Spéciales walked into the brasserie, and dallied by their table for a few minutes.

It appeared to Lafarge that they all liked to dress in the manner of Chicago organized crime figures, sharp double breasted chalk grey pinstriped suits, plain shirts and striped ties, while to a man they had their hair slicked back.

All very presentable, the sort of look that would win over any local girl's parents if their daughter was to invite them over for Sunday lunch, but that was till they opened their mouths.

All seemed determined to outdo each other in uttering profanities, squalid jokes of a sexual nature and often relating back to the powerless suspects they had tortured or raped that day, for nothing was beyond them in the search for what to them was the truth.

Mind you, Lafarge thought, truth was not something that came easily to these creatures.

At least Bonny and Lafont's gang barely pretended to be something they weren't, although they reveled in the title of the French Gestapo, but their avarice and criminal activities were carried out in the open.

The Brigades Speciales were sullying the reputation forever of the French police, although Lafarge had to admit even without them, the regular police services were doing a good job of that themselves.

The headquarters was less frenetic than the previous day and Lafarge wondered what had happened to those lost souls that he had seen crowded on the benches.

Best not to think about that, he reflected as he knocked and entered Guillemot's office. Guillemot pulled up a chair for his colleague and poured him a coffee, which tasted like a real one for once, not the muck that they drank in Quai des Orfèvres.

The BMA had accrued a good reputation, but unlike the Brigade Spéciales, they didn't resort to outright brutality but more on creating good relations with the populace and then prying for information, the majority of it undercover.

Lafarge and Guillemot chatted amiably for a few minutes, the latter revealing that Limoges appealed to him more because his family had come from the region and a few still lived in Oradour–sur–Glane and its surrounding farms. Also he admitted Paris had never attracted him overly, even after being a student there in the early 30's.

"I'm more a Marseille man," he said smiling.

Lafarge laughed at Guillemot's gentle joke at the expense of he the Parisian, the rivalry between the two biggest cities in France never far from the surface of any conversation.

"I'm more a Nice man myself. That is, my family live there now," said Lafarge resignedly.

"Ah I thought you were more Vichy," came Guillemot's riposte.

"You're well–informed Inspector," said Lafarge admiringly.

"It's my job, Gaston. I wouldn't be much use if I didn't do my research, would I?" said Guillemot, smiling again. "Now to business," he added, changing the tone completely.

"We have had no firm sightings of de Chastelain for a few days now. However, before you get too dejected, I can tell you with almost complete confidence that he is still in the area," said Guillemot, his tone supporting his statement.

"How so?" asked Lafarge.

"Instinct born of several years of intelligence work added to the little slivers of information that we have been able to piece together. I have to admit it's not a complete picture but then I am afraid we have loads of other cases on our desk and this one came to us late," he said apologetically.

"That's fine. If you can furnish me with the information you already have, any people who you feel might be co–operative and talk to me that would at least get me started. I believe for instance there are two terrorist groups known to be operating in the region," said Lafarge.

"Yes at least two of them. I think we can discount the Armenian–led largely communist group given someone like de Chastelain, despite his reputation for taking on the state in court, would not appeal to them as they are a pretty exclusive bunch and rely on cultural as well as political fidelity.

"Thus we are left with the group mainly made up of confused intellectuals and lost professionals.

THE TORTURED DETECTIVE

"There we have easier access, if you understand my drift. They can be more malleable, as while their antennae might make them naturally suspicious they are also proud people who would take kindly to us paying tribute to their pre–war reputations. Their egos react well to being caressed.

"The only thing is finding them, as there are plenty of lawyers, doctors and professors, mostly at a loose end in Limoges, god knows why they chose this dull place, and they are not all plotting against the state.

"However, we have files on most of them and it is there where you may find a link to de Chastelain. There might be an old colleague or former law professor of his."

Lafarge thanked him and said he would await delivery of the files in his office and get cracking straight away. He turned to leave having drained another cup of the excellent coffee but Guillemot told him he hadn't finished.

"I believe you prefer to work on your own, Gaston. Here it will not be possible, a smaller town means no information or act goes unnoticed. It would be better for all concerned that you keep all the services informed of your plans and your progress, even though I know you are answerable really to one man and he is in Paris," said Guillemot affably but firmly.

"You never know but if you play it that way, then information will also come in your direction. We all for better or for worse are working for the same government, and I believe the same goal, so I would advise restraining your normal modus operandi and being a team player.

"Things will work out for the better for all concerned. It may mean even having to converse with the Brigades Speciales. I too loathe them but they do get results and if it helps catch your man then you should have no qualms about how they extract the information.

"Don't worry, though, I am not going to be shadowing you, your social life when you manage to have one is your own affair. Just tread warily there for while we have strength, so do they, and traps there are aplenty.

"Lord knows you are going to have plenty of time to learn that.

"I don't know if Bousquet has given you a deadline but I would suggest letting him know that you could be here for several months. The way these cases generally go and the hostile atmosphere out in the countryside makes me think you will be our guest for a long time," said Guillemot with a tone that suggested to Lafarge he was happy at the thought of that, which was an encouraging sign at least.

Lafarge had reckoned as much about the duration of his stay, he just didn't know whether Bousquet had.

Mind you, Lafarge thought as he wandered down the corridor to his office, the longer he was away from Paris, the happier Bousquet would be. He too was happy because it gave him the time to get to know his own actress acquaintance, Aimée de Florentin, much better and he would be calling on her at the earliest possible moment.

Not only because he wanted to, but also the couple that had greeted her at the station intrigued him and who they really were, for neither had for sure ever ploughed a field or milked a cow by the very nature of their appearance that day and the smoothness of their hands when he shook them.

CHAPTER FOURTEEN

Lafarge had leafed through countless dossiers in three hours and he was already bored. None of them really revealed much of an insight into how or through whom he could start making progress into tracking down de Chastelain.

The one thing he did glean from reading the files on some of the more notable people in the town and its surroundings was that the unattractive spirit of denunciation was as virulent here as it was in Paris.

The funny thing, though, was that they were busy denouncing themselves. Thus a farmer called Benoist Bouchard had written to headquarters relating that one of his farmhands, Lionel Cretillon, was sloping off from work at odd hours during the day, usually post lunch.

Bouchard apologized that owing to his duties on the farm and providing provisions for the security forces in the area, he had not been able to follow his errant employee. About the same time, good old yeoman Cretillon, Lafarge noticed, had filed a similar report with the police regarding his employer.

"Farmer Bouchard is not the most reliable of employers, for having given us our instructions for the day if we have finished by lunch we can rarely find him to give us further work for the afternoon," he said in his statement deposed with the gendarme.

It had transpired, when the gendarmes decided to take action, that Cretillon was screwing Bouchard's daughter on a regular basis while the farmer, who had higher ambitions for his offspring than a lowly farmhand, had informed on him to try and have him arrested.

Cretillon, having been warned by his lover, had decided to counter attack by filing a similar complaint. The result for both was a telling off for wasting police time and ordered to carry on working together.

With so few men of working age available as so many French males had been kindly sent by Vichy to work in Germany, Bouchard had little option but to ditch his ambitions for his daughter and keep his unwanted prospective son–in–law on at the farm.

That was one of the funnier ones that Lafarge had read, there were a lot of others that were far less amusing and had ended in serious repercussions for the person that had been denounced.

Those who did the denouncing rarely got severely punished even if they were proved to be wrong, as the state did not wish to discourage the practice. Similarly, they also did not want a deluge of false information that would distract them from real leads, and there was a suspicion that some resistance cells were deploying this tactic, as it was effective and not harmful to them.

Lafarge tossed the umpteenth file onto his desk which now resembled the bazaar that was Broglie's, even to the extent of the overflowing ashtray and the half full bottle of red wine, though, his was a better quality. The plethora of denunciations revolted him and illustrated once again that the French were no different to other human beings, that even with their culture and appreciation of the best things, whether it be art, food, women and wine, they had a very dark side.

These files and the information within them showed clearly a neighbour who had been a smiling and pleasant person to live beside in happier times became a vengeful and envious personality once things deteriorated. Sometimes it was for the tiniest of benefits, like adding a chair to their home because their neighbour had been arrested on their say so and the house had been declared open for anyone to take the accuseds' goods and chattels.

Lafarge, like any policeman, had always had use for informants, without them it made cases almost impossible to solve, but these sort of informants revealed within the files were totally unreliable and were meriting an equal punishment to their targets.

Lafarge was contemplating strolling down to the brasserie 'Le Chat Gris' where he had been invited the previous night, when Broglie, who he hadn't seen all morning, came in with a thunderous look on his round face.

He acknowledged Lafarge but headed straight for a cupboard just behind his desk and from it retrieved a bottle of red wine.

He pulled the cork and poured it into his unwashed, grimy glass before downing it in one. Lafarge kept his thoughts to himself, allowing Broglie time to gather himself and tell him what was on his mind if he so wished. It took another two full glasses before he did so.

THE TORTURED DETECTIVE

"Sorry Gaston, it's just I have had it with the creeps from Brigades Spéciales," he said, spitting the words out venomously.

Lafarge raised his hands in a gesture of why now, why are you so angry with them?

"I arrested a fellow and his wife this morning, a couple we have been watching closely for some time, pretty much since they came down from Paris. We acted on information provided by a reliable source that they were involved in a cell who were printing anti–Nazi pamphlets and were planning a similar thing here, even though their co–conspirators had been arrested by the Gestapo.

"Well, I preferred to wait until they did set up their new operation and I shared that intelligence with Guillemot, who agreed to the plan. Thus we pounced this morning... I didn't tell you because their arrival was well before your fugitive came here, and caught them red–handed. They surrendered without any resistance and we brought them back here.

"I was in the process of presenting them to Guillemot, having registered them with the desk sergeant, but unfortunately I must have been overheard or one of my fellows blabbered something to one of the thugs.

"No sooner were we having an initially cordial discussion in Guillemot's office than in strode de Blaeckere, the head of the Brigade Spéciale in charge of tracking down communist insurgents, and two of his sidekicks and demanded that we hand the couple over to his authority.

"Obviously, I protested in the strongest of terms as did Guillemot, but de Blaeckere would have none of it.

"He sneered at me that I was just a yokel from the country and had no say in what he, an aristocrat from Normandy and educated at the Sorbonne, decided.

"I went to take a swing at him, but fortunately, Guillemot prevented me from doing so and using his more subtle arts of diplomatic persuasion, tried to reason with the man.

"However it had no impact whatsoever and he simply ordered his men to take the couple, who had calmed down after realizing that Guillemot and myself were more interested in talking them into a confession than beating it out of them.

"In any case, having caught them with the printing press, there wasn't much to confess. Now I hate to think what he and his men are doing to the couple in the basement cells. I don't have much sympathy for what they were doing but at the same time, I still believe in the due process such as it is these days.

"Treason is treason and the penalty is death, but at least with me and Guillemot, they would have gone there unharmed. Those sadists are going to make them regret ever having lived," Broglie hissed and wiped away beads of sweat that had broken out on his forehead.

Lafarge sympathized with Broglie, relieved that his remark about the Jews and the stars appeared to be just to ingratiate himself early in their relationship, perhaps testing his Parisian colleague's sentiments.

His fury here was genuine and as he knew he was helpless to do anything about it. Of course, it could have been injured professional pride at being ridiculed by the arrogant de Blaeckere, but here Lafarge saw an opportunity for himself, a risky one but he was determined to take it.

Lafarge ran down the corridor and descended the steps into the basement where the Brigades Spéciales spent most of their time, appropriately close to the sewers and the rats, for that was where they belonged.

Here was where they did their brutal, savage interrogations, only legal because laws had been imposed that permitted them to go to any lengths to exercise their duties.

On reaching the basement, he had to cover his nose such was the stench of sweat, human excrement and burning flesh, a smell he had got used to during the desperate days of fighting the Nazis.

He brushed aside two of the blood spattered thugs brandishing his ID and demanded to know where de Blaeckere was. One grumpily pointed in the direction of a cell on the right, and Lafarge shoved open the door with full force.

A scene of utter depravity greeted him. De Blaeckere and two more of his goons were standing against the wall laughing as another leant over the woman.

Her pretty floral dress had been shredded, her pants were round her ankles and her bra was below her breasts, which were both now covered in cigarette burns while her face was turning purple, her nose a mix of blood and cartilage.

THE TORTURED DETECTIVE

One of the thugs was at that moment thrusting an object up between her legs, her moans issuing forth from lips that barely moved and were bloodied and swollen.

They had left her eyes untouched, perhaps to let her witness the terrible things they were perpetrating on her, and in them Lafarge did not see submissiveness or terror, pain yes, but there was also a determined look, and that was the only consolation.

"What the hell do you want!" shouted de Blaeckere at Lafarge.

Lafarge didn't hesitate and strode over to the woman, hauling the thug off her and retrieving the object, which he saw was a ruler, from within her.

Lafarge pulled her up into a sitting position against the stone wall and turned to de Blaeckere, who hadn't moved, although his men were edging towards him.

"Tell your lapdogs to desist, de Blaeckere. It wouldn't be wise to hurt an emissary from Paris, one who has absolute authority where Parisian fugitives are involved," snarled Lafarge.

De Blaeckere laughed, a totally humourless one, and took a drag on his cigarette.

"Total authority! On whose say so?" smirked de Blaeckere.

"As far as I am concerned, I have the authority here.

"You are outside your jurisdiction my friend. In case you haven't got accustomed to it, you are now in Vichy controlled France and we go by no–one else's authority, least of all that of some plain clothes detective who chases ordinary criminals, not those who threaten the state's existence," he grinned smugly.

Lafarge noted that despite de Blaeckere's confident statement, he had halted his men in their tracks, though they remained like attack dogs on their toes, ready to pounce given the order.

"I would suggest de Blaeckere that you place a call to Paris to secretary–general Bousquet's office and ask on whose authority I am here," said Lafarge icily.

However, he knew he was taking a huge gamble as should Bousquet not be convinced the woman and the man, who was nowhere to be seen, were anything to do with the de Chastelain case, then they would be left in the hands of de Blaeckere.

However, to his relief, his ploy appeared to have worked because de Blaeckere paused, not quite so sure of himself, and stroked his chin and then put a hand through his greased back blond hair as if deep in reflection.

Lafarge eyed the three men around him and noticed they too weren't looking quite so threatening as before, they turned towards de Blaeckere looking for guidance.

"Well you can't argue with that can you," said de Blaeckere with a smile.

"We're done with her anyway. There's not much more fun we can have with her, she's all used up, and she's just fit for the firing squad which as you know, detective, is where she will end up," he added.

Lafarge knew it was true, there was no alternative, as Broglie had said she and her accomplice had been caught red–handed with the printing press.

Still, that wasn't the point, treated differently, she may have given them more information. As it was now, she was little use to anyone and the determined look he had seen in her eyes suggested that even if she was given time to recover she would never volunteer any pertinent information.

It was pointless telling de Blaeckere this as he knew only one way to interrogate his prisoners and that was by fulfilling his sadistic fantasies, which didn't say a lot for his good education and aristocratic upbringing.

"Well, at least my way she will be able to die with dignity and not in this hellhole surrounded by you and your brainless thugs," snarled Lafarge.

"The next time you interfere, Lafarge, you may not be received with such understanding. Our secretary–general is a great admirer of our work and our results, hence why we are allowed some fun from time to time," said de Blaeckere proudly.

"Fun, you call this fun! You really have betrayed your family, your class and stained our country's reputation if you regard this as fun. I wouldn't mind having a few minutes with you alone de Blaeckere and showing you what fun it is to be treated in such a way!" yelled Lafarge.

"That I am afraid won't happen. But please, tonight, when you are at peace with yourself and lying alone in your bed, why don't you masturbate over that thought, because it's the only weapon you

THE TORTURED DETECTIVE

are going to use against me," chortled de Blaeckere, his brown eyes dancing merrily.

His men too thought it hilarious, and with that they made to leave, rolling down their sleeves over their bloodied arms and picking up their pinstripe jackets from the chairs before making for the door.

"Oi de Blaeckere, where is the man?" asked Lafarge.

De Blaeckere turned and shot him a look of triumph.

"He's next door. However, you won't really be able to tidy him up much, I think he would prefer to be buried alive the state he is in. What's that saying, the cat got his tongue!" said de Blaeckere with a belly laugh.

Lafarge was seething but resisted the urge to hurl himself at the sadistic brute.

He waited until they had left before making the woman as comfortable as possible and checked her breathing, which reassuringly was returning to some form of normalcy, and then he went next door.

There the scene was indescribable, the man's face was a pulp, and as feared, his tongue was pinned to the door of the cell.

His hair was soaked, a mixture of sweat and water, for they had ducked him into a cold bath not out of any compassion but to make him believe they were drowning him. He dragged him out of the cell and then went back for the woman, before charging up the steps to get some help in carrying the two broken bodies upstairs.

*

Lafarge was back at his desk after lunch, a whole new set of files had been delivered in his absence and these were the ones compiled of the doctors, lawyers and other bourgeois professionals who had drifted to Limoges from Paris since the Occupation had begun.

The couple of wannabe William Caxton's had been taken under guard to hospital, and he was waiting to learn from Broglie what their condition was.

Truth be told, he hadn't felt like eating anything but had gone along with Broglie and while his colleague had wolfed down a tete de veau and a healthy looking chocolate mousse, he had simply helped him finish two bottles of good red wine and downed a cognac to settle himself.

He couldn't really care less about upsetting de Blaeckere, why he had already accrued the powerful enmity of Bousquet, but it had been the first time he had seen for himself how the so called elite Brigades Speciales operated.

He had managed to successfully avoid them in Paris but here he had found it in his best interests to witness firsthand quite how sadistic they were.

One bonus for his interfering, was that he had earned the eternal loyalty of Broglie.

This Lafarge marked up as a victory, for further down the line, he could count not only on Broglie but his dozen or so detectives should he need to operate independently of de Blaeckere, no matter what Guillemot said to the contrary about inter service co–operation and all that rubbish.

Thus it was a largely content Lafarge who sat back in his chair and started poring over the files, which he had to admit were of more interest and induced a feeling of admiration for Guillemot and his section for their research. Broglie had wandered off in a semi sober state to the hospital allowing Lafarge time on his own to absorb the information contained in the files.

Lafarge was astonished at the talent that had opted to quit Paris and reside in what went under the name of Free France and as Guillemot had said in such a town as this. There were several judges, numerous state prosecutors and as for defence lawyers, it would have been a criminal's paradise were these men and women still operating.

Some were of course, but not at the rate that they would have been had they stayed in Paris or gone to Marseille, the city where crime proliferated and sometimes he thought it probably had originated there as well. However, what buoyed him was that there would certainly be someone here who had had close contact with de Chastelain and surely would have heard from him since he fled Paris.

It didn't take too long before he alighted on a surefire candidate: Henri Gerland, who had been a renowned defence lawyer before the war.

He was not someone who was known to be an anti–Vichy rabble–rouser or indeed unfriendly to the Nazis. Perhaps, more pertinently, he was on good terms with Bousquet. Indeed, he would

THE TORTURED DETECTIVE

be an ideal lawyer to defend de Chastelain and yet, he had followed a mass of refugees to this unlikely destination.

Lafarge knew him as well, and indeed, despite being technically on opposite sides, he respected him and they had also shared some convivial times together, unlike those he had spent with de Chastelain.

His links with de Chastelain were plentiful, for they had teamed–up on several cases.

The fugitive had usually played second fiddle to the baritone of the Paris bar, but on occasion, the master had allowed the apprentice to take centre stage and he had not been left disappointed.

However, where Gerland deployed charm and wit, de Chastelain, merely harangued the victims or the witnesses, using sarcasm when he felt it necessary to resort to humour. Hence Gerland was still regarded as the better of the two advocates, and perhaps the reason why de Chastelain, had chosen Limoges as his initial destination.

This was a stroke of luck and Lafarge could sense for the first time that he had not made a wasted journey. He noted down the address, for he didn't want to forewarn Gerland of his interest in him, and waited impatiently for the return of Broglie, so he could drive him to the house.

CHAPTER FIFTEEN

Gerland looked surprised when he opened the door to find one of his old adversaries standing on his doorstep.

However, he greeted Lafarge warmly and ushered him in. Gerland had fared rather better than the majority of the almost 200,000 refugees who had made their way to Limoges following the Nazi invasion, for he was living in a three storey Second Empire style house on the Rue Bonaparte in the centre of the town.

Clearly too he had managed to 'retreat' in some order unlike Lafarge and his regiment, for on entering his drawingroom he noticed that the shelves were well–stocked with books, legal as well as literary, and it was not lacking in furniture.

Gerland too had not lost his impressive shape, slightly overweight, but his face was finely–honed, a Romanesque nose with piercing blue eyes and topped by a mop of badger coloured hair. He gestured Lafarge to take a seat in a comfortable looking armchair, and offered him a coffee, a real one he added with a self–satisfied smile.

Lafarge would have preferred a drink but as it was 10 in the morning decided even for him that was a bit much and readily accepted the coffee. He had decided to leave his visit till the morning as Broglie only returned to the headquarters near on six, having waited till the woman had been operated on.

She would live to meet her executioner. She had a badly broken nose, a broken jaw and one of her legs had been all but snapped in two, but apart from that she was alright, Broglie had said in his matter of fact way.

As she wasn't going to be going anywhere fast with her injuries they were going to allow her to heal for a while, so at least she could stand on her own two feet when she was shot.

The man, though, had not even made it to surgery, for despite doing their best to staunch the bleeding from his mouth he had passed away before the surgeon could get to him.

"That'll set the tongues wagging round town!" Broglie had joked, to which Lafarge had replied: "Let's hope it doesn't make them hold their tongues!" which had elicited a laugh from his colleague.

THE TORTURED DETECTIVE

Broglie and Lafarge both concurred that gallows humour was the best weapon to try and inure oneself from the ghastly goings on. Trouble was the fanatics in the Brigades Speciales didn't see it that way, everything said was taken at face value and used against you later on or if they were drunk almost immediately.

"So Gaston what brings you down to this pretty but overcrowded little town?" asked Gerland, who had come back into the room carrying a tray with the boiling coffee and several Madeleine cakes on it.

"Have you come here because you need a good defence lawyer? There are still some in Paris you know, although they get even less of a hearing these days than in the pre–War years," said Gerland with a chuckle.

"Ha ha, no Henri, I am not in need of one yet, although, that may not be the case before too long," said Lafarge not altogether untruthfully.

"However, a former associate of yours is in more immediate need of one, well that is when I catch him he will need the best there is."

Gerland raised his bushy eyebrows, which looked like a pair of otters wishing to meet in the middle and copulate, and steepled his fingers together waiting for Lafarge to divulge the name.

"De Chastelain is the man I am after. I have sound information that he came here after fleeing Paris. Knowing how close you were and on hearing you were here, well, naturally I thought you would be someone who he would contact in a town that to my knowledge he has no ties to," said Lafarge crisply, keeping his eyes on Gerland to register his reaction.

Gerland had unsteepled his fingers and put one of them to his mouth and brushed it along his full lips. His eyes hadn't even flickered in surprise when Lafarge had informed him the name of his quarry, which told the detective that he was at the very least aware of something.

The lawyer would have known that Lafarge was in charge of the case, for if Aimée de Florentin knew from the newspapers then Gerland, who liked to know everything that was going on, especially now being in voluntary exile from Paris, would have certainly heard about it.

However, de Chastelain's name had been specifically withheld from any connection to the enquiry in the newspapers, Lafarge and Massu both agreeing that if he read he was the number one suspect then that might provoke him to flee further south.

"Pierre–Yves has been here Gaston, indeed he spent a few nights sleeping in the guest room," said Gerland in an even tone.

Lafarge felt a mini surge of excitement and relief that Drieu had not been telling a tall story to set him off the trail, however, he knew there was a but coming.

"However, he left a week ago, to where I do not know, although, I have a feeling he has not gone far," said Gerland.

"How, Henri would you come to that conclusion?" asked Lafarge.

"Well, he left some of his belongings here, and being a man of some fastidiousness and who takes pride in his appearance, I would venture that he would have need of fresh clothes, his own that is, soon enough," replied Gerland.

"Very good. However, my informant didn't mention anything about him travelling with luggage, he was in quite a state apparently and was desperate to leave Paris."

"Quite so, Gaston. However, a friend of his delivered a trunk and various other items a few days after he deposited himself on me. I was mildly surprised and not a little annoyed as I came to Limoges to avoid these sort of problems. Lord knows I have defended some scoundrels in the past and some totally innocent people too I might add, but I seldom took my work home with me," Gerland chortled.

"However, having kept a relatively low profile since I arrived here, a few minor cases apart, I decided that the less I knew the better, but I wouldn't turn my old colleague away," he added.

"Do you know this friend?" asked Lafarge, although he pretty much guessed who it was.

"Drieu La Rochelle. He explained that he could not cut all ties to his old friends and furthermore he believed that he was totally innocent.

"As usual with Drieu he couldn't keep his anti–Semitism out of the conversation for long, commenting that as 30 percent of lawyers before the war had been Jewish and were now stripped of their power to practise, France could ill afford to lose another lawyer," said Gerland.

THE TORTURED DETECTIVE

"Ah so you did discuss the problem, de Chastelain's I mean not Drieu's concerns about the sudden lack of lawyers," interjected Lafarge, who recalled the unwelcome experience – police detectives were obliged to – of having to visit the disgusting exhibition of 'Le Juif et Le Francais' in Paris the year before where the Jews were exhibited as being greedy, overly ambitious and controlling certain professions and so on and so forth.

Gerland nodded, looking totally unflustered by his betraying a confidence.

"How deeply did you discuss this problem, Henri?" asked Lafarge, not wishing to allow Gerland a moment to cover his tracks.

Gerland sighed and thought for a minute.

"Well, actually, we, the three of us, had a quite in depth conversation about it. There was little choice, for I said to de Chastelain that unless he was totally open with me then he could find somewhere else to lodge himself," said Gerland firmly.

"I see, and before we go into the depth of this discussion, for you are the first person I have seen who has heard his side of the story, I would like to know whether Drieu, who said he didn't really get a coherent account from de Chastelain, mentioned me," asked Lafarge.

"Just in passing. He said that you had been put in charge of the case concerning the murder of Marguerite Suchet and that meant no rest for de Chastelain, for you were not easily managed," said Gerland gently.

"So your relative surprise at seeing me this morning was no more than an act, Henri," said Lafarge.

"Not altogether. I did not realize that you were aware that Pierre–Yves had come to Limoges but once I saw you on the doorstep, I guessed that you being the excellent detective that you are, you had only one reason for visiting me," said Gerland with an appreciative smile.

Lafarge felt relieved that at least Drieu had not revealed their own discussion, probably more to preserve his own friendship with de Chastelain than to keep a confidence, and felt also that Gerland was willing to divulge some important information, if he didn't press him too hard.

Gerland, preferring to keep the discussion on the cordial side, made a suggestion.

"Look Gaston, why don't you dispense with your colleague who is sitting patiently outside, serving no purpose to our discussion, and I will drive you back later.

"In the meantime you can look through de Chastelain's things upstairs and I will get the cook to put some lunch together. That way we can discuss discreetly the matter and enjoy ourselves at the same time," said Gerland affably.

"My word, you have a cook, Henri! I must say you have not suffered unduly unlike most of our compatriots. I don't know whether to be impressed or despise you," said Lafarge half–jokingly.

"My dear Gaston, as I said, there are plenty of rogues out there who greatly appreciate the sterling defence I put up for them in court.

"Happily, quite a few of them found themselves here and being not without resources or resourcefulness, they look after me, for they never know when they might need to call on my services again," said Gerland with a hearty laugh.

*

"So Henri, tell me how much de Chastelain told you and Drieu about the night of Marguerite's murder," asked Lafarge as they tucked into the first course of duck liver pâté and fresh bread, itself a luxury even in Paris where Lafarge often found himself queueing for hours to get one baguette.

"Before I do, did you find anything of interest amongst his luggage?" shot back Gerland.

Lafarge shook his head, although, he had done so, for he had found a piece of scrolled up paper inside the cloth of the top of de Chastelain's trunk. Having unrolled it, he had seen a list of names with question marks beside them.

There was Lescarboura's, von Dirlinger's, Bousquet's even, Mathilde and to his surprise his own with two question marks beside it.

Lafarge complimented himself on being deemed worthy of two question marks but wondered why he had one more than the others.

THE TORTURED DETECTIVE

Drieu's was also on the list as was the aristocrat who had featured in the photograph on the side table of the dinner at Maxim's, de Chambrun, and Bonny's name was there as well.

It almost seemed like de Chastelain hadn't left Paris at all and had instead been shadowing Lafarge throughout the investigation. He knew that wasn't the case because both Drieu and Gerland attested to him being in Limoges for several days now, but still he had the impression that de Chastelain had been kept informed of the progress being made.

"No surprise there, then," said Gerland.

"Pierre–Yves was always very secretive about evidence compiled in the defence case, almost paranoid that the prosecution had eyes and ears everywhere.

"It made it a nightmare for me when I was joint counsel, because suddenly from nowhere he pulled a rabbit out of a hat. Infuriating really," harrumphed Gerland.

"Yes, it wasn't to my taste or my colleagues either," said Lafarge.

"Now back to my question, how deeply did you discuss that evening with him, or rather how much did he say about it?" asked Lafarge as he helped himself to the delicious pâté and poured himself the excellent sweet white wine that Gerland had produced from his cellar – another luxury Gerland had taken care to bring with him.

"Truth be told, once he started he couldn't bring himself to stop. He was grief stricken at her death, even, though as he told us, he realized that she had no intention of resuming their relationship, at least not until things took on a rosier hue politically," said Gerland sadly.

"She told him that she needed protection and the Abwehr colonel provided that, and was also extremely kind and caring to her and that was sufficient for her," he added.

"So she was still in love with de Chastelain? That is what you seem to be inferring," said Lafarge.

Gerland nodded.

"De Chastelain didn't mention whether she had suggested she was tired of the colonel and wanted to be free of him?" asked Lafarge.

"Absolutely not. She made it clear that this German was her protector and it would remain that way until such time as things changed politically. He, de Chastelain, I recall laughed bitterly after he said this, for he made a remark that sounded odd," said Gerland.

"What was that Henri?" asked Lafarge, barely containing his curiosity.

"He said 'The German is only hanging around until she gives him a present of diamonds!' to which I laughed and remarked 'but Pierre–Yves surely it is the other way round!'" said Gerland.

"How did he react to your remark?"

"He sneered and said that it wasn't just good enough for the Germans to come in and take our country, strip us of our pride but also now our women and then use them as common thieves. He said that von Dirlinger, that's his name isn't it, was no different despite his title and outward charm and grace.

"De Chastelain was extremely agitated by this, I thought he was going to have an attack," said Gerland.

"So he was claiming that von Dirlinger was a mastermind behind some theft? That he had manipulated Marguerite into committing some crime?

"Did he say whether he had told her this after she made what to me appear rather odd claims for her, regarding politics that is, as she wasn't known to be interested by them, and enlightened her on her German lover's real motivation for keeping her sweet?" asked Lafarge, his heart racing.

"Yes, he said he did, and what's more he said that it had been his strategy for his defence of the man accused of the crime, Lescarboura, but that had all been prevented by her providential call on him to warn him of his own impending arrest," said Gerland.

Lafarge was seeing part of the case become clearer now, although it still didn't rule de Chastelain out of murdering her, given the anger and frustration he must have felt. He was also a little confused over the claim that von Dirlinger had been the mastermind behind the burglary as Lescarboura had told him it had been de Chastelain's idea.

"Did he say how she reacted to this unpleasant piece of information?" asked Lafarge.

THE TORTURED DETECTIVE

"Not very well, she told him to get out, that he was just a bitter loser who had no future and but for their previous intimate relationship she would have called the police. However, she then burst into tears and he was in the process of consoling her when her telephone rang.

"She pulled herself together and answered it and all de Chastelain could ascertain was that whoever was on the other end of the phone was insisting on coming round.

"Suchet tried to dissuade the caller, but to no avail.

"When she put the phone down she appeared nervous and distracted, and told him that he had to leave, but then hesitated and ushered him upstairs to her maid's room. She told him to hide there just in case he was to cross paths with her visitor. She gave him the key to the room as she said the maid had probably gone out," said Gerland.

Lafarge was so engrossed in the discussion that he had not even noticed he had left most of his second helping of pâté untouched. It was too late to consume the rest as the cook had now entered the dining room to serve the main course, magret de canard with various vegetables and some potatos.

He helped himself to the food and then a generous glass of a fine Burgundy red, which had been opened and left breathing by his host while he was upstairs, and returned to the subject.

"So was the maid there? And did he say how long he spent hiding?" asked Lafarge.

"No, she wasn't there and feeling tired and angry, he lay down on her bed and waited for Marguerite to come and get him. However, after about two hours, he got fed up and ventured out and looked over the banister to try and see whether he could just make a run for it.

"He decided he would, seeing that there was no guard outside her apartment, for he didn't know whether the visitor was a high up official meriting such an escort, and descended the stairs."

So why did he end up with blood all over his shirt if he said as he told you he made a run for it?" asked Lafarge.

"I'm just getting to that Gaston. But please allow me to enjoy my lunch as well," said Gerland good humouredly.

Lafarge raised his hands apologetically and watched Gerland as he put a healthy helping of the duck and the vegetables inside his large mouth. Being the bon viveur that he was, Gerland took his time to enjoy it too, washing it down with a good dose of the red.

"Anyway, he was on his way down and noticed her front door was ajar. Naturally being the inquisitive type that he is, he entered quietly and found Marguerite lying on the sofa, with her head staring towards the window.

"He called out her name softly and received no reply. Not really thinking he went towards her and then saw that her hand was touching the rug and saw that she was bleeding and barely breathing. He tried to resuscitate her but it was no use and then kissed her on the lips and left, hurrying away to seek out Drieu. The rest you know," said Gerland returning to his overflowing plate.

Aside from the rather colourful and sentimental ending to the tale, which Lafarge reckoned was a nice piece of embellishment from his host, it certainly appeared a credible sequence of events.

However, it was not what either Bousquet or von Dirlinger would want to hear. For this account implicated one of them certainly for the jewel heist and perhaps the other for her murder. Bousquet lived close by and it must have been his imminent arrival that forced Marguerite to tell de Chastelain to go and hide in Mathilde's room.

"One thing more before we move onto dessert and lighter matters, did de Chastelain mention who he thought might have been the caller?"

"No, why?"

"Only that I know for a fact there were three men in the apartment that night, von Dirlinger, de Chastelain and god help me René Bousquet," said Lafarge puffing out his cheeks.

"I think it was in that order, which leaves me with the extremely unappetizing possibility that my boss, Berlin's darling, is the murderer and the other fellow is the mastermind behind a jewel theft that may or may not have provoked this whole sequence of events."

"That's not all Gaston, for I would surmise you were sent by them to catch Pierre–Yves, no?" asked Gerland, his tone gentle and his eyes sad.

Lafarge nodded glumly.

THE TORTURED DETECTIVE

"Never two without three! And Pierre–Yves is their scapegoat and you my friend are collateral damage or will be if you don't deliver him to them," said Gerland grimly.

Lafarge nodded again and thought to himself that although he had not wanted to believe it, it had been pretty clear that von Dirlinger and Bousquet's almost zealous enthusiasm for him to go after de Chastelain had not been in the common goal of catching a man guilty of murdering a mistress and a friend respectively.

No, it had been to absolve themselves of their own crimes that even they could be punished for, though by all accounts far worse ones were being perpetrated all over Nazi Occupied Europe.

However, Lafarge had never knowingly sent an innocent man or woman to death and even in these immoral and rancid times, he wasn't going to start afresh regardless of what it cost him. He was going to find a way of setting de Chastelain free...after he caught him.

CHAPTER SIXTEEN

"You still want to take him back to Paris, Gaston? I'm amazed. Why not just let him be? You can easily bluff your way through it and tell them you were on his trail but he found out and scarpered," said Gerland sternly.

Lafarge shook his head.

"I have to return with him to Paris as much for my own good as anything else. If I can at least show that I captured him and had him on his way back to face justice, then it should be sufficient to save both him and me," said Lafarge.

Gerland, who along with Lafarge was now digesting some cheese with a glass of extremely good Bordeaux claret, looked at him quizzically.

"How on earth can that be beneficial to both of you? I mean you are not steering him and yourself away from trouble you are heading straight into the storm. If you could explain your strategy it would be most welcome," said Gerland sounding totally confused.

Lafarge chewed on his bread and cheese and took a sip of wine before enlightening his host. It was, he admitted to himself, a plan rather made up on the hoof but he could see it working out.

"I have a contact in Paris who has, so he says, a route to get people who have an urgent need to leave France, to safety.

"They are mainly Jews, criminals who have made the wrong sort of enemy, and others who simply can't countenance staying in any part of France whether it be under Nazi or Vichy's control," said Lafarge, prompting one of Gerland's otter–like eyebrows to shoot upwards in surprise.

"Yes, you may wonder why I would have such a contact and why he isn't in prison, or been deported. But not being ideologically convinced by our occupiers' views, I would rather see as many people who have committed no crime other than to have had the misfortune to be born of the wrong faith escape their clutches," said Lafarge by way of explanation.

"What about the criminals, though, Gaston? I didn't think you were the lenient type when it came to them," said Gerland with a reproachful tone.

144

THE TORTURED DETECTIVE

"Besides, you are taking away my bread and butter! That won't do," added Gerland smiling.

Lafarge grinned at the gentle jibe.

"Yes Henri, I can see that you are suffering from the loss of several of your potential clients!" jested Lafarge, sweeping his hands over the table that had borne the weight of their excellent lunch.

"However, I am not going to endanger my contact's life and those of the Jews as well as other innocent people just because he is saving some criminals from the authorities," added Lafarge.

Gerland nodded in understanding and stroked his chin while Lafarge rose from the table to stretch his legs.

"Alright Gaston, so this is how you are going to try and get Pierre–Yves out of the country.

"Very well, but how on earth are you going to be able to organise all this from here, and also as you have no idea if or when you will have Pierre–Yves in custody, you can't simply set up the transfer into your contact's hands with a definitive date," said Gerland.

"Besides, I take it once you have de Chastelain in your keep, you will have to inform Bousquet at the very least that you have him and are bringing him back.

"That leads me to the next problem. Your ambitious boss will want to ensure there is no chance of him evading capture a second time and will either instruct you to have him heavily guarded on the train or send a strong force to the Gare d'Austerlitz to wait for you."

Lafarge was standing with his back to Gerland, staring out the window onto a large well–tended garden which was just starting to spring into full blossom, with red roses especially prominent, and a rhododendron bush at the bottom of it.

"That's where you come into the plan, Henri," said Lafarge crisply.

"Me? I don't really see how I can help you defy Bousquet," said Gerland.

"Well, in fact you can on two counts. Firstly, you can deliver de Chastelain into my hands, and then you can activate some of your old friends who are still in Paris to arrange for them to meet us at the station, and 'ambush me', taking the prisoner off my hands, temporarily of course," said Lafarge.

Lafarge could hear Gerland sucking in air and then expelling it as he listened to the plan. Lafarge knew he was placing an awful lot of trust in this man, who he had known and liked before the War but now under such different circumstances, it was asking a lot of him.

He was just hoping that Gerland's friendship and association with de Chastelain would prompt him to fall on the side of the good people in the story.

"I would need them to hide him in a safe house if they have one, allowing me to first of all square the story with Bousquet and then to arrange for de Chastelain to be spirited away.

"I know I am asking a huge amount from you Henri, but I think you would accept it is under exceptional circumstances and if it is just to save one innocent man from the guilty ones, then I believe it is worth your while," said Lafarge.

Gerland too had risen from his chair and came over to stand by Lafarge's side, surveying with some pride the state of the garden, although the detective somehow doubted that it had been his host's hands that had created such a beautiful and fertile environment.

"It's lovely to see things come to fruition, or rather blossom after a long hard winter Gaston, and I wouldn't mind seeing several more of these occasions," said Gerland tapping at the window pane.

"I am running a great risk, if I help you with this ingenious but devilishly risky plan, that I will end up propping up these plants should it fail, which to my mind is very probable.

"However, there is also a time when people have to stand up and do their bit to hurt those who by their very actions and behaviour are staining the reputation of one's own country.

"I couldn't really give a damn about the Nazis, it is for their own people to reflect on what they allowed to happen. But I am buggered if I am going to sit idly by and be a bystander to the crimes that Bousquet and Laval are committing in our name. I was no great admirer of the Third Republic but Jesus, it at least observed basic human rights and laws.

"Thus yes, I will help you on both counts. Pierre–Yves is like me, better at fighting with his mouth than his hands, so it shouldn't be too hard to persuade him to come back here and place him in your custody. Obviously it may take time as I have little contact

THE TORTURED DETECTIVE

with the people he has gone into hiding with, and it may also take some convincing him to believe in your plan.

"However, bide your time and I will get him here. I will also put into place the necessary arrangements with the people I can still trust in Paris. Again, it won't be easy and it could be expensive, but I am prepared to cover the costs.

"All I will say to you is that should things go badly awry, the only involvement I would wish imposed on me afterwards is you hiring me as your lawyer! I think you understand me clearly on that," said Gerland in a clipped but friendly tone.

Lafarge felt like embracing Gerland and kissing him on both cheeks, so elated was he that his gamble in placing his faith in the lawyer had been well worth it.

Instead, he slapped him on the back hard enough that Gerland's head hit the wooden part of the window frame, but instead of reproaching him he laughed and said: "I prefer to enter the garden by the door Gaston, no matter how eager I am to get out there!"

*

Gerland, as he had promised, dropped Lafarge off at the police headquarters after they had drunk a couple of cognacs to finish off the afternoon in pleasurable style. Gerland squeezed his arm warmly when he made to get out, a gesture of friendship as well as a warning to be careful, and Lafarge nodded.

There was pandemonium when he entered the building. What's new pussycat he thought to himself, with a new group of tired and harassed looking people aligning the benches whilst they waited their turn to descend into de Blaeckere's receptacle of Hell.

There was nothing that Lafarge could do about them. He'd fought his battle and now his mind was totally focused on his plan, although he would still have to go through the motions of searching for his prey, but at least it would be in the firm knowledge that he would get his man whatever happened.

He was greeted by Broglie, who was putting on his jacket as he entered their office, who asked him how the day had gone, to which Lafarge said it had been very productive without obviously going into details, save to say they had enjoyed some excellent wine.

Broglie said on that note he was going off for the night and would he like to join him for a drink at the brasserie. Lafarge thanked him and said he would think about it but he had some matters he needed to tie up before he clocked off. Broglie smiled and then stopped at the doorway smacking his head as if he was a dolt.

"I'm sorry, Gaston, but a lady called for you. I told her you were out on a work related matter and didn't know when you would be returning, so she gave me her number which I jotted down and left on your desk.

"She wouldn't leave her name but said that you would remember her from the stage," said Broglie shrugging his shoulders in wonderment at the games that people played.

Lafarge laughed and also felt a surge of excitement run through his body, and as soon as his colleague had left, he looked down at the note and dialed the number.

Lafarge was delighted when it was Aimée who answered, explaining that while it was not her house or place to do so, both her brother and his wife had gone out.

Lafarge kept the conversation to the minimum solely asking her if he came to collect her would she be willing to have dinner with him that evening.

It didn't take much convincing, although she insisted she would dine with him without having to force him to come and pick her up, as she could easily find her way into town, being more au fait with the area than the Parisian policeman.

Lafarge said he would meet her at his hotel at 8 and having replaced the handle of the phone, he let out a whoop of joy. As much as reality tried to bite he cast it aside, declaring that for one night only he could suspend his marital status, for should his plan unravel he would not have too many more occasions to enjoy the pleasures of the opposite sex.

However, as if to salve his conscience ahead of the dinner Lafarge decided to call Isabella, as it had also been a while since they spoke and if she had tried him at the apartment, she might have started to worry as to where he was.

Getting a connection was never easy but that evening it was not a problem, his perfect day, as he was coming to describe it, continuing in seamless fashion.

"Hello," came a young male voice after it had rung for several rings.

"Ah Philippe, it's your father. How are you?" asked Lafarge rather awkwardly.

THE TORTURED DETECTIVE

"I'm fine dad. Do you want to speak to Mama?" came the reply from his son.

"Yes, that would be great, thank you Philippe. I will try and come and see you as soon as I can, I miss you," said Lafarge sadly, regretting making a promise that he knew would be hard to keep.

"They both miss you," said Isabella once she had come to the phone.

"And you, Isabella, do you miss me?" asked Lafarge, eager but equally afraid to hear the response.

"Sometimes," she replied brusquely.

"Oh well, I will take what I can get. Anyway how are you and the children, not suffering I hope from the privations we have in the north?" asked Lafarge with a suitable air of concern in his voice.

"Everything is fine Gaston. We don't really lack for anything, your father helps us to obtain things that are difficult to get, he has been really kind, more present than you have been," she said coldly.

Lafarge recoiled at this barb, thanking his father in one respect but cursing him for making him look like an uncaring soul.

"What, he has visited you, or he has made arrangements for you?" asked Lafarge.

"Yes, he's been here to see his grandchildren on three or four occasions, sometimes with your mother, sometimes on his own.

"He says it gives him pleasure to have an excuse to leave Vichy and he can relax here. You should try it, it might be good for you.

"You know, blue skies, warmish water, laughter and there is still some crime so you wouldn't be totally lost and unemployed," she said laughing, though Lafarge could tell it was rather hollow and inside the joke, there was a message to him.

"Point taken Isabella, but you know that is what I wish to do. It's just at the moment I am involved in a very delicate and troublesome case and should I solve it, I will then ask for a transfer down to you and the children," he said with as much sincerity and confidence as he could summon up.

There was a silence at the other end of the phone and Lafarge wasn't going to invade it.

"I know Gaston, your father told me something about it. Not in much detail, but he did say that you would have to tread very

149

carefully and that he feared for you because you were not good at playing political games. I told him I was painfully aware of that," she said her tone changing abruptly to a tender one.

"He's right on all counts. However, I believe that I am nearing the end of it now. I'm in Limoges and have made significant progress and I also believe that I can emerge from this unscathed," he said reassuringly.

"Limoges? What a place to be at the best of times!" she said.

"Oh, it's not that bad. There are some old acquaintances here, the food is good and so is the wine, and as you well know, the china is excellent! I will try and get you some," said Lafarge trying to cheer her up with the promise of the town's most famous product.

"And the women Gaston, how are they in Limoges, any old as you put it acquaintances?" asked Isabella half in jest.

"No, Isabella none of them are female," said Lafarge, content that at least there he was being truthful.

"Good, I am glad to hear that. And before you ask, no I have not come across any old flames. I am being saintly and pure, and just going out occasionally with the children and on a couple of occasions with your father," she said.

Lafarge was relieved to hear her say that and also reassured that her coldness since leaving had nothing to do with finding a new male companion, indeed he chided himself for having arranged his dinner date now.

He had always thought a beautiful woman like Isabella, without her husband, down in the hotter climes of Nice would be like a magnet for any aspiring Lothario.

"So please come as soon as you can, Gaston, for I cannot remain a nun for the rest of my life, my South American blood wouldn't allow for that in any case. Guinevere wants her King Arthur back, this time alive not dead," she said sternly.

"Yes my Queen, I will obey you," replied Lafarge drily.

Lafarge felt a sudden urge to ask Isabella to come up and see him in Limoges, but then stopped short of doing so and as it turned out it was just as well he did.

"Gaston, I love you very much, you know that, but I want a new life for us after this case. I am not sure that Paris is where I wish to live and bring the children up in, and I certainly don't want to carry on being the wife of a detective," she said firmly.

THE TORTURED DETECTIVE

Lafarge was a bit taken aback by Isabella bringing up the topic, and didn't think it very wise to discuss on an open telephone line, so he bit his tongue and replied blandly.

"Ok Isabella let's just see how things turn out, shall we? And we can discuss the future after that," he said.

He heard her sigh deeply down the other end of the line, sensing she wasn't keen to delay the discussion. However, she was intelligent enough to realize there was a reason for his reticence and accepted she had been a little too blunt in what she had just said. However, not even the most zealous of Vichy officials could translate what she said into being critical of the government, he hoped so anyway.

"Alright Gaston, we shall leave it for now. I have to go and bathe the children anyway, and you I am sure have things to be working on, and the quicker you do so the better for all of us. Please, though, be careful my sweet, obstinate bull–headed principled husband," she said warmly.

Lafarge felt a lump rise in his throat, but pushed away the sense of sadness and loneliness, and pulled himself together.

"I love you too dearest Isabella, and no matter what happens that will remain the case, my love for you and the children and for our lives together now and in the future are paramount in my mind.

"Goodbye Isabella and kiss the children for me, after you have dried them down, for I know how nervous you get about having your clothes soaked when you are giving them their baths!" he said gently before placing the handle back on the receiver.

*

A couple of drinks later, his spirits had recovered sufficiently for him to approach dinner with renewed enthusiasm, and his heart skipped a beat when Aimée arrived in the small lobby of the hotel.

She had her long blonde hair pinned at the back of her head and was wearing a small but very chic black hat which covered just the top of her hairline, while she was wearing a long flowing black dress, with transparent sleeves, and a low neckline which accentuated her largish breasts.

Without much further ado apart from a gentle bow and lowering his face to her hand without touching it with his lips, he escorted her to the restaurant which was on the opposite side of the street to the hotel.

It was a small traditional style country restaurant, nothing fancy about the decoration or the cutlery, but the food, he had been informed by Broglie, was excellent and it was intimate enough not to be heard at the next table.

"I'm sorry the setting isn't up to the standard of your dress," Lafarge said apologetically.

She batted away his apology with a regal sweep of her right hand and smiled sweetly, before casting her eyes down to the menu. That prompted him to bashfully also eye the menu, which meant him leaning forward into the candlelight, as there was only one between the two of them, the restaurant being full which meant about 30 odd people, fortunately none of them known to Lafarge.

The owner, a well–built man of around 50 with a fabulous handlebar moustache, came over and took their order. Aimée ordered duck liver pâté and lamb with green beans while Lafarge, having had his fill of duck for the day, opted for goats cheese salad followed by calves brains, to which Aimée wrinkled her nose in mock disgust.

Lafarge shrugged his shoulders and laughed and that was how the evening panned out for the most part. Lots of laughter and stories, mostly from her, with tales of the stage and the stars and how Marais and Cocteau would lock the former's dressing room door before the curtain went up on opening night and the star would emerge looking flushed but in the best of spirits for his performance.

"Wow, I saw them only the other night, but it was too dark to see if Marais was flushed or not," said Lafarge laughing.

"Oh really, where?" asked Aimee with an air of curiosity, leaning forward so her breasts rested on top of the table.

"Careful, you'll get crumbs in there," said Lafarge jokingly.

She smiled and retreated a little before brushing the crumbs from the table and pushing herself forward towards him again.

"Coast is clear, I'm all ears Gaston!" she said soothingly, while running her fingers round her wine glass which was all but empty as was the bottle.

Lafarge ordered another bottle as well as the bill, time was moving on and as ever in the provinces and even more so after the Armistice, 10 at night was considered late for them and it was now 9.30

THE TORTURED DETECTIVE

"I saw them at Suzy Solidor's place on the Rue Sainte Anne. I'd never been there before, it was quite a place, full of the great and the not so great and also the worst types as well," he said.

"Yes, I like it a lot. I go there as a customer now, but before I did an act there. Still Suzy was very kind to give me a break, or at least give me the chance to earn some money, but in the end I was just pleased to move on," she said.

"Yes she is certainly a character, a livewire. However, I'm not sure I like her rendition of Lili Marleen, the original is great but I don't really think it necessary to have a French version. Besides, it's not as if we have soldiers sitting on the frontlines needing morale boosts, we're either in camps or at work in Germany," said Lafarge bitterly.

She smiled at him and held out her hand and stroked his, to which he didn't pull back and allowed her to continue, for it was nice to have the physical touch of a woman after such a long time. His earlier loving thoughts about Isabella seemingly banished.

"Were you a prisoner of war?" she asked gently, still stroking his hand.

Lafarge nodded, but didn't want to expand upon the experience, which apart leaving him feeling humiliated had also been very tedious.

"So you find the theatre more to your taste then. Certainly it is a step up the ladder in terms of prestige even if you are not in the limelight yet," said Lafarge.

"Yes, it certainly gets me more invitations to better parties," she said smiling.

"And the prospects of meeting a better type of guy," quipped Lafarge.

He regretted saying it almost immediately as even in the relative darkness of the restaurant he could see the colour rise in her face.

"I'm sorry, I didn't mean it in that way. I wasn't suggesting you had chosen this career so as to gain social standing or for that matter a husband," said Lafarge apologetically.

She smiled but it was a sad one.

"I can tell you Gaston that not all actresses are like Marguerite Suchet, Arletty or Mireille Balin and seeking an intimate alliance with the enemy. They killed my fiancé so I am not really too keen to pursue any sort of relationship with them," she said wiping a tear away.

Lafarge kicked himself under the table for his crass remark. Maybe he was becoming a bit overcome with the case, imagining that Marguerite was no different to any of her rivals, that they were all seeking a German protector. He was obviously profoundly wrong and had caused great upset.

"I'm so sorry," he said again, desperately seeking to put the evening back on its former relaxed and intimate tone. Trouble was, he couldn't think of what on earth could achieve that goal, so he let the silence drag on and waited for her to break it.

"What about you Gaston, are you married, or are you hiding away using your work as an excuse to avoid such a commitment?" she asked with a glint in her eye.

Lafarge would have said no half an hour ago, but now the manner in which the evening had turned he thought it best to be truthful rather than play her and end up feeling even worse than he had done when he made his flippant but offensive remark.

"Yes, I am married, actually got two young children, but they felt it best or rather my wife did to leave Paris and go to the south.

"It has its advantages because I know they are safe, but on the other hand, it makes life rather lonely. So I guess the second part of your question or suggestion is also correct, I use up all my time or the majority of it on the job," he said glumly.

"Hence the reason you are regarded with such respect. A man of integrity and probity both in his personal and professional lives, and that you cannot say for many people these days," she said warmly.

Lafarge could feel himself blushing, although, he wasn't so sure on reflecting on the remark whether she had been slightly disingenuous.

"That's very kind of you, or whoever you heard say that. I can't attest to being totally convinced that I am like that in my personal life, but maybe it's not for me to judge," he said.

"So, are you enjoying yourself in your temporary absence from the stage, are you taking to farming, milking cows and cleaning out stables?" Lafarge asked changing the subject he thought rather adroitly.

THE TORTURED DETECTIVE

She laughed heartily at that, her eyes regaining the sparkle that had disappeared just minutes ago.

"Well, thankfully, my brother doesn't call on me to do hard labour such as that. I was never a rural girl, but I do help out in the house and cleaning out as you say the stables and feeding the animals," she said laughing.

"However, the way things are going we soon won't have much to farm. The animals are being sequestered, whether they be horses for Vichy to supply their allies in the north, or cows for being killed and used as food supplies. So my days of farming experience may not be for long," she said with a note of relief in her voice.

"Yes I can imagine it is tough for your brother to keep up his enthusiasm for something that is little by little being forcibly and illegally taken away from him," said Lafarge sympathetically.

"I would like to come out and see it sometime, see how good you are at farm work," he added smiling.

"I am sure you will be impressed! I'm about as good at that as I am at house work! Of course you must, I already said you were welcome. I will come in and take you out there whenever you want. You just give me a call no matter how short the notice," she said.

"That would be terrific, a day in the countryside away from all this and the depressing atmosphere would do me the world of good," said Lafarge wearily.

"Yes, I can imagine that even for someone who immerses himself in his work there are limits," she said softly.

"Look let's make a definite date, why don't we organize it for two days from now, because I have made enough progress on the case for the moment and aside from a couple of things tomorrow I am sure I can spare one day," he said, eager to pin her down as he was both keen and intrigued to see how much her brother knew about farming which he ventured was not a lot.

For a second she looked a little taken aback by his determination to settle on a date, but she slipped back into sweetness and light mode quick as a flash.

"That sounds fine by me, but I must check with my brother, because he may have plans that day visavis the farm, but I am sure we can work something out," she said.

"Good, good, I can't wait. Now I think our host is getting a bit twitchy about closing up so let me settle the bill and if is ok with

155

you we could have a nightcap in the hotel before you take off for your greener pastures," he said grinning.

Their host's handlebar moustache twitched with delight at the tip that Lafarge left him, the detective thinking that it was an investment for being given special treatment the next time he ate there.

"Thank you sir, you have been very generous, I have to say I never know when your like comes here whether they are going to pay or not.

"Often I am told it will be the next time or that I am lucky to be allowed to stay open as some obscure law that I have broken should have me closed down," he said grumpily, shrugging his shoulders at the same time as if to say there's not much I can do about them not paying.

"Well, I am different to them Monsieur Fremont, I pay my bills and from now on I will use what influence I can to see that they do as well. Good night and thank you for an excellent evening," said Lafarge courteously before ushering Aimee out the door.

He took her arm as they walked the short distance back to the hotel, where lights were still shining in the bar area which pleased Lafarge no end.

"You are different Gaston, he was right. Not just because you pay your bills and don't throw your weight around with some spurious reason for not paying it. There is something of real humanity in you," she said gripping his arm affectionately, though her long nails threatened to draw blood so tight did she dig them into him.

"I'm touched Aimee. For these days one doesn't hear too many kind words, not that suspects or people you interview or interrogate are on their politest behaviour anyway! But thank you. Now for that nightcap," he said as they arrived on the steps of the hotel entrance.

"I think I will forego the nightcap Gaston, thank you," she said fumbling in her bag.

"Oh well I will escort you to your car then," he said sadly.

"There's no need for that Gaston, I took the precaution of booking a room for tonight here in the hotel. I didn't want to risk running the gamut with the gendarmes over the curfew. Also with

THE TORTURED DETECTIVE

drink taken and car lights having to be dimmed because of fear of air raids, even here, I thought it the wisest thing to do," she said.

"Ah you are blessed with wisdom as well Aimee! So is that an invitation?" he said grinning malevolently.

She tapped him on the chin and the nose in a good humoured way of telling him off.

"We shall talk some more in two days Gaston, then things may become a little clearer for both of us," she said and gave him an affectionate peck on the cheek before sashaying up the stairs leaving him to drink his nightcap on his own and reflect on a great evening and interpret her tantalizing final remark to him.

The trip to the farm couldn't come soon enough both for seeing her again and also to get to the bottom of the mystery of the brother and what exactly he was up to.

CHAPTER SEVENTEEN

"Heydrich's dead," were the first words Lafarge heard the next morning when he descended the stairs feeling rather foggy–minded to be greeted by Broglie looking uncommonly flustered.

"Ah so," muttered Lafarge matter of factly.

Broglie stared at him, or rather at his back as he entered the breakfast room and settled himself at his table and waited for the pot of coffee to be brought. Broglie, though, arrived quicker than the waitress.

"If you forgive me Gaston I'm not sure you should be saying something like that," he mumbled.

"Sorry I don't understand you. What am I not meant to say, ah now I see, no you fool you think I said asshole. Dear oh dear Broglie you should clean your ears out! I said ah so," Lafarge said laughing heartily.

Broglie grinned shamefacedly and pulled a chair over, about the same time that the pretty but very young waitress, Mabel, arrived with the coffee, whose only quality was that it was hot as it bore little relation to real coffee in taste.

Lafarge poured himself and Broglie a cup each and munched cautiously on a stale croissant waiting to hear what else Broglie had to impart whilst also scanning the room for any sight of Aimee. There was no sign much to his disappointment.

"As a result of Heydrich's death we are, like you saw the other day when you arrived, on a state of high alert. Further to that Guillemot has summoned all of us to a meeting in his office at 9 sharp, which means in 20 minutes time," said Broglie, who even though it was not that hot had started to sweat.

"I see and I take it I am to be present at the meeting and you are here to ensure I am there," said Lafarge, and received a nod from his colleague.

"Good. Any idea what it might be about this meeting?" he asked but this time Broglie was supping down his coffee, though, Lafarge could detect he was shaking his head at the same time.

"Very well Watson, the game is afoot as Sherlock would say! Let's go," said Lafarge and sprang to his feet and left the room leaving Broglie to follow in his wake.

THE TORTURED DETECTIVE

*

"René Bousquet has designed this as a day of mourning, following a request from the Germans. However, whilst we will dutifully don black armbands so as not to offend the Nazis I want this to be a day of action as well, for it will be recognized by Paris in the most positive of ways," said Guillemot solemnly.

Guillemot received several nods of appreciation for this, from de Blaeckere, who was present with his number two Yann Caullenec, a physically impressive looking fellow from Brittany but who was as coarse as they come. Broglie and his number two Gervaise Filbru, an amiable if lightweight detective to Lafarge's eyes, kept silent.

"Thus all three services plus the uniforms and you too Lafarge are going to combine on a raid on a terrorist cell that I have good information is due to meet today on the outskirts of Limoges. They are a group of lawyers and doctors, and believe that they are not known to us.

"The reason I want you coming along Lafarge is that there is a chance your fugitive might show his face, so we could come out of this with two objectives achieved," said Guillemot his face creasing into a smile.

"I want all available forces assembled outside in an hour and we hit them as soon as everyone is in position.

"I have already sent on an advance party to reconnoitre the surroundings and to keep an eye out for the various personalities who we expect to be gathering at the house.

Now as you can see from the map I have drawn up it is a big house, three storeys high and with a large garden which is ringed by bushes and trees making getting a clear sight of what's going on inside or indeed in the garden difficult.

"However, we expect them to be all there by midday, after that any latecomers we will either sweep up or it will be their lucky day because we will have already gone in.

"Needless to say cock your weapons but only resort to them if you are fired on. The main objective is to capture them and bring them back here for interrogation," said Guillemot firmly.

Lafarge put up his hand to attract Guillemot's attention, and noticed Caullenec whispering something in de Blaeckere's ear which provoked a snigger from the Brigades Spéciales chief. He ignored it and proceeded to speak once given permission by Guillemot.

"Forgive me for pointing out, Guillemot, but it sounds as if the odds against us are quite sizeable.

"I mean if we have no clear sight into the house or indeed the garden then we are going in blind. Unless of course you have someone planted on the inside?" asked Lafarge, disappointed at the cavalier plan devised by Guillemot, whom he had thought of as being pragmatic and wise.

Guillemot looked Lafarge straight in the eyes not flinching for a moment.

"Yes, I have someone on the inside and who is to hang a sheet outside the central top floor window, which we can see clearly, to tell us that everyone is there and we are good to go," said Guillemot.

"Good good. But how are we to recognize your informant if shooting does take place? Surely you want him to be kept out of harms' way. I mean losing a top informant when it appears we don't have many reliable ones would be quite a high price to pay for such an operation," said Lafarge.

"I have made arrangements for the informant to keep safe should shooting break out, but I don't envisage too much resistance from this group.

"For the most part, they prefer talking and conspiring than action. However, being quite wealthy they also contribute money towards weapons and deliver intelligence gleaned from their contact with the likes of us. They are very effective in winning our confidence and over a few glasses tongues relax a little bit.

"We are lulled into a false sense of security that such men are not capable of conspiring against us...We think because they earn their living from work we provide, whether it be legal or medical, that we have bought their loyalty.

"However, nothing could be further from the truth, the doctors especially have taken against us because of the state of the patients they have seen after muscular interrogations," Guillemot said fixing his gaze on de Blaeckere, who shot him a look of disdain.

"We get results, Guillemot, unlike you and your more cerebral approach to intelligence, footwork and fake charm when you come to interrogate prisoners," said de Blaeckere sulkily.

THE TORTURED DETECTIVE

"Well de Blaeckere, we all have our different approaches, that's what makes us such an effective and happy ship," said Guillemot sarcastically.

Lafarge was not entirely comforted by Guillemot's assurances on the operation, but he was delighted that he had brought up de Blaeckere's perverted modus operandi.

"On that note, I demand that should de Chastelain fall into our hands that I and only I get to interrogate him. Paris would not look kindly on the type of interrogation utilised by de Blaeckere," said Lafarge, enjoying the sight of de Blaeckere's features reddening.

"You have my word on that Lafarge, there is to be no interference with de Chastelain. Do you hear me de Blaeckere?" Guillemot said in a tone that brooked no argument.

De Blaeckere was seething and could only summon up a grunt acknowledging the order before allowing his temper to get the better of him.

"I am not entirely happy with that, but provided de Chastelain is caught and arrives here alive, I will leave him in the care of our colleague from Paris, the patron saint of sanctimonious bullshit!" hissed de Blaeckere, receiving a slap on the back from his number two.

"That's enough de Blaeckere! You will focus your mind on the task ahead of you and restrain yourself from making asinine and abusive remarks in the future, clear!" said Guillemot in a clipped tone.

De Blaeckere's features took on a petulant look but he nevertheless yielded and nodded.

"Right, that's all. Broglie, gather your men together, Lafarge go with him. Once we are in situ, I want de Blaeckere to lead the initial assault on the house, and you, Broglie, to hold the side entrance to the garden and block off any possible escape route from there.

"I will cover the road on the front and the back just in case the nimbler members of the cell try to vault the walls," said Guillemot.

On that note, the five men picked up their hats and coats and filtered out into the corridor to go and round up their men.

Guillemot talked to the head of the uniformed gendarmes and filled him in on what his men's duties would be, which was largely to drive the vans that would convey the prisoners to headquarters after the raid.

Lafarge was ambling down the corridor on the lookout for another cup of coffee when he sensed there was someone on his shoulder. He turned to see the unwelcome sight of de Blaeckere.

"What the hell do you want de Blaeckere?" asked Lafarge angrily.

"What I want is to have both you and de Chastelain in my sights and to let loose two rounds that take you both out, that's what I want Mr Paris man!" he said in a low vicious tone before he turned on his heel and trotted off.

Lafarge snorted derisively at the threat and having procured himself a cup of coffee proceeded to sit down at his desk and on an impulse, dialed Gerland's number. To his relief the lawyer answered after just two rings.

"Morning Henri, just thanking you for an excellent lunch yesterday and for your help on my divorce case," said Lafarge who heard Gerland breathe deeply in surprise.

"It's a painful enough event to experience on one's own but when you have as astute a lawyer as yourself to hand extremely fortunate and comforting," added Lafarge quickly hoping Gerland would bite.

"Yes I have experienced two divorces Gaston and neither a very pleasant experience, not least for the social shame they bring so it is pleasant for me to be able to help you navigate such a painful procedure," said Gerland his tone calm.

"Being that the case and Isabella not being as yet aware of my wishes, I was keen to make it as fast as possible and I was wondering whether I could drop by today, say around two o'clock," said Lafarge.

There was silence at the other end of the phone.

"Henri, you are still there?" asked Lafarge impatiently.

"Yes, I am. I had been hoping to meet with some friends for lunch, one of whom has recently decided like myself to avail himself of the freer air down here," said Gerland sounding disappointed.

"Well, I normally wouldn't insist but what if you were to get them to come to you, after my visit, for a late lunch? I am sure you have some of that excellent duck left over, probably better than anything they can provide," said Lafarge hoping his tone was as calm as that of Gerland's.

THE TORTURED DETECTIVE

"That could present problems Gaston, for it means a great deal of phoning around and some do not possess a telephone and will already have set out," said Gerland.

"That is a shame as I dearly wanted to make more progress on the personal matter. Normally I wouldn't insist but given I have so little spare time I thought it best to take any opportunity I had to draw up the necessary documents so I can then send them to Isabella and her lawyer in Nice," said Lafarge.

There was more silence from Gerland's end as he mulled over Lafarge's request, the detective hoping his warning had been understood by his friend.

"Very well Gaston, I will wait here for you, but please don't dally. Sadly I don't think it will be possible for me to contact my friend which means I might miss him entirely on this occasion," said Gerland, who appeared to Lafarge to be warming to the cloak and dagger game.

"Very well Henri, I have some business to attend to and I will try and not be too tardy for our appointment," said Lafarge warmly and replaced the handle.

Lafarge was delighted. Firstly his hunch had been correct and Gerland was due to go to the meeting of the lawyers and doctors cell and secondly should his conversation with Gerland have been listened to by Guillemot's men or by de Blaeckere and his gang that it would have sewn confusion amongst them.

Mind you he was a little confused himself as to why he would have used divorcing Isabella as an excuse to warn his friend off going to the rendezvous.

Perhaps he was just becoming more adept at lying to suit his own ends, he would prefer that as the reason and not wishful thinking on his part.

What worried him more for the moment was that Gerland's inference regarding his recently arrived friend suggested de Chastelain would be at the meeting, and there was no means to prevent him going.

It was now left to Lafarge to save him from being hurt, and that he could see was going to be extremely problematic.

*

Guillemot's confidence that there would be little trouble proved to be wide of the mark as Lafarge had suspected. It wasn't clear as

163

to who started the shooting but given that de Blaeckere had been leading the assault, it left little to Lafarge's imagination as to who was to blame.

He was left idly examining his gun as he, Broglie and his men waited by the side entrance as the shooting intensified. Despite increasingly frenetic pleas to Broglie, his colleague refused to breach the door and go to the aid of de Blaeckere.

Broglie instead told his dozen or so men, mainly middle aged and overweight and dressed in sad looking suits in comparison to the Brigades Spéciales, to fan out and hide behind the several cars parked in the non–descript street, with the aim of arresting anyone who exited by the door.

It wasn't a bad tactic but Lafarge thought it was the worst one for him as it negated him being able to at least gain access to the house and the garden and see if de Chastelain was indeed there.

They were also in a total state of ignorance as to what was going on inside the grounds, the only sounds alerting them to what could be taking place was machine gun fire and the occasional grenade explosion.

Unless Lafarge was mistaken not even the Brigades Spéciales were supplied with grenades, machine pistols yes, so the peaceful lawyers and doctors were certainly putting up a fight with ammunition that had not been part of Guillemot's informant's information.

Suddenly, the side door opened with a shout coming from inside of not to shoot, and with Broglie yelling to his motley group to hold their fire out stumbled one of de Blaeckere's bloodhounds, Etienne Castelnau.

He was not a pretty sight, one side of his face and body was streaming blood, but he somehow managed to stagger over to where Broglie and Lafarge were hiding and gasp some information to them.

"You've got to come, de Blaeckere demands it!" said Castelnau, showering Broglie and Lafarge with specks of blood that exited his mouth as he spoke.

"We've taken a real beating in there and we need your back up, if only to get our wounded out," he added, his words faint and Lafarge could see there was little point in running to get him medical aid for this young man was not due to see his next birthday.

THE TORTURED DETECTIVE

Broglie shook his head, prompting Lafarge to lose his patience.

"For pity's sake Broglie, we've got to do something, or at least I have to!

"If they eventually take the house, de Blaeckere is not going to stand on ceremony and he more likely than not is going to shoot all the prisoners he takes in revenge.

"If de Chastelain is in there, then the only hope he has got is me, and indeed the only hope I have of saving my case is to get him out alive," said Lafarge, his tone underlining his frustration with his obstinate colleague.

Broglie looked at him and then down at the dying Castelnau and bit his lip.

"Ok Gaston, you go, but I am under orders to hold the line here and that is what I am going to do until I hear otherwise from Guillemot," said Broglie, who was sweating even more than usual and Lafarge ventured it wasn't just because of the heat in the air.

Lafarge nodded his thanks and jumped to his feet, then ran in crocodile fashion across the street and hurled himself through the open doorway. What greeted him was a fusillade of machine gun fire from one of the second floor windows. Thankfully it hissed past him and hit the wall, showering him with little pieces of shrapnel that tore into his suit jacket.

He rolled over on to his back and withdrew his gun, cocked it, and then rolled over again so he could survey the scene. He could see five bodies lying scattered across the garden, difficult to tell whether they were de Blaeckere's men or their opponents, whilst from the bushes and from behind trees there emanated a constant volley of gunfire at the house.

The house itself was scarred by the incoming fire, the white walls pockmarked with rounds of ammunition that had failed to hit its human targets but destroyed a once attractive façade.

He scanned the garden, desperately seeking de Blaeckere or Caulennec, and saw that they were not so far away from him, skulking down his side of the garden behind a rosebush.

Aha two extra pricks to watch out for in that bush then, joked Lafarge to himself, as he made his way carefully down to them.

Truth be told, the gunfire coming from the house appeared to be less intense than a few minutes before but that wasn't much comfort for their targets, as hidden from sight, the cell members were perhaps saving their ammunition for when the police emerged from their hiding places.

After much crawling and jousting with various plants and other barriers he reached the two chiefs and found both to be untouched physically but mentally in shock at the ferocity of opposition they had met.

It was one thing to cut some powerless fellow's tongue out and another to have to fight to catch their prey. At this precise moment, however, Lafarge needed them both to come to their senses and organise a counter–attack, for his own safety counted on it.

For the first time since they had met, de Blaeckere actually looked like he was genuinely pleased to see Lafarge, slapping him on the shoulder amicably as if they were long lost comrades. Caulennec couldn't even muster that gesture as he lay slumped against the brick wall, useless to all.

"Where's Broglie and his men?" asked de Blaeckere, staring desperately over Lafarge's shoulder, his eyes wild with fright, his normally neat swept back blond hair an untidy mess and his immaculate pin stripe suit covered in earth and reeking of sweat and urine.

Good business to be had for the tailors of Limoges, mused Lafarge, after this mess is over, before focusing himself on the task in hand. He had been handed a great opportunity, if he gained access to the house, of seeking out de Chastelain on his own. For de Blaeckere and Caulennec were clearly in no state to launch a fight back, let alone keen to go anywhere near the house.

"They're not coming, I'm all you've got. As for Guillemot, I have no idea whether he will change his plan and come to our aid but for the moment we have got to make do with what we have and draw up an alternative plan," said Lafarge authoritatively, hoping this might at least provoke de Blaeckere into some form of clear thinking.

De Blaeckere simply shrugged his shoulders and pointed at Caulennec as if to say what could they possibly do just the two of them, Lafarge and himself, to turn the tide. Lafarge tended to agree but knew he had to take a risk in getting into the house rather than trying to save his skin.

"Look, all I'm asking is for you to give me covering fire while I try to enter the house. I need to if only to resolve whether de

THE TORTURED DETECTIVE

Chastelain is there or not. I need you also to transmit that message to whoever is left of your men, although, I can see that will be difficult," said Lafarge.

"What the hell do you think you are going to achieve if you do find this bloody de Chastelain in the house? They're not going to let you walk out of there with him. You'd be better off going back and telling Broglie and Guillemot to bloody well come and rescue us!" pleaded de Blaeckere, spittle covering Lafarge's face.

"I tell you Lafarge, Guillemot is finished if I get out of here alive. His informant sold him out or perhaps he even knew that, hence why he is outside and we are here, it was a plot to destroy us in a little power game. He will regret this," added de Blaeckere viciously.

Lafarge shook his head in wonderment at how conspiracy theories about in–house betrayal could cloud a man's mind when they were in such mortal danger. He repeated he was going in and if de Blaeckere wanted to survive his only hope was for him to cover him and then lie low until he had either come out or the gunfire stopped completely.

"You're a fucking lunatic Lafarge! Always seeking a cross to crucify yourself on aren't you! Ok then go on I will provide covering fire, but only until you get inside the house. You will be lucky if I am still here when you come back out," said de Blaeckere, the look of fear in his eyes not reassuring Lafarge that he was even capable of firing at all.

Regardless of that, Lafarge preferred to choose his own place of death and with whom he died and it was surely not with these loathsome scoundrels. He turned his back on de Blaeckere and crawled on all fours back to his original starting point and surveyed the house for potential weak points.

The side of the house was the answer, for whilst there was obviously someone at the second floor middle window, if he managed to unleash a burst and then ran for it he could make one of the lower windows. Then either he could throw himself through one or force it open, which was obviously the preferred option.

Hesitating no longer he stood up and fired off five bullets at the second floor while some covering gunfire also protected him. He made ground fast enough to pin himself against the side wall of the house, which eliminated any possibility of being shot at, though if there was a grenade to hand he was in a whole load of trouble.

He twisted round and tried the window to his left, but it wouldn't give, so he used the butt of his gun to break the panes either side of the lock. He looked into the room and saw no sign of life, opened the window and climbed into what was the reading room of the house.

It was certainly well stocked, a tranquil and comforting room to retire to in happier times he ventured. However, now was not the time to idle and admire the collection the owner of the house had acquired and probably would never enjoy again.

He gently opened the large wooden door and listened out for any sound of movement in the passageway or sign of people and registered neither. He stepped out cautiously and inched his way along the right hand side towards the front of the house meeting no opposition along the way.

He could hear bursts of fire from above and some shouting, though it was incomprehensible what was being said. He himself hadn't really worked out what he was going to do when he came across one of the gun toting lawyers, if indeed they really were the so called professional resistants cell.

For de Blaeckere had been right about one thing and that was Guillemot's information had been woefully inaccurate.

Lafarge had the time to reload his gun, although he would prefer not to have to actually shoot someone, given his mixed feelings about the present political state in France and who was right and who was wrong, but the people above him were probably not thinking about the complexities of that at the moment as they were just thinking of fighting their way out of the dire situation they found themselves in.

He edged his way into the hall and saw there were a couple of corpses lying either side of the main door, both young but definitely not de Blaeckere's goons. He looked up the central staircase and onto a balcony overlooking the hall and saw it was deserted.

All that changed suddenly as three men and a woman emerged from a room or perhaps a corridor to the right hand side diagonally across from him and all were easy targets to take out should he wish to.

THE TORTURED DETECTIVE

All the incoming fire had ceased and the quartet were keen to take advantage of this by making an exit, but from where, Lafarge had not an earthly idea. They may have successfully fought off the assault but if they showed their faces outside they would either be shot or arrested on the spot.

He decided to bluff it out with them, for as far as he could ascertain they were not aware of his presence.

"I've got you covered! Put down your weapons and come down the stairs slowly," yelled Lafarge in as authoritative a manner as he could manage.

He heard derisory laughter aimed at his direction, which hurt almost as much as if bullets had come his way, so he decided to show them he was not joking. He launched himself out of the shadows and fired three bullets which hit the man on the right full in the chest, sending him toppling over and down the stairs.

The three remaining resistants stood stock still, but one of them made the idiotic move to go to his jacket for what Lafarge could only imagine was a gun and he too took the full force of a bullet.

The other two were now in no doubt that their attacker was deadly serious.

The woman and the man, both of them young, good looking and well dressed and under any other scenario could have been mistaken for a loving couple about to go out for a romantic walk round town, raised their hands and walked carefully down the stairs.

There was still shooting coming from upstairs, but Lafarge was not interested in that. For it suited him as it meant he had time alone with the couple and to ask them questions without having the sudden arrival of colleagues who had miraculously rediscovered their courage. He addressed them civilly and calmly after having taken them down the corridor back to the reading room.

"Listen, I have only one real interest in this whole affair and that is whether Pierre–Yves de Chastelain is among you, and if he is, is he still alive?"

Both the girl and the man looked at each other nervously and then the man looked back at Lafarge and answered.

"Yes, he is on both counts and we can take you to him. That was where we were going when you murdered our two friends," he said coldly.

169

Lafarge ignored the latter remark, neither side it appeared had sole rights on lying, and ordered them out of the room.

This time round they turned left and walked to the end of the corridor, which Lafarge noted admiringly had what looked like some original prints or paintings of Napoleon and his troops at various battles. Not all of them were victories as some were of scenes from the retreat from Moscow and the Emperor brooding on the ship carrying him to St Helena after Waterloo.

So they had invaded a house and property belonging to a proud patriot, well one that had been so until the Germans came to pay their respects to France for the third time in 70 years and this time found enough French people to see things their way.

How truly surreal things had become that the situation now had patriot fighting patriot. It was a dreamlike scenario for the Nazis but a true nightmare for the French and however things turned out globally Lafarge thought to himself it would be years before France made peace with itself.

The couple indicated to Lafarge to take the stairs down to the basement and the detective nodded and told them to go ahead of him in case he was being led into a trap.

They progressed slowly, aided only by a bare light bulb hanging from the ceiling half way down the steps, and aside from the smell of damp, Lafarge had to cover his nose with his free hand because of the sickly sweet smell of death emanating from below.

Once they got to the bottom, there was barely any light at all, just the half–moon windows giving some illumination and in the half darkness, Lafarge could make out several bodies lying with their backs propped up against the wall.

The couple paused briefly by them before walking along the passage towards the far end of the house. Lafarge wanted to know whether they had been killed in the assault or had been hidden there for a few days, victims of some other resistance activity, but realizing that time was pressing and impatient to set eyes on de Chastelain, he followed them without mouthing a word.

Once they came to the end, they stopped at the door and then knocked twice.

There was the sound of two bolts being withdrawn and then the door swung open revealing in the light that shone from behind the figure who greeted them that it was indeed Pierre–Yves de

THE TORTURED DETECTIVE

Chastelain. His look of surprise when Lafarge stepped forward was a moment of sheer unadulterated pleasure for the policeman.

CHAPTER EIGHTEEN

"Lafarge, Lafarge!" yelled Broglie as he slapped his Parisian colleague's face in an effort to rouse him.

Lafarge opened his eyes to discover Broglie and his stained teeth bending down over him, and fearing he might be given the kiss of life by his rustic partner, blinked three times to show he was alive if not fully compus mentus.

His head hurt like hell and as he glanced around him, he could see that he was lying inside the room where he had come across de Chastelain.

He had asked de Chastelain not to hit him too hard. Whether the lawyer turned fugitive had misheard him or else had put all his pent up frustration and fear into the one punch, it had been worthy of Germany's former heavyweight champion of the world Max Schmelling.

Cursing de Chastlelain under his breath, he groggily raised himself onto one elbow and managed to ask Broglie in a reedy voice how long he had been lying there.

Broglie looked rather shamefaced as he prepared his answer.

"About 90 minutes I would say. When the shooting eventually died down, de Blaeckere came stumbling out and muttered that you were in the house but he thought you must be dead," said Broglie.

"I then enacted a search of the house from top to bottom, finding several corpses on the way, thankfully none was yours, and we got here a few minutes ago. I thought you were dead when I first saw you," he added with a relieved sigh.

Lafarge nodded his thanks and was also satisfied that such a length of time would have allowed de Chastelain and the other two to make their escape.

He was happy too that Broglie had come for him, because if he had been relying on de Blaeckere, he could have lain here for days or as was the Brigades Spéciales habit, might have been burnt to death when they punished Resistance fighters by burning down their houses in revenge.

"Erm I know that you are a bit shaken but what happened to you?" asked Broglie.

THE TORTURED DETECTIVE

Lafarge replied saying he had escorted two of the 'terrorists' down to the basement to see if there were any more down there. In the gloom, he had not noticed another figure come up behind him and pin back his arms while one of the other two, he took it to be the man not the woman, had slugged him.

Evidently, in order to hide evidence of him being down there, they had dragged him along the passageway and dumped his body behind the door where Broglie had found him.

"Did you find anyone else alive?" asked Lafarge.

Broglie shook his head.

"No, we found eight bodies upstairs and three in the passageway down here. However, I have my men searching the tunnel that seems to lead from this room to god knows where, just in case there are others hiding or trying to escape," he said.

"Tunnel?" asked Lafarge hoping he sounded convincingly surprised.

"Yes, it seems that this cell have been very busy. They have been planning for such a day to come and there is a tunnel stretching for rather a long way. Given the time it took us to find you I would imagine there is little chance of finding them if there were any survivors," he said.

"Yes, they seem to have been well prepared. Here, lift me up will you Broglie, I can't spend the rest of the day lying prone staring at your cherubic features," said Lafarge.

Broglie duly obliged, although he noticed Lafarge grimaced as he finally stood up and suggested he accompany him to the hospital. Lafarge said that would be nice but he didn't think it would reveal any serious damage.

"Where's Guillemot by the way? I would have thought he would have been interested in what was found in the house?" asked Lafarge.

Broglie smiled and shook his head.

"Guillemot and de Blaeckere were engaged in a colourful exchange of words when I left them, the one blaming the other for the disaster, which is an understatement for what happened here," said Broglie, not looking unduly unhappy about how things had turned out, but Lafarge didn't comment just in case he was being lured into a trap.

173

PIRATE IRWIN

"And Caulennec?" he asked, although he didn't particularly care one way or the other but felt it would seem odd if he didn't ask.

"He didn't make it. De Blaeckere said he took a bullet in the throat, his dear leader had his blood all over his piss–stained trousers as proof," said Broglie not entirely sympathetically.

At that point Broglie's search party – all of two men and not exactly the bloodhound looking types – returned from their search, shaking their heads and saying that they had got to the end of the tunnel. Apparently it led to a ladder which took them up to a manhole in a street several kilometers away and there was no sign of anyone.

Broglie looked at Lafarge, raised his eyebrows and bared his grimy teeth.

"Well, it's not my mess, I will leave it to the others to explain their actions," he said looking content with himself, although Lafarge thought rather too much so as inaction by him had perhaps cost de Blaeckere several men.

On that note, Lafarge picked up his gun which lay the other side of the doorway and he and Broglie, with the two men, walked back down the basement corridor and made their way out of the house, passing in the hallway the two people Lafarge had shot.

As he passed them he said a prayer to himself wishing that he could have disabled them without ending their lives.

As they emerged into the dusk which was starting to cover over the evidence of the shootout – although there were several emergency medical staff lifting bodies onto stretchers some zipped up totally, others with their faces exposed – Broglie turned to Lafarge.

"By the way, you didn't see your man, did you?" he asked.

"No, after all that I didn't. Quite a wasted and costly day, wouldn't you say Broglie," commented Lafarge laconically and wandered off towards the gateway feeling extremely happy at the way things had turned out.

*

The hospital visit had been as Lafarge had expected a mercifully short one. Even a cursory inspection by a rather harassed young doctor, who had far more seriously wounded patients to attend to, diagnosed there was no concussion and that a couple of headache pills and a good night's rest should suffice.

THE TORTURED DETECTIVE

Several of de Blaeckere's men had been brought in while Lafarge had waited with Broglie. Three looked as if they would be fortunate to see the next dawn, while five others were due for longish convalescences. That should clip his wings a bit, thought Lafarge, who also found it strange that he wasn't present at the hospital to greet his men.

Of Guillemot too there was no sign, which suggested that their colourful exchange, as Broglie had put it in his understated way, was still being played out.

Lafarge enquired after the woman whom he had 'rescued' from de Blaeckere's torturers and was told that she was making progress and would make a full recovery. That would not be music to her ears mused Lafarge, a rare time when the words full recovery meant nothing better than a death sentence.

Still, there was nothing he could do for her now, and instead he felt like treating Broglie to a good bottle of wine as he was enjoying one of those days so rarely experienced during this ghastly dark period, one which he could look back on and say it had been a success.

He had managed to warn Gerland, who he suspected had in turn warned the people at the house, de Blaeckere's men had taken a severe mauling, he had seen and talked to de Chastelain and he had emerged without the slightest suspicion cast on him.

There was also the date at the farm with Aimeé and her mysterious family to look forward to the next day. That had him feeling both excited and expectant like a young teenager but also wary of what he might uncover.

Of course, they too were fully aware he was a policeman and would no doubt try and behave as normally as possible so as not to alert him to any possible shenanigans they might be up to.

Lafarge sighed deeply at this last thought, for he didn't really know what he would do were his suspicions about them proved to be correct.

Compromises there were aplenty in this war and in the situation the French in particular found themselves to be in, but sometimes one had to draw the line and the last thing Lafarge appreciated was being made a fool of.

"Hey Gaston, wakey wakey what about that bottle of wine you promised your savior!" said Broglie offering him one of his sadly unforgettable toothy smiles.

"Of course Broglie, where would I be if it wasn't for you and your insatiable appetite for the best and most enjoyable things in life! Let's go," said Lafarge, affably throwing his arm round Broglie's shoulders and striding to his colleague's battered old car.

Both of them got a bit of a shock, though, when they entered the brasserie and found Guillemot propped up against the zinc bar. He did not look his usual suave and composed self, and although he greeted them warmly enough and said how glad he was Lafarge was alright, there was Lafarge saw in his eyes a sad look.

Lafarge told Broglie to take him outside to the terrasse while he ordered the bottle from Jean–Jacques, the owner, who was holding court with some local farmer types down at the other end of the bar.

Lafarge eventually gained his attention and ordered a fine bottle of red Burgundy and in the process of paying for it, Jean–Jacques plucked up his courage and informed him that Guillemot had told him he had been recalled to Paris over the incident.

"Has he indeed? That certainly explains his doleful look as it rounds off a truly dreadful day. Thanks for that Jean–Jacques," said Lafarge with an appreciative smile.

Lafarge dutifully joined his colleagues plopping the bottle down on the table and filling their glasses. They allowed Guillemot time to drink some of it before tackling him about his being recalled and his argument with de Blaeckere, of whom there was still no sign.

It was only after the second glass that Guillemot felt relaxed enough to speak about the day's events.

"I've got to return to Paris on the first train tomorrow," he said grimly.

"I spoke with Bousquet and he was to say the least not happy at the way things had turned out. He may always look well turned out and chic but he has a vocabulary that would do one of those farners in there proud and a vicious streak to boot.

"De Blaeckere obviously didn't help my cause by phoning him first, and alleging that it had all been a set up to get rid of him but thanks to the foolhardy bravery of his man, meaning Bousquet's man and therefore you Gaston, that had been avoided."

THE TORTURED DETECTIVE

Wonders will never cease thought Lafarge, de Blaeckere praising him must have rankled with Bousquet, but he had been delivered Guillemot on a plate so he would suffice as a consolation prize.

"I see Guillemot, so instead of me being hauled back to Paris in disgrace it is to be you," said Lafarge sympathetically.

"Yes that's about it really. Although Bousquet consoled me by saying that it may only be temporary and that he felt sure there was a mole within, who had tipped off the terrorists. Indeed he said that wire taps out of our headquarters might lead us to him," said Guillemot, his tone taking on a more optimistic lilt.

Lafarge and Broglie both grunted at this, Lafarge taking a large gulp of his wine to quell the fear he suddenly felt rising in his gut. However, he calmed himself down by reasoning that his conversation with Gerland could for the large part be explained innocently enough.

However, it hung on whether Bousquet would miss the reference to the newly–arrived friend, if he didn't, then there would be serious questions posed to both him and Gerland.

He thought he could withstand the questioning but Gerland was another matter.

A man who was accustomed to living comfortably and being able to avail himself of the best things in life might not be the most resilient of suspects under possible threat of torture.

"These wire taps, are they the real reason you are returning to Paris?" asked Broglie.

Lafarge looked at Guillemot for his reaction, and noticed he looked over their shoulders as he replied, a sign that Broglie had arrowed in on the essence of his recall.

"That is certainly one of the matters up for discussion in the review of the terrible events today. Obviously also there is my role to be looked into, I mean my intelligence or rather my unreliable insider has led to the deaths of nine men and eight wounded and without the slightest sniff of any interesting information having been secured," said Guillemot sadly.

"So while I can hope that it was a result of a mole within our ranks I also have to prepare myself for the possibility of being assigned to other duties which may lead to a safer and gentler pace of life, but will bore me to tears."

Broglie and Lafarge nodded sympathetically, but they were both equally keen to discover why Guillemot hadn't altered his plans once he realized they had been caught in an ambush. Rather than letting the discussion become a blame game should Broglie ask the question, Lafarge put it to Guillemot.

Guillemot sucked in his cheeks and held them there for a matter of seconds.

"I am or at least I thought I was a master of accruing intelligence and then devising a plan to intervene and ruin the actions of those trying to put theirs into place," he said.

"However, I am no military man and once the trap was sprung on us today I admit I became paralysed, for I had no alternative strategy to put in place, I am sorry for the men who lost their lives, I am only glad it didn't cost you two yours.

"I think next time I will restrict myself to barracks. As for you Broglie you have nothing to reproach yourself over your inaction, for there would only have been more bloodshed. We can't all be nerveless devil may care types like Gaston," he added smiling.

Broglie grunted and disappeared inside, Lafarge could see that he was ordering another bottle of wine. He hoped it would be the same one for it was doing wonders for his sore head, and took the opportunity to try and get some more information out of Guillemot.

"Aside from de Blaeckere's surprise praise for me, did Bousquet have anything else to say about me?" he asked.

"Yes, he said that he would much appreciate an overdue call from you for an update. He also wondered whether de Chastelain had been seen at the house either by my informant or by you," said Guillemot.

"Obviously there is no point in me seeking any evidence from my informant for the moment as he is plainly unreliable and so I leave that to you to fill in our leader. He sounded rather more interested in you than the overall turn of events truth be told. I would say that there was a glacial tone to his voice when he talked about you despite de Blaeckere's favourable comments.

"I venture that if you don't come up with anything soon that you too will be on your way back and to a job of similar interest to the one I may be allotted. He also all but implied that if there was a mole that it would be you, as your loyalties despite your father and sister's faithful adherence to Vichy are questionable.

"I of course defended you. But my word counts little at the moment and de Blaeckere's gratitude will dissipate all too quickly once he gets wind that there is a suspicion on Bousquet's part that you might have been the one who betrayed us."

All the confidence that Lafarge had been feeling after the initial discourse had rapidly evaporated as he heard the fuller debrief of Bousquet and Guillemot's conversation. His fear over his phone conversation with Gerland coming to light and what could be read into it returned.

Thankfully Broglie had also returned armed with the bottle, and it was indeed the same one, so Lafarge quaffed the remainder of his old glass and poured himself another one.

He knew from experience that too much drink, while it would settle his nerves now, would only make them worse on awaking in the morning but for now, he saw no other option of quelling them.

All he knew was that his finely–hatched plan with de Chastelain would have to come to fruition soon and be trouble free for him to allay doubts over his loyalty, especially if Bousquet was to interpret his conversation with Gerland in the way he wished to.

Should he do so, then it would mean Lafarge would not be joining Guillemot at some menial clerk like job but be delivered into the hands of the Special Brigades in Paris and that would mean only one ending for him.

CHAPTER NINETEEN

"Ah Lafarge, how kind of you to spare me some of your valuable time by ringing me," said Bousquet, his tone dripping with sarcasm.

Lafarge thought "go fuck yourself", but restrained himself. He had even hesitated whether to call the odious man but thought better of it, as he felt with himself already under suspicion, there was no need to exacerbate the situation by making him think he was avoiding him totally.

He could have refused to, for which he would have been justified in doing so as Bousquet was still a suspect in his case.

However, three strong cups of black coffee had persuaded him otherwise and besides, he wanted to go to the farm house free of having to fret over what Bousquet might do at another affront from his least favourite and least pliable detective.

"It's my pleasure secretary–general. I am sorry to have kept you waiting," said Lafarge with an equal dose of sarcasm.

Lafarge could hear the displeasure this had provoked down the line and pressed on before he received a telling off.

"There's nothing really to report to you apart from I have set the wheels in motion to trap our suspect and bring him back to Paris. I would prefer not to go into the minutiae of the details as others may be listening in," said Lafarge pointedly.

"How soon do you think these wheels will start spinning in our direction, Lafarge? It would be a shame should there be a derailment or a puncture like there was yesterday," said Bousquet coolly.

"I would say in the next couple of days, sir," replied Lafarge, plucking a figure out of the air and then swearing at himself for doing so.

"I see. That is rather optimistic isn't it? I mean as far as I have been told since you have been down there, you have upset the Brigade Spéciale's commander and aside from that spent most of the rest of your time drinking and whoring," said Bousquet brutally.

That sent Lafarge into a towering rage, and he fought to combat it.

THE TORTURED DETECTIVE

"No, it is not an optimistic forecast sir. Furthermore I would strongly protest at that summary of my activities down here. Yesterday's actions by myself, totally on my own behest, saved what was left of that riff raff bunch of hoodlums and clowns," said Lafarge forcefully.

Lafarge could hear the deep sigh at the other end of the line and awaited the full force of Bousquet's ire.

"I would ask you to temper your language Lafarge, we are not in some school playground," hissed Bousquet. "I would remind you that the riff raff, as you arrogantly describe them, lost a great deal of men in doing their duty in attempting to bring terrorists to justice. They are the riff raff, Lafarge, those who are trying to undo all the good that we along with the National Socialists are doing to France, in repairing the damage done under the Third Republic," added Bousquet, his tone assuming a level of self justification that made Lafarge want to throw up at.

The hypocrisy of the man knew no bounds thought Lafarge, for he had willingly accepted to be prefect of a region under the very same Third Republic he was now decrying. Oh well, so be it, just keep calm, Lafarge, he told himself.

"Well, forgive me for using such intemperate language sir but I don't like my character being impugned either," said Lafarge hotly.

"Hmm well, there will be time enough for that later anyway. Let's try and get back onto the main business, shall we? For which your future depends on aside from any other difficulties that may crop up," said Bousquet, not bothering to hide the menace within the phrase.

Lafarge shrugged that aside and did as he was told by returning to the pursuit of de Chastelain.

"I can promise you sir that you will have de Chastelain on a train with me back to Paris in the next three days," said Lafarge.

"Good, well if you keep to that schedule then that will be satisfactory. The sooner this business is wrapped up, the better it will be for all parties concerned.

"Now if you do have him with you, I suggest you do not contact me until you are back in Paris, that way no–one can bugger up things again. Also I have a very busy schedule over the next three days, with high matters of state, and not even great personal business such as de Chastelain can take priority over them," said Bousquet pompously.

"What does that mean, you are not going to greet me with a bunch of flowers and a bottle of champagne then?" asked Lafarge.

"Cut the sarcasm, Lafarge. I am involved with something that will only bring even more harmony between France and Germany and be a story told proudly by all French people in the decades to come.

"It will set an example to those future generations and to other countries who are undecided about which way they should go on such matters," said Bousquet, his tone assuming such a level of conceitedness that Lafarge whilst wanting to put the receiver down was also intrigued by what this great event might be.

"Well sir, I can't wait to return to Paris to see what this example to all is," said Lafarge.

"For once I believe you. Now go about your business and get me de Chastelain," said Bousquet abruptly and put the phone down.

*

Lafarge drove himself out to Oradour–sur–Glane, quite a pretty little village near Limoges, where he was then to be met by Aimée and given a lead to the farm house.

He settled himself at a café and ordered a pastis, and brooded over the conversation with Bousquet which had gone as badly as he had predicted but he didn't feel any the worse for it. Bousquet could interpret the phone call with Gerland in the worst possible sense but it wouldn't get him very far.

Lafarge had drawn up divorce papers after his conversation with Bousquet, backdated of course. He had then driven over to Gerland's who he had found at home, sitting out in his garden, and whose gratitude for being forewarned over the attack made him into a willing accomplice in the deceit.

The papers of course were only to be used in the event that Bousquet questioned Lafarge's role in the leaking of the information. Gerland promised Lafarge he would draw up legal documents, also backdated, and that there could be no argument about their authenticity and thereby their phone conversation.

Lafarge had thanked him and then asked whether de Chastelain had been in touch, whilst revealing to Gerland that he had seen him and told him to make his way to the lawyer's house. They could

THE TORTURED DETECTIVE

then put into action their plan while assuring him that he would not fall into Bousquet's hands.

Gerland told him yes he had and he would be there the next day. Lafarge said good and told him he would be back at his desk early afternoon, and to call him.

Thus he now sat at the café and looked on as the local folk took their midday strolls with their children. Some stopped at the café to enjoy their pre–prandial aperitif, usually on seeing a friend that became plural indeed several, and he started to wind down and look forward to his hostess's arrival.

He was on his third pastis by the time Aimée showed up, some newly–acquired goods in the wicker basket on her arm. She looked stunning, even without too much make–up, enhanced by the simple blue gingham dress she was wearing which was not so conservatively cut that it blinded one to her fine bosom.

He downed his pastis, after she declined his offer of a drink, and he indicated where his car was as she said her brother had dropped her at the village but had returned home. The drive was only a short one, 10 minutes down winding peaceful tree–lined lanes, a wonderful contrast to the grimy buildings and noise of the urban neighbourhoods he had become so used to.

They chatted away gaily, without touching on anything to do with his work, while he asked about any sign of her returning to Paris, to which she replied there was no set date but Guitry was keen for her to return soon. For sex or for professional reasons mused Lafarge as Guitry's libido was almost a match for his ego, though nothing beat the size of that.

Their chattering almost made her forget to tell him to turn into the driveway of the farm house. Fortunately, he was adept at making awkward sharp turns from his times in pursuing criminals through the streets of Paris. The drive snaked along for about half a mile, passing, contrary to what Aimee had told him, well–stocked fields, 20–30 cattle and a flock of sheep munching on fertile enough looking pasture.

As they drew into the yard at the back of the farm house, which was a well–kept three storey grey stone building, chickens and ducks and geese scattered. Certainly no hunger rations here, thought Lafarge, already looking forward keenly to lunch.

As if reading his thoughts Aimée laughed.

"Yes, Gaston, there is no danger of famine here. One of the joys of leaving Paris is there are no long queues for shops that rarely have anything in them. Here everything, almost, is just outside our front door, or rather back door," she said grinning.

While they were getting the shopping out of the back of the car, Bernard and Lisette both emerged from the house, greeting him warmly.

After dumping the cheese and other food in the large kitchen, Bernard suggested, as it was a warm sunny day, to have a drink on their terrace which looked out over a neat and well–kept large garden.

Aside from his soft hands, Bernard was an impressively built man, about six foot in height with black hair, steely grey eyes, broad shoulders and no belly on him.

Lisette, Lafarge wanted to say, was coquette but reproached himself and said less of the humour. She was cute looking, of average height, brown straight hair, grey eyes as well, a longish upturned nose, full lips, large bosom and shapely legs. They were both friendly, quite witty but careful in their language and topic of conversation noted Lafarge.

He didn't know whether that was because they thought he preferred not to have questions asked of his work or whether they were on their guard over their own political affiliations and loyalties. In any case there was enough superficial chat to be had that such questions disappeared to the back of his mind for the moment.

Aimée was very attentive to him, almost as if they were husband and wife or lovers, of which they were neither, but even so he enjoyed that enormously, not having been used to such undivided and affectionate attention for so long.

It being so warm they decided they would eat lunch outside and so both Lisette and Aimée repaired to the kitchen, leaving the two men alone.

The amiable atmosphere continued as they discussed their families, Bernard offering the information that his and Aimée's parents had gone to live out the war in Switzerland while he had been left to look after the farm and Aimée could pursue her love of dramatics in Paris.

THE TORTURED DETECTIVE

"They wanted to leave this behind? I would have thought this would be an idyllic place to see out the war," said Lafarge, incredulous that anyone would wish to leave such a spot where the war appeared to be in another world.

"Well, they are ageing and things might be ok here for the moment, but they are old enough to remember firsthand the two previous visits by the Germans and a third time was just too much," said Bernard.

Lafarge nodded, empathizing with what must have been for people of their generation too much to endure the horror and the shame for a third time.

"I know you are a policeman, so I do not wish to be impolite or impolitic but they just couldn't bear the humiliation of France collaborating with the invaders. The Huns or Boches, as my father gleefully taunted them with when they sequestered his house in Neuilly," said Bernard bitterly to which Lafarge could sympathise at the loss of their house in one of the smartest suburbs of Paris.

"Luckily for him, the German officer who took over the house, rent free of course, was a cultured and almost one would say humane man. He issued the passes for my parents to leave the country, on condition of course that they were not to return."

"I understand their sentiments, I can't of course sympathise with them, but they are not alone in the way they feel," said Lafarge, wishing not to go any further lest he compromise himself.

Bernard smiled and poured himself and Lafarge another glass of passable red wine. Lafarge had brought three very fine bottles that he had procured from the brasserie owner, at double the price but still worth it, and had set them aside for lunch.

Lunch was duly brought forth by Lisette and Aimée and Lafarge was not to be disappointed.

They tucked into a duck terrine followed by a gigot d'agneau and flageolets with mashed potato and a salad and cheese followed by a chocolate mousse made with real chocolate and not the ersatz stuff one got in Paris if one was lucky enough to find any at all.

Lunch was conducted to the background of the noise of the sheep and lowing of the cows, a gentle breeze cooling the hot afternoon temperature. The conversation remained lively and not stilted, based largely round tales of the family of Aimée and Bernard and the fun days they had had down on the farm.

Lafarge remarked that little was asked of his family and their background or where they were, which he found slightly suspicious. However, he surmised perhaps with their parents not with them anymore, they just wanted to remember the good and happy days when they were all together.

Lisette's, it turned out, were living in Toulouse, her father was a banker but had resigned when his largely Jewish clientele started being victimized and persecuted.

He and his wife had thought of leaving France too but with a lovely chateau down in the Toulouse area, they had opted to stay and felt that they were safe despite his public protests over the maltreatment of the Jewish clients and the theft by the state of their funds.

With the evening drawing in and the lunch cleared, Aimée asked Lafarge if he would like to go for a walk. He accepted willingly and accompanied by a black Labrador, they strolled arm in arm down into the wood that bordered the garden and the rest of the property.

They progressed through the wood, mainly oak and elm trees and alighted upon a little lake.

Aimée produced a bottle of champagne from the basket which she rarely seemed to be without.

She also laid out a rug and having shooed away the Labrador so that he moodily prowled round the edge of the lake, they lay on it and drank from two flutes.

She told him how much Bernard and Lisette had taken to him, he replied it was mutual, and apologized for the conversation having been so dominated by their family and their nostalgic stories.

He said it didn't matter and that in any case, describing his family would be best done to a psychiatrist rather than three normal rational human beings.

"I guess generations before us were just the same, I mean my parents probably lay in this spot discussing happier times during the Great War, although they were already married and had us to worry about," said Aimée sadly.

"I guess so, and now their daughter is doing it but with a married man, and a policeman to boot, employed by the invading Boches," said Lafarge smiling.

THE TORTURED DETECTIVE

Aimée shot a glance at him and Lafarge did not hesitate this time, pushing himself up off his elbows and taking her head in his hands and kissed her passionately, Aimee offered no resistance and kissed him as vigorously.

A couple of hours later, after as passionate a session of making love as he had ever experienced even with Isabella, and then a quick swim, they made their way back to the house with the Labrador ambling along in front of them.

There was no regret from either party, Lafarge did not feel the slightest pang of guilt for, for him, Isabella no matter how much he loved her was far away looking after his and her future, the children. For Aimée it was a blissful moment before she had to return to the challenge of life in Paris and fighting for a role, one that sometimes necessitated such acts but without the feeling.

Dusk was falling as they walked up to the house where they could make out Bernard standing on the terrace illuminated by the lights on inside.

"We thought we'd lost you both! Or that you had been arrested, Aimée," joshed Bernard as he moved aside so they could enter the house.

They both laughed and waved their fingers at him. On entering the drawing room they were greeted by a smiling Lisette and a table covered in canapés and four champagne flûtes. Bernard popped the cork and they sat around before dinner was served.

Everything was as sweet and harmonious as it had been until Lafarge returned to the table after excusing himself for a quick bathroom break.

In fact, he hadn't taken one at all but instead, suspicious of this Utopian atmosphere, he thought a spot of eavesdropping might either assuage his suspicions or confirm them. It was to be the latter.

"Christ sake, Aimée, I'm getting weary of all this pussyfooting around. I am nervous he is going to rumble us soon," said Bernard, his tone a long way from the amiable and equable one he had employed through the day.

"Yes, you've got to get rid of him tonight. We've got to go out and we don't want him around because he might follow us or worse, pretend nothing has happened and then once he returns to

Limoges, alert his colleagues," interjected Lisette, her tone nervous.

"Look, calm down both of you. He's fine, he's different to the majority of them. I wouldn't have risked bringing him here if I thought he would cause us trouble. Besides he's staying and I will keep him occupied," said Aimee.

"Why do you trust him Aimee? You hardly know him for heaven's sake. Of course he is very charming and good company, far more so than any of the ones I have met, but it could all be an act, a ruse, so he snares us," said Bernard.

"Look Bernard, I wouldn't do anything to endanger you or Lisette, and I vouch for Gaston. I really feel he would rather be on our side than the one he works for. I haven't felt like this about a man since the death of Eric. I assure you I will ensure he doesn't stray from the house tonight," said Aimee her tone emphatic.

"Alright Aimme your instinct is usually correct so I will give in to you. However, you better make sure he stays in the house, because if he does cause us any grief then I am afraid we will have to act, regardless of the potential consequences," said Bernard.

"Okay, okay, leave him to me. There'll be no trouble I promise you," insisted Aimée.

Lafarge pushed the door open to the dining room and they all resumed their previous sweetness and light expressions. He had decided to take another course of action to ruffle a few feathers and they weren't those of the birds outside in the yard.

"Forgive me, Bernard, but with my policeman's instinct I noticed your hands are very soft, too much so for daily chores on the farm. I was wondering who you got to do all the work. I mean coming from Neuilly as you did, farm labour wouldn't have come naturally to you or to Lisette," said Lafarge, his tone cordial.

Bernard didn't let his mask slip one instant, nor for that matter, as Lafarge noticed, did Lisette. As for Aimée, she was opposite him but he was more interested in his hosts' reactions.

"Well, you are right Gaston, and I raise my glass to you for your powers of observation. No, neither myself or Lisette would be naturals at tilling the land or milking a cow, so we have several more experienced hands to help us out and for that they get the reward of being regularly fed," said Bernard.

THE TORTURED DETECTIVE

"It also stops the buggers from poaching as we look after them," he added smiling.

"Quite, quite. That is a sensible strategy, but what about the more lawless elements that are quite prevalent in the region, like the resistance fighters? They must be fed and I imagine with the severe penalties in place for doing so, you run the risk of being regularly pillaged," said Lafarge.

"Oh they, if they are near here, haven't troubled us and I haven't heard of any such incidents. I'm sure they have their own resources, hunting in the woods or fishing," he replied evenly.

"If they're good enough to cause the local police trouble, then they are more than capable of getting the better of some animal.

"Besides, perhaps some of them are farmers too!" he added chortling at his own joke.

Lafarge laughed along with him, thinking he is a cool customer indeed, and wondered exactly what was his and Lisette's game.

He wondered too whether all the stories about their respective families were true and even if Aimée and he were siblings. It was all rather confusing but also becoming clearer if that were possible.

"Anyway Gaston, at least few people if any go hungry round here, not like in Paris where starvation is never far away.

"Even before I left Paris, there were queues lining the pavements to the butcher and the baker for the smallest slice of bread, or morsel of meat which was usually gristle. You of course wouldn't have to suffer such indignities and deprivations, being a member of the collaborationist establishment," said Lisette in a sudden vitriolic outburst that caught all by surprise.

"Lisette please, don't be rude to our guest. He is not responsible for the food shortages or for the policies, he acts for those that are, but then many reasonable people do," said Bernard, admonishing his wife.

"I'm very sorry Gaston, Lisette tends to get quite emotional like her father did and she has these occasional losses of temper," said Aimée.

Lafarge laughed it off and got to his feet and by way of easing the atmosphere, picked up one of his bottles from the elegant oak table which was situated against the far wall.

They sat round drinking it, Lafarge even started to tell them tales of police cock ups, from before the war of course, and by the time he came to bid them farewell, he was told to sit himself back down and Bernard suggested they round off the evening with a bottle of cognac.

Thus it was seemingly four rather drunk but happy people who rose to their feet near midnight and made their way to their two bedrooms, Aimée having insisted that Lafarge should stay, to which he put up little resistance.

What he hoped no–one had noticed was that while they had been throwing back the cognac, he had been sipping his and pouring the rest into a potted plant just beside him.

He had to remain sober for what was to come for the rest of the night, the pleasure that lay ahead in the bed and for the more serious business that lay outside the house.

*

Lafarge rose from the bed a couple of hours later. Aimée was sound asleep, the concoction of drink, sex and conversation had weakened her resistance and she had drifted off around 20 minutes before.

Lafarge, not exactly too far from lapsing into the arms of Morpheus's warm embrace either, had stirred himself when he heard the floorboards outside the bedroom creaking as someone or perhaps people made their way down the corridor and to the stairs.

He threw some clothes on and with his shoes in his hand crept to the door and as silently as possible opened it. He was met by complete darkness but he heard clearly enough stepfalls on the stairs.

He waited until they had reached the bottom and then he furtively crept along the corridor, something he was increasingly getting used to over the past few days in Limoges and its environs.

He had enjoyed his previous forays into corridor creeping.

But that had been years ago when he had stayed at girlfriends' houses and despite every possible barrier being put in front of him, by suspicious parents, he had risen to the challenge almost every time and successfully reached his target's bedroom.

That was until he had upset his hosts and been cast out into the night, fortunate to have his clothes with him but with no money and had to walk back across Paris in a sorry and dejected state feeling humiliated.

THE TORTURED DETECTIVE

For he had inadvertently chosen the wrong room and crawling into bed, he had fondly kissed the female who lay there and started caressing her only to be greeted by shrieks. When the light was turned on he saw to his horror that it was not his girlfriend but her mother and her father was the other side looking distinctly unamused. Needless to say he had never seen his girlfriend again.

The opening of the front door, for the stairs led down to the hallway, woke him from that particularly disgraceful memory and he progressed to the top of the stairs and then swiftly down them in case he lost sight of whomever it was that had just left the premises.

Thankfully there was a full moon which lit up the hallway through the two large windows either side of the entrance, so he didn't lose his footing coming down the stairs. It also aided him to make out two figures walking down the drive. Helpfully, the drive was not a gravel one, but a dirt track so his footsteps didn't make too much of a noise.

He kept his distance as the couple walked, without glancing backwards, to a building that was hidden by a large bush.

They knocked and went inside. The moon could only give Lafarge so much guidance but it was enough to see that there was space between the wall that marked the farm's boundary and the hut for him to hide and hopefully listen to what was being said or done inside.

Having safely negotiated the clearing between the bush and the hut and settled as comfortably as possible by the building he listened in.

"I'm telling you it's too dangerous to go out tonight. Aimée brought the detective here and he's stayed the night," Lafarge heard Bernard say.

"Jesus what did she go and do that for? She's a real pain in the ass that one," said a man, whose voice he vaguely recognized.

"I'll thank you not to say such things about my sister," said Bernard bluntly.

Lafarge sighed with relief that at least some of their story had been true.

"The cop needs to be got rid of Bernard. He has already caused us trouble and he's likely to cause us even more," came the man's voice again, someone whom Lafarge was fast taking against.

"No, I can't do that. Aimée has him under control anyway upstairs and I think that he doesn't suspect anything," said Bernard.

Lafarge could hear a scuffing of feet as whoever Bernard was addressing mulled over whether he could accept his hosts' assurances.

"Very well, I will take your word for it. However, having met him albeit briefly and at the end of a gun, I am warning you that whilst he may appear to be one of the better ones he is far from being on our side," said the man.

"I will vouch for him too. I had an ill advised outburst at dinner and he took it very well. To be honest, I think he is more addicted to alcohol and women than he is to running down resistants," giggled Lisette.

"Well, you may laugh Lisette but my sources tell me that he is not to be taken lightly. He may not be playing the game according to his superiors liking but he is far from being committed to our cause either. He's a maverick and more dangerous for being so, as you don't know what side he is going to pick," said the man.

Lafarge was beginning to like the man more now after that description, but he also realized he had stumbled upon a haven for the résistance. The man was probably the one he had held at gunpoint yesterday when he had finally seen de Chastelain, but he wondered if that was the case was his quarry still with him, and where was the woman?

"Well all I can advise for you at the moment, Gilles, is to sit tight here, along with Christiane, and we will be rid of the cop tomorrow morning and then tomorrow night, we will start on our plan. I take it the other fellow, the one that Lafarge was interested in, won't be joining us," added Bernard.

Both the man, Gilles, and Lafarge thought, Christiane laughed.

"No, he has other things planned. It appears your policeman has top level orders to bring him back to Paris and he is going to gamble that his guardian plays fair. More fool him," sneered Gilles.

"At this rate, there will be three of them in the compartment, Aimée seems to be besotted by our Parisian detective," said Lisette.

"She isn't, Lisette, she is acting a role just as she does when she is in costume in Paris," said Bernard sternly.

THE TORTURED DETECTIVE

"If you say so Bernard, but I wager her feelings are stronger than you believe them to be," retorted Lisette.

"Anyway, we're not standing around here to debate Aimée's real feelings or love life, there are more important things to talk about. Best if we relax a little and have a drink while we are doing so, don't you think?" said Bernard rhetorically.

Lafarge heard a general buzz of approving noises to Bernard's suggestion and whilst he would have liked to stay around and hear more of their conversation, he felt it wiser to make good his return to the house lest he be discovered.

He crept back, hoping that Aimée hadn't awoken and was looking for him, for whether she really did have strong feelings for him or not, her first loyalty would be to her brother and their cause. He need not have worried for he re–entered the bedroom to find her sleeping as soundly as when he had left her.

Sleep did not come easily to him, for if what Lisette had said was true, female intuition and all that, then he faced a real dilemma with Aimée.

His being married had nothing to do with it, for he had broken his vows the moment he made love with her by the lake.

The real problem was, could he save her without alerting her sibling and his wife?

Or would he have to sacrifice her and use her as a decoy to aid his goal of getting de Chastelain, a man he held little regard for, onto the train without the knowledge of de Blaeckere and his wounded pack of bloodhounds?

CHAPTER TWENTY

He returned to Limoges alone and in a sombre mood, for his farewell with Aimee had been a tortuous one for him, realizing that it was probably the last time they would see each other.

She had been the only one present at breakfast, no doubt Bernard and Lisette were exhausted after their late night sortie, and conversation had been awkward at best. The only positive thing was she made no remarks to suggest she knew he had got up in the middle of the night.

As he drove back to Limoges he mulled over whether there was any opportunity for him to get Aimee away from the farm before he alerted his colleagues about the cell operating out of there.

Aimee after all wasn't wholly implicated, she was to his mind guilty only for being the sister of a man who was.

However, Lafarge knew well enough that whole families were paying for acts that were perpetrated by siblings or their children and were perceived as crimes against the state. Thus unless he acted to help her she would not be spared if she was taken in with Bernard and Lisette, and with him gone he could only shudder at what perverse and debase acts would be performed on her.

Nevertheless reluctant as he was to sacrifice her, his own future good health depended on delivering, or at least making a semblance of doing so, de Chastelain to Paris. It was clear he could only achieve that untroubled if de Blaeckere and his men were out of the way, and he had the means to ensure that happened.

He raged against himself for having allowed himself to get so intimate with Aimee, for it had seriously complicated an already complex situation and he could only blame himself for that, quite apart from the feeling of guilt he would carry around with him from now on.

He had thought he could keep himself serenely above the moral conflicts, aside from being his usual judgmental self, but now he could see that not even those who wished to distance themselves from getting their hands dirty could do so.

His temper was hardly improved when he got to headquarters and found de Blaeckere had moved into Guillemot's office, which pretty much confirmed the spy chief would not be returning.

THE TORTURED DETECTIVE

"Ah hell isn't to your liking anymore then de Blaeckere," said Lafarge coldly.

De Blaeckere, who looked to have recovered all his former arrogance after his loss of control the day before, looked up at him and smiled thinly.

If Lafarge had been expecting at least a thank you for his actions during the bungled raid then de Blaeckere had left them behind in the phone call with Bousquet. It had probably been a ruse on the young man's part anyway as he aimed his vitriol first at the weakened Guillemot knowing that Lafarge was only a temporary irritant.

Now with Guillemot out of the way he could assume control of all operations in the area.

"Local politics, don't you just love them," grinned Lafarge and carried on down the corridor towards the fresher air of his and Broglie's office.

"Oi Lafarge, come back here," shouted de Blaeckere, to which Lafarge paid scant notice and turned right into the detectives' office and thence to his where he saw Broglie was already in situ, grunting a pre aperitif good morning.

Lafarge had barely sat down and poured himself a thick looking cup of black coffee when de Blaeckere burst in.

"Lafarge, I warn you, you are on borrowed time here, any more impertinence such as that and I will have you drummed out of here and on a train back to Paris to your good friend René Bousquet," seethed de Blaeckere, panting as he spat out the words.

Broglie made as if to leave but Lafarge told him to stay put.

"Well that's a fine way of thanking someone for saving one's life, and those of his men who were at risk of being carted off to the morgue thanks to the foolhardiness of their leader," said Lafarge curtly.

"That is in the past, and I have said as much to the secretary–general, who put your bravado down to other more sinister reasons. Whether that is true or not I don't know, but as he knows you rather better than I do, then I am willing to take his word on the matter," said de Blaeckere, his tone adopting a new level of high–handedness.

"Thus I suggest what is better for all parties concerned is that you catch de Chastelain as quickly as possible and piss off back to Paris

195

and annoy those who have the time on their hands to put up with your meddlesome habits," said de Blaeckere, enforcing his point by tapping Lafarge's desk with his middle finger.

"Furthermore, I am under strict instructions to be present when you do arrest de Chastelain in case there is an unfortunate incident and you allow him to slip away…again," he added with a knowing smile, which disconcerted Lafarge momentarily.

He recovered quickly enough, thinking there was no way de Blaeckere knew he had seen de Chastelain. For the only witnesses to that were for the moment temporarily safely ensconced in Bernard's hut, thus the guy was obviously on a fishing expedition, albeit along the right lines.

"Well, I am touched by your concern for my future well–being and my travel plans de Blaeckere, but I'm a big boy and I can look after myself. As for de Chastelain, his apprehending is an inexact science, I know I will have him but when and where is not decided," said Lafarge in as condescending a manner as he could manage.

De Blaeckere looked even more furious than when he had first entered the room and Broglie cast a look at Lafarge warning him to go easy. For he was dealing with a highly intelligent sociopath, who could just as easily dispose of him and believe he could clear it afterwards with Bousquet.

Lafarge, though, was in control of himself and was about to dangle a carrot so appetizing to de Blaeckere that it would erase the sour memories of the previous part of the conversation. Lafarge was reluctant to do so but he saw little option and compromise being the operative word of the war he was now going to offer one.

"Now, moles and other such annoyances aside, de Blaeckere, and our own personal antipathy to each other, I do have some cast iron intelligence for you that will help in our battle with 'terrorists', or the Résistance, depending on how you look at things," said Lafarge.

"Regardless of whether it was Guillemot's fault regarding placing too much trust in the intelligence or not, your reputation took a blow with those you want to impress in Paris and probably to a lesser extent in Vichy.

"Thus I can point you in the direction of a farmhouse not too far from here, well closer to Oradour but still in your catchment area

THE TORTURED DETECTIVE

where there is a veritable vipers' nest of terrorists, plus an excellent wine cellar as booty," added Lafarge smiling warmly.

De Blaeckere looked at Lafarge searching his face to see whether this was a wind up and whether to trust him or not, as this seemed a most unlikely offering from someone who appeared to be so lukewarm to the present regime.

However, Lafarge remained stony–faced and de Blaeckere, evidently convinced, gestured to Broglie to bring a map from his desk so he could get a proper idea of where the property was situated.

Lafarge had noted down the directions he and Aimée had taken from Oradour so he would not be obliged to go on this operation. Quite aside from getting hold of de Chastelain, he did not wish to see the look in Aimée's eyes when she and her family and friends were rounded up.

 He could just about cope with the sense of guilt and shame, and the irony he was sacrificing a woman in his pursuit of solving the murder of another one.

However, he didn't think he would be able to handle physically being there when she was arrested, the Judas kiss and all that didn't play with him let alone from the fact he was not religious at all.

He had long ago forsaken his beliefs and besides what good had they done to anybody, did they provide succour when you were loaded onto a train to be taken god knows where or was it just emotional baggage best left behind on the platform? He thought the latter but then as he acknowledged that that was a problem he would not have to face should he ever be sent east.

De Blaeckere wrote everything down fastidiously and marked all the relevant points of the farm and its landmarks such as the lake and the hut, which he had Lafarge also do a rough drawing of, and then posed the question the detective had been waiting for.

"You are remarkably well–informed Lafarge, for a man who hasn't travelled very much outside this town, how do you know all this?" he asked.

"I spent last night there de Blaeckere. They were very good hosts, too good in fact, and that aroused my suspicions. Thus I took a late night walk and stumbled upon their little secret," said Lafarge evenly.

PIRATE IRWIN

"Excellent. Was there a woman involved that kept you overnight?" asked de Blaeckere leering at Lafarge.

"Yes, there was as a matter of fact. A charming lady, an actress actually, well regarded by Guitry and other leading friends of our partners," replied Lafarge, hoping the emphasis on Aimee's well–regarded metropolitan friends would play in her favour with de Blaeckere.

"Hmm, well she is a stupid girl then isn't she. Mind you, most actresses aren't blessed with brains equivalent to their talents. That doesn't excuse her being mixed up in terrorist activity either. So she will get no mercy from me," said de Blaeckere.

"I would advise you to not be too trigger happy with her de Blaeckere or to place her downstairs in one of your hellhole torture chambers before you refer back to Paris," said Lafarge icily.

De Blaeckere shook his head disdainfully at Lafarge and turned to Broglie.

"Right Broglie, I will want you and your men, who are all fit and well after yesterday's disgraceful lack of action on your part to be ready in an hour," he said taunting Broglie, who bristled at the criticism but nodded his head.

"As for you Lafarge, you can sit this one out, and before you start thanking me, it isn't any philanthropic act by myself but just in case you became all sentimental once you saw your tart," said de Blaeckere viciously.

"I have to say, though, you are a funny one Lafarge. One moment a holier than thou crusading knight coming to the rescue of that woman downstairs, the next charging like some Great War poilu into an enemy house and now delivering on a plate a woman you were only fucking a few hours ago.

"I may be in your eyes a vicious, fanatical diehard, whose university education should have taught him the difference between right and wrong. However, if you opened your eyes you would notice how many of our German friends are from a similar background, and lawyers to boot.

"You on the other hand don't seem to know which side you are on and that makes you dangerous for everybody. A loose cannon is the last thing either side should be relying on, whose mood swings dictates what side he plumps for on any given day.

198

THE TORTURED DETECTIVE

"You are a cold fish Lafarge, one not for eating lest it poison those who do so.

"I will make sure that your actress friend knows exactly who was responsible for her and her family's untimely deaths. For die they will whether it be before they have been tortured or after will depend on their level of resistance when we move in, though, I would prefer we get the chance to interrogate them.

"Why perhaps your name might come up in a compromising and unflattering manner.

"In the meantime to ensure you don't have regrets while we are en route I will leave one of my men here with you so as you don't make a phone call. Alright?" and with that de Blaeckere sarcastically doffed his hat at Lafarge and left the room.

Once he had left the offices Broglie without saying anything poured them two glasses of red wine.

"Thanks, Broglie. I need this," said Lafarge appreciatively and downed it in one.

Broglie patted him on the shoulder and poured him another one.

"I will explain it to you another time if you don't mind. For the moment, I am too confused to really explain myself, save that it will make my own plan easier to achieve," said Lafarge, feeling profoundly angry and depressed.

"It's alright Gaston, we have all done things which ordinarily we wouldn't have. I mean obviously there was always before the war the odd fit up of a suspect, but I am happy with myself in that they were always guilty. It was just a case of having the evidence in place at the right time," said Broglie.

"Anyways, sometimes it is best to just go through the motions every day, dull it with a good drink or three, and hope that sometime it is going to come to a halt and normal service will resume," said Broglie.

On that note he made his excuses and left to round up his men and prepare them for the assault on the farm house. He left Lafarge to his own dark thoughts, and hoping that Gerland and de Chastelain would at least come through and ease his conscience ever so slightly, as he dearly didn't wish to still be in Limoges if Aimée was brought back alive to headquarters.

*

Broglie, de Blaeckere and their men had been gone for a good hour, leaving Lafarge in the care of a young fellow from the Brigade Spéciale, Luc Barenthoen. He lounged around looking bored, not saying very much except to reproach Lafarge for being responsible for him not being able to go on the raid which would have allowed him to release all the pent up anger over the fiasco two days before.

Lafarge shrugged his shoulders dismissively and flicked through an old copy of the newspaper Aujourd'hui, which was virtually unreadable as it had become a propaganda tool of the Nazis and Vichy under the editorship of the venal collaborator Georges Suarez. He had left the novel he was reading in his hotel room, having packed it with the rest of his things before he went to meet Aimee the day before, as he hoped that today would deliver him his prize asset. The bill was paid, so everything was set, just the phone call remained.

He tossed the paper to Barenthoen, who reluctantly thumbed through it, and so it went on for another half hour, save the two of them downing a glass of wine from Broglie's amply–stocked war chest.

At last Barenthoen had to excuse himself for a call of nature and probably an opportunity to stretch his legs. Lafarge was relieved that he didn't have to accompany him, although he asked him what should he do if the phone rang.

Barenthoen replied that he could answer it for by this stage the police must have arrived at the farm so even a warning wouldn't help his friends. Lafarge protested at the use of the term friends but Barenthoen merely sneered and said everyone knew he was soft on the terrorist elements.

He was gone just 10 minutes but by happy coincidence the phone rang the moment he returned. Lafarge let Barethoen pick up the receiver, which resulted with him being handed the phone.

"It's your divorce lawyer Gerland, he wants a word," leered Barenthoen revealing finely polished teeth, which made a nice contrast to Broglie's rotten stumps but that was about the only thing better about him in comparison to the local policeman.

"Yes, Gerland. What do you want?" asked Lafarge brusquely.

THE TORTURED DETECTIVE

"Hello Gaston, just to inform you that the papers you need to sign are indeed here, delivered this morning in fact as expected," replied Gerland in a businesslike tone.

"I wish I could say terrific, but in the circumstances its hardly worth celebrating. Do you want me to come round and sign them?" asked Lafarge.

"Well I think that in order to rush this through and given the difficulties in the postal service it would be wise," said Gerland.

"Alright, I may be accompanied but I am sure he will stay outside," said Lafarge eying Barenthoen.

Barenthoen surprised Lafarge by shaking his head and mouthing that he could go alone.

"Actually scratch that, young Barenthoen doesn't feel like accompanying me on a strictly personal matter, he has a heart after all," said Lafarge laughing.

Barenthoen grunted as Lafarge put down the receiver and said that he may have been asked to play nanny for the day but there were limits.

Lafarge slapped him on the back in jovial fashion and walked briskly out of the office, hoping that this was probably the last he had seen of the poky little office and he wouldn't be shedding any tears over that.

Much that he cared about his welfare Barenthoen wouldn't suffer unduly. If Aimée and the cell had been swept up, then de Blaeckere would be in such a good mood that letting an irritant such as him leave would be a bonus and besides he would now be Paris's problem.

Lafarge breathed in deeply as he left the building and felt for the first time in ages that things were now turning in his direction. He had the key about to be placed in his hands and the mystery surrounding Marguerite Suchet's murder was set to be unlocked.

CHAPTER TWENTY ONE

"I could at the very least arrest you for assault, de Chastelain, you hit me bloody hard," griped Lafarge as the train chugged smoothly out of Limoges station.

"You deserved it Lafarge, that was years of resentment and added to by your reprehensible decision to work for the Nazis. To be frank, you disgust me," retorted de Chastelain.

Lafarge sighed and reflected that what he had taken to be a blemish free record as a policeman had attracted enemies from both sides of the fence, though, he admitted de Chastelain's punch was a good deal milder a punishment than what Bousquet would inflict on him.

He was relieved they were even on the train. Events at Gerland's house had not gone according to plan initially as de Chastelain had signalled he was not going to honour his promise to return with him. He was keener to risk going his own way and trying to reach Spain, adding that he had no guarantee Lafarge would honour his side of the bargain.

Lafarge had reacted furiously, barely restraining himself from blurting out that he had sacrificed a family, and the people who had given de Chastelain safe refuge, so as to fulfil hiis pledge about accompanying him to Paris and then facilitate his being taken to a safe haven.

It was Gerland who rescued the situation. His emollient tones persuading de Chastelain that should Lafarge not honour his promise when they got to Paris there would be two of his acquaintances waiting at the Gare d'Austerlitz who would ensure he did.

Lafarge had commissioned a first class compartment all to themselves. He made clear to the elderly guard that he was on official business and no one was to be given access to the compartment even if they had seats reserved in it.

It was clear, though, that de Chastelain was only travelling back to Paris with him because he was the least worst option, and he needed to ease the atmosphere if he were to gain any useful information about what took place the night of Suchet's murder.

THE TORTURED DETECTIVE

Thus he withdrew from his pocket his gun and laid it to the side, and pulled out a bottle of Armagnac from his suitcase, with two glasses he had purloined from Gerland. De Chastelain raised his eyebrows at this.

"You drink too much Lafarge, you know that. You always did but now it must be to assuage your shame and guilt for having thrown your lot in with the enemy," chided de Chastelain.

Lafarge shrugged his shoulders and sneered back at him who, if he continued in this vein, would only find himself holed up in a cell alongside Lescarboura.

"I think you would be better refraining from constantly making niggling remarks, for if you need reminding, it is you who is under arrest and not me," said Lafarge coldly, and he was pleased that his remark appeared to have its desired effect as a look of resignation crossed de Chastelain's face.

Despite his protestations, he poured them both a glass, commenting he never liked to drink alone, which he knew was a bald–faced lie but nevertheless he felt it worth making, and sat back studying his prisoner's face.

De Chastelain looked tired, as one would if one had been on the run from a murderous regime intent on pinning a murder that two of their members may well have committed themselves. He could see also determination in his eyes and the firm set of his jaw suggested that it was not going to be easy to prise information out of him, especially given his evident dislike of his captor.

The only thing he had going for him was that de Chastelain disliked Bousquet even more than he did Lafarge, and the threat of being handed over to him was a useful weapon to hold.

He certainly wasn't going to divulge any details of how he had managed to come alone to Gerland's house and pick him up without anyone interfering. De Chastelain would probably go for Lafarge's gun were he to learn that he had got such an easy passage out of Limoges because the Parisian cop had offered up the lawyer's fellow Resistants as sacrificial lambs.

"So you are Bousquet's little poodle now, how endearing Lafarge," said the lawyer with a bitter smile on his face.

Lafarge was stung by the comment but let it slide, hitting back with one of his own.

"And you, de Chastelain, escape from Paris hiding in the trunk of the car of one of the most notorious collaborators and virulent anti–semitic writers of our generation, and that is saying something," he said enjoying the moment.

De Chastelain snorted derisively and looked out the window, which didn't yield much of a view as they were rolling through a part of the journey where either side was overshadowed by steep rock faces.

"Needs must when one is being wrongfully pursued by the law, for something that had nothing to do with me. Furthermore Drieu may have his faults but at least he remembers his friends when they are in deep trouble," said de Chastelain quietly.

"You needn't worry on that score, for we were never friends before the war and this is certainly not going to change that. But let us at least try and enjoy a professional relationship on the journey, for your future as much as mine counts on it," said Lafarge, offering a small olive branch.

De Chastelain shrugged and took a sip of his Armagnac. Evidently it was to his liking because he quickly took a bigger slug, lit a cigarette and laid back stretching his long slender legs across the compartment, blocking off Lafarge from doing a similar thing.

"Ok, I guess I don't have much choice here, given you have the gun and I am in your charge, so let us begin the interrogation, no rubber saps, though, please," he pleaded sarcastically.

Lafarge smiled, pleased that at least his prisoner was showing a hint of willingness to co–operate with him.

"I heard your version of events from Gerland, so all I really need to know is did you hold any information back from him? If so, I would like to know what it is," said Lafarge

De Chastelain appeared relieved that Lafarge had taken his story as being the truth, and letting his guard down as the detective had hoped, he visibly relaxed by topping up his glass.

"I didn't hide much from Gerland, but what information I did hide was only to protect him," said de Chastelain, staring straight at Lafarge for the first time since their journey had started.

"Very considerate of you, and that was?" said Lafarge.

"I saw Bousquet leave her apartment, my inquisitiveness got the better of me, or perhaps my lack of patience did and I came down the stairs as he was leaving," said de Chastelain.

THE TORTURED DETECTIVE

Lafarge groaned inwardly, seeing the nightmare scenario unfolding before his eyes and lessening the chances of his being able to let de Chastelain go. For how could he appear before Bousquet firstly without his much sought after prisoner and secondly then accuse him of being the murderer himself.

"You are sure about this?" said Lafarge, knowing it was a stupid question.

"Of course I'm bloody sure, I'm hardly likely to mistake him, am I?" replied de Chastelain forcefully.

"Yes, but it is in your interests to implicate him and, apart from anything else, suits you very well that the man responsible for wanting you arrested should be the very person you turn round and accuse of the crime. Were you the only witness to this?" asked Lafarge, hoping there had been someone else who had seen Bousquet.

"Yes, the maid," replied de Chastelain, taking Lafarge aback with his answer.

"What, Mathilde Langlois?" asked the detective, seeking confirmation as if he needed it.

"Yes, her. Funny one she is, extremely attractive but frigid as an igloo, more's the pity as she could have been an interesting replacement for Marguerite," sighed de Chastelain regretfully.

Lafarge did not feel like filling in his prisoner on why she was as she was, and pursued his line of questioning.

"Funny she didn't mention that to me, she said the last time she saw Marguerite was at nine that evening before being told she would not be needed any further that night," said Lafarge.

De Chastelain shrugged nonchalantly.

"Well, she was with me, or rather just behind me when Bousquet exited the apartment, maybe she preferred to keep her own counsel. I mean upsetting Bousquet is only a thing a fool or fools like us would do," smiled de Chastelain.

Lafarge nodded, for once finding common ground with de Chastelain, though not ground either of them could feel comfortable treading on. However, something troubled him about Mathilde, the air of mystery surrounding her, how von Dirlinger had got her the job with Marguerite, all seemed too down pat, contrived even.

205

"You know that she came to be taken on by Marguerite because of your replacement von Dirlinger," said Lafarge.

"Yes, I am painfully aware of that, but I don't really see the relevance of it," said de Chastelain truculently.

"No matter, it's just an observation. I mean her reticence may have more of an edge to it than simply not wishing to make an enemy of Bousquet, that's all," said Lafarge.

A look of alarm flitted across de Chastelain's face before once again his stony expression returned, but Lafarge was satisfied that his remark had hit home and his prisoner was suitably discomfited.

"Bousquet, I take it, didn't see you?" asked Lafarge.

"Lord no. Do you think I would be sitting here now if he had? He would have had the gendarmes around in no time," replied de Chastelain, all but sneering at the stupidity of the question.

"Hardly if there was a corpse lying in the apartment he had just come out of," interjected Lafarge incredulously.

"How did he look, was he flustered, was he rushing away or was he just his normal arrogant self?"

De Chastelain paused before replying, running his bony hands through his black hair.

"To be honest, he looked as he always does, relaxed, usual erect gait, not a hair out of place, cigarette in his hand, clothes unruffled, yes not a hair of that slicked back oiliness out of place," said de Chastelain bitterly.

"Did he close the door behind him?" asked Lafarge.

De Chastelain looked at him bemused.

"Well, yes of course he did. He was well brought up, you know. Also he's hardly likely to leave the door open to an apartment where he has just murdered the owner," he replied dismissively.

"Really Lafarge, you should reduce the old alcohol intake you know. It may do wonders for your guilt trip but it doesn't for your grasp of the matters in hand," added de Chastelain disparagingly.

Lafarge once again waved aside the needling remark, and as if to spite de Chastelain, he poured himself another glass.

"Did he say anything as he left the apartment?"

De Chastelain scratched his head.

"Yes he did, but it was in German so I didn't really understand it. I just thought he was being ironic referring to Marguerite's present lover's native language. Although of course he is quite an

THE TORTURED DETECTIVE

admirer of all things Teutonic himself as we know," said de Chastelain darkly.

"Quite. But it's interesting he should speak in German, for it suggests that there was someone alive inside the apartment when he left. I mean, it may not have been Marguerite, but it could have been someone else.

"Also Bousquet didn't know he had an audience. So there is no reason for him to go through some Agatha Christie type scene of pretending he is addressing someone who is already lying dead inside," said Lafarge.

De Chastelain for the first time nodded his approval at Lafarge's line of thought.

"Of course that largely depends on at what stage you entered Marguerite's apartment," said Lafarge.

"Well I didn't go in there immediately. I went back up to Mathilde's shoebox of an apartment and decided it was best to lie low there for an hour or so," said de Chastelain.

Lafarge puffed out his cheeks in some relief, for a time lapse such as that would have enabled someone else to murder Marguerite and make good his escape.

Mathilde had told him that her employer had said she was expecting von Dirlinger for dinner and perhaps that was why Bousquet had spoken in German on leaving the apartment.

Obviously, de Chastelain still remained a suspect but the manner in which he told the story was convincing and it would just take asking Mathilde one direct question to clear that up. Whatever, de Chastelain had earned himself a reprieve from Bousquet's clutches for the moment.

He just hoped that Gerland had organised the welcoming party at the other end and that Bousquet had not been apprised of the likelihood that he was on this train with him. For despite him saying he had higher matters of state to deal with he could probably spare two of his most trusted men and send them to the station.

Anyway, they still had several hours remaining before he had to confront that situation, maybe even longer if the Allies launched a bombing raid and delayed the train. So he returned to his questioning of de Chastelain, who he noted with some satisfaction had refilled both of their glasses.

"Did both you and Mathilde go down to the apartment?"

207

De Chastelain shook his head.

"No, it was just me. I think you know all about this part because Gerland would have told you," said de Chastelain, somewhat exasperated with having to repeat his version of events.

"I'm sorry if this is irritating you but I need to check the statement or rather the account you gave your friend Gerland with the version you are giving me. It's equally important for you as it is for me, because it will decide in whose hands you are placed when we get to Paris," retorted Lafarge sternly.

De Chastelain looked surprised at the way in which Lafarge had couched his reply.

"Hey I thought you assured me there would be no double cross?" he asked, a note of alarm in his voice.

Lafarge smiled, enjoying his prisoner's moment of discomfort, and told him to answer the question.

"Ok well, I found Marguerite lying on the sofa, I called out to her and when I received no reply I went over to her and found her unconscious. She was still breathing, I leant over her and tried to revive her and that must have been when my shirt became covered in blood," said de Chastelain confidently.

"And Mathilde never entered the room? I mean she can't support your claim?" asked Lafarge, leaning forward as if this was the crucial moment as to whether he turned him over or not.

De Chastelain sensed this, Lafarge could see, as his demeanour took on a downcast look.

"I am afraid not, no. She never came into the apartment. I ran upstairs and told her what I had seen and told her to stay where she was as there was no point her getting involved," he said forlornly.

Lafarge could tell he was telling the truth vis–a–vis that and resolved to honour his word and hand him over to Gerland's men were they to show up, but he wasn't going to tell him that now.

There still remained questions over his role in the burglary. Besides he was enjoying in a sadistic way the fact de Chastelain was co–operating because he was afraid and there was no sign of the insufferable self–confident persona he usually adopted.

"Very well, and it was from there that you made your way to Drieu's place?" asked Lafarge.

THE TORTURED DETECTIVE

"Yes, I was as you can imagine very upset at seeing Marguerite in that state and I didn't think too clearly about where or to whom I would go to.

"I couldn't stay there because if I was found, despite my protestations of innocence I was already a fugitive. Bousquet would also have realized that I could well have been in the building and seen him," said de Chastelain mournfully.

"There was little option but to flee and hope I found sanctuary somewhere before getting out of Paris. I thought of Drieu finally because he remained a friend despite our enormous differences. Also he would be the last person anyone would think of who would help a fugitive flee from the Nazis or the police.

"At least I got that bit right!" he remarked bitterly.

Lafarge nodded and mused what a funny fellow Drieu was. An arch collaborator but unlike many of his fellow travellers one who remained friends with those who ideologically were totally opposite to him. De Chastelain and André Malraux were too such examples, although his close friendship with the communist poet Louis Aragon had not survived.

"Very well, that chapter is closed. However, don't believe for one moment you can relax, de Chastelain. There are other questions regarding the burglary of the diamonds and your association with the unfortunate Arnaud Lescarboura and Marguerite, a collusion that may very well have brought about her death," said Lafarge brusquely.

De Chastelain looked alarmed at this and as if to prepare himself, asked if he could be excused to go to the bathroom. Lafarge said he could but he would accompany him to the door.

"I'm not going to jump out of a train in the dark for God's sake Lafarge!" he protested but to no avail as Lafarge dangled handcuffs in front of him as an alternative.

Ten minutes later, they were back in the compartment, having shuffled back without seeing a soul, the other first class compartments had their blinds down as their occupants enjoyed unlike them a peaceful night's sleep.

Lafarge took the opportunity to open a bottle of red wine this time, not the right order at all, but he hadn't felt it was fair to divest Gerland of a second bottle of Armagnac. There were limits after all to his generosity.

209

"Right. Tell me how you came up with this bizarre idea to go the way of so many of your clients and become a common criminal by robbing the Countess?" asked Lafarge.

De Chastelain scratched his clean shaven chin and closed his eyes as he looked for the least inculpatory answer but there was none.

"Alright, theft doesn't bring one a death sentence. Well at least it didn't and even the Nazis don't normally impose such a sentence for it. So yes I was part of the burglary with Arnaud and Marguerite," said de Chastelain.

"Just the three of you? You were the puppeteer and the other two were your puppets?" asked Lafarge, sensing that there was someone else at the very least involved.

De Chastelain looked uncomfortable with the question, gulping back the red wine and smoking two cigarettes before he would answer it.

"Is it important? I mean, the three of us are big enough no? Lescarboura is banged up, Marguerite is dead and you have me," he said, his voice losing its confident air.

"Of course it is important. The very thing you just said highlights how important it is, for none of you who played an active role in the burglary are now at liberty. Indeed one of them, the person you loved the most in the world, is dead because the mastermind or the masterminds wished it so, and the diamonds have gone missing," said Lafarge.

De Chastelain's face clouded over with grief and also concern as he sought to extricate himself from a situation where there was very little to gain from it for him.

"Listen, if it will make it any easier for you to say the name, I will tell you that your unfortunate client Lescarboura nodded when I asked him whether Bousquet was involved. He was just as frightened as you seem to be and lord, he was actually in prison, you by contrast are not surrounded by aggressive guards or listening devices," said Lafarge trying to encourage him to come clean.

De Chastelain's face froze at this.

"Arnaud said that? I'm amazed, you must possess some sort of hypnotic powers that I didn't give you credit for, Lafarge! Well

THE TORTURED DETECTIVE

why then would Bousquet wish me to be arrested?" asked de Chastelain.

"I don't know but I would like you to tell me," replied Lafarge fixing him with a firm gaze.

De Chastelain hadn't, it seemed, expected Lafarge to throw it back at him, for his self satisfied grin disappeared quickly.

"Wow, you must really not care about your job at all, Lafarge! Or you hate Bousquet more than your job security," said de Chastelain incredulously.

"I'm just a professional detective doing my job. Not enough of us are doing that these days but I still have a sense of duty and integrity regardless of what you think my motives are," said Lafarge cooly.

De Chastelain eyed him warily, and swept back his hair in a bid to cover the fact that, as Lafarge had observed, his hands were shaking and it certainly wasn't for want of drink as they had had a plentiful amount.

"Lafarge I don't think I dislike you enough to give you the information that would enlighten you on the subject but at the same time consign you to an early grave," said de Chastelain.

"Try me!" said Lafarge in a firm tone that left no room for de Chastelain to wriggle out of.

De Chastelain smiled grimly and held his hands up.

"Okay Lafarge. I will tell you all that I know regarding the jewel theft. It is a pretty sordid tale and one that doesn't make me proud with my involvement in it, but even the most honest of people appear to be losing their sense of right and wrong these days," said de Chastelain.

Lafarge thought to himself, what a self–righteous prig, taking him to task for resuming his duties as a policeman when he was going around committing crimes.

"I am an admirer of the Countess de Marchand but my passion for Marguerite was such that any other feelings were secondary. Thus I thought if I could successfully steal her jewels and sell them on, then I would have the money to make a secure future for myself and Marguerite, and wrest her away from the German.

"All she ever sought was security. Hence why she ditched me because she was afraid that my defending perccived enemies of the state she would be implicated by association and lose any chance of furthering her acting career.

"Thus I thought I would bring the plan to her thereby enlisting the services of Lescarboura and with his expert criminal skills I would succeed in both my goals.

"I must admit the idea of getting her to invite the Countess to dinner was a sweet touch by me. It gave us both alibis as well as my chance to play one off against the other as they were both terribly in love with me," said de Chastelain, positively warming to the task of talking himself up.

"*Were* in love with you," said Lafarge taking him down a peg or two.

De Chastelain looked angry at this remark but collected himself and continued with his account.

"Well everything went terrifically well up to the point that Marguerite then confided in me that she had let slip to the German colonel, and he to Bousquet, about the plan," said de Chastelain, his tone turning bitter.

"No doubt you are wondering why would she go and do something like that. Well obviously it was this sense of security she sought. She was afraid that there was a chance of being caught so if she had the support of her colonel and Bousquet all would be alright.

"In a sense she was correct, regarding herself. But it meant a smaller share of the booty for all of us and evidently she saw no future with me."

Lafarge mulled over the detail and saw that this band of thieves certainly had no honour, what a mixed bag they were.

The insecure starlet, the professional burglar devoted to his childhood friend, the former lover and self–righteous lawyer, determined to win back her love, the playboy intelligence Abwehr colonel, outwardly charming and carefree, and towering over them the careerist opportunistic head of French police Bousquet.

No wonder de Chastelain was so sought after by that duo, for he was the last of the dispensable three still at large. Both von Dirlinger and Bousquet had placed a great deal of faith in Lafarge and his renowned sense of duty, not to them but to his job, to bring them back the missing piece.

THE TORTURED DETECTIVE

"Did you ever all meet together to sort out the finer details of the burglary?" asked Lafarge.

De Chastelain looked at him with an astonished look on his face.

"What all five of us? Hardly! It would likely have ended in a murder," he said sardonically.

"An unfortunate choice of words there. I think it did, don't you?" retorted Lafarge.

De Chastelain nodded realising his gaffe.

"So how do you know that both Bousquet and von Dirlinger were implicated in the plan?" asked Lafarge pressing for something more concrete than he had been given so far.

"Marguerite told me so, and I have no reason to doubt her word on that. Of course it may have been a ruse to scare me off from going through with the plan, but she was most insistent that they knew and what they wanted as their share," replied de Chastelain, his voice firm.

"But I don't understand why a rich man like Bousquet and it appears von Dirlinger isn't short of cash either would risk their reputations on a high profile burglary," said Lafarge.

"Hell I don't know Lafarge. You can only ask them when you present your evidence, though, I don't envy you that task!" said de Chastelain acidly.

Lafarge grunted and silently agreed with him that the task ahead was going to be an unenviable one but he was determined to see it through.

"One thing surprises me above all else Lafarge, and there are many things that surprise me about this case, and that is why Bousquet has put you in charge of the investigation when we both know that your mutual dislike dates back years," said de Chastelain, his tone taking on a suspicious note.

"I mean he must realise that if you captured me alive you wouldn't sit on a train for several hours idling away the hours with tittle tattle and drinking sociably with someone he knows you despise. No he is counting on you posing questions surrounding the murder."

Lafarge had to agree with de Chastelain again.

He had been aware of this from the start or at least once he discovered the cigarette case, but he couldn't understand why Bousquet would allow him to continue the investigation. Unless of course he was innocent of the murder and he didn't think he would widen the enquiry to include the burglary.

Surely, though, he and von Dirlinger had taken into account that de Chastelain might divulge details to Lafarge that could embroil them in an almighty scandal.

They were if nothing else both intelligent men, which made Lafarge fearful of what might await them at Gare d'Austerlitz.

For whilst he had not phoned to say he had de Chastelain he had little doubt that once de Blaeckere returned from his raid he would note his absence and alert Bousquet. The secretary–general would, if he were not too occupied with his matter of state, work out which train they were on and when it arrived in Paris.

However, with the diamonds still apparently missing, hence Bonny's surprising intrusion at the apartment, de Chastelain had some currency still to keep him alive in case he knew where they were.

Or von Dirlinger and Bousquet hoped that if he would not tell them, then he would inform Lafarge. That was a bargaining chip to keep in storage for the undoubtedly tough times to come.

"So tell me, how come you all fell out so quickly?" asked Lafarge intrigued as to the circumstances of this unholy quintet's falling out.

De Chastelain smiled but the lack of mirth in his eyes told a different story.

"Because unfortunately, you are not the only diligent cop in Paris," said de Chastelain.

Lafarge raised his eyebrows and leaned forward.

"A detective called Purevoy was assigned the case and quickly picked up Lescarboura, a man whose talents he was already a connoisseur of. It was too late for Bousquet to intervene as the paperwork was done and the fool was in custody.

"Lescarboura logically thought I would be the best man to defend him, given my intimate knowledge of the case, and I accepted, primarily because I was very keen to find out where the missing diamonds were.

"He knew as little as I did about where they were, and so I contacted Marguerite and threatened that at the trial I would make sweeping allegations about her lover and Bousquet. Faithful as

THE TORTURED DETECTIVE

ever to her protectors she duly relayed the information to them and from that moment I was a marked man.

"Hence Bousquet's piece de theatre surrounding my arrest. However, for some unknown reason the German intervened and hijacked it. It appears that not even those two powerful men could stick together," commented de Chastelain drily.

Lafarge smiled, though, his heart was beating double its usual rate for the information he had succeeded in extricating from de Chastelain was astonishing.

It could destroy the careers of two men, one of them one of the most powerful men in France and seen as a potential replacement for Laval while the latter, the German's pet French bulldog, replaced the octogenarian Pétain.

However, it was also extremely dangerous information to possess and he could see that he too was expendable if he was to hand him over to Bousquet's men.

For he was dealing with two callous characters, one of whom was possibly a murderer, though that was a moot point as both had enough blood on their hands already.

This was different, though, as both were suspects in personally murdering Marguerite, not just signing a paper condemning a person not known personally to them to death.

However, as they had both fallen out with each other, that remained like the missing diamonds, a potential bargaining counter were things to become extremely tricky.

The only thing he could do for the moment was to ensure de Chastelain's safety, Lescarboura the poor sod was beyond his help wherever he was, and pray that one day the case came to trial.

"Do you think that von Dirlinger saved you only to set you up for Marguerite's murder?" Lafarge asked after a pause.

"But of course Lafarge. I haven't heard of too many philanthropic gestures by Germans have you during this war," replied de Chastelain sardonically.

Lafarge nodded in agreement and looked out the window. Noticing that it was getting lighter and that they must be nearing Paris, he decided to tell de Chastelain what their course of action would be.

"Obviously I should be taking you straight to Quai des Orfèvres. However, I think that this would be the worst solution to our problems.

"Thus this is what is going to happen, or at least I hope will unfold when we arrive at Austerlitz. There will be two men there to greet us and they will take you away to a safe house, where you will lie low. I will come for you later and tell you how you are going to leave the country.

"Obviously should the Allies fail to liberate France, then I would recommend you never return, and I will expect our meeting at the safe house to be our last, for I doubt I shall see my way to retirement.

"You needn't worry about the two men who will take you away as they have been organised by Gerland and so are trustworthy. I will explain to Bousquet why you are no longer with me. I will of course relate some of what you have told me. It promises as you said earlier to be a stormy meeting," said Lafarge smiling sadly.

De Chastelain looked stunned at Lafarge's plan, but then in an equally surprising gesture he held out his hand. Lafarge somewhat reluctantly took it and then they shook before filling their glasses and toasting each other, in what was their first ever convivial drink over a period of jousting of a decade or more.

Lafarge refrained from telling him that Bousquet's men might also be there but he assumed that de Chastelain already thought they would be.

"Look, I know friendship between us is not a term one would use but while I see a jewel thief in front of me I also see at heart a man of integrity, though prone to defending those who are indefensible.

"However, sometimes one must make compromises, especially nowadays, and while it is a first for me to let a self–avowed criminal escape, and I won't make a habit of it, this is a case of good against evil and we are on the right side," said Lafarge.

De Chastelain laughed and patted him on the knee, the realisation he wasn't being tricked and would indeed be given a chance of escaping releasing all the tension in the compartment.

"No don't make a habit of it Lafarge, you wouldn't want anyone to think you are a bent cop!

THE TORTURED DETECTIVE

"I appreciate enormously your gesture, I know it doesn't guarantee that I will escape from the country, but I am eternally grateful for this opportunity.

"You too are a damn fine policeman, a bit self important, distant and priggish, but maybe you are softening. Don't worry I won't tell anyone!" said de Chastelain, laughing heartily.

The laughter died down and de Chastelain paused before he broached a subject that had obviously been gnawing away at him.

"I just don't see why you would risk your life and career for me, someone whom you openly disliked and had contempt for. What is your motivation?"

Lafarge sighed and sipped from his glass.

"Let's just say I am fed up with the hypocrisy and the crimes being committed by a government headed by a man who claims to have saved France for a second time when in fact he is staining our name for ever," sad Lafarge passionately.

"Thus I am not going to do all in my power to avert another state sponsored murder orchestrated by a man who along with Laval are the main progenitors of this odous period of collaboration with one of the most appalling regimes in history.

"And don't think de Chastelain that I have no blood on my hands, for I too have had to make a choice which I would rather not have had to do and indeed if it had been peacetime I would never have had to make.

"However, I have done so and now I must live with that, which makes me even more committed to seeing this through, saving you first will do something to salve my conscience," he said biting back tears, as he thought of the horrors that Aimee might be experiencing as they sat in comfort on the train.

"Well I thank you for that again and I do have some sympathy for your predicament, and I won't ask you any further about what this sacrifice might be," said de Chastelain sincerely.

The increasingly cordial chat continued for another half hour until the conductor came by and informed them they would be arriving in 10 minutes. It sobered them up and left them to their own thoughts, Lafarge praying that there were not two reception committees waiting for them, for then it would entail some quick thinking on his part so as not to let de Chastelain fall into the hands of Bousquet and probably hasten both their ends.

Both Lafarge and de Chastelain got off the train the worse for wear. Their lack of sleep and enormous intake of alcohol had taken effect even on the usually impervious detective, but they succeeded in ambling, albeit slowly, along the platform.

They were swallowed up in the mass of people, a mix of civilians and Germans in all types of uniform returning for the most part from some welcome time resting in the South of France.

Lafarge looked round to see if by chance von Dirlinger was amongst the mass of Germans, given de Chastelain's account of the events it wouldn't have surprised him that he had been tracking him all this time.

There was no sign of him and Lafarge chided himself for being so neurotic. They reached the sanctuary of the designated meeting spot, the bar at the station, ordered two glasses of red wine and positioned themselves at the end of it so they could have a good view of who entered.

Even at that ungodly hour of the morning, it was just after seven, eyebrows were not raised if one ordered alcohol. The French tried to justify their enormous consumption of their finest product by claiming wine was not categorized as alcohol, Lafarge being one of those saying it was fermented fruit juice.

Not that he accompanied the wine with a croissant as was customary with the usual liquid served at most breakfast tables, but then he reasoned he wasn't the norm.

The bar was pretty busy.

The majority were grey suited types waiting for their train to be readied for departure, some travelling lightly others accompanied by what appeared to be their wives. Some were with their children as they headed for their holidays in the south, refusing to allow the changed circumstances of the period to interfere with their annual ritual.

Celebrating their new found camaraderie Lafarge and de Chastelain clinked glasses and spent the time making observations about the others in the bar, though, as time wore on the conversation became edgier as Lafarge began to wonder whether their rendezvous had been aborted or Gerland had failed to get through to his contacts.

THE TORTURED DETECTIVE

However, at the same time he was relieved that there had been no official welcoming party. There had been what he felt a larger than usual police presence at the station but they had paid scant attention to two weary looking gentlemen having trouble walking in a straight line.

Finally after what seemed hours, but in fact had been around 45 minutes, two well–dressed, well–built middle aged men came into the bar, unencumbered by baggage but carrying about them an official looking air.

Both made their way immediately to Lafarge and his companion, who were indulging in their second glass of red, and introduced themselves. Lafarge knew one of them already, a former inspector in his division from before the war, Gilbert Huariau, known for his honesty and diligence, but who he had lost touch with.

The other introduced himself as Florian Conti, whose accent confirmed Lafarge's initial reaction when he heard his name that he was from Corsica. By the look of him he was certainly the muscle of the duo. Scars on his face and light bruising on his hands indicated he knew how to handle himself, and the large bulge on the inside of his jacket suggested he knew how to use a gun as well.

Both of them weren't in any mood to move off quickly and gladly accepted the offer of a drink, before Huariau explained why they had been held up.

"While you have been travelling back from the no no zone here in the ja ja zone things have been getting busy," said Huariau, using the pejorative terms for the Vichy controlled area and the Occupied Zone.

"There's a massive police operation going on in Paris this morning. We must have been stopped three or four times by uniforms, but once we flashed my old police badge there was no problem. They didn't really look at it very intently, just saw police and waved us on."

Lafarge grunted and thought perhaps that was why there had been no–one to meet them, for this was the big event that Bousquet had alluded to when they spoke on the phone. That was good news but it also meant that were they to be stopped de Chastelain might be in danger of being arrested as he had no papers that he was aware of.

219

"Don't worry Lafarge we have papers for your friend here. When we have a client we leave nothing to chance. Besides I think the road blocks will have lifted soon, it appeared also they were only interested in our yellow star wearing friends," said Huariau.

"Why are they suddenly so interested in the Jews and where they are, there hasn't been an uprising since I left has there?" asked Lafarge half hoping that was the case.

Huariau laughed grimly and took a gulp of his wine before ordering another round.

"No, it looks like our colleagues, or rather your colleagues and my former ones, have decided to round them up, make Paris a safer place for all non Jews! Makes you want to laugh huh Lafarge! If they took a sample of the religious break down of the people I arrested before the war I doubt the percentage of Jews would have come to double figures," said Huariau clearly disgusted.

"To be honest I never looked at it like that, for a criminal was a criminal and nothing to do with his ethnic background, but yes it makes a mockery of their justification for what they are doing," said Lafarge.

"Still I can't believe it is anything but giving the Jews a prod, a humiliating sort of kick in the butt and then letting them go about what little business or socializing they are allowed to conduct these days," said Lafarge gloomily.

"You're naïve if you think like that Lafarge," said de Chastelain.

Lafarge turned to him annoyed at being contradicted and belittled by him in front of his former colleague but it didn't have the desired effect of shutting de Chastelain up.

"Even you must have heard of the stories of how the Polish Jews and the others who have been steamrollered by the Nazis have been first maltreated and then disappeared in their thousands, never to be seen again.

"They were transported, so the Germans say, for crucial work in the east, preparing the way for their faithful German people to move into their homes as they depart. Judging from what Huariau is saying they are starting on them here too now and what is worse relying on us the French to round them up.

"Yet another dark stain on our nation and one that won't be easily erased. Of course for you and your colleagues it is just another

THE TORTURED DETECTIVE

example of the efficient teamwork between two allies. It makes me sick to the stomach," said de Chastelain spitting on the floor.

"For Christ's sake de Chastelain, don't be so dramatic and unnecessarily critical of the French police, I am sure that they are not engaged in anything as illegal as you suggest. The vast majority of policemen are at best ambivalent about the Nazis and would certainly not volunteer for such an appalling task," retorted Lafarge.

Huariau grinned and drank the last dreg from his glass, licking his lips to make sure nothing had escaped his attention.

"Now, now you two. Listen we better be making a move regardless of what is going on in Paris, as we have to take your friend to his safe house.

"You have the address already Lafarge, and you can contact me at this number when you feel that it is alright for taking him to the person who is going to put him on his way to freedom," said Huariau handing Lafarge a slip of paper.

Lafarge thanked him and Conti and walked with them to the main exit of the station and bade de Chastelain farewell.

"By the way Lafarge, I would suggest you walk back to Orfevres, not only to clear your head a bit but also to see what is really going on. I think you will find de Chastelain's version is nearer the truth than what you hope it to be," said Huariau softly before the trio disappeared into the sedan car that was waiting for them.

Lafarge absorbed what he had said and without further ado he began his journey on foot with a deep sense of foreboding at what lay ahead.

CHAPTER TWENTY TWO

The first thing that struck Lafarge was the huge amount of buses that were on the streets. A succession of the green and cream coloured vehicles winged their way through Paris, when normally one waited hours for one to come along, shortage of petrol being the main reason.

There were hundreds of them. He wondered at first whether this was a new national day imposed by the Nazis, ride a bus day and promoting the values of public transport where everyone could be together and not the individualism and hence independence of driving one's own car.

However, that was a laughable thought as if he were not a detective he would be hard pressed to be able to afford to run a car.

However, it took him a while to realize that all the buses were either completely empty and heading in one direction, that of the largely Jewish neighbourhood of the Marais, or were packed.

None of them either empty or full were stopping at designated bus stops.

Lafarge decided to head to the Marais to see what exactly was going on. His heart sank, though, as he took a closer inspection of two buses that passed him on their way to their destination, for on both, situated at the rear, were uniformed policemen.

However, what shocked him was that these passengers were not your average Parisian going to work with their habitual expressions of fatigue or resignation. Nor were they engaging in the social discourse that some people, Lafarge could never cope with them, found easy to come by so early in the morning.

No, almost to a person their expressions were glum.

Some were crying – not even the most humdrum of jobs could possibly induce that, mused Lafarge in an attempt to introduce some levity into his thoughts – while others were banging on the windows as if they were desperate to escape the mass of people they were crammed in with.

For those lucky enough to not be inside they were standing on the small platform space at the rear of the buses, guarded – for that was clearly the intention – by two policemen.

Drink had clearly dulled his powers of observation.

THE TORTURED DETECTIVE

For it took him a while to register that a surprisingly large percentage of the passengers were children, or perhaps he just didn't want to accept what was taking place before his eyes, and that all bar the policemen were wearing the yellow star.

The cargo, for that was what it was, were all Jews.

He felt physically sick, nausea gripped him, and he retched but nothing came up. He strode on, and reached St Paul near the Bastille – where nearly 150 years before the people of Paris had struck the first symbolic blow against the Bourbon monarchy – which marked one of the boundaries of the Marais.

There he came to a halt and tried to suppress his nausea by lighting a cigarette, while looking around to see if there was a café open where he could get himself a drink and try and glean information. He knew deep down that this was the highly important event that Bousquet had hinted at.

The walk and the shock at what was taking place had sobered up Lafarge, but for him this was not a moment to be sober. This was an event that was darkening the image of France forever and would make every French person ashamed that they were part of it, for they were as guilty as the uniformed police carrying out their orders.

This was open collusion in persecuting people because of their religion, rounding them up and taking them off to be dealt with by the Nazis as they saw fit. Work camps they had said previously, but were they really that?

Lafarge grimaced and then to his delight he espied a café that was open on the opposite side of the street on the corner of the Rue Vielle de Temple. He entered and saw that it was populated by some uniformed policemen and others in plain clothes, while the mustachioed barman and one harassed looking waiter struggled to serve them all.

He managed to secure himself a place at the end of the bar and ordered a cognac and a coffee, and settled in to listen to their conversation. They ignored him and chatted among themselves.

"We cleared this building, they didn't know what was happening and were in shock. I was a bit reluctant to order their children to come with them, but then what would happen to them left on their own, so I forced them out and into the bus.

223

"They brought some belongings but that is all a sham, for they will be taken away from them once they get to wherever they're going," said a middle–aged officer with blotched features.

"So what? Let them be, for they have had a good life, compared to most of us, for years. They have hoarded their money, profiting from the misery of honest French people. It's time for them to pay a price for that," commented a younger officer.

"Well I am not one who signed up to be a policeman to round up children," replied the older officer, his humanity a welcome oasis in this desert of human feelings.

"Well old man perhaps it is time for you to go into retirement for you won't find too many of us who sympathise with you. They're Jews, the lowest of the low, who have remained rich while others have barely had enough to eat. I am delighted that we are bringing them to order," said the younger officer.

Lafarge had had enough of this exchange and, whether it was the brandy or just fatigue, he laid into the younger policeman.

"What's your name officer?" he asked leaning across the older man.

"Who's asking? A Jew? Why haven't you got your star on?" replied the younger man.

"Chief Inspector Lafarge, Quai des Orfevres," said Lafarge triumphantly and producing his badge at the same time so as not to leave a smidgen of doubt in the officer's mind.

The older officer smiled, while the younger one bristled but felt compelled to give him his name which was Pierre Durand.

"Your conversation repels me officer Durand, and I have a good mind to report you. It may not strike you at the moment but you are participating in an illegal act for which hopefully you will one day come to regret and be held accountable for," said Lafarge.

"You are a disgrace to the force, your colleague at least possesses a modicum of human feeling, you, heaven help us I hope do not accurately reflect the feelings of the men enforcing this crime today," sad Lafarge with such force that the rest of the bar fell silent.

Durand came round the back of his colleague and confronted Lafarge, hatred contorting his face.

"So there are Jew lovers in the force! A plain clothes one to boot. Well sir, you and your woolly liberal conscience disgust me too.

THE TORTURED DETECTIVE

"Why don't you take it with you as you get out of this bar right now? Otherwise I might just have to throw you out myself and then have you reported for espousing anti state remarks," Durand said his tone full of contempt.

The older policeman stepped in between both of them, facing Lafarge he gestured with his eyes that it would be best to leave, and he took the hint and made for the door after chucking some cash on the bar.

He could hear Durand making some sort of disparaging remark as he exited which was greeted with a cacophony of laughter, but he didn't stop to make a riposte, for it was pointless.

Durand was reflective of a group of people who were indoctrinated to the ways of the 'new world order'.

They couldn't see that what they were doing that day destroyed the image of the country that had drawn up the 'Rights of Man' and made a mockery of the idealistic credo that adorned government and court buildings: 'liberty, equality and fraternity'.

With the screams of terror and misery emanating from within the Marais, Lafarge trudged despairingly away from them, and made his way towards the centre of where this evil had sprung the Quai des Orfevres and its Mephistophelian chief René Bousquet.

What he had orchestrated today he would hopefully answer for in the years to come but Lafarge was now determined that Bousquet should be held to account for the murder of Marguerite Suchet if he was indeed guilty – even Vichy could not justify that as a state ordered assassination.

*

"Alright Huariau I will be round in an hour, have him ready to go," said Lafarge before replacing the receiver and taking a sip of his favourite red wine from his cellar.

He had made little headway at Quai des Orfevres.

His determination to bring Bousquet to heel had failed miserably. Firstly he was unavailable as he was overseeing the operation for rounding up the Jews from another office and secondly Massu had told him to go home when he saw what a state he was in.

Massu, who was playing no role in the criminal events in Paris whilst not interfering with the smooth brutal running of the operation, had given him a cup of coffee and told Lafarge kindly but firmly that he was better off going home and getting some rest and returning the next day if he wished to see Bousquet.

As ever Massu preferred not to hear the details and didn't ask Lafarge about his time in Limoges.

Massu had told him that Lescarboura had disappeared to some camp in Germany, as part of the workforce the Germans had demanded the French supply. As ever they had acquiesced without receving anything in return except for some prisoners of war coming home.

With regard to von Dirlinger, Massu had chanced upon him once at the Lutetia where they had exchanged pleasantries, though, Lafarge found it instructive that the Abwehr officer hadn't apparently asked for his news.

Either he didn't care, which Lafarge doubted, or else he knew perfectly well he was still in Limoges and that information could only have come from Bousquet which suggested that maybe a common interest had brought them back together again.

He shuddered at the thought that he would remain their unifying force once they learnt that de Chastelain had slipped from their grasp, hopefully from his point of view for ever.

He would have to hope that his father could help him one more time by preventing him from being tortured and shot or worse sent on one of the trains to the east. Lafarge had toyed with the idea of seeking out Mathilde to confirm de Chastelain's story but refrained from doing so.

He was not certain where her loyalties lay and that she would repeat her conversation straight back to von Dirlinger should she see him at Solidor's club that evening. He needed time to get de Chastelain on his way and running the risk of having an Abwehr officer after them would not help their chances of succeeding.

Besides he reasoned to himself his instinct told him that de Chastelain was innocent of the murder and that was all he was really interested in.

The burglary he was complicit in. However, it was a minor offence in the greater scheme of things and he wasn't about to deliver a scapegoat into the hands of the two people who were more than likely responsible for the death of Marguerite.

THE TORTURED DETECTIVE

Thus he had taken Massu's advice and returned home where he had washed, taken a nap and now felt refreshed enough to aid de Chastelain's second effort at escape.

Truth be told he hadn't seen the man who held the fugitive's future in his hands for several years, but if he was anything as effective in getting the people out as he had been as his and his wife's doctor then de Chastelain was in very good hands.

Lafarge had been surprised that the good doctor had become the head of an escape ring but then lots of people had assumed roles that one would never have suspected them capable of performing.

Indeed 'Doctor Eugene', or Doctor Petiot which was his real name, appeared to have adapted really well to his second occupation judging by the paperwork that he demanded, though, he did not come cheap with 200,000 francs cash the going rate.

Of course Lafarge had nothing like that amount of money and de Chastelain's account could not be touched so the reliable Gerland had vouchsafed for it.

Lafarge had picked up the cash when he collected de Chastelain, other arrangements such as passport photos of de Chastelain had been furnished by associates of Gerland's to Petiot at his medical practice in Rue Caumartin near Gare St Lazare.

Departure, though, was to be from a far more respectable address up in the 16th arrondissement on Rue Sueur where Petiot had a townhouse. Such riches didn't surprise Lafarge as the prices he was charging he could easily afford a smart address.

However, he thought it was uncomfortably close to Gestapo headquarters on Avenue Foch but then perhaps the unimaginative types that seemed to dominate the ranks of the Gestapo could never think the respectable 16th would be the epicentre of such a huge escape operation.

Why the majority of the people who lived in the 16th had been very welcoming to the Nazis. Those who hadn't been, the rich Jews for example, were for the most part now housed in far less salubrious surroundings and their apartments had been taken over by German officers or French people favoured by either Vichy or the Nazis.

By coincidence Petiot used an Argentinian diplomat to get him the fake papers and visas and it set Lafarge wondering whether this pliable diplomat, admittedly no doubt having his palm greased by the doctor, was his father–in–law.

Lafarge was in a much better frame of mind once he swung by the safe house to pick up de Chastelain. His passenger wasn't ready and it was Huariau who greeted him, and listened to his description of what he had seen after they had parted that morning. He smiled sadly and told him he expected there to be a repeat the next day.

Lafarge couldn't believe it, hoping that after one day of this disgusting work that older heads like the one he had come across at the café might protest and say this type of action was not what the police were meant to do.

However, Huariau reproached him for his altruistic view of the uniformed police, saying they had even less brains in general than those in plain clothes, Lafarge excepted of course.

Huariau added that in any case what they lacked in brains they made up for in animal instinct. They were not going to risk their jobs for a group of people they didn't have anything in common with, for the majority of those picked up were foreign Jews.

Lafarge shook with rage at this.

For in a way this made it even more reprehensible. People who had sought refuge from persecution in their own countries were now being hunted down for the same reasons by French policement, and without a German present as far as Lafarge could see from what he had witnessed that morning.

Their sombre discussion was interrupted by the arrival of a refreshed looking de Chastelain. He looked the way he had been when he wooed the Parisian courtrooms, clean-shaven with a fashionable haircut and dressed dapperly in a well-cut grey suit.

Lafarge doffed his hat and sarcastically bowed before ushering him out the door and into the car. Huariau said to him as he was leaving that if he ever needed similar help to just call him to which Lafarge nodded and felt good that there were still people around like his former colleague. Sadly they were all mainly like Huariau now outside the force.

The trip wasn't going to take long and for the first part of it they travelled in silence, Lafarge hoping there weren't too many checkpoints while de Chastelain seemed apprehensive at stepping into the unknown, in handing his future to a man he did not know.

THE TORTURED DETECTIVE

Lafarge tried to lighten the atmosphere by whistling some old tune which had been popular before the war, even for once unifying the different political factions, and offered de Chastelain a cigarette and some cognac from his hip flask.

"Bloody hell Lafarge, do you ever go anywhere without a drink?" asked de Chastelain, who nevertheless seized the flask and gulped down a large portion of the contents.

"Easy tiger. You want to be conscious and at your sharpest for the journey ahead. You are not going to have a decent cop like myself after you the next time. Chances are if you do fall into the wrong hands they will just shoot you. I would say your last chance at a trial – fair or not – disappeared the moment I handed you over to Huariau," said Lafarge.

De Chastelain sighed and stared out the window cracking his knuckles at the same time and Lafarge wished he would stop because his nervousness was having an effect on him.

"Look you have nothing to fear from the guy who is going to help you. Not for the fee he charges, it wouldn't be worth his while to get on the wrong side of me. I could have his operation closed down within minutes," said Lafarge trying to reassure de Chastelain.

De Chastelain remained silent, absorbed in his own thoughts, it dawning on him that this was the point of no return. He could of course change his mind still and risk being put on trial, but there were few judges who would contradict the will of the government now.

Besides de Chastelain hadn't made too many friends among the judiciary during his barnstorming days at the bar, his acerbic humour having ridiculed many of them. That was something, being extremely self–important to a man, they often didn't forget. Turn the other cheek was for other people, not for them.

Lafarge tried once again to boost his passenger's morale.

"You won't be gone forever de Chastelain, and when you are able to return, why you will be feted as a hero, not as someone who escaped the guillotine after murdering your former mistress. I will see to that, even if I too have to disappear. I will write it all down and leave it with someone I can trust. It will be the official record," he said.

"To be truthful Lafarge, I don't see myself returning here, and I'm not being fatalistic," replied de Chastelain.

"I can feel that this is my last ride across Paris, it's a pity it is in the dark, for this truly is the most beautiful city in the world and where I have experienced my happiest and most successful moments.

"But like those experiences I now will put Paris into a locker marked 'the past' and see where life takes me," he added.

Lafarge said nothing, simply grunted and inwardly praised de Chastelain for his pragmatic outlook.

They were making good progress, hardly a uniformed policeman was to be seen, obviously sleeping off their hard work of today and preparing for more of the same tomorrow Lafarge guessed.

Eventually they entered Rue Sueur and Lafarge purposefully slowed the car so he could get one last word in with de Chastelain before he handed him over.

"Look Pierre–Yves," he said using the lawyer's first name which was the first occasion he had done so in the entire time they had known each other.

"This must be serious Lafarge, or perhaps I too should enter the spirit of the moment and address you as Gaston," said de Chastelaine smiling.

Lafarge gave a short genuine laugh.

"Yup it's funny when old habits get thrown aside, but hey there's no need for formality or indeed hostility between us now, for I'm achieving a lifetime's dream…I'm finally seeing the back of you.

"No more de Chastelain style minute dissections of my evidence, nor character assassinations of me and my colleagues. I should have brought champagne," joked Lafarge which he was glad to see de Chastelain too saw the humourous side.

"However, on a more serious note I swear to you Pierre–Yves that I will go as far as I can to bring either or both Bousquet and von Dirlinger to justice, for what that is worth these days. I will get the utmost pleasure in doing so, as much good it will ultimately do me," he said taking his hand off the wheel and patting de Chastelain on the shoulder.

De Chastelain seemed moved by Lafarge's promise and gulped.

THE TORTURED DETECTIVE

"Listen not that I am hopefully going to my death but this old warrior wouldn't mind a last smoke and a final gulp of cognac if you don't mind.

"Where I'm going cognac may be in short supply and Argentinian liqueur I am not terribly au fait with," he said.

Lafarge willingly provided both, then gestured that they were at journey's end as his eyes having got used to the dark alighted on number 21 and the large double doors that served as an entrance to de Chastelain's temporary haven of safety.

They both climbed out of the car and Lafarge helped de Chastelain with his three suitcases, a number he thought was hopelessly optimistic if the lawyer thought he would be able to take them all on his travels.

Anyways that was for him to debate with 'Dr Eugene' for his role in the escape was now at an end.

He rang the bell and waited until the door swung open creaking on its hinges, and he half expected Bela Lugosi or Boris Karloff to appear out of the darkness.

In the end rather disappointingly in terms of drama it was just the dark bearded dapperly dressed figure of 'Eugene' who emerged and shook both their hands.

"Ah Chief Inspector, good to see you again, although of course in rather unusual circumstances," said a smiling Petiot.

Lafarge smiled too and offered him the case he had been carrying which he took, and rather strangely, to the detective's mind, opened it and looked inside, his face registering disappontment.

"Is there a problem Doctor?" asked Lafarge, who glanced at de Chastelain and saw he was shifting from foot to foot.

Petiot looked glum and a little angry, his brown eyes had lost their warmth.

"I don't see the money," his voice a whisper, but the tone glacial.

Lafarge sighed and gestured at de Chastelain's midriff, the lawyer helping him by lifting up his shirt to reveal the cash strapped round his body, a precautionary measure they had taken with Huariau.

Petiot laughed, Lafarge thought rather hysterically, before leafing through some of the notes attached to de Chastelain. The lawyer didn't look best pleased at having his honesty questioned,

231

quite apart from the fact he was a fugitive standing out in a street in the middle of Paris and with curfew due to come into force soon.

"Very good, very ingenious. Right well then everything is in order, best to get you inside," said Petiot, his air of bonhomie fully restored.

De Chastelain picked up his suitcases and moved inside the courtyard, Lafarge made to follow but Petiot stepped in front of him barring his way.

"No need Chief Inspector, the less you are implicated or know about my operation the better," he said.

"Yes, you are right Doctor." said Lafarge stepping back.

"Please do not worry I will be in touch once he is safely arrived, or at least he will send you a postcard to let you know," smiled Petiot.

"Just one thing Doctor, I was wondering whether you could give me the name of the Argentinian diplomat who is helping you. As you know my wife is the daughter of the Ambassador and I had a mad thought it might be him," said Lafarge grinning.

"I am afraid again I cannot reveal such information, too dangerous for all concerned. Please pass on my regards to your delightful wife, and of course if ever you or she need anything medically please feel free to call on me at my usual address," said Petiot before stepping back to make to close the door.

Lafarge called after de Chastelain, who turned and put down his suitcases before striding back to him and giving him a hug. Then just as quickly he was gone and the door swung back leaving Lafarge staring at it with a strange feeling of loss.

CHAPTER TWENTY THREE

Lafarge awoke from a fitful sleep, which had been dominated by the sad, shocked and tearful faces of the Jews on the buses the day before, to hear loud banging and screams coming from within his apartment building.

At first he thought it was a continuation of his dream, then that it was a fire that had taken hold but he couldn't smell any smoke. He got out of bed and wandered to the door passing a table that bore the evidence of a hard night's smoking and drinking which would have done justice to two people rather than just himself.

He winced as he passed it but it was nothing to how he felt once he opened the door.

Stepping out he peered over the banister, his apartment being on the third of five floors, and looked down to see a family of five, the Berkowitz's, being forced down the stairs by uniformed police, while plainclothes detectives climbed the stairs towards his floor.

He withdrew towards the sanctuary of his flat but it was too late as the detectives were already on the top step and looking at him. He didn't know either of them personally, but he'd seen them around Orfevres and thought they were from the Brigades Speciales.

Both were mid–30's Lafarge reckoned, smartly dressed but with a mean look, one had a bulbous nose, like a boxer turned to heavy drinker, the other was an athletic looking type. The bulbous–nosed one approached him, surprising Lafarge as he looked more like the muscle than the lead cop of the two.

Lafarge told himself to keep cool and not react as he had yesterday because these two looked like they would gladly throw him over the banister and claim he had drawn a gun on them.

"Good morning Chief Inspector Lafarge, I'm Chief Inspector Roland Dumont. Sorry for the noise but some of them get unnecessarily anxious and argumentative when we ask them to come with us," he said smiling revealing a surprisingly good set of teeth.

Lafarge noticed they both had folders in their hands with a list of names hence how they had known who he was, although perhaps too they had taken more care than he had about putting a name to a familiar face at Orfevres.

Lafarge was repelled by the terminology Dumont had used.

He made it sound as if they were being asked gently to go off with their local friendly policeman and answer questions about a run of the mill matter when they were being illegally and brutally thrown out of their homes. Still Lafarge felt it better to hold his hands up and smile amiably before turning his back and going inside his apartment.

He was about to close the door when Dumont's large foot intervened stopping it from doing so.

"Sorry Lafarge, one more thing," said Dumont softly.

Lafarge could barely contain his annoyance, but displaying uncommon patience he swung the door open and stood on the threshold waiting for Dumont to speak.

"Listen we have just three families listed here as being foreign Jews, I was just wondering, you living here and being one of us, you knew whether that was correct or not," said Dumont.

Lafarge kept his composure and did try and rack his brains as to whether there were any others in the building, but truth be told he didn't know. Most of the inhabitants of his block apart from saying hello kept their business to themselves, especially these days, afraid as they were of being denounced for the mildest of slights.

"I have to say I haven't made it a habit of asking someone's religion before conducting a conversation with them, or as a means of vetting them before they took an apartment here, so my answer is I don't know" he replied.

Dumont stepped back, whether it was because of surprise at his colleague's unwelcome disinterest in his neighbours' religious convictions or the smell of stale alcohol Lafarge didn't know and he cared even less.

Dumont didn't look pleased at all and looked to his silent partner as if for an answer of what they should do next, but all he got was an unhelpful shrug of the shoulders. If anything Lafarge thought that the silent one looked is if he would have preferred to be doing something else rather than harassing helpless people.

"Look Lafarge, you may not like what we are doing, but these are orders from our government, from Bousquet himself, and there is no room for flexibility on this. So I am asking you politely one

THE TORTURED DETECTIVE

more time if you know of any others in this building that we need to take away," asked Dumont, his tone firm but civil.

Perfect, thought Lafarge, no flexibility, orders are orders, allowing no moral judgement on the part of the executors of those orders, but he wasn't going to fall into line.

He played it out, scratching his head and even taking time to search in his pocket of his dressing gown for a cigarette, thankfully he found one and then scratched around for a light, which Dumont supplied him with.

"Thank you. Truthfully, flippancy aside, I don't know of any other families living in this building that should be taken away," he said smiling, hoping his equivocal answer wouldn't be picked up by either Dumont or Mr Silent.

He needn't have worried, Dumont appeared happier with the manner of the answer and indicated to his partner that they should move along as the other two families were on a floor above. Dumont yelled down the stairs for the uniforms to come up and help them just in case there was trouble, and thanked Lafarge for his time.

Lafarge at last was able to shut the door and wandered back to the kitchenette where he was able to find enough coffee to make a pot. He left it to come to the boil while he tidied up the drawing room and emptied the ashtray, stashed the bottles down by the stove and washed up the glass.

It was as he was doing this that it came to him.

The fog of the effects of last night's bacchanalian excesses had eased and he smacked his head with his hand cursing himself. For there was a couple down the corridor who he vaguely remembered had a name like Rosenberg, and could not be anything but Jewish.

They had moved in late last year but perhaps their names had not been registered with the local town hall. The constant flux of people moving in and out of different apartment buildings, and a lot of people fleeing, had sorely tested the famed efficiency of French bureaucracy and this seemed to be one instance where it had failed.

Lafarge was surprised that the concierge hadn't provided the police with their names, but then she was an unpredictable character and if they had spoken to her in what she perceived was a patronising manner she would have given them short shrift.

235

Maybe Dumont had left it to his sidekick, whose lack of enthusiasm had led him to ignore her information, or not relay it back to his superior. Whatever Lafarge was going to ensure they didn't fall into their hands just in case their names did crop up from another tenant.

He left the coffee to cool and as quietly as he could he stepped back out into the corridor. He heard Dumont's voice booming out above him, he was on the top floor and having a ferocious argument with the head of the family he was coercing to go with the uniformed men, so Lafarge crept along to four doors down, right at the end of the floor.

He knocked gently and waited, his breathing seemed to echo down the passage which he hoped didn't reach the ears of Dumont, though, he was still engaged in conversation with Papa Horowitz.

To Lafarge's relief the door opened, playing silent inside wouldn't stop Paris's finest from breaking down the door, and Hal Rosenberg's narrow good looking face peered out. He looked surprised and at first relieved to see that it was one of his neighbours but then his face clouded over with despair as he remembered that this neighbour was a policeman.

Realising this must be the case Lafarge put his finger to his lips and gestured to him that he wanted to come in. Rosenberg opened the door wider and Lafarge entered.

He was immediately struck by the beautiful antiques adorning the tables and mantlepiece and striking paintings hanging on the walls and thought this was a collection worth protecting and not giving oneself up lightly.

Mrs Rosenberg appeared from a room to the left of the hall, she was as good looking as her husband, long golden hair surrounding an oval face with a pair of striking brown eyes and a figure as shapely as anything Lafarge had seen in his life.

He had to shake himself away from that splendid sight to focus on what he had to tell them, though, he regretted that Hal Rosenberg was there.

"Mr and Mrs Rosenberg forgive this intrusion. But I feel I have no choice but to warn you that you are in danger and I want you both to follow me and come to my apartment," he said breathlessly.

Naturally both the Rosenberg's looked wild eyed with fright and not a little bemused by their previously anonymous neighbour,

THE TORTURED DETECTIVE

suddenly appearing on their doorstep and urging them to trust him and come with him.

They looked at each other and then at him and asked if they could confer among themselves in the next door room. Lafarge replied in the affirmative but told them not to take too much time as his colleagues might arrive at any moment.

They took a bit longer than he would have liked, but it was for a good reason for both returned 10 minutes later fully–dressed and with a suitcase each.

"We've decided to trust you Chief Inspector, and we hope we will not be disappointed," said Hal.

Lafarge shook both their hands warmly and without further ado opened the door and indicated to them to stay there while he checked if the coast was clear.

He made his way down the corridor, which was around 60 metres long and looked up the stairwell. He could hear Dumont's raised voice as with all pretence at courtesy shunted aside he openly threatened Horowitz.

He could hear a woman shrieking, which he took to be Mrs Horowitz and frailer voices crying while he heard things breaking from within the apartment.

That was good news for the Rosenberg's and himself if not for the Horowitz's so he rushed back to their apartment and gestured for them to follow him.

Hal Rosenberg double locked the door and then the trio made their way slowly down the corridor and with one last look upstairs, and seeing the coast was clear, Lafarge ushered the couple into his apartment.

Once inside Lafarge suddenly came to his senses and wondered what the hell he had done for he had no plan B should Dumont call on him again, although, if he didn't answer they were hardly going to break down a colleague's door.

He looked at the Rosenberg's and then all three of them smiled with relief and as a means of celebrating he served them up a cup of coffee which was just about drinkable. He then beckoned them into the second bedroom, where his children had slept, and told them to stay there until the police had gone.

He returned to the drawing room and then his inquisitiveness getting the better of him he once again went out onto the corridor.

237

The noise had not abated but there was movement as the uniforms dragged the Horowitz children down the stairs while the parents were pushed on their way by Dumont, who was yelling insults at both father and mother.

They passed Lafarge, who had to step back to let them pass, and he ashamed at his inability to help them averted his eyes and stared down at the parquet floor. The looks on their faces as they had come down the stairs, bewilderment and misery from the wife, anger on the face of the husband, were seared into Lafarge's memory.

The three children – the oldest could not have been more than seven – were all in tears and clinging to their teddy bears.

Dumont paused briefly, as he passed Lafarge sighed deeply and shrugged his shoulders, as if to say look at these people they are impossible. Lafarge remained expressionless and simply shut the door on Dumont, of his silent partner there was no sign.

*

Lafarge came upon similar distressing scenes when he walked down Avenue de la Republique, children being led out of their schools and packed into buses, at least the Horowitz's had gone together, these children weren't even given the solace of another family member to accompany them.

Lafarge stopped and watched from the other side of the Avenue, the heart wrenching scenes proving too much for him to just walk by and try and ignore. Indeed people from the apartment buildings which were on the Avenue had poured outside and were like him watching as these innocent young things were escorted sometimes not too gently by the gendarmes.

The teachers offered no resistance.

Some just stood mouths agape, some in tears, on the steps of the entrances to the two schools, that were only a few metres apart, as girls and boys, as young as six, were aggressively plucked from a place which they considered a place of safety and offered them protection.

The children – the eldest of whom were 11 – looked confused and bemused as they were manhandled by people they had largely been brought up to respect and consider protectors into buses that were taking them away to destination unknown.

THE TORTURED DETECTIVE

Most offered little resistance, why would they and indeed how could they, save two cheeky looking lads, their heads covered by caps, who broke away from their two guards. One of the gendarmes held his hand as if he had been bitten by one of the boys, while the schoolboys sped down the road chased by several of the uniformed police.

Despite the police calling out for them to be stopped, not one civilian intervened, and the two then turned left into Rue Servan. Lafarge ran down his side of the Avenue to see the denouement, there was little he could do to interfere and he didn't wish to attract attention now he had a couple of undesirables in his apartment.

Three gendarmes turned into Servan and gave chase, two others halted and breathed in heavily, perhaps wishing to play no part in this unedifying pursuit of two little boys. Lafarge crossed the road and stood on the corner, resisting the urge to venture further down the street.

He couldn't see the two little boys for the three policemen still giving chase crowded out any view of them, but he saw one of the gendarmes withdraw his service pistol and fire a warning shot into the air above where Lafarge took their heads to be.

It didn't appear to have had an effect as the gendarmes continued running, but then to his horror he saw the same one who had fired the warning shot go down on his knees and aim at body height.

Lafarge yelled 'stop stop' but his words either failed to register or were ignored for the gendarme fired off two rounds and then stood up and inserted the gun in his holster. The other two gendarmes looked at him with a mixture of anger and shock on their faces, one made to go for him but was restrained by the other, while from further down the street Lafarge could hear screams.

The trio of gendarmes walked down and returned a little while later and resumed their work at the schools, prompting Lafarge to go and see what had happened to the boys, although he already knew in his heart that it wasn't good.

He arrived to find a crowd gathered round and forcing his way through he saw the two young boys both on the ground, each with a bullet hole in their back.

Both were dead. He felt like throwing up and he staggered to the side of the street and disgorged his guts.

He went into a café just to the right of where the bodies lay and asked the barman whether anyone had rung for an ambulance and he was told yes.

Preferring not to wield his badge as he thought that would not be the best idea he ordered two cognacs, offered one to the barman, who readily accepted, and downed it while he debated whether he should go back and confront the gendarme who had shot the boys.

"Bloody disgraceful what that policeman did, bloody murderer, and to think he is French!" said the barman shaking his head as he dried the glasses.

Lafarge nodded glumly and asked for another cognac which the barman said was on him and refilled both their glasses.

"Thanks. Two little boys, they probably thought it was some sort of game and even if they didn't anyone would run rather than be bundled into a bus without ones parents being there," said Lafarge.

The barman sensing he had a sympathetic ear to bend didn't hold back.

"He should be held to account for that. It's one thing to follow orders and round up children, although it's not something to be proud of, it's quite another to shoot them in the back. I know the Germans are capable of that, I fought against them in the Great War but that Frenchmen should do this, it makes me ashamed! Trouble is there isn't anyone of any stature in the Vichy government who will stand up and take responsibility and tell the Germans it is plain wrong," he said.

Not one normally to take the advice of a barman, save when it came to recommending a particular wine or telling him that he had had enough to drink, Lafarge decided to break the habit and act on it.

He reasoned that the police were unlikely to search his apartment in revenge for what he was about to do. If they were to do so and found the Rosenberg's he would say that they had asked for shelter because they had lost their keys and were waiting for a locksmith to come and let them in.

They had already agreed on this story before he left them in his apartment so on that score he felt confident he could argue his way out of it.

THE TORTURED DETECTIVE

Lafarge found the gendarme lounging against the bus, which was only half–full, with a couple of angry–looking colleagues either side of him.

The gendarme, who looked to be in his early 30's of stocky build and with an oafish face, waved them off dismissively and with a self–satisfied look on his face and turned to Lafarge when he called out to him.

He gestured for Lafarge to give him his papers, which Lafarge ignored as he planted a left hook into his stomach provoking the uniformed policeman to crumple to the ground.

His two colleagues rushed at Lafarge, who quickly flashed his id forcing them to step back. Gasps emanated from the children within the bus, and more erupted when Lafarge pulled his gun while he placed a foot on the felled gendarme's hand so he couldn't reach for his pistol.

"What's your name officer?" shouted Lafarge.

The officer sneered and spat, the spittle staining the lower hem of Lafarge's navy suit trousers. This earned the officer a kick in the ribs, and Lafarge waited patiently for him to recover his breath before asking him again.

"Captain Monnet you prick!" he replied wheezing.

Lafarge ignored the insult.

"Right Captain Monnet, I am Chief Inspector Lafarge from Quai des Orfevres and I have the great pleasure to arrest you for the murder of the two boys in Rue Servan. So up on your feet and put your hands behind your back," said Lafarge, his voice trembling.

Lafarge gestured with his pistol for the policeman to get up, and asked one of the other two gendarmes to relieve Monnet of his gun just in case his temper got the better of his judgement.

This done Lafarge withdrew his handcuffs and snapped them around Monnet's hands and walked him back down to his apartment building where he had left his car, as he had preferred to walk to work, leaving Monnet's subordinates stunned at what had just taken place.

*

The reaction from the desk sergeant at headquarters was equally one of surprise and it took Lafarge a quarter–of–an–hour to persuade him to book Monnet and throw him in a cell.

241

The sergeant, who was one of the rare policemen that Lafarge enjoyed cordial relations with, took him aside, after he had Monnet taken away. He warned him that his chances of getting the two gendarmes to testify or even produce a statement regarding the incident were slim. Lafarge had smiled and replied he knew but he couldn't let an act of cold blooded murder go unnoticed.

Lafarge didn't have to wait long before there was reaction from up above. Sitting in his office, drinking a cup of coffee, Bousquet's deputy, the equally objectionable Jean Leguay, who had followed his boss from the Marne where he had been his assistant when Bousquet was the Prefect, came storming in.

"What the fuck do you think you're doing Lafarge! Interfering in state business is an offence. I am ordering you to go downstairs and apologise to Captain Monnet and then you are to present yourself at the secretary–general's office," he shouted.

Lafarge's colleagues pretended not to hear, continuing on with their business, bur he jumped to his feet, heart pumping, and approached Leguay.

"He shot two boys in the back which to anyone's mind, well those that are real policemen, is a capital offence. You should be preparing the guillotine for him not demanding I go and apologise, which for your information I am bloody well not going to do," said Lafarge.

Leguay waved his finger angrily at Lafarge brushing the tip of the detective's nose.

"You better do what I said Lafarge or otherwise I will have you replace Monnet in the cells," he said coldly.

Lafarge laughed and brushed past Leguay.

"Well Mr Deputy after what I have seen the past two days I think you are the one who belongs in the cells.

"You disgust me, but I tell you what, I will do one thing you asked me to and that is go and see your boss. Not to discuss the rights and wrongs of state orders but another matter that also involves murder but which has nothing to do with you," sneered Lafarge, who made his way out of the office leaving Leguay to mutter some expletive–filled invective aimed at him.

Lafarge stormed around to Bousquet's office where he told the secretary that he had been ordered to see him, whereupon she

THE TORTURED DETECTIVE

looked rather uncomfortable and asked him if he could leave his pistol with her before entering the room.

Lafarge handed it over and she put it in the top drawer before rising and ushering him in.

Bousquet was sitting behind his desk and on the phone but gestured for Lafarge to take a seat opposite him.

Lafarge indicated towards the drinks cabinet to which Bousquet nodded and relieved Lafarge helped himself to a large cognac. It could be the last one he enjoyed for a while given he had had to surrender his gun and their meeting was to take place in a confrontational manner on opposite sides of the desk.

Bousquet, though, appeared to be in a rather better mood than his pitbull Leguay, or at least on the phone he was. The conversation intermittently littered with bursts of laughter and also with smiles of satisfaction spreading across Bousquet's handsome narrow face.

Lafarge had no earthly idea who his boss was talking to but whoever it was was obviously a superior, one who was heaping praise on his subordinate.

Eventually Bousquet replaced the receiver after a final 'thank you Karl' and giving Lafarge one of his opaque looks he lit a cigarette and smoked half of it before he addressed him.

"Well that was the pleasant part of the morning Lafarge. I have received the official thanks on a job well done from Himmler's representative here Karl Oberg. July 16 and 17 will be days in the years to come that French people will look on with as much pride as July 14, we could make it several days of national holidays starting with Bastille Day," he said, a self–satisfied smile creasing his features.

"Yes indeed Bastille Day followed by holidays to remember 'Operation Spring Breeze'. A delightful name don't you think for our well–planned operation over the past two days, when we have liberated our compatriots of an evil as dangerous to their wellbeing as the revolutionaries were to the Bourbon Monarchy.

"I should really draw up a statement of gratitude to issue to all the men who participated, though, of course I will have it posted in public as well, but I will leave that till later," he said purring like a cat that had had its stomach tickled.

Lafarge felt nothing but revulsion for the man opposite him. Disappointment had long faded from his list of feelings towards

243

Bousquet, who had allowed his ambition to override any sense of morality and used his undoubted administrative talent and energy to be directed into aiding and now actively enforcing the crimes of the Nazis.

However, his self–righteous belief was such that he probably thought he was doing nothing wrong and just helping France to get a better deal from the Germans eventually.

Whatever the reasons Lafarge knew that he was sitting rather lonely on the other side of this large moral divide and that anything he said to the contrary of what Bousquet believed would only make his situation worse.

Nevertheless, he wasn't one now for biting his tongue, things had gone too far on either side for there to be any need of diplomacy. Besides he wasn't totally helpless as he had evidence that could ruin his superior's career if he were to be allowed to bring it up.

Bousquet had helped himself to a drink and returned to his desk. He pushed to one side several files that lay heaped on his desk and placed a decanter of cognac on the now cleared space. He then settled back in his chair, steepling his fingers, and looked intently into Lafarge's face.

"So Lafarge I won't bring up your behaviour from this morning, I think that it is clear how I felt about it, and besides you are not here for that reason," he said his gaze not leaving Lafarge's face, though, the detective didn't flinch and stared straight back at him.

"So, what I would like to know Lafarge is where is de Chastelain? Unless he has withered into a small enough object for you to carry in your pocket I don't see any sign of him," said Bousquet.

Lafarge simply smiled.

"Well I would have thought you would be congratulating me Bousquet. I half expected to see him waiting for me in your office, unless of course you are going to click your fingers and he is going to pop out of the cupboard, or is he in the decanter?" said Lafarge, content to see Bousquet's confused look.

"Why on earth would you have expected to see him here Lafarge? It was you who brought him back from Limoges, and since then he has not been seen," said Bousquet.

"Well I wouldn't have thought that any Parisian policemen would have been looking for anyone other than those with yellow

THE TORTURED DETECTIVE

stars on their clothes to be honest, secretary–general," said Lafarge.

Bousquet blanched and looked away for a second. Surely not embarrassment thought Lafarge, not from the always so assured head of police.

"Where the hell is he!" hissed Bousquet.

"Well I want you to answer that one because I handed him over to two of your men at Austerlitz yesterday morning. They presented their ID, we had a couple of drinks at the bar and then they went off with de Chastelain. Ask the barman, he will confirm it," said Lafarge settling back into the hard leather chair.

Bousquet snorted with derision at the response, but then picked up the phone, ordering whoever was at the other end to go to Austerlitz and get confirmation from the barman.

Lafarge hoped the barman was on duty otherwise he envisaged a long night ahead of him probably in the cell that the murderer Monnet had vacated. Silence descended for a moment as Bousquet pondered what to ask next, whatever it was it would make uncomfortable listening for him.

"Well as he is not here to tell his story, why don't you enlighten me Lafarge?" he said.

Lafarge cleared his throat, took a gulp of cognac and refilled his glass, before he related to Bousquet the story as he had been told it word for word by de Chastelain, who he hoped was already well away from Paris.

Bousquet listened poker–faced, initially silently but as the details got to involve him more he started making grunting noises, shaking his head vehemently and running one of his fingers across his mouth. Lafarge consoled himself that as yet he hadn't run his finger across his throat, although, such a thuggish gesture probably wasn't part of his repartee.

Lafarge left nothing out, which he had never intended to do anyway, but he could see that by the end Bousquet was starting to look uncomfortable.

"Perhaps it's best if he doesn't turn up then," he said smiling.

"However, I hope he does so I can repudiate every single thing he told you.

"It's not just a case of my status against that of a discredited lawyer, it's because it is the truth. I did not murder Marguerite

245

Suchet and furthermore any connection between me and the jewellery burglary is quite ridiculous. What on earth would I be doing getting mixed up in something as tawdry as that?" he said.

"I don't know Bousquet. But all I will say is I would never have imagined you, despite my personal animosity towards you, of being responsible for what I have seen take place over the past two days. So yes I believe de Chastelain's version of events," said Lafarge.

Bousquet recoiled at that, a furious look in his eyes, and drummed his fingers on the desk.

"Lafarge, be careful. You are on precarious territory here, the dossier on you is large enough that you don't want to push me so far that I take the severest action against you, regardless of your father's position," said Bousquet.

Lafarge sighed and laughed bitterly.

"What's so amusing? You seriously thought you could accuse me of murder without any possible consequence. You really are delusional!" said Bousquet.

"Well it is interesting that you have not even offered an alternative account or an alibi for that night, nor have you even shot down this story, " said Lafarge.

"All you have done is utter threats and use your position as defences. Now I know you were never a policeman but this should be obvious to anyone. When confronted with such an accusation, one that I haven't actually uttered yet, the suspect has a viable account of their movements at the time of the crime," said Lafarge coolly.

Bousquet was obviously not prepared for Lafarge refusing to back down and looked flustered as he sought to come back at his subordinate.

"Please take your time. After all I'm not going anywhere yet, oh, and before you start thinking of disposing of me I have noted down everything and put it in a safe place," lied Lafarge.

Bousquet didn't reply or display any emotion, his intelligent technocratic brain searching outside the narrow confines of imagination that such people possessed for a plausible answer. Lafarge doubted he would come up with one.

"Listen Lafarge I'm sorry but I'm not prepared to account to you for my whereabouts on that night.

THE TORTURED DETECTIVE

"I have no compulsion to do so. Indeed I find it reprehensible that you should have the temerity to suspect such a thing of me when in fact you are here to answer serious questions over your own behaviour in the past month," said Bousquet.

Lafarge groaned and held his hands up making to get up and leave, for he wasn't going to endure the risible experience of a murder suspect give him a lecture about observing the law and on morality.

"Sit down Lafarge, you are going to hear me out and then you can leave," ordered Bousquet.

Lafarge smiled grimly and sat back down, but afforded himself one more glass of Bousquet's excellent cognac to which his superior raised his eyebrows.

"Perhaps your drinking has got the better of you. I see before me a man who is losing his sense of where his priorities lie, someone who is increasingly intransigent, impudent and also unpredictable.

"Perhaps you should seek a cure for your attachment to drink," said Bousquet contemptuously.

"What now you want me committed? Or you want me to seek a cure at the baths in Vichy? I think they already have a full complement of sick people down there, incurably collaborationist I think they term the illness.

"I wouldn't want to catch that, I mean even you don't spend all your time down there for that reason," said Lafarge.

To his surprise Bousquet laughed, for him it appeared to be a genuine one.

"Anyway Bousquet touched as I am by your concern for my well being, I feel perfectly fine. Yes, I drink a lot, I always have done, the nature of the job incites one to do so, you can't deal with misery on a daily basis and not become immune to it. So drink rather than other diversions suits me fine thank you," he said.

"In any case I am surprised that you haven't become an alcoholic given the orders you draw up and issue from this office. My you must be a hard man to be able to dismiss all you do so glibly," said Lafarge.

"That's not for you to comment on Lafarge. What you have reacted to so emotionally both in Limoges and here is simply putting into effect laws that have been brought in under the new

247

government. What I am doing is simply executing them," said Bousquet.

"Nicely put. Anyway before you cut me off and lecture me further I would just like to put on the record that what you have done is execute laws that no civilized country would ever dream of imposing.

"I don't know if you think you are the re–incarnation of St Just but I would remind you that he ended up being guillotined, that's how far his lust for blood under the pretext of flimsy laws got him.

"The people will have enough of you as they will have enough of our conquerors. Then there will be nobody to protect you from the vengeful mob. Believe me I got a taste of it today when Monnet shot those boys in cold blood, the crowd were not supportive of his actions at all," said Lafarge.

"Maybe, but they did nothing, right? That is the nature of the people, they may not like what they see but they also prefer firm leadership and government. Overall they are getting just that, not the pathetic ineffectual government that led us to humiliating defeat and who directed over nothing but chaos before the war," said Bousquet.

Bousquet shrugged and picked up one of the files on his desk, a large one as he had told Lafarge and at least on that score he had not been lying, and opened it.

"Fine words Lafarge, that I do give you credit for. However, you will find it hard to come up with the right ones for the following misdemeanours, and there I am being unnecessarily generous, that you have committed since you left for Limoges," said Bousquet with a smug smile.

"Please I'm all ears."

"Preventing the interrogation of a couple of terrorists, one of whom subsequently died before information could be fully extracted from him, as you had had him removed with his accomplice to hospital.

"Secondly abusing an officer of the Brigades Speciales for carrying out his duty, though, he has decently said that a verbal reprimand would suffice," said Bousquet his pompous disapproval drifting through the air so densely Lafarge all but ducked to avoid it.

THE TORTURED DETECTIVE

How kind of de Blaeckere mused Lafarge sarcastically to have just asked for a verbal reprimand, must remember to thank him when I get to see him next.

"Thirdly having listened to the recorded conversation between yourself and the lawyer Gerland we have strong suspicions that it was a coded warning not to be at the house when the attack took place.

"However having interviewed Gerland, and given him credit for delivering de Chastelain, regrettably for the moment we are willing to accept that it is indeed linked to your impending divorce with Isabella," said Bousquet.

"Well that's very kind of you to believe that somebody might have other matters to deal with even at a time of war. As you well know Isabella is clinical when it is time to rid herself of an unwanted man," said Lafarge, reveling in the pain that would have caused Bousquet.

Bousquet, though, ignored the remark.

"Where are we? Ah yes, fourthly consorting and sleeping with an enemy of the state, the actress thingy, Aimee. However, again you get the benefit of the doubt because you provided evidence of a terrorist cell and its location and which proved to be both true and extremely rich in information.

"Before you ask, no, we didn't get Aimee. She appeared to have scarpered, but it was her brother and sister–in–law who provided the background on your affair. They cursed Aimee for having allowed you to come to the farm house, and no doubt she does too now.

"As for them they weren't as lucky as she was, they were executed but not till after giving us information on other cells in the area which de Blaeckere acted on and achieved notable success.

"It was fortunate we got them alive as there were two others hiding in a barn. They were burnt to death as they refused to come out and de Blaeckere was obliged to try and smoke them out.

"Returning to your actress friend, though, I would warn you to be careful Lafarge as she could turn out to be a more effective enemy than even myself," said Bousquet a broad grin covering his face.

Lafarge was pleased in one way that Aimee had escaped. But he could see Bousquet's point should they meet again it wouldn't be a cosy nostalgic chat but potentially a lethal encounter.

"What advice would you give me then Bousquet? You seem to know the most effective manner in dealing with vengeful actresses.

"Was that what Marguerite was bitter about? Something you had done, probably to do with de Chastelain," said Lafarge.

Bousquet's narrow pallid face went red as he realized he had made an error in commenting on Aimee and her coming after Lafarge.

"As I said Lafarge we are not here to pepper the air with false accusations, it was merely a humourous aside my remark about the actress.

"Now let's move on as time is pressing and I have to meet with my men to get a more in–depth debriefing about how today went. Apart from Monnet's unjustified detention I don't know too much else," he said drily.

"Well I'm sure the rest of the children went along like little lambs," said Lafarge.

Bousquet flashed him a look of such visceral hatred that for once Lafarge thought better of saying anything. Let his conscience, if he has one, eat away at him. That is the best solution.

"Fifthly and I think finally there is to compound everything the disappearance of de Chastelain, but that is in abeyance until we receive confirmation or not from the barman.

"Perhaps it will be one time you can congratulate yourself on having stopped for a drink," said Bousquet.

Lafarge lit a cigarette and remained silent, save from tapping a leg of the chair with one of his feet. Bousquet stayed in his chair, filled his glass with cognac and unexpectedly poured one for Lafarge.

However, that apart not a word passed between them. They were like two strangers sat waiting for a train that might never arrive, though, they both wished that it would.

Lafarge spent most of the time observing Bousquet. He was trying to keep busy by leafing through folders, the fate of the people listed in them a mere signature away from death dependent on the mood of the man wielding the pen.

THE TORTURED DETECTIVE

Someone no doubt like Arnaud Lescarboura. He could expect little in the way of salvation from one of the men implicated in what he had thought was a get rich quick run of the mill burglary but had evolved into a deadly affair of state corruption.

Bousquet looked completely at ease with himself, going about his business with a matter of fact air. He showed little emotion, save for calls that came from his good friend Abetz, and one from René de Chambrun, whose parents Lafarge recalled had been in the photo with Marguerite the night of the dinner at Maxim's.

Finally the phone rang for a third time and on this occasion Bousquet's tone took on an official air. He listened intently for a couple of minutes, then thanked the caller and hung up. He looked at Lafarge and smiled.

"Well Lafarge you are fortunate for the barman supports your version of events. He says that the two men presented themselves and flashed IDs and after some lively conversation, mainly between you and de Chastelain, they departed with him. So again you get the benefit of the doubt," said Bousquet clearly disappointed.

Lafarge was hugely relieved, he hadn't expected the barman to back him so thoroughly and made a note of returning there some time and giving him a huge tip.

This time he was ready to leave and he sensed Bousquet couldn't wait for him to be gone so he rose and picked up his hat but was stopped in his tracks.

"That is not quite all Lafarge. You may not be facing charges, for we don't have enough cast iron proof to hold you on the most serious offences. But in view of your overall behaviour it is my duty to dismiss you from the police force for good," said Bousquet his tone clipped.

Lafarge felt a surge of relief course through his body, for it was the least worst result he could have hoped for once he handed over his gun to the secretary.

Of course he was angry that he, an honest policeman, should be sacked but as Huariau had said there was no room for them anymore. That being said there were good men like Broglie around but they were able to play the game better than he and Gerland's man were capable of doing.

251

He was exhausted too and there was a grain of truth in what Bousquet had said that his drinking was becoming a problem, no matter that he thought he could control it.

Time away and with the family could rectify that and rebuild his strength. But it wasn't going to deter him from solving the Suchet case one day and Bousquet surely knew that. Just to be sure he disabused any notion the police chief might have had of it being to the contrary.

"Bousquet you may feel that you are untouchable and I may be as popular here as a pork chop in a synagogue – a phrase no doubt that pleases you – at the moment but things will change. The war will turn in the Allies' favour and then you may ask yourself whether it hadn't been better to side with the terrorists as you disparagingly refer to them.

"For the record I am not a member of the Resistance. But from what I have seen in the past two days there are many like me who will have been persuaded that yours is not the right way and that the answer to our future lies across the channel.

"But before that day comes Bousquet I will be back here in the same office and I will hold you to account for your part in Marguerite Suchet's murder. For if I am certain of one thing it is that you are involved to the extent that criminal charges should be brought.

"I will grant you a certain amount of capital for handling my charges with a surprising equanimity and fairness, qualities I thought you no longer possessed. But that does not mean I will forget the case nor will it prevent me from bringing to account those who I believe to be guilty.

"You can be judged by a higher person than myself for those actions you have permitted in your role as head of the police, but on one case of murder I will be the man responsible for your fall."

With that Lafarge opened the door and left.

He passed briefly by the office to collect some personal items and without so much as a goodbye even to Massu he rode the lift down to the ground floor, stepped out into the sunlit afternoon and breathed his first breath of Parisian air as a liberated man.

THE TORTURED DETECTIVE

PART TWO

CHAPTER TWENTY–FOUR

"Please wait here Gaston while I go and see if the Marshal is ready to see you," said Pierre Lafarge.

The former chief inspector smiled and took a seat in the lobby of the Hotel du Parc Majestic where Petain and his increasingly isolated and delusional Vichy government held court.

Despite the decline in their power the hotel still buzzed with activity. Well–dressed men and women strutted to and fro with folders under their arms, no doubt with reams of grandiose statements inside them ready to be signed and counter–signed by the relevant ministers.

Whether any of them made any difference to how the country was run was a moot point as the Germans now controlled all of France.

With their usual sense of trampling over history and symbolic dates, the Nazis had taken over the Vichy controlled part of France on November 11 of 1942, Armistice Day when the last World War had finally come to an end with the defeat of the Germans and their allies.

Fifteen months had passed since Lafarge had been dismissed by Bousquet, and they had been long but useful ones for him.

Walks with the children and Isabella in the afternoons, early dinner usually in their large house, paid for not by him but by her father, and then long hours reading or listening to his wife play the piano, had restored the bonds both matrimonial and paternal.

However, lately he had started to brood and resume his heavy drinking.

His festering resentment at the manner in which he had been drummed out of the police force, at the behest of a man who he suspected of conspiracy to burgle and perhaps murder, had resurfaced.

His mood hadn't been lightened by the sight of Bousquet appearing in a photograph with Leguay and SS officers in Marseille prior to the southern metropolis' own experience of 'Le Rafle' – not something that one entered to win a prize – but the term used for rounding up the Jews in the city.

THE TORTURED DETECTIVE

Not that you would have known the Vel D'Hiv in Paris had been used as a temporary prison for the Jews rounded up in Paris. Just three months after 'Operation Spring Breeze' the great and the good – the term of course used by Lafarge in its most sarcastic form – had trooped there to watch a European welterweight title fight featuring France's darling Marcel Cerdan.

His fight with Jose Ferrer was at least fought on equal terms – less blood spilt too – as opposed to the cycling tracks' previous 'show' the incarceration of unarmed Jews by armed gendarmes. But by September with the blood dried or washed away it was as if it had never happened.

Lafarge, though, had not forgotten about those crimes or the one he had been close to solving before his investigation had been unsatisfactorily interrupted. Even, though, Bousquet had said that he would put someone else onto the case, Lafarge had never heard from his replacement so he concluded it had simply been dropped.

Lafarge bided his time and eventually told Isabella that he was going to try to get reinstated by using his father's influence over Petain. That way Bousquet could not block his return, even if the secretary–general sneered about the Marshal to the Germans he was still technically in his post thanks to Petain and was therefore obliged to obey his orders.

Thus Lafarge now found himself in the lobby awaiting his audience with the hero of a previous war, who now looked like he was going to end this one as a villain. Unfortunately for Petain the Nazis were taking a beating almost everywhere, from the desert in North Africa to the Eastern Front where the Soviets had not caved in as had looked likely to start with and now had the upper hand.

The war was not over, far from it, but that crucial moment where one could say the tide had 'turned incontrovertibly' had arrived and this Lafarge hoped would help his case. It might also make Bousquet's position that bit weaker.

His father Pierre was a lifelong civil servant who had risen to a prominent position and had married a wealthy banker's daughter.

However, despite his closeness to the Marshal it hadn't stopped several members of his wife's family being rounded up after being falsely denounced as having Jewish blood, and only released by payment of a large fee to Bousquet and De Brinon.

This had hardly warmed relations between the Lafarge family and Bousquet and on the several occasions Pierre and Antoinette Lafarge had visited Isabella and himself, Lafarge had played upon this with his father and pleaded with him to get him reinstated or at least facilitate an audience with Petain.

Aided by his mother – whose hatred of Bousquet even out–rivalled his own – they had succeeded in persuading Pierre to circumvent Laval. He had convinced Petain that Bousquet and his Prime Minister were colluding in trying to have him replaced as Head of State with the latter taking his position and Bousquet becoming Prime Minister.

Petain didn't take much convincing as the Germans had already once forced him humiliatingly to recall Laval after he had dismissed him.

With the Prime Minister being Bousquet's political godfather Petain knew where the latter's loyalties lay.

He remained loyal even though he had been undermined by Laval's enthusiastic embracing of the Germans' idea to raise a new French militia, called the Milice, as he agreed the police were not to be trusted with both the French people's and Germans' security.

Several of these diehard ideological loyallists now guarded the hotel and some stood outside the lifts by the lobby, their long floppy blue berets distinguishing them from the other uniformed security forces.

Lafarge espied Laval at one point across the lobby, typically a cigarette was hanging from his mouth, while he held his silver–topped cane in his hand and dictated some comment or statement to his harassed looking secretary.

Laval thankfully didn't notice him and if he had done he did not give any indication he had recognized him otherwise he might have insisted on his being present at the meeting.

Eventually he walked off into the hotel bar accompanied by some German officers and their lady friends, he was not going to be defecting from his friends any time soon, Lafarge ventured. In any case it would be impossible for him to do so as he had stated publicly on the radio the year before that he was praying for a German victory as the alternative was Bolshevism.

Time Magazine's man of the year of 1931 had no hope of a repeat honour mused Lafarge, more likely the next time he featured on

THE TORTURED DETECTIVE

the magazine's front cover it would be in a rogue's gallery line–up.

Finally his father returned and gestured to him to come with him. As they went up in the lift he patted his arm sympathetically and told him everything should be alright, though, the Marshal was sometimes, because of his age, inclined to lose his temper as he forgot things.

Lafarge Junior nodded and braced himself for his first ever meeting with the hero of Verdun, who had saved France once but now faced ignominy and vilification for the manner in which he had tried and failed to save the French a second time.

Petain's office bore no relation to Bousquet's. It was much smaller and certainly less ornate and Lafarge could not see a drinks cabinet, although he was not to be disappointed as the Marshal's military aide asked him if he would like a drink to which he readily said yes and ordered a cognac.

Petain himself was not there yet. He finally emerged from a little side door dressed in his blue Marshal's uniform, looking younger than his 80 plus years, his blue eyes alert, and his handshake was firm while he held the taller Lafarge in the eyes with a steady gaze.

Lafarge remained standing until Petain offered him to take a seat and both sat silent for a few minutes, Lafarge sipping his cognac while the Marshal fiddled with several pieces of paper, browsing through them before placing them neatly in front of him.

"Well Lafarge I hear you want to return to Paris and make a nuisance of yourself again," he said with a twinkle in his eye.

Lafarge smiled and brought out his cigarette case and asked the Marshal if he could smoke to which he nodded.

"I think Lafarge that once you get to my age and having fought one major war, not to mention subdued an uprising in Morocco, and led the country in a second one that if you haven't already been taken by a bullet a cigarette isn't going to make much of a difference," he said.

"I take your point Marshal. Now with regard to Paris, yes, I am keen to return there and to resume my duties because I feel frustrated that I was not able to resolve the case I was working on at the time of my unfair dismissal," said Lafarge laying the emphasis on unfair.

Petain said nothing and opened the folder that lay before him.

"I have to say Lafarge that reading the report filed by the secretary–general about your behaviour and suspect activities it gives me little in the way of justification of restoring you to your previous post.

"To be frank it makes for grim reading and if you had been serving under me I am certain I would not have been so lenient as Bousquet in simply dismissing you," said the Marshal.

Lafarge shivered a little as he didn't doubt that he would have been facing a firing squad rather than a reunion with his family if it had been Petain's choice. However, he wasn't going to let Bousquet's one–sided report be the end of the matter.

"I would insist sir that this report is heavily biased and is based on personal animosity and also self–interest in that Bousquet was one of the main suspects in the case I was investigating," said Lafarge.

"These allegations that he has included in his report he even cleared me over them, but I see he has still seen fit to include these calumnies.

Petain waved his hands as if to calm him down, Lafarge hoped it was that and he was not being dismissed.

"Come come Lafarge. Do you really think a man as ambitious as Bousquet would risk ruining his career, not to say putting his life at risk, by murdering some harlot who advanced her career through her good looks and her body," said the Marshal.

Lafarge wasn't enjoying this meeting at all. His father's confidence appeared to have been dreadfully misplaced, for so far he had been told he would have been shot and had had his defence dismissed out of hand. He didn't see how he could convince the Marshal that he justified being sent back to Paris.

"All I can say Marshal is that my talents lie in being a detective, my record clearly shows I am very good at what I do. My instinct and the evidence I had collated told me that unfortunately for your government one of its senior members and rising stars was heavily implicated in the murder, not to say also the burglary that preceded it," said Lafarge.

Petain took a sip of what looked like water and swirled it round his mouth as he pondered what Lafarge had said. Lafarge by contrast lit another cigarette and took a gulp of the cognac.

THE TORTURED DETECTIVE

"Very well Lafarge. However, the one pertinent witness to these tawdry unwholesome events is now I believe no longer in our custody and could even be outside our jurisdiction.

"If that is the case, what use is it me provoking trouble with Bousquet and by extension Prime Minister Laval in sending you back to Paris where all you can do is repeat the same things and still without a witness?" said Petain.

Lafarge tugged at his lip, reflecting that no wonder this old bugger held the Germans at Verdun, he didn't give a bloody inch even in debate.

"Well there is not a lot I can say to that. Save there is other means and another witness who can at least verify most of what de Chastelain said to me.

"There is also a German officer from the Abwehr, who I need to speak to again as I believe he too is involved.

"Finally with regard to the burglary, the burglar, Arnaud Lescarboura, could still be alive despite being transported abroad. I would ask you to demand his return so I can speak to him again and offer him guarantees that I was unable to the previous time we spoke," said Lafarge.

Petain sighed and stroked the back of his bald dome.

"In terms of demanding the return of this burglar, you are asking the impossible," said Petain.

"Why last year when I was in a stronger position I couldn't even get an old friend Senator Pierre Masse released by the Germans. They replied saying that under no circumstances would they release one of the most dangerous Jews in Europe.

"Do you really think now that they have taken control of the whole of France they will listen to me and go looking for a common jewel thief among the millions of people that have been sent to Germany or to the East!

"On the other hand Lafarge, thanks to your father's undying loyalty to me during the time here, where he has shielded me as much as he could from these petty little court disputes and intrigues and alerted me to any possibility of revolt, I am prepared to allow you to go back to Paris," he said.

"I am not, however, doing it out of altruistic reasons, because I don't think you have a solid enough case against Bousquet.

"The thought that you might also seek to bring down this Colonel von Dirlinger, yes Lafarge I know his name for I have read the full report, fills me with horror on your behalf. I don't know if you have a death wish but if you do I believe that I am fulfilling it for you by agreeing to your reinstatement.

"Furthermore you will be doing me a service as it is time that Laval had his wings clipped. By taking Bousquet out of circulation you will be achieving that goal for me because he has been his eyes and ears up in Paris and has also collaborated with him to perpetrate crimes that have shamed France.

"I have played my role in those I agree but I did not order them. The hero of Verdun disappeared a while ago, but I still possess some fight in me and if it is just to see Laval humiliated a bit then I am willing to help.

"It is bizarre isn't it how destinies don't pan out the way that they look like doing.

"Look what would have happened if all three of us had died before the war. I would have received a state funeral, Laval would have been revered for having been a great statesman and Bousquet would have been feted for the Legion d'Honneur for extraordinary courage he showed at the age of 20 for saving all those people in the floods.

"Now all that probably awaits us are paupers' graves and the enmity of the French people. It would be funny if only it weren't so damn tragic," said Petain a sad smile on his lips mirrored by the look in his eyes.

Lafarge didn't know what to say, the unlikeliest of solutions had been delivered and yet he was being told that it was most likely leading to his own demise but in doing so he would be helping the old man in front of him.

He helped himself to another cognac, the bottle having been helpfully left on the tray. Reluctant as he was to admit it, he had to agree with Petain over his self–pitying soliloquy about the trio of Vichyistes. The irony was that having thrown his lot in with the Nazis, Petain's finest moment in winning the last War was for obvious reasons not permitted to be celebrated anymore.

He raised his glass not in honour of them but to thank the Marshal, downed it in one, and thought to himself I will be

THE TORTURED DETECTIVE

responsible for the downfall of one of them at least and that will salve my conscience.

I am not going to my death, thought Lafarge, I am going to my salvation and that is the destruction of Bousquet.

CHAPTER TWENTY FIVE

Lafarge sauntered down the corridor feeling extremely happy with himself, only to be stopped by his father and ushered into his tiny little office.

The only redeeming factor about the small room was that it had two windows, which allowed a lot of light in. This was crucial these days as there were constant power cuts, a good analogy for France's present government thought Lafarge.

His father poured them both a large cognac and gestured for Gaston to sit in a comfortable armchair, while he sat on an unstable looking wooden chair.

"So you got your wish then?" asked Pierre, his full head of silver hair gleaming in the midday light.

Gaston nodded and thanked him for his help, while mentioning almost as an aside that Petain had said he was probably sending him to his death.

"Well Gaston I believe he may be correct. I think you are being stubborn and foolish in insisting in resolving this case which quite honestly can sit gathering dust until the war is over, and not cost me one of my sons," said Pierre.

"Don't be so pessimistic papa, I am returning at a good time when Bousquet is not the force he was and this Abwehr colonel, well I am not sure yet how deeply involved he was. If it is just the burglary then I might let it slide.

"I am more interested as to whether you have had any news of Leon," Gaston asked referring to his brother.

"The limited news I get he seems to still be alive, so let us hope that remains the case. I just pray that if we all survive the war that he will still talk to me," said Pierre.

"Yes, well it looks like he will be the one who collects the victor's spoils now, doesn't it, so we will have to kneel before him," said Gaston dryly.

"As for Vanessa, well all I hear is bad stories about her lover Bonny and his gang of thugs. You know that Lafont has actually sworn an oath to Hitler and goes round wearing SS uniform! I mean we may have collaborated in the interests, rightly or wrongly for

THE TORTURED DETECTIVE

France, but this common criminal has gone beyond the pale," said Pierre grimacing.

"Vanessa of course thinks it is all hilarious and fun, of course she would as she is getting rich from all their crimes.

"She won't find it so amusing if the Resistance get hold of her. I keep on telling her to break off with Bonny but she refuses to contemplate any such thing. She always was a bloody fool," he added.

Gaston nodded in agreement but truth be told he couldn't feel the slightest bit of sympathy for his sister, who had always sought out the richest man in the room or the most powerful and paid scant regard to advice from her family.

She deserved a good lesson and he told his father as much.

"However, Gaston don't you think that this girl, Suchet, deserves about as much sympathy as Vanessa. Ok von Dirlinger might not be in the same category of criminality as Bonny but he is still a German and that girl must have been aware of the risks she ran of consorting with him," said Pierre.

"Your mother and I are concerned that perhaps this case has had a detrimental effect on your health and your mind.

"Antoinette of course detests Bousquet as much as you do, but she isn't risking her life by opposing him so openly and in accusing him of a capital crime.

"If you think that by achieving a condemnation of Bousquet that you will receive clemency or better justice from the Allies should they win then I think you will be sorely disappointed.

"You have after all served the regime, and done so after returning as a prisoner of war which should have convinced you not to work alongside the Germans," said Pierre.

Gaston was irritated by his father taking the moral high ground, given he had collaborated at a much higher level than he had done, and after all he had been spending most of his time back in the police deliberately ignoring dubious orders.

As for his mother he could barely believe that after helping him convince his father to talk to Petain now she was anxious for him to return to Nice and see out the war performing mundane domestic duties.

"Papa I will speak openly with you. Your lecture would be all the more effective if it was not for the fact you have spent the majority of the war bending over for the Nazis, allowing your superior to pass laws that would have shamed Robespierre and the Committee for Public Safety during the Terror," said Gaston.

He could see his remarks had angered his father but he persisted.

"I mean if you had seen what I did in July last year. Your secretary general of police, the man chosen by Petain, implementing acts that made me physically sick and ashamed of being French then you would regret ever being associated with this regime, this joke of a government that exists here.

"I think that you would do well to visit one of the spas here and cleanse yourself of the crimes that have been committed in France's name not just by the Nazis but willingly by Frenchmen.

"You can sneer at Lafont and Bonny, and by god they are execrable, but don't you dare use them as a moral guide, for you have made them possible.

"You and Petain hide behind the fact that laws were passed so they are legal, well I'm sorry but what democratic body passed them, did the people vote for them?

"No, an elderly former war hero and a bunch of second rate ideologues and profiteers voted to pass them into law, even decreeing Jews were no longer entitled to be French citizens before it was asked of them by the Germans.

"So don't sit there and preach to me about Marguerite Suchet and was she worth risking one's life for," said Gaston.

His father looked shocked at this outburst, but he pulled himself together and stood up.

"Gaston, you are my son and I love you because of that. However, your comments are reprehensible and go beyond what a son should say to one's father, a man who has always served France as he believes is best," said Pierre his tone calm but glacial.

"I cannot allow you to remain here and continue to insult me and one of France's finest men. But for him France and its allies would have lost the last War.

"We have stood and done our best again for France while others fled across the water and moaned and whined and falsely claimed they were the government in waiting. We have remained to try and give the young of France a future albeit in the hardest of circumstances.

THE TORTURED DETECTIVE

"Yes, certain things have taken place, which are, in normal times, illegal but we decided that a little bit of give here would allow us to survive as a country.

"Those acts you refer to well I'm sorry you were a witness to them but they were not crimes committed against French people. They were for the most part foreign Jews, who had overstayed their welcome and many lest you forget were not even legally residents of the country.

"So I have no regard for your remarks as I find them totally disproportionate and grossly defamatory.

"I would like you to leave now Gaston, what becomes of you in Paris well I leave to you, but honestly unless you change your attitude I fear that it will be your funeral the next time our paths cross.

"It goes without saying that you disappoint me, that you at the age of 39 think like a naive adolescent. I would prefer that you did not stop by at our room and wish your mother goodbye for it would only upset her gravely.

"I will not mention this discussion with her for as you can see she is not the strong person she once was. I also would ask you not to contact her or me again until such time as you have come to your senses."

With that Pierre opened the door and with his eyes bowed beckoned Gaston to leave.

This he did willingly, too stunned at his father's vicious defence of himself and his superiors to offer any kind of response. In any case he realized that it would be pointless to do so for his father had pinned his colours to the mast of Petain and he was willing to sink with him.

Gaston for his part was not willing to join his father and sister in the dock either of history or if it came to it, show trials.

Solving the Suchet case or at least feeling he had enough evidence to accuse someone officially with the murder would suffice he believed to avoid such a fate.

The only problem now was that he really was on his own. There would be no safety net were Bousquet or von Dirlinger to turn on him using their power to crush him and that made him feel extremely uneasy.

*

Lafarge returned to Nice crestfallen over his row with his father, realizing that while they may make up eventually, their relationship would never be as warm as it had been prior to that.

He worried too that should Bousquet hear of their row he would feel he could do as he wanted with Lafarge without being concerned of the reaction from Vichy.

At the same time Lafarge felt he had the tacit support of Petain to bring down Bousquet and that would not change, though, were the Germans to oppose such a move then he really would be alone.

How Bousquet would react to to his being reinstated would be interesting, would he feel that it was another sign that he was finished in his present role or would he have Lafarge arrested on some spurious charge?

All these questions swirled round Lafarge's head as he entered the house, but the confusion and anxiety were swept away once he heard the tinkle of the piano and the laughter of the children playing upstairs.

He entered the library where Isabella was playing and saw from behind that she had a student with her.

For Isabella had decided that it wasn't fair for her wealthy father to pay for everything. Thus being a talented pianist she had advertised for students, and there were many, both male and female, who had availed themselves of this opportunity at the reasonable rate his wife charged.

Isabella heard him enter the room and turned, he raised a finger to his lips and made to leave but his wife touched the woman's arm to stop her playing and got up to kiss her husband on the lips.

He enjoyed the moment until he saw over her shoulder who her student was. It was Aimee. His legs nearly gave way but he steadied himself and smiled at her as she too rose up from the piano and made to come over to him.

"Well hello again Gaston," she said smiling, her tone warm, and lit a cigarette.

Lafarge looked at her and observed that being on the run had not left many marks. While her face was made up it didn't appear to be hiding any marks. Nor did money seem to have been a problem as she was smartly–dressed, a dark green suit highlighting her perfect figure.

THE TORTURED DETECTIVE

He by contrast felt his pangs of anxiety return and he made straight for the drinks cabinet to fix himself a stiff vodka and tonic, offering the women one as well, which they both accepted.

The way Isabella had kissed him suggested that Aimee had not revealed much, but he would have to be careful about what he said so as not to make a mistake about how well they knew each other.

What he really wanted was to be alone with her and find out what she wanted from him. Was she there to put a bullet in him, which he could understand after betraying her, her brother and sister–in–law, or simply to destroy his marriage?

He had to admire her investigative powers, of tracking him down when she herself was on the run, but all these questions would have to wait.

"My my Gaston you are a discreet soul. You never told me that your line of work involved meeting such beautiful women," teased Isabella.

If only you knew the truth, thought Lafarge.

"Yes, well darling there are some bonuses. These days they are few but I shared an enjoyable few hours with Aimee on a train journey last year. No doubt she told you that," replied Lafarge to which thankfully Isabella said she had.

"So Aimee how impressive that you came and found me," said Lafarge, thinking it best to pay a compliment to start with.

She smiled and took a sip of her drink.

"Well as you know Gaston my acting career was not going in the direction I wanted it to and so I decided that I would prefer to live in a warmer climate far away from Paris, then of course the Germans took a similar decision.

"I came across the advertisement for piano lessons by a Madame Isabella Lafarge and I thought hmm there can't be too many of that name living in Nice.I don't know if you remember but you told me all about your domestic arrangements," said Aimee still smiling.

Lafarge winced and tried to recall if he had, and then thought he must have at some point.

"Of course well it's a lovely surprise to see you again. Are you planning to stay here long? I imagine it will take you a while to become a good enough pianist to change career," said Lafarge, hoping that she would say she was leaving for another destination soon.

PIRATE IRWIN

"No, I think I will stick to the day job, I am stubborn as you know and I believe with change certain to come I can benefit from that.

"So I am thinking of returning to Paris and seeking out Guitry again for he can perhaps at last help me properly. Although I know you also have acquaintances in the theatrical world so perhaps you could help too," she said flashing her catlike smile again.

"Do you know people like that Gaston? Another secret kept from me," said Isabella playfully.

Gaston heaved a sigh of relief that his wife was so relaxed, for it had always been a rule between them that his cases were his alone and not to be shared with her. The Suchet case was exceptional because he had had to explain why he had suddenly turned up last year and without a job.

However, details about nights in Suzy Solidor's cabaret and sleeping next to a lesbian maid were not ones he was willing to divulge. She didn't really appreciate why he had returned to the police service so any hint of sordidness would only confirm her prejudices.

"Ah well as it happens I too am returning to Paris so maybe our paths will cross there, though, I would have thought you might wait a bit before making your grand entrance as change is still some way off," said Lafarge.

"Well Gaston, thank you for your advice but I feel it is time for me to take a chance on that and besides, Guitry offers some form of protection. Why, he might even convince your friend René Bousquet that I am not worth the bother," she said, draining the last of her drink.

The mention of Bousquet deepened Lafarge's sense of foreboding.

Having to cope with him was bad enough but to also have a vengeful Aimee prowling the streets would mean he could never relax for a minute.

Being an actress and having access to all sorts of different disguises she could follow him without him knowing. It made him wish all of a sudden he did have a partner to watch his back.

Still too late to change a lifetime's habits old son, he told himself. He would just have to look out for himself everywhere he went. He felt like answering that Bousquet had a penchant for actresses but

THE TORTURED DETECTIVE

thought better to keep his dry comments to himself in case he sparked an unwanted revelation from her.

"Ah yes our good friend the secretary–general. I take it from the fact you are returning to Paris your meeting went well Gaston," asked Isabella as she gestured to her husband to refill their glasses which he obediently did.

Early evening sunlight filled the room as Gaston handed them their glasses and he suggested they go out to the garden and sit there, but both laughed and said the sun may be out but it was early December and they didn't feel like catching a chill.

He shrugged his shoulders and returned to the sofa and took his place beside Isabella.

"Yes the meeting went as well as I could have hoped for, and I am to leave in a couple of days. Hopefully it won't take too long and I can return within a matter of weeks," he said, suddenly feeling weary.

They carried on chatting for half an hour about South America mostly, anything but the case and the war which came as a relief to Lafarge, before Aimee said she should be leaving as she had a dinner to attend with some of her old theatrical friends.

Lafarge walked her to the door and down the steps to the gate, while Isabella said she would get the children ready for bed. He felt huge pangs of guilt as he opened the gate for Aimee and wanted to explain everything but as he opened his mouth to speak she took his arm and raised her fingers to his lips.

"There's no need to explain Gaston, well at least not now. I just wanted you to know that I haven't disappeared. You will get to explain yourself someday whether it be to me or to some court, I will let you mull over that conundrum while you kiss your children good night," she said.

With that she kissed him on the lips and walked with her usual confident gait down the road leaving Lafarge to ponder whether returning to Paris really was such a good idea, or would it be best to leave France behind and try to get on a boat to Argentina.

269

CHAPTER TWENTY SIX

In the end Lafarge decided to take the train to Paris, but at the same time realised that if he came back alive he and his family would have to leave France for a while.

Isabella was delighted with his decision as she was disillusioned with the France she had once so loved and found to be the most cultured and magical place she had visited in Europe.

Despite her father having Fascist sympathies, born out of his fervent admiration for Argentina's own despot Juan Peron, she had wearied of their ideology and found their hatred for anything but pure Aryan stock repellent.

She had already helped to hide several Jews and Communists and fund their trips over the border into Spain. But now the time had come for her to think of her children and their future and it did not belong on a continent that whatever the outcome of the war would take years to recover.

Lafarge was relieved too that Isabella had agreed with him. Whilst he had not got too many things right of late with regard to giving advice to family members he knew that he was on a winner when it came to suggesting Argentina as a destination.

Thus he climbed onto the early morning train to Paris in a brighter mood than he had experienced of late, but it soon darkened when he saw that he would have to share his compartment with two Wehrmacht officers.

The train was surprisingly not very full and the officers quickly found themselves another compartment much to his relief, courteous, though they were.

It struck Lafarge that if these two were representative of the Wehrmacht they looked a lot less self–confident than their fellow officers had done a year ago and normally they would have suggested it be he who looked for another compartment.

Thus nicely settled on his own, he read two of the woeful papers that had acted as odious mouthpieces for the Nazis since they entered Paris.

Le Nouveau Temps, owned by another of Abetz's old friends Jean Luchaire, whose daughter had a Luftwaffe captain as her lover, and Aujourd'hui, edited by the loathsome anti–Semite Georges Suarez.

Of course there were no commentaries about the less confident air of officers in the Wehrmacht or their colleagues in other services, only that everything was progressing as planned, though, here Lafarge noted with glee, slower than expected in the East.

By that very admission even the diehard supporters were conceding that things were not alright at all. Aside from that there were the usual vicious diatribes against all enemies of Vichy and the Nazis : Jews, gypsies, communists and freemasons.

There were tasteless cartoons about US President Franklin D Roosevelt and his wheelchair. But the least wholesome part of all were the classified pages where 'valiant' French people hiding their courage under the cloak of anonymity denounced people they knew to be Jews, who were either neighbours or had sought refuge in their town.

This made Lafarge nauseous, a quick nip of cognac putting that to rest, as he read through some of them. The Germans may not be winning the war but it wasn't stopping people from continuing their patriotic duty in either going down to the local gendarmerie or sending these poisonous notes to the newspapers, none of which would be checked for their veracity.

Not many policemen were industrious in researching the information provided to them and would simply have the people who had been denounced picked up. Robespierre would be proud of them, for they had not learned anything from the terror that he had created under the false premise of protecting the state.

He sighed deeply and looked out the window as the train sped along under its own steam through the countryside. Every now and then he would spot a group of German tanks or armoured columns either motoring along or taking a break in the fields, the young men looking like any other human being but for their uniforms and heavy weaponry.

How much longer, mused Lafarge, will this be the case? Will I or the people who occupy this compartment in the years to come have the same sight confront them? His thoughts were interrupted suddenly as the door to his compartment was drawn back and looking up expecting to see the conductor he saw instead Aimee.

Oh Christ he thought as he flashed a look of despair and he also felt fear rising inside him, for perhaps she had followed him with the sole purpose of killing him. Perhaps she had dispensed with the idea of him facing judgment by legal means and thought it was too good an opportunity to pass over. She must have sensed this because she burst out laughing.

"Ah Gaston you look as if you died! Or that I was about to perform a grisly execution ritual on you, a drama worthy of Shakespeare or Marlowe! Well you can rest easy, I have not come here armed with anything more powerful than my handbag and a packet of cigarettes," she said still laughing.

Lafarge smiled thinly, breathed a sigh of relief, but still questioned her motives. For she had hardly boarded a train simply to frighten the living daylights out of him. It was too risky for her to have had that as her only motive.

Undeterred by his silence she took the seat opposite him and lit a cigarette.

She once again looked superb, a finely designed blue wool two piece suit with a cream taffeta shirt and adorned by an elegant mother of pearl necklace. He noticed too she was wearing stockings, which were hard to come by for most women these days, and for those on the run even more so.

"There's one thing missing from this reunion on a train, Gaston," she said, merriment in her eyes.

"What's that Aimee?" he asked evenly.

"Why a drink for your travelling companion. You were very generous with it the first time we met, perhaps having conquered me you feel it isn't worth it this time round," she said.

Lafarge smiled sheepishly and stood up, withdrawing a bottle of wine from his suitcase. The cognac could come later.

It was after all only just past 10 in the morning and his nausea had subsided. He opened the bottle and poured them two healthy sized glasses and they clinked them together and sat in silence. She looked out the window while he looked at her and tried to gauge what it was that she was after from him.

"Aimee I cannot expiate my guilt over what happened in Limoges. I don't expect you to ever forgive me for betraying you and your family, all I can say in mitigation is that I had to sacrifice something so as to survive myself.

THE TORTURED DETECTIVE

"Unfortunately that is the situation I found myself in, and it has caused me a lot of pain since as I did have strong feelings for you. I mean sleeping with you was not done lightly, as you can see I have a very special wife, but I really felt something strong between ourselves," said Lafarge.

Aimee flashed him a look of such disdain that he resisted making any further comment.

"So Aimee what is it that you want? Obviously you are not going to kill me, but you must have a reason for placing yourself in danger by taking the train," said Lafarge.

She didn't answer, simply crossed her legs so they were barring him from leaving the compartment, and carried on looking out the window.

He filled both their glasses again and tried to resume reading his book, The Man in the Iron Mask by Alexandre Dumas. It wasn't exactly adult reading but he had always found the author an exciting read and for him a well observed account of previous French rulers and their endless deadly intrigues.

After about an hour of the train crawling through the countryside she finally broke her silence.

"You know Gaston, being an actress doesn't just mean I perform on stage or in front of a camera. I am always performing a role of some sort, no more so than when it is really needed. Thus it was the day your charming colleagues turned up at the farm house," she said, her eyes not meeting his.

"However, unbeknownst to you I knew that something was pending. I saw you slip out that night and follow them across the driveway. I don't know what you heard but obviously it was enough for you to report back to your colleagues.

"I really don't want to know why you felt compelled to do such an awful thing, but in any case I made my own arrangements to escape, by making my way down to the lake and rowing across it to safety. Hence I feel a little guilty too because I left my brother and his wife to their fate. But at least I did not betray them.

"I was stopped but I was fortunate for it was that colleague of yours Broglie, who does not seem to share the enthusiasm for the Nazis as some of your colleagues do. He put me in his car and drove me to the lawyer chap in Limoges, Gerland, who looked after me very well and explained that you had been by and taken away your prisoner.

"Of course that all made sense then, why you had done what you did, but it still doesn't make it right. Gerland managed to get me new identification papers which got me as far as the south and from then really I have been able to live a normal life to the extent that I have reassumed my real name.

"Of course there is an inherent risk in doing so, but I do not feel like fleeing as so many have done. No, I want to stay and hope that in a short time things will be almost back to what they were before. Then I can enjoy the sight of seeing those who benefited from the Nazis rule being judged and even executed publicly for that is what they deserve.

"It's ironic isn't it that in pursuit of solving a case regarding a slut of an actress you were prepared to sacrifice one that refused to go down the same road so as to advance her career.

"That I am sure is not lost on you.

"But then your whole behaviour over the murder has been from what I am told by those who know you, for I have done my research, been unpredictable. Whether it is because you have been blinded by your crusade against Bousquet or some other motivating factor heaven knows.

"All I can tell you is that it could cost you dearly, even if the case is solved. That is sad because I really thought you were different to the others, rather special in fact, but then I was never too good at picking the right man," she said her eyes brimming with tears.

Lafarge dismissed her observations and her amateurish efforts at psychology and stared out the window, his indifference to her clear.

She smiled a bitter smile and poured herself another glass of red wine, settled back in her seat and sat observing him. He found it unsettling and eventually unable to handle the heavy atmosphere he stood up and told her he was going to stretch his legs.

"Going to find the nearest Gestapo man or German and deliver me up again are you Gaston?" she sneered.

"How easy that would be for you. Get some credit ahead of your unpopular return to Paris, make sure you rid yourself for good of an irritating character who you enjoyed an unwelcome adventure with and would prefer you hadn't. Go on then do it," she hissed.

THE TORTURED DETECTIVE

Lafarge shook his head in exasperation and stepped out into the corridor. He walked to the end of the carriage and was about to progress into the next one when he saw that the conductor was coming down it checking the tickets.

It was not so much that that alarmed him with regard to Aimee but that the conductor was accompanied by two members of the Milice. They were so fanatical and violent that even Bousquet regarded them with disgust, whether because it challenged his authority or was even too extreme for him Lafarge didn't really care but at least there they agreed on something.

Renowned for their brutality they were largely sociopaths, who were little better than the Lafont and Bonny outfit, and gave no quarter to French people believed to be anti–Vichy.

Lafarge thought quickly of how to avoid Aimee falling into their hands, but then reflected on how it would look for him if he were to be caught in the same compartment as a wanted terrorist.

He couldn't claim ignorance about her links to the Resistance as one phone call to Paris and a subsequent look at his file would reveal that he had slept with her on a previous occasion prior to the destruction of the cell.

He could just imagine Bousquet's glee on hearing the news. Aside from his investigation coming to a definitive end, he could face much worse than that if he were to be charged with aiding and abetting an enemy of Vichy.

He was perhaps developing a paranoid streak because he wondered whether this had all been a set up from the get go, her turning up at home just after he had his meeting in Vichy and then on his train.

It was too late to move compartment as he didn't have the time to go back and get his luggage. All he could hope for was that she had left by the time he returned, but he was to be disappointed as she was still sitting by the window.

"I'm afraid that without any help from me, though, you may not believe me, that you are about to be picked up Aimee," said Lafarge coolly.

"And before you get mad with me I might add that I too am screwed because of having you in here.

"What deal did you do with them to set me up Aimee? No death sentence, a light punishment if you delivered me to them and prevented my return to Paris?

"So your holier than thou remarks about me being judged by a higher court was all bullshit, you couldn't wait or rather you had already set the trap when you made them!

"Revenge sweet is it Aimee? Well before you start congratulating yourself and enjoying the moment I would counsel you to take their word lightly. They are about as honourable as the snake was in the Garden of Eden," he shouted.

Aimee remained impassive.

"For Christ's sake Aimee can't you see what you have done? You've screwed everything up, Bousquet will be the only one to benefit from this. I really pity you!" he shouted again.

"What's going on?" came a gruff voice from behind him.

Lafarge turned round to see the conductor flanked by the two milice officers, who because of his rant he had not heard pull back the door.

Lafarge tried to calm down and smiled pathetically at the conductor, an old man who had probably seen these type of disputes aplenty down the years, and then at the two milice men. Their demeanour didn't suggest they were going to fall for such a ruse.

The conductor checked their tickets and franked them leaving the milice officers to check the identification papers and that they had the obligatory travel permits.

The older of the two, middle aged with beady mean eyes and a pencil thin moustache which made him look like a mobster, checked Lafarge's papers. He eyed him warily when he saw that he was a policeman, and made a derogatory remark about lily–livered detectives to his younger partner, who was checking Aimee's papers.

The younger one, who had a pockmarked face as if he had suffered from a bad dose of chickenpox early in his youth, handed the papers back to Aimee without any fuss at all.

"Enjoy the rest of the journey, I would suggest that you go easy on the drink as it's never conducive to an even tempered debate," said the younger one with the hint of a smile on his face.

THE TORTURED DETECTIVE

"Paris isn't the worst of destinations after all. It's not as if you are packed into a cattle truck like the Yids! So think yourselves fortunate and calm down.

"We don't want to have to intervene in a domestic dispute when we might have Jews and their like to arrest on the train.

"So Monsieur and Madame Lafarge I would recommend you sleep this off, there are several hours to go. Why not even take advantage of the fact you have a compartment to yourselves, if you know what I mean?" winked the younger one.

The older one clearly didn't share in the levity of the situation and looked at Lafarge with contempt.

"Ah Jean now you see why we had to be asked to step into help with the security of our country, when you see the degenerate and lax way our so called professional police behave. No wonder the terrorists and other lowlifes have killed so many of our patriots, because the police drink and whore their way through the war," he said.

Lafarge bit his tongue so as not to lash out at the older Milice man, and sensing this the younger one, Jean, pulled his colleague out of the compartment apologising and shutting the door behind them.

Lafarge was stunned. Firstly at the vitriolic attack by the Milice man and that Aimee had successfully passed herself off as his wife.

He looked at her for an answer, but all he got was a belly laugh. It was perhaps the best response in case the middle–aged Milice man had stayed outside the door eavesdropping hoping to hear an explosive argument.

Disregarding the young pup's suggestion about laying off the drink, Lafarge poured them both another glass and withdrew a second bottle from his suitcase. In fact he was willing to ignore most of the advice so unhelpfully proferred but he still wanted answers from his 'wife'. Eventually her laugh died down as she reveled in the moment.

"Gaston, you really thought I would offer myself up as a sacrifice just to trap you! You really aren't worth that much. I did enjoy your outburst, though, it was a performance worthy of Vigan more than a Guitry soliloquy, which is a compliment by the way!" she said before breaking out into another bout of laughter.

Lafarge didn't feel like joining in, he felt ridiculed and that he had made a fool of himself, and he slumped down thoroughly deflated in the seat nearest the door.

"Oh come Gaston, look better to be fooled by me than to be carted off by those two gangsters and tortured before facing execution. The worst you can be accused of now is that you are a bigamist, which many Frenchmen would be envious of!" she chortled.

A bigamist, terrific, thought Lafarge. Married to a fiery Argentinian and also a wanted terrorist, and he doubted Isabella for all her relaxed airs would find this amusing. However, once he started to calm down he too began to see the funny side of it but he still needed an explanation.

"Ok Aimee you had me there. I apologise for thinking that you were setting me up for your own satisfaction, it was uncharitable of me to think that you should do something like that. But then as you say or as people have told you I have become a little neurotic," he said gently.

"However, how on earth did you manage to pull this off? I guess it explains why you were so confident that you could return to Paris without any problem, I take it that seeking Guitry's protection was a ruse, but still you have a nerve," he said.

"Ah well Gaston, being an actress puts you in touch with all sorts of characters, not just the ones one plays! Hence there was an assortment of colourful characters I could call on in Nice to help me in my predicament, who because of affairs in the past and friendships formed were only too happy to help me create a new identity," she said.

"It helped obviously that you or at least your wife was living in the city. So I went to work on such details as date of birth, ages of children etcetra, just in case I underwent a stiffer examination than those two fools performed. What better security for an active member of the Resistance than to go round as the wife of a senior detective, albeit one who does his best to be an outcast.

"What fun it has been putting all this together! Rather malevolent of me, no? Brilliant, though, perhaps my finest role awaits me in playing obedient and submissive Madame Lafarge! Now I have the perfect cover to go about my business in Paris, for nobody will suspect me of 'terrorist' activities."

THE TORTURED DETECTIVE

She smiled contently and sat back with a triumphant look on her beautiful face.

Lafarge had to admire her for her chutzpah in going into such detail and pulling it off for now. But what if she came into contact with people who knew the real Madame Lafarge? Admittedly there were very few still in Paris, and one of those, Bousquet, was not likely to be seeing her.

Ordinary gendarmes stopping her in the street would not know her so she would have a free pass unless she was caught in the act of transferring messages or whatever duties she had been assigned to carry out – duties he did not wish to know about.

"Well Aimee I have to hand it to you, you are quite something. If you survive I can see you enjoying a terrific career as an actress. However, once we are in Paris how are you going to carry on this charade, I mean we will be separated and you will have to explain why you are not living at the address on your ID papers," said Lafarge.

She didn't flinch.

"Ah but this is the sweetest part of it, and this is the payback for your betrayal.

"We are going to live as a married couple in your apartment and to all intents and purposes we will be Monsieur and Madame Lafarge.

"You will deal with the concierge in whatever way you wish to, money or some story about changed circumstances, and we will carry on our daily lives separately but we will live together.

"Isn't it terrific, the cop and the terrorist living under the same roof. How your colleagues would laugh if they knew.

"No, maybe they wouldn't. So this Gaston is my bill for what you did in Limoges. If it succeeds then I will deem it that we are even, if it doesn't then I guess it won't matter for both of us will be dead. Sweet no?" she said with a seductive smile.

Lafarge smiled grimly and settled back in the seat opposite his 'wife' and reflected that he had made one of the worst decisions in his life in deciding to return to Paris.

Not only did he no longer enjoy support from his father but he was now lumbered with a fugitive from both Vichy and the Nazis as well as he still probably had the Jewish couple living in his apartment.

He thought probably because obviously contact had been cut once he left Paris. He hoped they were still there because if they had been arrested he already had a serious charge awaiting him once he set foot back in the 'City of Light'.

God what an inapposite name for the place as it was now, he thought. He wished that it was in total darkness when the train pulled in at Gare de Lyon so he could lose Aimee and slink back home unnoticed.

Also what on earth was he going to tell the Rosenbergs? He suddenly turns up and informs them that he has reluctantly agreed to host an undesirable and that having three of them was too many!

Not that he was far off being registered in the same category given his relentless pursuit of Bousquet. At least he and Aimee had done things that had made them personae non gratae in the eyes of the government, whereas the mistake the Rosenbergs had made was to be born Jewish!

Well he was damned if he or Aimee for that matter were going to be the cause of their death. So the Rosenbergs would have to return to their flat and pray that the worst was over, which if he took care of Bousquet might prove to be the case.

Whoever came after him would, Lafarge hoped, be less supine with the Nazis especially as their hold everywhere apart from France seemed to be weakening.

That was the positive side to things, but it nevertheless didn't solve his major headache, how to retrieve something out of the ashes of his investigation once he resumed his job.

He had had several brief conversations with Massu, the latter always courteous but clearly uneasy about his younger colleague's desire to return and stir things up again.

However, the chief of the Brigade Criminelle was now so well practiced in the arts of turning a blind eye without overtly collaborating that he couldn't actually come out and give a firm opinion about anything, save if it involved a case and a suspect, in which he remained a master.

Lafarge could at least console himself with the fact that Massu would act as a layer of protection so long as he didn't overreach himself.

That was the problem, though. Would he be able to restrain himself and also what incontrovertible proof could he obtain to

THE TORTURED DETECTIVE

implicate Bousquet, in either the burglary or the murder, and avoid being drummed out of the police force for a second time?

For he accepted that this was the end game, one of the two of them would fall, and he was determined that it would not be him.

After that well he would also go but on his own terms, and if it needed him to betray Aimee again then he would do it, for she might be sitting there looking all content and smug but she forgot one thing.

She did not have anything on him that could pose a threat so she remained expendable. He certainly wasn't going to ruin her moment of triumph but he would bide his time.

CHAPTER TWENTY–SEVEN

As luck would have it there was a power cut when they arrived at the Gare de Lyon, but they were fortunate that with Lafarge flashing his badge they were allowed to go to the head of the long line of people queuing for taxis.

After a surreal drive through pitch black streets where they were checked by one grumpy looking gendarme, they arrived safely back at Pere Lachaise. The walls to the famous cemetery looked even more sinister without any light on them, and Lafarge shivered at the possibility that he could be checking in there permanently sooner rather than later.

Well if he was lucky he would end up alongside several Napoleonic generals, people of the arts and other luminaries of past generations. The normal burial ground for those who were victims of the state were far less salubrious, unmarked graves usually, so the crimes committed by Vichy or the Nazis could not be unearthed.

They were met at the doorway by the ever alert concierge Madame Grondon, who had a lit candle, and she looked very surprised when she saw that Lafarge was accompanied by a woman, who was not his wife.

However, having been well looked after by the policeman through the years she was not going to comment. Besides what she had witnessed just in the past year was enough to make her discretion personified. So she bade him hello, nodded at Aimee, and escorted them up the stairs as she possessed the only means of lighting their way.

Lafarge held his breath as he turned the key in his door awaiting the shrieks of surprise or fear or both from the Rosenbergs, but instead he and his two female companions were met by utter silence, and the whiff of fresh polish.

"The lady down the corridor and then me, after she and her husband left, looked after the apartment for you Mister Lafarge just in case you did come back with your wife and family," said the concierge, casting a quizzical look at Aimee.

Lafarge smiled and patted the elderly lady on the shoulder, his way of thanking her for her not mentioning the Rosenbergs.

THE TORTURED DETECTIVE

She smiled, relieved also her remark about Lafarge's family had passed off lightly, and then shuffled over to a drawer in the kitchen and pulled out a candle which she lit and handed to him.

She said goodnight and Lafarge thanked her profusely and said they would talk in the morning for he was desperate to find out if the Rosenbergs had been arrested or if they had left of their own accord.

Once left on their own Lafarge did the best he could to show Aimee what was what in the apartment and where she could put her clothes. To his astonishment she had not just come with her handbag but had stowed a huge trunk in the luggage compartment of the train.

This joy still awaited him downstairs but having ascertained to his relief that his 'wife' had all she needed for the night he put that task off till the morning when at least he would be able to see his way up the stairs.

He could also get someone to help him for Madame Grondon, helpful as she was with the housework, was not physically capable of helping with a piece of luggage as heavy as that.

Aimee had been unusually, but thankfully, quiet but she appeared to be impressed by her new home.

"Ah Gaston this is perfect for my first matrimonial home! The only pity is that you didn't carry me over the threshold, and I thought you were a dyed in the wool romantic," she cooed.

"May I remind you Aimee this is role playing, and just in case you were entertaining doubts about that, this is your bedroom," said Lafarge determined to impose his house rules from the start lest the boundaries between reality and fantasy became blurred on either party's behalf.

He could sense that she was disappointed for she let out a sigh, part actress part real he couldn't tell but he had a feeling she had hoped that they would fulfil their roles down to sharing a bedroom.

Still he was not willing to do so, not for the moment in any case. If he felt she needed reassurance then later, depending on how long this was going to take him, he would provide it but only to keep her near him should he feel that he could use her as a bargaining chip.

Even so he did play the role of the perfect host, finding other candles left in the same drawer and lighting them in her bedroom, the bathroom and the drawing room.

He waited for her to freshen up and then offered her a drink which she accepted gladly, asking for a glass of champagne.

This Lafarge thought would be impossible until he looked in his fridge and saw there were three bottles, the year was still good for drinking and they were still cold enough despite the power cut. There was a note pressed in between them, which he took out and read before opening one of the bottles.

"Thank you Inspector Lafarge for your kind gesture which cannot really be repaid, certainly not with three bottles of champagne, but they will have to do unless we should meet again under happier circumstances. With our undying gratitude, Hal and Lotte Rosenberg."

Lafarge gulped, genuinely touched and also marked by the irony of the term undying gratitude. He hoped it would be the case so long as they eluded the grasp of his colleagues and the Nazis.

He wiped away a tear, for their gratitude for a single and perhaps fruitless gesture said it all about the low expectations of the hunted and harassed, and served them both a glass, though, quite what there was to celebrate escaped him.

So he left it to his uninvited guest to make the toast.

"Here Gaston is to the end of tyranny and to the rebirth of French democracy and following along that line of thought to a blossoming acting career starting with my finest role to date as your wife!" she said giggling.

Lafarge laughed too and shook his head, wondering how this woman could maintain her permanent air of optimism and gaiety when things were so dark and gloomy.

He got swept up by her positive attitude and they chatted for about an hour about endless subjects until Lafarge, his eyelids drooping, apologized and said their discussion would have to be held over till the morning.

He escorted her to her bedroom, albeit it was adjacent to his so he had to pass by there anyway, and kissed her on the cheek. She moved her lips towards his, but he adeptly removed his face from pressing on hers, so as to avoid an embarrassing moment.

THE TORTURED DETECTIVE

"Ah well, can't blame me for trying! Still we have time on our side so watch out!

"However, seeing the manner in which you even have old ladies like your concierge swooning around you I think I may be way down the queue.

"One thing I can say for you Gaston is that you have a very loyal female following no matter how cruelly you treat them. Good night dear husband," and with that she smiled sweetly and closed the door on Lafarge.

He shrugged his shoulders and tried to distract himself from thinking about her by reading another chapter of the 'Man in the Iron Mask' but it proved a losing battle. He reflected on what she had said and while she had made sense she was wrong about one thing.

The most important one in fact, that they had time on their side.

No Aimee, you idealistic dreamer, we do not have time on our side thought Lafarge. It is very much against us and I have to hurry if I am to try and wrap this up before the clock runs down otherwise we will both be doomed.

The following morning he let her sleep in as he washed, dressed and with the aid of one of the other tenants, who he knew well enough that he wouldn't ask questions, brought the trunk up to his apartment.

She stumbled out of her room, wiping the sleep from her eyes, but even in her half asleep state she looked stunning, her hair ruffled but shining.

He was amazed at how well she had managed to look after herself throughout the months of being on the run. Not even the fear she must have felt at being found or betrayed at any moment had not left a mark on her face.

"Your former husband has been delivered safely to you madam," Lafarge said drily.

She laughed and thanked him for bringing it up before she made it clear she wanted a coffee before anything else was said.

Lafarge obediently performed this task and watched her as she settled cosily into one of his battered armchairs, sipped the coffee, and lit a cigarette, all seemingly in the same seamless movement.

He was anxious to get going, but nevertheless had a cup of coffee himself, surprisingly good quality, another present from the

285

Rosenbergs' he ventured, and outlined to Aimee his plans for the day.

He had to remind himself at one point that he was not talking to Isabella but to some woman that was not close to being his wife.

Well ok they had slept together and he was also on probation because he had set her up, but all the same the less they behaved in private like a married couple the easier it would be for him.

As for what she was going to do he preferred not to know. The less he knew the better and the thought of her being arrested, carrying papers saying she was his wife, frightened him.

He didn't even want to think about how he could explain that a woman he had known down in Limoges, and who was part of a terrorist cell, had by happy coincidence turned up with papers pretending that she was his wife. She saw the concerned look on his face and smiled.

"Look Gaston, I'm going to be a good girl I promise you. I am here to carry out a few tasks which will be simpler to complete now the Germans are starting to lose their grip on the city.

"Other than that I'm going to try and see Guitry discreetly, and friends who share my political goals as well. Don't worry I will remain faithful to you hubby. If I'm bold you can spank me," she said her eyes twinkling.

Lafarge laughed nervously, not sure whether it was because she swore she wouldn't be doing anything too risqué or about the spanking bit. He bade her farewell, after telling her the spare keys were hanging up in a cupboard by the entrance to the flat.

She obviously still didn't trust him as she checked the keys were there before he left, though, she also took advantage of the moment to give him an affectionate peck on the cheek.

On his way out he paused to speak to Madame Grondon to find out about under what circumstances the Rosenbergs' had left.

She stopped sweeping the courtyard and ushered him inside her tiny quarters, which was always so neat and tidy and put him to shame.

She offered him a cup of revolting thick coffee, the sort where the spoon couldn't break through the surface and he sipped at it politely as she recounted the Rosenbergs' tale.

"You needn't be worried sir because they left under their own steam.

THE TORTURED DETECTIVE

"It was perhaps six months after you had left when he came to the door and told me that he and his wife had had enough of taking advantage of your generosity.

"Knowing they could not realistically return to their apartment, in case the police came back again, they were going to leave Paris altogether and try and reach Switzerland. Apparently Madame Rosenberg has family living there.

"They asked me to look after the apartment for them just in case they were able to return one day and left me the keys," said Madame Grondon.

Lafarge was relieved and once again thanked Madame Grondon for not divulging their presence to his colleagues. She said they had been around on several occasions asking questions about the Rosenbergs, as they had realised they had missed them the first time.

"I told them of course that they had left a long time ago and that their apartment was in the hands of a proper French person, now, and that was me.

"Though, of course taking pride in my job I preferred to spend my time in my more modest abode so I could keep an eye on the comings and goings of this block.

"They believed me of course because they stopped coming here and also never insisted on going up to the apartment," she said proudly.

Lafarge grinned and thought what a wonderful example for many of our fellow citizens who have allowed cowardice and bigotry to overwhelm them, thinking mainly of those denunciations he had read in the newspapers.

Maybe Madame Grondon will get the apartment in the end anyway should the Rosenbergs fail to return. She would certainly be entitled to it thought Lafarge. He told her so too to which she smiled warmly.

"Well sir you and I are on the right side aren't we, so hopefully for both of us there will be a reward at the end. I just hope that it comes soon. You coming back suggests that might be the case," she said.

Lafarge laughed, he hoped it didn't come across as patronising, and shook his head.

"No, Madame I am not the advance party of some heavenly body set to sweep through and wash away the evil spirits. I'm here for business, an unresolved issue that I won't allow slink away quietly into the night," he said.

She smiled faintly, a slight look of alarm on her face.

"It's not to do with the lady upstairs is it?" she asked, clearly hoping it was not as she had been very fond of Madame Lafarge and the children.

"Good Lord no! She is an actress who is alive, I am here because of one who is not.

"On that note Madame Grondon, I have to rush but would you erm keep an eye out on the lady upstairs, discreetly of course, and let me know if you see anything suspicious?

"It would be a shame if as you say we don't get our just rewards when the real heroes sweep into town," he said with a conspiratorial wink.

THE TORTURED DETECTIVE

CHAPTER TWENTY EIGHT

Lafarge was actually looking forward to his resumption of duties – well that was slightly false as he only had one case and then it would be all over, so he regarded it as up to him how he went about business.

He hoped many of his colleagues were beginning to think in the same way as him and starting to become more relaxed in their treatment of alleged terrorists, Jews, homosexuals, communists and gypsies, to name but a few sections of society that didn't gel with the Nazis sense of order or racial purity.

Whatever next might the loonies in Berlin and their acolytes in Paris come up with, people with dark hair?

For of course they were not archetypal ideals of the Aryan race.

If they wanted to be then from the top man down the Nazi regime would have to start dying their hair or shave it off entirely. For apart from the now thankfully very much dead Heydrich none of them had the slightest hint of blond hair.

Oh well he thought leave it to them what they decide on next, I will just go humbly along and revisit some of the characters I came across in the first part of the investigation.

He didn't feel like dropping in at Quai des Orfevres, but then reflected that he would be best advised to, at least to recover his gun, for he didn't possess another one and he felt he may have recourse to use it.

He didn't see him and Bousquet having a duel but there were plenty of others who would feel less reluctant to settle a score with him. He was principally thinking of Bonny and he didn't envisage his sister protesting too much at his being targeted. Wealth and its trappings came before the family as always with her.

Thus with some trepidation he returned to headquarters hoping to avoid any uncomfortable reunions with Leguay or Bousquet. Fortunately neither of them were around, nor Massu, as he did him the courtesy of swinging by his office only to be told he would be in later as he was attending to a personal matter.

Lafarge then had the pleasure of being able to commandeer a car for himself and decided the best thing he could do was to go back to Suchet's apartment block and pay a visit to Mathilde, the pleasure loving lesbian maid. It was time to confront her over de Chastelain's different version of events.

Surprise was the strongest element he possessed and he wasn't going to waste a phone call on her, that was even if she was still working for the new proprietor of the apartment.

Suchet hadn't left a will, even in wartime young starlets didn't expect to be a name on the long list of the dead, and flats where murders have taken place have a grisly value. He imagined some ghoul had stepped in and bought it from her estate and would like to have kept a maid on, especially one of Mathilde's looks and bearing.

However, it was Lafarge who was surprised when he arrived at the elegant block of flats and saw the name on the buzzer which had been Suchet, and had now been replaced by none other than his old acquaintance von Dirlinger.

Aha so someone has benefited materially from the murder, Lafarge thought.

Still it was puzzling, if not a little morbid, that the German would wish to leave the security of the Lutetia and move into the flat belonging to his dead mistress, a crime for which he remained a suspect.

However, perhaps Lafarge's enforced absence had been a good thing after all. For believing the case to be buried one of the suspects had moved in to the crime scene itself.

Even better for him and his desire to wrap up the case as quickly as possible. He might be able to question two of the small number of people he needed to speak to, under the same roof, and perhaps within minutes of each other, if von Dirlinger had not already left for his office.

He could not ascertain whether Mathilde was still in residence as maids, even high born ones, were not deemed worthy of having a buzzer or a name plate.

Visitors for such people – who were not openly encouraged to receive them – had to rely on the benevolence of either the concierge or another owner to be allowed access into the building.

Lafarge struck lucky as the door was held open for him, after he flashed his badge, by a smart looking gentleman. Lafarge decided that Mathilde would remain as his first target, and if von Dirlinger

THE TORTURED DETECTIVE

was not in when he descended he knew where he could find him, unless of course he was away on business.

Thus he rode the elevator up to as high as he could go – they didn't of course go as far as the hired help's level for they could walk the rest of the way – and thanked his good fortune he didn't cross von Dirlinger as he made his way up the final flight of stairs.

He knocked twice before he heard the bolt being withdrawn and Mathilde's attractive face poked itself round the door. She looked extremely surprised to see him, whether it was a pleasant or nasty surprise he couldn't tell. However, he made it clear he wanted to come in and just for official purposes he flashed his ID card. She opened the door wider allowing him to enter.

For a maid, albeit an untrained one, the place was a mess when he compared it to how Madame Grondon kept her equally small living quarters, but he wasn't there to pass comment on how she looked after her room.

It was just he had remembered how tidy it had been the night he had slept there, but he conjectured maybe it was because she had had a late night and hadn't been bothered to put things away.

He ambled over and leant against the wall, which had the only shaft of natural light coming into the apartment from a skylight type window which slanted down.

He shuddered to imagine what would happen to her if there was a fire. Scrambling up to try and open that window was challenging enough if one was just opening it for air but if you were in a panic lord knows.

For the moment, though, all he was interested in was having the best possible position to observe how she reacted to his questions, of which there were not many.

Although it was already 10 in the morning he was surprised that she was still dressed in her silk dressing gown and not dressed for work. Indeed it didn't look like she would be wielding the feather duster down at Colonel von Dirlinger's apartment any time soon.

She sat down on her bed, crossed her legs, and lit a cigarette, reaching back to get an ashtray from the side table.

He had to admit the past year had not been kind on her looks. She looked stressed, tired and wrinkles had sprung up around her eyes and by the sides of her mouth – perhaps the effects of her

291

carousing late into the night with Suzy Solidor, or maybe just age, surmised Lafarge.

"Not going to offer your old bedmate a coffee?" smiled Lafarge.

If he was hoping for either a smile or a cup of coffee he was to be disappointed on both counts. All he got was a thick cloud of smoke hitting him full in the face.

"Wow haven't seen so much smoke since I came under fire in 1940," he joked but again it fell on fallow ground.

Christ, thought Lafarge, well I'm going to have to play the tough guy now, for she looks as if she can't wait for me to leave and my jokes haven't broken the ice.

"Didn't think I would be seeing you again Lafarge," she said all of a sudden.

"Well thank you for your warm welcome Mathilde. It makes me wonder whether I shouldn't have left it like that. All the same as you are a key witness in a murder enquiry I think it would be remiss of me not to come back and ask you further questions regarding the death of your former employer, don't you?" asked Lafarge.

She shrugged her shoulders with total indifference and stared down at the floorboards.

"Well, I see that you treat your new employer with a more relaxed attitude than Marguerite Suchet, judging by your informal look at this hour of the morning," chided Lafarge.

"What's it to you? You're not responsible for coming round and telling me what to do, it's none of your business.

"The colonel is very flexible about the hours I work and besides we are more friends than employer and employee.

"We go to the club most nights anyway which means I don't get back till late. So I'm hardly going to rush to get out of bed and start cleaning up after him, when he's probably sleeping it off too," she said.

Very cosy arrangement thought Lafarge, wish Bousquet had been like that with me, though, of course that was never likely to happen.

"Gosh Mathilde I could almost see you killing Marguerite just to have better work conditions," said Lafarge.

"That's not even funny Lafarge. Can you just get on with it so I can get ready," she said.

THE TORTURED DETECTIVE

"For a start Mathilde you can address me as Chief Inspector, not as Lafarge," he said, trying to assert himself.

"Secondly I have the authority to charge you with obstructing the course of justice or of giving a false account to a police officer, both of which carry penal terms. While you may not be inside for long I can make it extremely uncomfortable for you.

"For if it was to become common knowledge about your sexual predilection you will suffer badly," he said.

"You bastard! You're as twisted and manipulative as all of them. I didn't trust you from the first time I set eyes on you with your fake charm and macho attitude, why not even drink softened you," she said.

"Yes, well I can accept that from you, because of course you are antagonistic to men so you are bound to have a rather jaundiced view.

"Nevertheless you are still obliged to answer my questions, and count yourself lucky that my macho side hasn't seen fit for me to denounce you as worthy of a pink star to the Nazis, which of course I can still do," he said.

She looked alarmed at that remark and fear swept over her hard but attractive features.

"Don't think that von Dirlinger would put himself out to save you either. He's probably done enough for you anyway and he may not in any case be in a strong position to speak up for you once we have finished here," he said.

That appeared to have the desired effect for she was co–operative for the next 20 or so minutes as Lafarge went over the events of the night of the murder.

Her version replicated pretty much the first account she had given him and all of de Chastelain's, save for one key part and this was where she once again retreated into her obstructive mode.

"De Chastelain said that you didn't accompany him down the stairs when he went to see whether Marguerite's guest had left, is that true?" asked Lafarge for the third time, his patience beginning to wear thin.

"I don't have to answer it. This is not a court of law," she said, her eyes flashing.

"No, it's not Mathilde. But if I bring the person to justice then you will have to answer such a question and there you will be under oath and liable to be charged with perjury if you obfuscate in a similar manner.

"So I would advise you to tell me. Not only will it make it easier for you in the long run it will also go some way to me finding who the killer of your former employer was. Surely you want that?" asked Lafarge.

She pouted, twirled her hair and all but squirmed on the bed as she sought to extricate herself from an increasingly tight corner, giving Lafarge some enjoyment at her discomfort.

"Okay okay. I accompanied de Chastelain down the stairs when he went to see whether Marguerite was alone. In fact I went ahead of him just so that he was hidden by me if her guest was still there or came out the door. Which is exactly what happened," she said.

"And?" asked Lafarge after there was a long enough silence to indicate that she felt that was a satisfactory answer.

"Well as he told you, somebody did come out the door."

Lafarge tapped his foot on the floorboard pushing her to come out with it all. She looked at him with contempt but she knew she had little choice.

"It was your great friend René Bousquet. And yes as de Chastelain told you he said goodbye in both French and German.

"I imagine that they, that is he, Marguerite and the colonel, were discussing the whereabouts of the jewels, so it can't have been the most pleasant of discussions.

"The rest you know, de Chastelain finding her body and then you being sent off to track him down and deliver him back here which of course you didn't," she said.

Lafarge nodded and reflected on her account, which was good news and bad at the same time for it seemed unlikely that he could pin the murder on Bousquet.

Of course as he had remarked to de Chastelain he could have been covering himself, if anyone had been around, by saying goodnight so publicly, with Marguerite's corpse lying inside.

However, whichever way he looked at it Bousquet was still bang to rights over being implicated in the burglary. That was good enough to get him sacked and hopefully charged too. Von Dirlinger now looked the most attractive target to charge with murder.

"So you can confirm von Dirlinger was there too?" prodded Lafarge.

THE TORTURED DETECTIVE

"Yes, he told me he was. But insisted that she was still alive when he left," she said.

"That's what they all say Mathilde!

"No, I am afraid you may be looking for your third employer in a short period of time, though, as you appear to bring bad luck, one employer dead and the other in jail, the next owner may prefer you leave," said Lafarge.

She flashed another contemptuous look at him, which didn't bother him in the least for now he had all he needed to go after the two main protagonists, an eyewitness attesting to the fact they had both been there on the night of the murder.

However, the problem was what to do with Mathilde. For going on past experience anyone who was a threat to Bousquet or von Dirlinger didn't have a long life expectancy. If he were to drop her name as the witness then he was putting her at risk.

He didn't like her, indeed he didn't trust her, but he was damned if she was going to be prevented from testifying.

He could of course charge her for obstructing an investigation and witholding evidence but then she would be right in the middle of Bousquet's vipers nest and be easily disposed of.

Similarly there was a problem in offering her protection. He could hardly bring her over to his apartment with Aimee there, and Madame Grondon really would have a fit with two strange women living in what she considered somewhat grandly her domain.

No, the best he could do was to ask Huariau to keep an eye on the apartment block, but he wouldn't tell Mathilde unless she informed von Dirlinger.

Instead he told Mathilde that she would have to look after herself until he had charged both men and warned her that she could be in danger, but she didn't seem too concerned.

"Really inspector, I have all the protection I need. Why do you think I'm still alive and living here?"

Lafarge scratched his head and thought about it but she put him out of his misery.

"Because Karl trusts me. That is why I got the job with Marguerite in the first place.

"It wasn't just to get me some work. I had to look out for his interests too, be his eyes and ears, keep a note of who came to see her when he wasn't around and if she had any dubious acquaintances," she said.

"However, I insist that I knew nothing about what took place in her flat the night of the murder. As I told you, von Dirlinger informed me he was there, and I also believe him when he says he didn't kill her.

"He was infatuated. It wasn't a case of him keeping her sweet until they sold the jewels, and as far as I can tell he didn't seem to be too concerned they had disappeared.

"As for de Chastelain I trust his account as well but it would have been better for you if you had brought him back to Bousquet. Indeed it would have been better for everyone.

"I would be very careful with what you accuse him of, because you have no protection and you could well be arrested should you go to the Lutetia with such accusations."

Lafarge thought about this and acknowledged that walking into the headquarters of Nazi intelligence in Paris and accusing one of its senior officers of a serious crime might not be one of the wisest things he had done.

But unless he confronted von Dirlinger he would not be able to resolve the case satisfactorily.

"Thank you for your advice Mathilde, and thank you for at last being honest with me," he said.

"However, I would turn your advice on its head and say to you is von Dirlinger the sort of protection you need now?

"I mean you're an intelligent woman. You must hear people say that the Germans are no longer certain of winning the war, that they are now in a fight just to survive and their enemies are massing on many fronts.

"It will only be a matter of time before the Allies attempt to take France and then do you seriously think von Dirlinger's thoughts are going to be to take you with him!

"I sincerely doubt it. No, he will leave you to the mob that will take its revenge on those who helped the enemy, for the Germans will not be around to take the force of their anger. I don't even think he will shed one tear for you as he drives off towards the border, that is of course if he is still alive," said Lafarge.

THE TORTURED DETECTIVE

She looked pensive for a moment as his words sank in, then stood up and wandered over to her small cooker to see if there was any gas still left with which to heat the water.

"I appreciate your counsel inspector, but last time I looked around I didn't see anything but German uniforms guarding the buildings, marching through the streets or parading as they like to do down the Champs Elysees," she said.

"Yes the 'good guys' might feel they are in sight of winning but there is a world of difference between that and them actually being here.

"Until then I think it would be wisest to keep one's opinions to oneself and not to overplay the threat of what might happen in a year or more's time.

"Besides after what von Dirlinger tried to do to you and will no doubt try again I would bet against you witnessing the day when Paris is liberated.

"I think that you have a lot to thank me for Inspector, not just my honesty, and that in itself requires you to be there for me," she said.

Lafarge was intrigued and wondered what she had done to deserve his protection...

"Do I? And what is this great debt that I owe you Mathilde?"

"You remember the night you stayed over and then came upon Bonny in the apartment?"

"Yes of course I do," answered Lafarge.

However, he wondered whether he remembered it more for failing to persuade Mathilde that being heterosexual was actually quite fun, or that he had found his sister's loathsome lover ransacking Marguerite's apartment looking for the jewels.

"Well von Dirlinger set all that up.

"When he learnt that I wasn't going home with Suzy that night and you were accompanying me home he became very agitated in case you stayed over. He had told Lafont and Bonny about the jewels and asked them as they were experts in, how would one put it delicately, 'finding such things' to go to the apartment.

"Well Lafont was too drunk so Bonny came. If I let you stay I was to keep an eye on you.

"However, if you were to go down the stairs to the apartment then I was to follow and to take care of you, I was to say your name get you to turn round and shoot you with your own pistol.

"I was to claim that you had tried to force yourself on me after luring me into the apartment on the pretext of your investigation and I had defended myself.

"It was von Dirlinger's creative side, although others might call it paranoia. He wasn't certain you would go after de Chastelain, that you were keener to shadow him.

"It made him feel exposed and he believed that if you discovered one of the Lafont gang in the apartment you might get them to talk and it would lead back to him.

"Of course the fact you are here now is because I am not going to shoot dead a policeman. I don't trust Karl to the extent that he would have backed me up.

"As I say I don't care for you, but risking the guillotine is going too far."

Lafarge was genuinely shocked by her story, because while he hadn't trusted von Dirlinger totally he hadn't thought he was capable of ordering his murder.

Naively perhaps he couldn't see an aristocratic German, working for by Nazi standards a relatively principled outfit such as the Abwehr, conniving with such lowlifes as Lafont and Bonny.

On the first point perhaps he was at fault because he had so wanted to pin the murder on Bousquet, but on the second one he could barely believe the association with the French Gestapo.

"I'm sorry but I don't believe this story Mathilde. I find it hard to connect von Dirlinger and Lafont and Bonny. Furthermore I can't see why he would wish to involve more people in the jewellery affair. Especially those two who would swindle their own mothers if they had ones that recognised them as their sons," said Lafarge.

Mathilde smirked and returned to the bed armed with a piping hot cup of coffee, Lafarge remarking that her generosity still did not extend to offering him one.

He waited patiently while she settled herself, briefly glancing at his watch to see that it was already half eleven. While he wanted to try and find both Bousquet and von Dirlinger he was intrigued to discover the connection between von Dirlinger and the French Gestapo.

"You are obviously not very close to your sister, for then you would know why," she said.

THE TORTURED DETECTIVE

"Skip the personal observations Mathilde! You have no right to make remarks about my family," said Lafarge.

She smiled at having hit a raw nerve.

"Well they have been partners for a long time.

"Von Dirlinger relies a lot on their persuasive interrogation powers to get him information, as he doesn't like to get his hands bloodied and it is not really the Abwehr style.

"Initially it was for intelligence gathering. The Abwehr paid them on a scale for the value of the information, higher still for it leading to the arrests of resistants, communists etcetra.

"However, once von Dirlinger saw first–hand the luxurious lifestyle and riches that Lafont and Bonny gained either through extortion or as a result of information gleaned from their interrogations he wanted to become a partner of theirs. A silent one of course.

"Von Dirlinger believes it is a win win situation for him. Good intelligence for his employers and financial security for him in the event that the war is lost. That is why he would have brought them in with regard to the jewels. He can trust them as they are partners, and that is why he was so nervous about you probing deeper.

"You would be justified to ask if he was getting so rich why get involved in the burglary? I would venture greed and his love of risk–taking. I say again, though, I don't think he murdered Marguerite, it just doesn't ring true. He was capable of ordering your murder but you are a man and you were also a threat to him.

"Yes, the charming cultivated colonel is quite an operator," she said.

Lafarge was scandalized by this, he could still barely believe it but then the story was so fantastical that he couldn't see why Mathilde would make it up.

He was beginning to see now that von Dirlinger was not worried by him pursuing his investigation into Marguerite's murder. It was the possibility he might uncover his financial links with Bonny and Lafont that was exercising his mind.

Sure rumours were rife that several German officers got a percentage of the French Gestapo's takings, ensuring they turned a blind eye to their criminal activities. But von Dirlinger's involvement appeared to go deeper. Perhaps he even singled out people for Bonny and Lafont to pick up and torture to get them to reveal where they had hidden their paintings or cash.

Poor people did not feature on the list of the endless stream of people they were believed to have picked up and murdered or delivered to the authorities for transportation after being tortured for hours. No they were rich Parisians, Jews or rivals of Lafont and Bonny's.

What he couldn't figure out, though, was why von Dirlinger had demanded Mathilde kill him, not one of Bonny's men. Perhaps he had set her up as she feared, and that after she had shot him Bonny would have taken care of her.

Their two deaths would have cleared up two problems for von Dirlinger. He could continue his lucrative relationship with Bonny and Lafont while another member of the group that knew of the burglary would also be dispensed with and the shares for those left would increase. That was obviously more important to von Dirlinger than catching Marguerite's murderer.

So much for the Abwehr being a gentleman's club, thought Lafarge bitterly when they resort to getting women to do their dirty work.

He mulled over whether it was worth going after Bonny and Lafont.

However, aside from lacking the manpower Lafarge thought if I am to tackle von Dirlinger, he is likely to send them after him in any case.

Would he have a word with his sister about the danger she might be in, as he felt sure she would sooner or later become expendable?

Despite her public disapproval of him they might try to use her as bait to lure him into a trap but if this failed he felt sure that Bonny would take out his frustration on her

No was the simple answer. She had had enough opportunities to leave but she had always refused to and so let her suffer the consequences.

As for Mathilde well he had no idea how deeply she was involved, for her knowledge alone suggested she was more heavily implicated than she had let on.

The fact she was still alive despite failing to go through with his murder suggested that she was of some importance in the whole ghastly operation.

THE TORTURED DETECTIVE

He sensed her willingness to talk now was down to a basic survival instinct, her insurance policy to play both sides and make herself of use.

However, if he were to keep her on his side he would have to flex his muscles and go after von Dirlinger. Preferably arrange a confrontation between the three of them as soon as possible, that is once he was able to track the colonel down.

However, he had to be assured that Bousquet was not privy to this arrangement between von Dirlinger and the French Gestapo. Otherwise were he to ultimately arrest him he would be released within seconds and be free to take care of Mathilde.

"Do you know if Bousquet was aware of this arrangement?" asked Lafarge.

"Good grief no. Why would von Dirlinger complicate matters by involving Bousquet?

"The cock up over the jewels, a rare freelance effort by him in not using Lafont and Bonny, illustrated that there was no point doing business with people who you weren't used to dealing with.

"That is why also he pulled in Bonny for trying to find the jewels in the apartment. Lafont and Bonny were none too pleased that he had not included them in the first place.

"However, he calmed them down and said the partnership, as in the amount of people who were originally in on the burglary had been reduced to just two so there was plenty of profit to be made from them helping him find the jewels.

"He assured Bousquet that he would track down the jewels without telling him who would be conducting the search, as there is no way he wanted your 'friend' to know the types he was in business with.

"Even Bousquet might have raised an objection to that.

"The truth of the matter is that Bousquet is of no importance to him. Karl thinks he is a capable poodle, whose eagerness to please the Nazis is of more importance than posing questions over his links to dubious French characters, so long of course that the jewels are recovered.

"So there Inspector you have the whole story, well in as much as I know, regarding the outwardly charming and carefree colonel.

"It's certainly a case of not taking anyone on face value. You backed the wrong horse in terms of suspect number one and you certainly underestimated the ability and the character of suspect number two.

"However, while you may think the lady doth protest too much I repeat that he is not the murderer of Marguerite. I am certain, simply because he does not have the courage to commit the crime personally. This was no hit," she said.

Lafarge winced at her reference to a 'hit' as there might well be a contract out on him.

He wondered whether this clever and calculating woman had deliberately dropped that term into the mix so as to either warn him off or to tell him to be careful. Maybe she didn't dislike him as much as she said, thought Lafarge.

However, hit or not he had returned to Paris knowing he was a marked man and he had come back to resolve the case and settle scores with those he had in the crosshairs.

Lafarge had so much evidence against von Dirlinger that he now felt emboldened rather than weakened in tackling him.

He left Mathilde, warning her firstly not to tell von Dirlinger he had been around and secondly to stay in until he came back, and deciding to leave the colonel alone for the moment he set off for his showdown with Bousquet.

THE TORTURED DETECTIVE

CHAPTER TWENTY–NINE

Of course to have his confrontation with the secretary–general of police Lafarge needed him to be at work. With Bousquet's position weakened he was apparently spending less time in his office, so Massu had told Lafarge in their most recent conversation on the phone when he had informed him he was returning to Paris.

Finding Bousquet, if he was not in his office, would be nigh on impossible as his movements were known by only his closest circle, which included the odious sycophant Leguay.

Fortunately for Lafarge – although the term was not one he often used in respect of Leguay – he was in his office at the Quai when he returned there.

His pig like and humourless eyes narrowed when Lafarge entered his office without even the slightest hint of a knock.

"Ah you Lafarge, back from your cure?" asked Leguay.

"Yes, and I suggest you try one soon Leguay. Although in your case it might be too late to clean yourself up," replied Lafarge.

Leguay smiled smugly, his thick lips thankfully hiding his tobacco–stained teeth.

"So what do you want with me Lafarge? You usually just jump the queue and go directly to the secretary–general. This is an unwanted displeasure for me, so be quick about it," said Leguay, who to emphasise the point indicated the files on his desk.

"Yes, I see you are loaded down with work to deal with the undesirables Leguay. So anything I can do to distract you from such an unpleasant task and delay their arrests will give me great pleasure," said Lafarge.

Leguay didn't rise to Lafarge's deliberate provocation and waited patiently for the chief inspector to come to the point.

"I went to see the secretary–general but his secretary said she didn't know where he was, and referred me to you" said Lafarge.

Leguay frowned and reflected for a moment.

"I am afraid the secretary–general has suffered a grievous personal loss and may not be here all day," said Leguay.

Really, thought Lafarge, what could that be? Was he already too late and Bousquet had been removed so as to avoid any scandal

303

which could only further besmirch the reputation of the increasingly ridiculous Vichy Government?

Whatever it was it wasn't good news for him and he felt deflated, all the optimism and determination he had felt on leaving Mathilde's was evaporating.

"Ah and what may I ask is the loss?"

"His political godfather, before Laval that is, Maurice Sarraut has been murdered and as you can imagine the secretary–general is beside himself with grief," said Leguay.

"Please Leguay spare me your faux sympathy for your boss' loss. Do we know who was responsible?"

Leguay shot Lafarge a look of such hatred that he told himself to be more restrained in his choice of words as he remained vulnerable until he could see Bousquet.

"Well yes someone was arrested but he has since been released by order of the Germans. We think that they and the Milice, whom Sarraut was bitterly opposed to as indeed we are, we have raised any number of protests against them but to no avail, were behind the assassination," said Leguay.

This was indeed a seminal moment for not only Lafarge but also René Bousquet, for his hold on his present positon now looked untenable as evidently the Germans had withdrawn their support.

If they had allowed the man, who had murdered his oldest mentor, be released then Bousquet must have realised that he was finished. Unless of course his stubbornness and arrogance convinced him he could stay on and he had run to Abetz and tried to persuade him to speak on his behalf.

Regardless of that, Lafarge now knew he hadn't missed his opportunity and he relished the fact he could apply the coup de grace.

The irony was not lost on him that he would be hammering the final nail into Bousquet's coffin – though he thought it was unlikely that he would end up tied to a pole and executed by the Germans – when he agreed with him that Sarraut's murderer should be brought to justice.

Oh well it was far too late to start commiserating with the parvenu who had bowed, scraped and connived with the Nazis to round up thousands of people and send them off to what appeared likely to be certain death.

THE TORTURED DETECTIVE

Lafarge hoped Bousquet would answer for those crimes once proper order of law was restored.

However, the problem was where to find him and so far Leguay had not proved very co–operative with him on that topic.

He knew he didn't have many cards to play in his favour, given their mutual loathing. He thought, though, he could perhaps drive a wedge between the two men, based solely on hoping Leguay did not know about his rupture with his father.

Lafarge opted for a horse racing analogy as he knew that Leguay's weakness on the social front, he had too many on the professional side to list, was a penchant for gambling.

"Look Leguay it appears that you may be backing the wrong horse here. One that has brought you much good fortune in the past but who has run too many races now and whose trainer wishes to put him out to pasture.

"It is probably against his will but nevertheless it will happen. Thus perhaps it is time for you to switch to another one and ensure you still have something that could win to bet on," said Lafarge.

Leguay seemed to warm to Lafarge's effort to convince him as he smiled and allowed Lafarge to continue.

"I mean this horse has been leading all the way in his last race at Auteuil, seemingly destined to end its career unbeaten, when bam, he unships his rider at the final fence.

"So instead of returning to the winner's enclosure and the acclaim of the crowd he trots back of his own accord, for he has his pride and refuses to allow his lad to take hold of him, to the stables. However, his final return to the stables is accompanied by the jeers and the whistles of the fickle public.

"The trainer too and the owner turn their backs on him and don't wish to know René Bousquet anymore and you as his principal punter are the big loser," said Lafarge, sensing he had Leguay in thrall to him now.

"Now I have the good fortune to have an in with the owner, as you know I am related to his closest advisor, who could of course have a word in his ear that a wealthy punter is keen to back him.

"However, that depends on the level of support that person is willing to give. No half measures especially when you are backing the favourite."

Leguay looking pensive fiddled with his pen and tapped it on the desk as Lafarge waited for his response.

Leguay was, for all his many faults, like Bousquet an intelligent man, which made his criminal acts all the worse to Lafarge. But above all he was a man keen on survival, it had been a feature thus far of his short career as a technocrat, so it really depended on whether he thought his boss was still the way forward.

Lafarge would have liked to have added that he would lose whichever jockey and horse he backed for the regime was doomed. However, he refrained from doing so as he didn't think that would help his cause, no matter the pleasure it would have given him to see Leguay's reaction.

"Very well Lafarge as you have put it so cleverly, perhaps it is time to shift my betting habit to another jockey and horse, you have made a persuasive case and I do so hate losing.

"I think that René Bousquet is a great man, and switching away from him is very painful for me. Indeed I think Vichy would have been a better government had it been him as Prime Minister and Laval as President, but fate did not decree that," he said.

"It appears that with the murder of Sarraut a clear message has been sent. Bousquet is no longer untouchable and certainly not the golden boy in the Nazis eyes either.

"Whatever you may think of us in the holier than thou world that you live in we actually saved lives, at the expense of others of course.

"The ones that we had to sacrifice were largely foreign Jews, people who would have stolen food from our tables and gladly pushed French Jews to the front of the queue instead of themselves.

"So you will not get an apology from me about the work we have done here. The Milice are far worse and less discriminatory than we are. French lives mean nothing to them, Jew or non–Jew," he said.

The look of pride on Leguay's face made Lafarge feel physically ill.

"Listen Leguay I am not a Roman Catholic priest come to hear your confession, you can save that for the real thing," said Lafarge.

"Besides no matter how you couch it, including your sickening claim you were protecting the French people, you have committed crimes that simply are not justifiable.

THE TORTURED DETECTIVE

"So tell me where Bousquet is and I will leave you to prepare for your new life. That is of course after you have signed off on those dossiers which look oh so impersonal but contain the lives of human beings, innocent for the most part," said Lafarge bitterly.

"Alright Lafarge, I am just as keen for you to be gone so I don't have to stare at your sanctimonious features anymore.

"Bousquet is due here for a meeting with his Special Brigades chiefs in an hour and as far as I am aware he will honour that, for he has never let down those people who have been loyal to him.

"So I suggest you fill up your time till then and return either before the meeting or wait till it is over," he said.

Lafarge had half a mind to actually attend the meeting, for it sounded as if it was going to be a valedictory one, which would make it all the more enjoyable.

However, he doubted he would be welcome and it could be seen as a direct provocation which was not wise in the presence of a group of sociopaths.

He could make a few calls, including one to von Dirlinger and also check in with Huariau to see if his man had reported any signs of suspicious comings and goings at Mathilde's apartment block. He should also be able to fit in a cognac or two before he settled his account with Bousquet.

Lafarge thanked Leguay, without wishing him well for his future, and made his way to the door.

"Oh Lafarge I do hope this is the last time our paths cross, for it has been most tiresome having you chipping away at the model police force we were trying to implement.

"You're a clever bastard, a fine detective. But you are a supercilious prick, whose head I would have gladly placed in a public square as an example to other policemen who were having doubts about following our path.

"You were never a horse worth backing because one didn't know whether you would ditch your jockey or not," said Leguay, not bothering to look up at Lafarge as he browsed through one of the files.

Lafarge shook his head in wonderment at this man's lack of understanding of the independence of human nature and exited his office without giving him the benefit of a response, for if he didn't see things clearly now then he never would.

Perhaps, Lafarge thought, that was why Leguay was the perfect deputy. An enforcer and yes man incapable of posing questions as to why the orders had been given and the morality of carrying them out when they were patently criminal acts.

Sadly for France there had been too many men of similar ilk.

*

Bousquet was neither chastened nor depressed when Lafarge finally gained access to his office three hours later.

His loyal special brigades chiefs had filed out stony–faced after a meeting which had finished with loud cheering and a rendition of the very English anthem 'For he's a jolly good fellow', the irony not being lost on Lafarge as he sat outside.

He had not been idle himself while he waited to be summoned, arranging to have a drink with Drieu later that afternoon at the Flore as before, while Huariau had assured him nothing unusual had been going on at the apartment block. A final call had confirmed that von Dirlinger had been at his office. His tone had been friendly and he had willingly accepted to meet Lafarge the following evening at the apartment.

Lafarge was surprised to see that his old enemy – one of many he reminded himself – de Blaeckere was one of those who had attended the meeting with Bousquet.

He hadn't changed much physically save that he wore an even more self–satisfied look on his face, one Lafarge hoped masked trepidation of the uncertain future, and flashed a venomous look at his troublesome Parisian acquaintance.

Lafarge smiled patronizingly back at him and resisted the urge to ask him if he had mastered his kidney problem which had manifested itself the day of the shootout in Limoges. Once that unwholesome gang had departed he was permitted entry to Bousquet's office.

Bousquet was seated on the sofa, empty glasses and filled ashtrays surrounded him and Lafarge guessed that his outwardly confident look had been bolstered by alcohol.

His certainly had been as he had also made the time to drink three cognacs at the café on the corner opposite the headquarters.

Lafarge noted that Bousquet, who was as well dressed as ever in a chalk pinstripe suit, navy blue shirt with a yellow tie and gangster

THE TORTURED DETECTIVE

style spats, had retained his lean physique but while his face hadn't aged he had dark patches under his eyes.

Bousquet did not shake hands but he did at least offer Lafarge a drink, which put him one up on the social graces of Mathilde and Leguay, but then that was relative.

However, things turned nasty from the outset as on Lafarge asking Bousquet if he would like a drink too, he declined saying he preferred to choose who he drank with and Lafarge was not on that list.

Lafarge shrugged, thought suit yourself it saves me having to carry two glasses, and sat himself down.

"In case you're wondering how I came to be here at a time when I could catch you, it was Leguay who told me," said Lafarge, enjoying seeing Bousquet's annoyance at his deputy's indiscretion.

"He was very forthcoming in fact once I told him that he was backing the wrong horse. It appears like many others he suddenly doesn't want to know you Bousquet. Must be a lonely feeling," said Lafarge, his tone totally devoid of sympathy.

Bousquet flinched at that, swallowed deeply and ran his tongue along his lip. Maybe he was regretting not having that drink after all thought Lafarge.

"Oh I don't know Lafarge, I still have plenty of support from my men here and the grassroots officers.

"Those that followed me are not regretting for one moment my time in charge.

"As you could probably hear and then see for yourself as my chiefs left they are not very happy at the thought of my being replaced.

"So I am not gone yet. They can threaten me by murdering those closest to me but that does not mean I will submit to them and go meekly," said Bousquet.

Lafarge quite admired his resilient attitude. It also pleased him for it meant that what he was about to say would have more of an impact as to whether Bousquet stayed or stepped down. He could after all land the knockout blow.

"So Lafarge I imagine that your return from the professionally dead is down to your father and that old man ensconced in his fantasy world in Vichy.

"I also would guess that you have come back for only one reason, to resolve the murder of that actress, Marguerite Suchet. Of course most people have forgotten about her by now, I mean really her talent was minimal and her films even with the support of Alfred Greven and Continental flopped.

"But you are incapable of letting it go. It's as if you were her lover and not von Dirlinger," he said, his eyes flickering like a snake.

Lafarge did not appreciate the remark but let it drop as he prepared to disassemble Bousquet's cocksure attitude.

"Well let me wipe that grin off your face Bousquet.

"I am here to arrest you in connection with the burglary of Baroness Marchand's jewels in 1942, a charge that if convicted would see you serve a minimum term of eight years.

"Of course that might just be the aperitif. By the time you are contemplating freedom the war may be over and you will inevitably have to face trial for far worse crimes, for which the penalty is as I am sure you are aware death," said Lafarge trying not to look smug.

Bousquet's grin disappeared as Lafarge had hoped it would, but in its place did not come one of resigned acceptance but one of fury, his face going a light crimson.

"You will, however, be relieved to learn that I will not be pressing a charge of murder on you, for lack of evidence," Lafarge added.

"You really are out of your mind Lafarge. I thought you were already crazy when I took the decision to have you leave the force last year, but sadly that spell in the south has not brought you to your senses.

"I am still police chief and you cannot walk in here and accuse me of something so, what would one say, risible, yes risible, as being an accomplice in a burglary.

"Why would I risk my career for something quite so absurd? Also I don't need the money, so where is the benefit for me in all of this?

"No Lafarge you spent too long in that train with de Chastelain and listening to his fanciful tales. I will let this go if you just get up and leave now," he said his eyes narrowing into slits.

THE TORTURED DETECTIVE

"Sorry Bousquet I won't be doing that. I will leave once I have your promise that you will resign, I mean perhaps we could come to an arrangement over why you stepped down but step down you will.

"Everyone that matters wants you out now. The Germans are fed up, which should be enough for you, and even Leguay is looking to leave. The game is up Bousquet and you appear to be the only one unwilling to accept that," said Lafarge, pleased with how he was not wavering from his line despite the intimidation.

Bousquet appeared to be taken aback by Lafarge's attitude and not a little bemused by his confidence.

He stood up, Lafarge thought somewhat unsteadily, walked to the drinks cabinet and fixed himself a drink whilst he brought the bottle of cognac over to the table and placed it in front of Lafarge. He slurped down a large measure of his drink and lit a cigarette.

Lafarge decided now was the time to finish him off before Bousquet could fight back.

"If you think that de Chastelain is my source then you are wrong.

"As he is now out of reach I had to look elsewhere and I found myself a reliable witness. That person can attest to the fact you were at Marguerite's flat the night of the murder and more crucially that you were involved in the burglary.

"Unlike de Chastelain this witness will not be going anywhere until after the case is brought to court.

"I don't think there is a move you can make to extricate yourself from this Bousquet," said Lafarge.

Bousquet drank the rest of his drink and sat back on the sofa, stroking his shoes with his hand. He sat for several minutes considering his options and eventually sighed and took a deep breath.

"Such stupid things we do us humans huh Lafarge?

"Everything is in place for a comfortable and fruitful career, happily married with a child, and then what an apple is dangled before one.

"An apple that one shouldn't dare touch let alone look at, and yet like a fool one does and from doing so you bring ruin on yourself.

"Maybe it was the thrill of being involved in something which was clearly wrong and believing I was untouchable. Also other matters were of more importance to the police than a burglary of

311

some middle–aged aristocrat! Well I was sorely wrong about that," he grinned sourly.

"I had the misfortune to have the two detectives, who I couldn't control, stick their noses in and from the moment Lescarboura was arrested I knew that trouble lay ahead.

"It didn't help that von Dirlinger decided to play the maverick and have de Chastelain warned off appearing in court. Then to cap it all that stupid hysterical cow gets herself killed and that brings you onto the scene.

"Having put one detective in his place over the Lescarboura arrest I wasn't in a position to interfere with your being in charge of the murder enquiry, so I made it look as if I had asked for you to lead it.

"However, I do not know where you got the idea from that I was responsible for the murder. I was close to throttling her that night as she threatened to come clean about the whole affair if Lescarboura wasn't released.

"I told her there was no way I could organise that as it would look suspicious. First de Chastelain disappearing and then the man he was due to defend being released when there was clear evidence linking him to the burglary.

"She couldn't see it that way and so I left. She was very much alive.

"Of course but for the stupid mistake of leaving the cigarette case there I would not have been directly implicated. Nobody, not even you, would have asked questions if I had occasionally poked my nose in and made helpful suggestions such as looking into de Chastelain as a potential suspect.

"As I said I wasn't especially keen to have you anywhere near it but Massu likes and respects you and wouldn't countenance you being removed, so I relented.

"The problem is that you are too independent and I was preoccupied with other matters so I let you go too far before trying to rein you in.

"Our mutual animosity meant that I was never able to cajole you to put your foot on the brakes.

"Von Dirlinger reprimanded me on several occasions over that but I dismissed him as some sort of lightweight aristocratic playboy going all wobbly.

THE TORTURED DETECTIVE

"I may be right about that, but he was correct about my having let you wander off the ranch and being unable to bring you back in. That was of course until you came back from Limoges and without going over that ground again gave me the reasons to get rid of you.

"I always expected you to come back, one of your few characteristics I admire, because I share it, is that you are persistent.

"You are fortunate too that your timing was good because with the murder of Sarraut regardless of my determination to continue it is clear that as you say they, the Germans, want me removed.

"Well so be it, and to be honest I am quite welcoming a rest, for this period of almost two years have been exhausting, time to take a back seat," he said his voice quavering.

Lafarge could see that despite Bousquet's act of contrition, and his sudden enthusiasm for stepping down, his eyes were brimming with tears, which he quickly wiped away, while his hands were shaking ever so slightly.

He had little sympathy. For him these tears were those of a man angry with himself for having been unable to control the one case that could bring him down, and for failing to see that to the Nazis he was not their equal and he had served his purpose.

The tears were not for the thousands of people – not just foreign Jews but French as well for in the end religion overrode any sensitivity to their nationality as was the case with the communists – he had had rounded up and sent to the camps in eastern Europe.

Lafarge was certainly not going to begin to lecture him over that, for he had already had his fill of self–justifying excuses from his father and Leguay.

The next step was to stand over Bousquet and get his resignation written down and signed, for without it he could quite easily renege on his pledge.

"Right Bousquet get your secretary in here now and we can finish this in an honourable way," said Lafarge.

Bousquet looked furious but he accepted that now there was no alternative if he wished to save some face and also avoid a prison term.

So wearily he got to his feet and went to the door and called in his secretary telling her to bring pen and paper.

He took his place behind his desk, as it was probably the last time he would conduct official business from it, and dictated his letter of resignation, impressing Lafarge in the way he managed to keep his emotions in check.

He wondered whether this was the same tone of voice Bousquet had used when issuing the orders to round up the foreign Jews, if so it said it all about the coldness of the man. His secretary looked stunned but in her efficient and orderly way she had the letter typed and ready for his signature in 10 minutes.

At that point Bousquet called Leguay and Massu and asked them to come to his office.

His Special Brigade chiefs, including de Blaeckere, trooped back in to the same office they had only left an hour before believing their boss was staying on.

They all looked on with disbelief as Bousquet told them that he had rethought his decision and decided in the interests of unity and the future of Vichy's relationship with the Nazis he was after all going to resign.

His unprepared speech Lafarge noted was delivered again in a neutral tone, his voice never faltered until right at the end when he extolled the virtues of the French police force during his time in charge and that he regretted nothing.

This earned a rousing cheer from Leguay, who may have had his bags packed but still showed some loyalty by turning up to his mentor's farewell, and the Special Brigade leaders, though, they were in effect cheering themselves, while Massu applauded politely. Lafarge remained seated.

Bousquet then told them all to leave except Lafarge, and as they departed Massu asked to see him afterwards.

Lafarge said he would try but he had an urgent appointment on the other side of the city. Massu repeated his request and for once made it sound like an order, to which Lafarge nodded and said he would be there as soon as he could.

He didn't stay long, taking advantage of the cognac for what he knew would be the last time, only to wait for whatever Bousquet wished to say to him.

Bousquet had also helped himself to another drink, returned to his desk, sat down and put his feet up on the fine mahogany–topped surface.

THE TORTURED DETECTIVE

"Well Lafarge I believe this is the last time that either you or I will be in this office, also I think this is the last time that we will see each other.

"You seem very confident that the Germans will not win the war, I remain unconvinced. But should we both survive it and you see me on the street one day, please cross to the other side because I fear what I might do to you.

"I may have resisted the urge to throttle Marguerite Suchet but I would not for one instant show such restraint if I see you. Goodbye Lafarge," said Bousquet and with that he waved him towards the door.

Lafarge left without saying a word, a broad satisfied grin on his face.

CHAPTER THIRTY

Drieu strolled into the Flore about 10 minutes after Lafarge had arrived, dressed aptly for the cold evening, with an overcoat topped by a fur–lined collar. Fascism might be losing the argument in the war but Drieu's fortunes economically hadn't taken a similar pounding judging by his appearance.

He greeted a couple of high ranking Wehrmacht officers before sitting himself down at the table Lafarge had taken, which in summer would have been on the terrace but was covered in winter. It gave them a good view of those passing by and more importantly for the detective, those coming in.

He had had the impression he had been followed from the Quai, but then dismissed it as him being neurotic.

"So let me say it is an honour to be in the presence of Bousquet's executioner!" said Drieu, a sardonic smile spreading over his face.

"News travels fast, how the hell do you know?" asked Lafarge, aggrieved he couldn't tell his friend the news first.

"Christ you think news like that stays within the Quai? That it will only be known after a radio broadcast by Laval? You are being naive if you believe that," said Drieu.

"You are a hero to half of Paris, and that number is growing by the day with the 'master race' starting to look anything but that."

Lafarge performed a mock bow, though, he was restricted by being seated and his head brushed the top of his cognac glass.

"Enough of that," said Drieu gesturing towards the cognac and after gaining the attention of a waiter he ordered a bottle of Dom Perignon, the most expensive champagne the Flore presently had in its cellar.

"Well come on Gaston it is not every day that I get to sit with a man who brought down one of the most powerful people in France. Even if he was technically speaking on my side and was effective initially in resolving the Jewish problem," said Drieu.

Lafarge sighed and prayed that he wasn't about to be treated to another of Drieu's monologues on the Jews, but thankfully their long friendship had taught the writer to hold his tongue.

"He was on his way out anyway, Drieu," said Lafarge.

THE TORTURED DETECTIVE

"What, he was on the way out of the office when you caught him?" said Drieu laughing at his own joke, which was par for the course.

"Come come don't be so modest. I would like to know how you managed to persuade the great man to vacate his premises," said Drieu leaning towards Lafarge and at the same time blowing smoke into his eyes.

Lafarge coughed and wiped his eyes to rid himself of the stinging sensation and told Drieu everything. He had given his word to Bousquet that he would guard for himself why he had stepped down, but now he was gone and he had got what he wanted he didn't feel he was beholden to him.

Besides it was the reason he had arranged to see Drieu. He would have told him even if Bousquet had refused to resign as he owed it to his friend who had been involved in the story from the start and had pointed him in the direction of Limoges.

Drieu sat quietly listening attentively until Lafarge had finished.

"Have you heard from de Chastelain since? Or this Doctor?" he asked.

"No, but I didn't furnish him with our address in Nice, so there is no way he could have contacted me. I'm not worried. No news is good news in my book," he said.

"I guess so. You still think that he was innocent? That you did the right thing?" asked Drieu.

Lafarge thought for a minute.

"Yes, I'm comfortable with what I did. As indeed I am with regard to pushing Bousquet to take early retirement," he replied.

"De Chastelain's story rang true when he told it to me and the maid supported his version, though, it took her some time to admit as much. She is pretty suspicious herself to be honest, seems to enjoy playing one person off against another," he added.

"So by the laws of elimination Gaston it has to be the German, von Dirlinger," said Drieu.

"Yup with the other two out of the running it looks that way, although Mathilde is adamant she doesn't think he did it. Of all of them I think the maid is capable of having murdered Marguerite but on the other hand she doesn't have the power to go after the rest of the group," said Lafarge.

"Well I wish you luck with von Dirlinger, he's a slippery character. I don't really think his heart is in the Nazi cause to be honest, only to enrich himself, but if he is indeed involved with Lafont and Bonny you better be careful.

"Mind you there are less and less people who seem as fervent in their support of the Nazis since their fortunes declined on the battlefield," said Drieu.

Lafarge raised his glass and mouthed 'Hallelujah', to which Drieu smiled.

"I crossed paths with two Wehrmacht officers in the train on the way up from Nice and they didn't look too cheerful, less of a strut to their step. However, you look around here and nobody either in or out of uniform seems too preoccupied with the predictions of imminent defeat," said Lafarge.

"Well that's because they are thanking their lucky stars they are not on the Eastern Front. I shudder to think about the conditions there, and we have our boys in the French Volunteer Legion fighting alongside them poor sods," said Drieu.

"You better be careful Gaston in case von Dirlinger punishes you by enrolling you in the Charlemagne and sends you out east!" added Drieu laughing.

Lafarge grimaced at the thought and reflected that Drieu might not be far wrong in that happening.

"No these people here are still cocooned in the relative comfort of a Parisian winter, though, many cannot afford or have access to coal or wood for their fires or heaters," said Drieu.

"Well perhaps not most of us drinking here this evening, but judging by the length of the queues for bread and other basic goods, the shortages are affecting more and more people. Of course if you can afford to go, the cinema is the best refuge to at least warm yourself for an hour or so.

"Talking of which, over there, yes that stunning blonde, is the actress Maryse Arley."

Lafarge looked over to where Drieu had gestured and saw that she was indeed striking, and surrounded by several admirers, none of them in uniform.

"Yes she is lovely looking, but so what," said Lafarge.

Drieu smiled and gave Lafarge a knowing look.

THE TORTURED DETECTIVE

"No, I didn't sleep with her! Only she got a role that would have been Marguerite's if she had lived. I don't know if you had time to see 'Les Corrupteurs' before you took your unscheduled break last year, but she definitely has potential," said Drieu.

Lafarge winced at the mention of the film, for though he hadn't seen it he had heard it was a truly awful production with its sole purpose to show how dreadful the Jews were. In a way he was delighted that Marguerite had not lived to have her name associated with such vile fare.

"And what now for you? Are you going to stay or leave?" asked Drieu.

"Me? I'm finished here, at least for the immediate future. Massu told me as much after I dropped in to see him following Bousquet's resignation. He didn't rule out me returning yet again but he said he felt it better for me that I take a leave of absence.

"Besides I promised Isabella that we would review the situation after I wrapped things up here. Also with Joseph Darnand replacing Bousquet I have no hope of being retained. He is even more dangerous because he is a zealot as is clear from the brutal manner his Milice have behaved."

Drieu nodded in agreement.

"Yes I think that would be good for you Gaston, Bousquet at least had a boundary he wouldn't cross. He cared about being seen in a good light by both Vichy and the Nazis, so taking you out permanently would never have been an option.

"Darnand on the other hand is a mad dog, a warrior, and would prefer probably to be in full German uniform. Although I hear he even approached de Gaulle through intermediaries to see if he could go over to him and was rejected. Anyway now he knows there is no way out he will be ruthless and unleash his dogs of war on whoever crosses him.

"You my friend would be near the top of the list because you are no good at holding your tongue and besides I would imagine your dossier is awaiting his attention as soon as he settles down behind his desk," said Drieu.

Lafarge grinned and attracted the waiter's attention to bring a second bottle. He looked at his watch and saw it was six thirty and thought he better call it quits after this bottle and get back to see how Aimee was coping in 'prison Lafarge'.

PIRATE IRWIN

"And you Drieu, what are you going to do?" he asked.

Drieu's expression changed from being cheerful, well with him it was relative, to a pensive look.

"Well that is an excellent question Gaston. What indeed does the future hold for me? The answer is not a very rosy one," he said with a sad smile.

"I referred to those who had shall we say lost their faith earlier on and you raised your glass to that.

"Well you may be shocked to hear it from my lips but I am one of those. I haven't lost my faith in Fascism as being the only ideology capable of installing order and combatting the baleful Satan that is Bolshevism.

"However, the Germans look likely to fail this time both in defeating the Bolsheviks and resolving the Jewish question permanently. Therefore it will be left for another generation to prove more effective and more clinical in the execution of these crucial conflicts.

"Obviously I am desperately disappointed by this. I thought for so long that it was possible, but my hopes have, as well as those of many others, been dashed.

"Some will cling to the increasingly unlikely possibility of the Nazis turning things round, a miracle weapon or maybe more likely Stalin dying, how I pray for that, but even Brasillach is having his doubts."

Lafarge was indeed surprised by his friend's admission and his pessimistic forecast of the way the war would develop, Of course Drieu was no military man, but he mixed with high ranking German officers, SS types and bureaucrats and no doubt information from them had contributed to his conversion from confidence in ultimate victory to abject defeat.

Lafarge would not regret the defeat of the Nazis and their French allies but he did worry about what would happen to Drieu when the Germans eventually left Paris, which could still be a matter of years.

However, whenever that moment did arrive people would come hunting for Drieu. His public support for the Nazis and virulently anti–Semitic articles had made him one of the most high–profile and notorious of the clique of literary collaborators.

THE TORTURED DETECTIVE

"Why not flee while you can Drieu? I can even help you, see if the Doctor is still operating," said Lafarge patting his friend on the arm.

Drieu smiled at Lafarge's unintended play on words, but his expression resumed its hangdog look almost immediately.

"No, that is very kind but I have decided I will stay. I have seen what I need to see of the rest of the world, and I cannot think of a country I could envisage hiding away in for probably the rest of my life. Besides it is not in my nature to bite my tongue and live quietly," he said his voice trembling.

Lafarge sighed and clinked his glass against Drieu's and when soon afterwards it came to say goodbye, he felt tears welling up as he knew that it would be the last time he saw him. Misguided and as unattractive as his opinions had been he would still miss him terribly.

While Drieu wandered off to hail a taxi and an evening at the Casino de Paris, another place Lafarge avoided owing to its tasteless notice posted outside 'No Jews or dogs allowed', he walked towards Rue Bonaparte, past the church of St Germain des Pres, to where he had parked his car.

He never reached the car. Waiting to cross the street he felt something pressed into the back of his spine. A man crossed the other side of the street and approached him while a black Citroen pulled up alongside them. The man stopped in front of Lafarge and smiled.

"Chief Inspector Lafarge. I'm Emmanuel Clausel, my colleague with the gun pointing at your spine is Florian Grandpierre, and you are to come with us," said the smartly dressed man, neither whose name nor face were known to Lafarge.

Lafarge cursed inwardly, for he had been right he had been followed to the Flore but the champagne had made him careless.

"I don't seem to have a choice do I? Although I wouldn't mind knowing where the hell you are taking me," he said.

Clausel smiled darkly as he relieved Lafarge of his service revolver.

"To Rue Lauriston. My bosses and indeed your sister are most anxious to see you," he said.

Lafarge groaned and shook his head in despair as Clausel and Grandpierre pushed him roughly into the back of the car before taking their places either side of him.

*

His kidnappers deposited him at Rue Lauriston after a troublefree drive through largely deserted streets. Not a word passed between them while Lafarge had to try and suppress the nervousness he was feeling about what awaited him.

Clausel both in his classy manner of dressing and comportment didn't strike Lafarge as a typical Lafont goon. But he didn't probe and it was he who escorted him through the marble–floored hallway, and away from what sounded like a raucous party taking place in a room off it. They proceeded down a red–carpeted passageway which led to what he took to be the chief's office.

This was pretty gaudy with mirrors on three of the walls and huge vases of lilies and orchids covering the Louis XV tables that lined the walls. There was a huge elegant mahogany topped desk with a chair like a throne behind it, and above it staring defiantly out over the room was a photograph of Hitler.

Lafarge breathed a sigh of relief that at least he hadn't been taken downstairs from where, he had heard, few people emerged alive. Clausel fetched him a cognac, good quality too he noted when he took his first sip, and then stood guard silently at the gold–flaked double door.

Suddenly the doors burst open and in marched Bonny, his ratlike features bathed in a triumphant smile, and the rounder figure of Lafont, who looked as if he was going to a fancy dress party dressed as he was in his SS uniform.

Lafont patted Lafarge on the cheek and smiled at him before he took his place behind the desk, while Bonny stood to the side and Clausel having served them both drinks and refilled the detective's glass exited.

Both Bonny and Lafont seemed to be well on their way to being drunk, which Lafarge didn't think was a good omen as he couldn't imagine they were good–natured drunks. Lafont, who had a good looking face which had gone to seed and was quite jowly, looked at him with a bored bleary–eyed expression on his face.

"So Chief Inspector I will get to the point as we have guests, influential ones too, and I don't want business to ruin the evening,

THE TORTURED DETECTIVE

although your sister Vanessa is doing her usual excellent job as hostess. She is most accommodating if we ask her to be extra friendly to some of our German acquaintances," said Lafont his voice crisp.

"So before I hand you over to Bonny, who I can't tell you how much he is looking forward to being on his own with you after your brief encounter in that slut's apartment, I would like to know what you intended to do about us and one of our German business partners."

Lafarge took a sip of his cognac puffed on his cigarette and considered his response trying not to allow his fury at the remarks about his sister affect him. So she wasn't just Bonny's mistress they were also hiring her out as a prostitute, surely even she had a limit to the humiliations she could put up with.

"With regard to you and him," he replied waving his hand dismissively in the direction of Bonny "nothing. However, tonight may change that. Von Dirlinger is another matter for I have other business with him."

Lafont took a large puff of his cigar, rolled the smoke round his mouth and exhaled the smoke slowly.

"I don't appreciate being threatened in my office Lafarge, better men and women than you have been very forthright in here and all of them have regretted it. All the same you are right. Tonight will indeed change things, but only in as much as you will no longer pose a threat to our arrangement with von Dirlinger," said Lafont.

Lafarge tried to restrain himself from laughing but failed lamentably prompting Bonny to move menacingly towards him, only for Lafont to hold his hand up to stop him.

"What the fuck is so funny? I heard you were a puritanical holier than thou prick, but I didn't know that you were also a bit soft in the head," growled Lafont.

"Well really Lafont, you are so predictable with your lame impression of Al Capone. Do you really believe I thought I was brought here for a polite chat and a pull yourself together lecture? I'm not a rookie Lafont, even Bonny would vouch for that. I would rather be blunt and frank than go downstairs regretting I had held something back.

"So it is a pity you felt obliged to pick me up as I had no intention of trespassing on your territory. It is only your renegade German

323

partner I wanted to punish. However, I see you have some sense of fidelity and are taking care of business for him. I am sure I will not be the first person you have helped disappear on his behalf."

Lafont grunted and looked at Bonny, who had retreated a few steps.

"Well that leads me on to the second and final question I wanted to ask you. That is where are the jewels?" asked Lafont, his beady eyes boring into Lafarge's.

Lafarge shrugged.

"I have no idea. Why don't you ask your business partner?" Lafarge said pointing at Bonny.

Bonny bristled and flexed his fists, but the detective could tell he had momentarily at least sown a seed of doubt in Lafont's mind.

Lafont turned his gaze away from Lafarge and stared at Bonny.

"What the fuck Lafarge! Of course I didn't find the jewels. Do you think I would screw you over René? This prick is trying to make trouble but he is lying," protested Bonny.

"Oh well if that's what your version is Bonny then so be it. I just wondered what all that clanking in your pockets was when I kicked your ass out of the apartment," said Lafarge.

This proved too much for Bonny who walked over and punched Lafarge in the jaw, sending him crashing to the floor. Lafarge rubbed it gingerly, sensed it wasn't broken, and rose to his feet his fists raised.

"Alright you two stop it!" said Lafont, who had remained seated enjoying the spectacle.

Bonny turned to Lafont and shook his head.

"Seriously René this guy is as you said soft in the head. He's making all this up, trying to be too clever for his own good. I didn't have a chance to search the whole apartment and I can assure you I didn't find them in the one room I looked in," said Bonny.

"We're making too much money for me to go out on my own. Now that we have wiped out our opposition we have a monopoly, there is no way I would jeopardise that."

Lafont nodded and looked at Lafarge raising his eyebrows.

"Well Chief Inspector? Do you have any actual evidence to support your accusation?"

Lafarge shook his head accepting that he could only play them off against each other for a limited spell of time.

THE TORTURED DETECTIVE

"So now that that piece of theatrics is over Lafarge. Where are the jewels?" asked Lafont.

"I haven't the faintest idea. I don't have them, neither does Bousquet and obviously von Dirlinger hasn't either so your guess is as good as mine, and it is not often that I have thought of us as equals," said Lafarge.

Lafont was not amused by the remark and rose from his seat.

"You are a real wise ass huh Lafarge! You are also or have been until now a lucky son of a bitch. Do you know that we sent a commando of our men down to Limoges to take care of one of our men, Jean Leroy for skimming money from us?" said Lafont.

"He died whimpering like a baby. Our men asked after you round town but of course we were too late, though, I think we would have been anyway if you had remained there. The Special Brigades chief appeared equally keen to get rid of you as we were.

"Well we've got you now and it is my pleasure to leave you in the hands of Bonny, who has already shown you a little of what you can expect. Only this time you will have your hands and legs tied together," said Lafont with a malicious grin on his face.

Lafarge grimaced while Bonny moved towards a pair of doors behind the detective and Lafont made to exit by the ones they had entered through.

"Von Dirlinger is behind all this isn't he Lafont?" asked Lafarge, hoping at least to go to his death knowing who was responsible for it.

Lafont stopped at the door and turned towards Lafarge, who by this stage was being manhandled out of the chair and towards the other room by Bonny.

"Him? No of course not. He is especially squeamish and doesn't like to know how we deal with problems, though, he must be aware of our methods. This is all our own idea and work Lafarge.

"Firstly we like to protect our partners and secondly we loathe your type, those that like to think they are incorruptible, or that their price is too high for anyone to pay. After all everyone can be bought, only you are not worth what you may think you are and we believe it is cheaper to get rid of you than to pay you.

"We already have one of your family on the payroll and she doesn't come cheap, especially her morphine habit. But the bonus is that she is more our type sexually speaking than you are and she repays us liberally with her favours," said Lafont flashing him one of his evil grins before disappearing out the door.

Lafarge would have liked to have run after Lafont and kicked the living daylights out of him. However, despite his wiry physique Bonny was strong and kept a tight hold of him before dragging him into the adjoining room.

"You bastards! You have turned my sister into a whore and an addict!" shouted Lafarge.

Bonny just laughed and threw Lafarge onto the white and black tiled floor while he called out to someone to come and help him.

"It might be a good thing your sister has such a liking for morphine because you will need some to ease the pain we are going to inflict on you," said Bonny bending down over Lafarge.

Lafarge spat in Bonny's face and earned a kick in the ribs. As he curled up in pain he saw two of the other members of the gang enter the room, which reminded him of a dentist's surgery with its white walls. However, instead of the seat one lay in while the dentist poked around inside your mouth there was a large white bath.

One of the men bent over it and started running the water while Bonny and the other well–built man restrained Lafarge, tore off his jacket and shirt and bound him with ropes.

Bonny asked whether the bath was ready and his accomplice nodded. With Lafarge now subdued the other man went over to another corner and wheeled over to the bath a device which looked like a seesaw on wheels.

Lafarge's eyes bulged when he saw this, his heart racing as he realized what they had in mind for him.

Bonny looked down on Lafarge's prostrate figure and reveled in his misery.

"Yes this is how it is going to end. But don't worry it won't be quick, I am a master at prolonging life until the victim is begging for death," he said smiling.

Bonny then gestured to the man who had helped tie up Lafarge to come and aid him in dragging him over to the seesaw. Lafarge was powerless to resist but refused to scream out as he didn't want to give Bonny the satisfaction.

They then lifted him onto the contraption where they briefly untied him before retying the ropes round the plank. Lafarge's head

THE TORTURED DETECTIVE

was at the end nearer the bath which meant he was staring up at Bonny's face.

"Bonny usually one is allowed a final request. Are those the rules here?" asked Lafarge, trying to suppress the fear he was feeling being reflected in his voice.

Bonny nodded.

"Well I would rather that the last thing I see in this life wasn't your face so please turn me over," said Lafarge, which provoked the other two men to burst out laughing.

Bonny was furious at being ridiculed and slapped Lafarge twice round the face.

"Right let's give the Chief Inspector a taste of what he can expect," said Bonny after he cooled down.

With that Bonny and the well–built thug tilted up the other end of the seesaw and Lafarge's head disappeared into freezing water.

He reeled from the shock as his body was racked by palpitations his heart rate slowing considerably while he couldn't breathe without water flooding into his mouth and entering his lungs.

After what seemed like several minutes, though, it was probably just a minute otherwise he wouldn't probably still be alive the plank was tilted back the other way and Lafarge came back up retching and gasping for air, his body trembling all over.

Bonny peered down at him, he was smiling in a self–satisfied way.

"Probably the first time you've been pleased to see my face after all Lafarge!" he said.

Lafarge didn't react, he was physically incapable of doing so. His whole thought process seemed to have shut down, dread at being dunked back into the bath was the only thing that filled his head. However, he desperately tried not to convey the fear he felt by shutting his eyes.

"Come come Lafarge open your eyes! You've kept them closed for long enough to the realities of the situation that you might as well die with them open," hissed Bonny before bursting out in a manic laugh.

Seconds later he indicated to the sidekick to take hold of the device and help him tilt it upwards again. Lafarge steeled himself for the shock, never one for church or religious thoughts he wasn't going to recite a prayer as he braced to depart the world.

He was just numb and he thought it best to die in that fashion. No thoughts of regret, of failing to have the time to make up with his father, how he would miss his family, just acceptance he was minutes away from death.

Down he went his head hitting the water with some force and then the same ripples of shock running through his whole body. However, this time it didn't appear to be as long as the first time under water, or maybe he was already getting used to it. Or of course he was just plain dead.

However, he could just about feel his heart beating when he emerged once again. This time when he opened his eyes it was to see a far from happy Bonny saying something he couldn't make out, as his ears were blocked, to one of the two gang members.

They moved towards him with knives drawn and Lafarge waited for them to plunge them into his body or to slit his throat like they would a pig.

Instead, however, they sliced apart the ropes tying him to the seesaw and lifted him up so he sat astride the device, leading him to cough up water which splattered on their shoes.

He was by this stage totally confused at the turn of events. But once he came properly to his senses and his eyes were able to focus properly he saw why he had gained such a reprieve, for standing in the doorway was Huariau.

Huariau put his index finger to his fedora and tipped the front of it in a kind of salute. All five men stayed in their positions, the Bonny trio encircling Lafarge, none of them saying a word until the detective had regained his ability to speak.

"Huariau what are you doing here?" asked Lafarge stretching out his arms as he tried to get some feeling back.

Huariau stepped forward, Lafarge noticed he didn't even have his gun, and held out his hand.

"I suggest we speak in the car. Can you walk? Otherwise I will ask these two gentlemen to help you to the door," said Huariau.

Lafarge sensing that perhaps his reprieve might be temporary unless he made his exit now tried to stand but his legs gave way, the blood not having fully recovered its power of circulation, and Huariau caught him.

THE TORTURED DETECTIVE

"Right Schwarzfeld and you Bonny, yes you you stupid bastard, take a shoulder each and bring him to the car," said Huariau, his tone brooking no argument.

Bonny was seething, his moment of revenge ruined and now humiliatingly forced to help his victim to the car, but he obeyed Huariau nonetheless.

It took some time to drag Lafarge back down the passage and into the hall. He could hear the party was still in full flow and wondered briefly what state his sister was in by this stage.

He thought it wise not to ask whether she too could come with them, and finally they managed to get him down the steps outside the front door and into the passenger seat.

Bonny slammed the door shut, probably vainly hoping that Lafarge's foot was still hanging outside the car, and engaged in a heated conversation with Huariau. The detective could not make it out clearly enough and frankly he didn't care for he was enjoying the fact he was still alive.

Huariau finally managed to rid himself of Bonny, who mounted the steps and stood on them with his hands on his hips looking hatefully at the car as it drove off, though, Lafarge thought he looked rather pathetic. However, he shuddered to think what was in store for Vanessa. For if what Lafont and Bonny had taunted him with was true then she was as much a victim as those who went downstairs or into the room he had been in.

On the other hand nothing he had heard from others about seeing her at these parties or out at clubs and restaurants on Bonny's arm suggested she had been an unwilling companion.

"Cognac?" asked Huariau, breaking Lafarge's train of thought.

Lafarge gripped the hip flask and his hands still shaking slightly raised it to his lips and drank half of the contents. Never had his favourite drink tasted better or more welcoming as it warmed first his mouth and then the rest of the top half of his body.

He took a cigarette Huariau offered him and managed to light it, the smoke burning his lungs at the first intake, but soon his body returned to something approaching normal.

"So Huariau do you mind telling me how you managed to track me down and secondly how on earth you succeeded in persuading that vile piece of shit to release me," said Lafarge.

"Well you can thank Gerland. He was concerned by the interest the Lafont and Bonny gang members showed in you when they came to Limoges to resolve their own internal problems," said Huariau, his eyes not straying from the road.

"Thus he asked me to put a couple of men on tracking you when he heard you had returned from Nice. I did so, and while you were not aware the gang were following you, they appear to have been similarly ignorant that we were shadowing them."

"Yes, but you still had to gain access to Lauriston and then persuade them to let me go," said Lafarge.

"Ah that was actually far easier than the tracking of you and them. Gerland has kept a lot of his old clientele, he probably told you as much when you were down in Limoges. He never misses an opportunity to tell anyone he comes into contact with as he thinks it is hilarious.

"Anyway one of his, as it turns out, best pre–War investments was he defended Bonny when he was thrown off the force in disgrace and then imprisoned.

"While he didn't keep him out of prison, Bonny thought he had done a fine job. Thus once he and Lafont started making serious money, he entrusted all legal matters to Gerland and a fair amount of their money to be kept safe in Limoges or secreted away.

"He has quite a hold over them, both personally and professionally. He told me, as they know me because I have been a go between for Gerland before, to present myself there and tell Bonny to release you otherwise he would never see a large part of his fortune.

"The fact all of it has been gained through criminal and violent means is purely secondary in this matter of course!" sad Huariau laughing bitterly.

"Bloody hell Gerland and you have some nerve. How could he or indeed you be so sure that Bonny and Lafont would dismiss the threat, kill me and you and then send his goons to Limoges to deal with Gerland?" said Lafarge.

"Well I guess Bonny perhaps has more regard for Maitre Gerland than to spit in his face, although I think the money is the key. Sheer greed," said Huariau.

"This bloody war has been far worse for France than the Great War, it has completely divided us.

THE TORTURED DETECTIVE

"Even worse it has made scum like Lafont and Bonny extremely rich. Profiteers are bad enough but thugs and gangsters are the pits, and decent people of integrity like Gerland have felt obliged to compromise and become involved with them," added Huariau.

"Well I am a stubborn son of a bitch and the last one to wish to make compromises but I am truly glad that Gerland did!" said Lafarge.

Lafarge couldn't believe his good fortune and he owed Gerland and Huariau a huge debt for stepping in and standing up to Bonny. Whatever Huariau said it had taken immense courage to do that.

He told him so but Huariau shrugged his shoulders as if to say I'm sure you would have done the same thing. Lafarge grunted a yes but in truth he didn't know if he could have done so.

Huariau appeared to know where they were going as he hadn't asked Lafarge for a destination, and to the detective's surprise his former colleague drew to a halt outside his apartment block.

Then it came to him, of course he had been tracked since he returned from Nice. He didn't really care whether they had seen him with Aimee on the first night as they were not going to denounce her.

Huariau helped him out of the car, but this time Lafarge was able to walk, albeit it was more of a shuffle.

"Erm Huariau I feel embarrassed to ask you this after what you did tonight, but could you keep an eye out for my sister? That is whenever you have to conduct business with them on behalf of Gerland," said Lafarge.

Huariau nodded.

"Good news is that you can call your men off watching the apartment block. There's no need to keep an eye on it anymore," said Lafarge.

He shook Huariau's hand with both of his to emphasise his appreciation.

"By the way Lafarge, Gerland said to pass on to you that he does do divorce cases for real," said Huariau winking at him and raisIng his eyes up towards the floor that Lafarge lived on.

For the first time in what had been an extraordinary day, and one which had almost culminated in his death, Lafarge laughed… and boy did it feel good.

PIRATE IRWIN

THE TORTURED DETECTIVE

CHAPTER THIRTY–ONE

Lafarge woke the next morning with his body and head aching. The former because of his experiences at Rue Lauriston the latter because having finally dragged himself up the stairs and into the apartment, aided by Madame Grondon, Aimee had poured drink down him to help dull the pain.

Normally a hot bath would have been the healthy option. But despite a generous offer of Madame Grondon to heat up some water, Lafarge was understandably reluctant to get into a bath.

Aimee hadn't pressed too hard to get him to tell her what had happened, but drink as is its way loosens tongues and he gave her a fairly detailed account of what had taken place, ending it on the brighter note of Bousquet's resignation.

Aimee said she knew already as it had been broadcast on the Nazi–authorised Radio–Paris, which as he lay back in bed he could hear blaring from the drawing room with some collaborationist politician droning on.

His aching head could also not blot out the memory of him and Aimee tumbling into bed, their making love brought about by a mix of drink, relief at having escaped certain death and also their mutual attraction.

He had no regrets, although he accepted that there was no future for them as a couple. Indeed if he was able to make his rendezvous with von Dirlinger that night then he wanted to be on a train back to the south the next day.

He was sure that Aimee was not under any illusions either. But he hoped the matter would not cloud their day together, for he wanted to spend a pleasurable time with her before he brought the investigation that had dominated his life for almost two years to a conclusion.

Funny he thought that this has been so important to me and I have paid scant attention to far greater events that will have a direct influence on the way the world is run for decades to come. Better to think in the short term than tempt fate as Hitler had and predict a 1000-year Reich which now appeared to have been one of the most inaccurate prophecies of all time

PIRATE IRWIN

Yet he reasoned that unless ordinary people, especially policemen like himself, went round doing their jobs even in times of war then anarchy and despotism would rule everywhere. Even if it wouldn't merit mentioning in history books – Bousquet would no doubt feature but not in the way he probably imagined it would be a year ago.

Lafarge sighed and then levered himself out of bed, putting on a dressing gown, which was hanging on the door. He walked out into the drawing room where Aimee, also in a dressing gown though hers was a far more glamorous silk one, was making coffee.

"Ahi there you are sleepy head! You know what time it is? Midday!" she grinned.

He smiled too and gave her a kiss before sitting in his favourite tatty chair.

"You want to go to the cinema Aimee? You must be bored out of your mind having spent all of yesterday cooped up here," said Lafarge.

"Besides it is warm there. The only thing is to be there early as the queues are almost as long as those for the baker and the butcher these days with so little food available."

Aimee laughed and wagged her finger at him.

"You don't have to get me out of the flat! I am not going to ravage you. Although that is a far more enjoyable means of keeping warm," she said.

Lafarge could feel himself blushing but vehemently denied that was the reason for his suggestion.

"No seriously Aimee it would be nice to do something normal, not anything that involves beating up people, arguing with anyone or even being tortured," he said.

"Also you can compare yourself with the actresses. That is if you are still intent on breaking cover and persuading Guitry to get you a role. I think it is a pretty stupid idea, but I will leave that up to you."

She flinched at his remarks about her announcement the night before that she was willing to trust in Guitry's ability to have her rehabilitated and get her roles.

"Well that is as you say up to me. But yes let us go to the cinema I heard on Radio–Paris of one called 'Goupi Mains Rouges' which sounds a decent tale of a family conflict, essentially between two

334

THE TORTURED DETECTIVE

brothers. One stays on the family farm and the other is told to return home from the city to marry a girl who is coveted by the boy who stayed in the country," she said.

Lafarge thought it sounded perfectly awful but its good point was that it didn't seem to be an ideological vehicle. To be fair to Greven he had not turned French cinema totally into a propaganda tool and some fine films had been made as he had discovered when he had been in Nice.

"Ok that is a deal then. Go and get ready while I finish my coffee and look in the paper, which I imagine Madame Grondon sweetly brought up this morning, for where it is on.

"We can go and grab some lunch and go to the mid–afternoon showing. How does that suit?"

Aimee nodded enthusiastically and rushed to the bathroom.

Lafarge added a drop of cognac to his coffee and listened to the radio.That was not a rewarding experience as the rabid far right journalist Jean–Herold Paquis spewed forth his daily dose of venomous outpourings against anyone and anything the Nazis despised.

By the time it came to Paquis' trademark phrase 'England like Carthage shall be destroyed' Lafarge had had enough and turned it off.

England indeed, sneered Lafarge, it was France that shall be destroyed…if it hadn't already been.

*

The film was pretty woeful as Lafarge had feared it would be but it passed the time. At least Aimee had enjoyed it, or it seemed she was the moments he was not snoring gently as the effects of their lunch took hold.

Now, however he was alert as he drove to his meeting with von Dirlinger. He hadn't told Aimee where he was going as he didn't want her worrying or causing a scene when he dropped her back at his apartment.

As a matter of courtesy he had phoned Massu and informed him where he was going but to not post a police presence. He would deal with the matter on his own as he had done pretty much from the beginning.

He was running about 20 minutes ahead of schedule. However, he wanted to arrive at von Dirlinger's apartment in enough time to scout around and ensure there were no Abwehr agents, or that Lafont and Bonny and their goons weren't in the vicinity.

Lafarge parked a cigarette smoke's away from the building. He glanced at his watch under the weak light in the car and saw he had 10 minutes till the meeting, but it was going to take longer to skirt round the ares in the pitch dark.

Even the wealthier areas of Paris lacked street lamps that worked and there was seemingly no great urgency to replace the bulbs.

Well, Lafarge thought, if the people cannot even get bread or other basic goods who is going to care about ensuring the well–off have enough light to walk their precious dogs or take heed of their pleas that it made them susceptible to being mugged?

He walked around for longer than he would have liked but he preferred to be at ease once he entered the building assured that there were no nasty surprises awaiting him should he leave unharmed.

He'd passed a couple on the opposite side of the avenue, but they had turned down a pathway soon afterwards and Lafarge had observed them unlocking the door into the block.

Thus satisfied and not a little relieved to get into the relative warmth of von Dirlinger's building he rode the lift up to where it had all begun almost two years ago and where now in a neat piece of symmetry it was all going to end.

He rang the doorbell and was surprised to see that it was Mathilde who answered and stood aside to let him in.

She wasn't dressed formally, a low cut dark blue woolen dress with a sparkling silver necklace round her giraffe like neck, so he surmised that she was there to be a witness to the conversation between himself and von Dirlinger.

That made him a little nervous, more so that her welcome had been even less cordial than the glacial one she had given him earlier in the day.

She did at least offer to take his coat. He declined and said he preferred to keep it on and if he got too hot he would just throw it over one of the chairs in the drawing room.

She then wandered off towards the kitchen and he did the same on the pretext that he thought she was taking him to von Dirlinger, but the real purpose was he wanted to discern whether there were others in the apartment.

THE TORTURED DETECTIVE

He noticed that the spare room door was shut as was the one to Marguerite's bedroom, no doubt it was now the German's which he thought was a bit much.

Mathilde on realizing he was behind her flashed him an angry look, by now a standard issue one for her with regard to Lafarge, and coldly told him that the colonel was in the drawing room. Fortunately she said this as she opened the door to the kitchen and Lafarge could make out that there was nobody in there.

He smiled and apologized beating a hasty retreat to the drawing room whose doors were also shut. He felt like cocking his revolver but reproached himself for being too neurotic. He opened the door to find von Dirlinger standing by the mantlepiece, a roaring fire going, with nothing more offensive than what looked like a dry martini in one hand and a cigarette in the other.

"Come in my favourite French detective. Take off your coat as you can see I do not want to share the privations of others and sit wrapped in several coats trying to keep warm. Not when I can avail myself of free wood for a real fire!" said von Dirlinger.

Lafarge smiled warmly and did take his coat off because the heat in the room would have done justice to how Joan of Arc must have felt at the stake.

Mathilde emerged from the door leading into the kitchen and offered him what was indeed a vodka martini, olive included. Just so he didn't get the idea she was fulfilling servile roles all night she picked up one of her own from a side table.

"Nice that we are drinking in rather smarter surroundings than the last time we had drinks in this apartment Mathilde," said Lafarge.

Mathilde smiled politely, which at least was an improvement on the scowls that he had got so used to.

"So Gaston tell me, I hear you have been very busy since you returned," said von Dirlinger.

"Claiming the scalp of Bousquet was quite some coup. I am impressed, no really. Knochen and Oberg were starting to think that they would have to send their men in and arrest him, which would really have been a most unfortunate sequence of events.

"There could have been a very tense stand–off between the former secretary–general's loyalists and our SS and Gestapo officers. It is the last thing that we would have needed at this delicate stage in our relationship," he added, all but adding a tut tut at the end of his sentence.

Lafarge would have liked to have replied 'don't you mean at this delicate stage of the war' but refrained from doing so so as not to upset the amicable atmosphere. That was going to change but for the moment he would go along for the ride.

"Yes well that would have been the worst option. The reaction of his loyalists to his resignation was one of disbelief and fury, but at least he told them himself. An enforced change would have resulted in a pitched battle, of that I am sure," said Lafarge.

"As for my role in it, well I wouldn't be too congratulatory. I don't think what I had to say to him would ordinarily have had a huge impact on him. He would have simply had me arrested on some trumped up charge or he would have sent me back to Nice. But he decided to acquiesce once I dangled the carrot in front of him of no charges being brought.

"Still it did give me a lot of pleasure," he added with a laugh.

Von Dirlinger laughed as well, before he turned towards the mirror and tried to adjust his black bow tie, for for once he was out of uniform and he looked as impressive in evening dress as he did in the Abwehr uniform.

Mathilde having disappeared to fetch him and Lafarge another drink, the detective thought it the moment to start turning the screw.

"You look very at home here colonel," said Lafarge.

Von Dirlinger cast him a glance in the mirror and smiled.

"Yes, you probably think it's macabre for me to come and live in the apartment where my love was murdered, but to me it was the logical thing to do.

"Better for someone who loved her to live where she died than a person who would not appreciate her and the history of the place," he said.

"Don't worry colonel I have seen some macabre things in my life and this would be low down the list. I would call it more a calculated move by a highly intelligent man," commented Lafarge.

Von Dirlinger had finished adjusting his bow tie and turned to face Lafarge, who had remained standing, profiting from the heat from the fire. He looked at Lafarge a little perplexed but his

THE TORTURED DETECTIVE

expression altered as Mathilde re–entered the room armed with three newly filled glasses.

"Ah my beautiful maid, Gaston was just remarking that moving in here was a calculated one by what was it? Ah yes a highly intelligent man.

"Well not so intelligent an example of the species that he hires a lesbian as the maid wouldn't you agree?" he said winking at Lafarge, who found it a pretty tasteless remark.

Mathilde just smiled and handed them their glasses. Lafarge, though, moved in between her and von Dirlinger and took the glass she was offering the colonel so he was forced to take the one he should have had.

Can't be too careful Lafarge thought. All too easy for them to have planned to dope or poison me prior to my arrival, so let's see how von Dirlinger reacts.

Von Dirlinger, to his disappointment, didn't bat an eyelid, taking a sip from the glass and complimenting Mathilde on her cocktail mixing ability.

"Suzy has taught you well Mathilde, I must thank her later," simpered von Dirlinger.

Lafarge had to agree that she was indeed a fine maker of cocktails.

"Your talents are wasted here Mathilde. You should see if Suzy couldn't keep you closer at hand and make you one of the first female cocktail makers," said Lafarge, a little unkindly but it hit its mark for Mathilde's cheeks turned red.

Von Dirlinger thought it highly amusing, but Lafarge was keen to take that irritating look off his face.

"Yes, I congratulate you on the efficient and calculating way in which you have played your role throughout the investigation colonel. This latest one is mere confirmation of your abilities," said Lafarge.

That wasn't enough to erase the smile from Von Dirlinger's face. To Lafarge it now appeared that Mathilde and the colonel were like a bad cop good cop partnership, she sulked, grimaced and scowled and he was all smiles and laughter.

This sort of behaviour was easily read by criminals and only served to get them to play a game with the respective detectives.

339

Oh well if it amuses them let them carry on playing, thought Lafarge.

"Right colonel I think it is time we moved on to the official reason why I am here, for you look as if you are due somewhere else. Mathilde, well we know where she has to be, and I too have an engagement," said Lafarge.

Von Dirlinger agreed saying he had a dinner with Cocteau and Marais which was being hosted by the American socialite Florence Jay Gould. It was only around the corner and he had said that he would be fashionably late, that is around 10.30.

Lafarge said that he might be later than that but he would try to be as quick as possible.

He preferred to stand leaving Mathilde to sit in one of the armchairs. Von Dirlinger flopped down on the sofa where Marguerite had died, the covers of which Lafarge noted the colonel had at least had the good taste to have replaced.

"So colonel I have heard through Bousquet and Mathilde, for there is no reason to protect her anymore, that you have throughout this investigation tried either to control me or if she is to be believed have me killed," said Lafarge.

Von Dirlinger remained impassive, although he shot a glance at Mathilde, who sat with a face like thunder on her.

"But that's ridiculous Gaston! Pure fantasy on both their parts, and Mathilde I really don't understand where you got the idea I wanted him dead from," said von Dirlinger.

Mathilde stayed silent, allowing Lafarge to fill in the gaps.

"Mathilde has no reason to lie von Dirlinger. She has told me all about your arrangement with Bonny and Lafont, your sleazy sideline in criminal ventures, and how if you needed them for dirty outside jobs they fulfilled the contract at a price.

"Thus it was with finding the jewels, although with your endless sense of the dramatic you wanted Mathilde to deliver the fatal blow to me. Something which she was incapable of doing because as she told me she didn't trust you enough to go through with it," said Lafarge keeping his tone calm and controlled.

Lafarge remarked that Mathilde would gladly honour the deal now the manner in which she was looking at him. But it was too late for that.

THE TORTURED DETECTIVE

"Mathilde, tell him you were spinning a yarn," said von Dirlinger sternly,

However, Mathilde refused to change her story and remained silent.

"Futhermore colonel I obtained first–hand evidence of your connection with Lafont and Bonny last night. I notice that was not part of my day you referred to earlier, although, I am sure they informed you about how things turned out," said Lafarge.

Von Dirlinger looked slightly uncomfortable and moved to speak, only for Lafarge to put his finger to his lips.

"Now I know that you were not aware of what they had planned last night but nevertheless I already have you on one charge of attempted murder thanks to Mathilde's statement. More could ensue as the evening goes on," said Lafarge.

Von Dirlinger sighed deeply and crossed his legs, stroking the neat creases in his trousers.

"That is complete rubbish. I admit I told Bousquet to keep a firm grip on you, which he patently failed to do. However, it was only so your attention did not drift away from pursuing de Chastelain, who quite clearly had murdered Marguerite, and who you let get away," said von Dirlinger.

"However, having you killed wasn't in my plan at all, why on earth would I want you to die when I had nothing to fear from you?" he added raising his eyebrows.

"Simple, because you were getting worried that I was doing exactly what you feared and which Bousquet had not taken care of. I was paying too much attention to you and you feared I would uncover how deep your links were with Lafont and Bonny.

"Now I know lots of Germans are tied to them, but you have a rather different relationship with them. You are a silent partner and the last thing you would want is for your compatriots to learn you were taking a lot of their money.

"It's probably why you went off that night at the club leaving me with Mathilde, because you were afraid if you drank too much you would slip up. Hence your quickly hatched plan to be rid of me. I have to admire its inventiveness but it fails on its practicality," said Lafarge.

"Well thank you for the compliment. But again you are missing the point, why would I wish you dead? As far as I was aware you were due to go to Limoges and see if you could track down de Chastelain.

"I didn't take your interest in me very seriously. I accepted that you had to look into my story, but there was nothing in your behaviour or questions that duly alarmed me.

"As for the Bonny and Lafont connection there was absolutely nothing I saw that would lead back to me as they for once weren't suspects. Even when Bonny showed up here, you thought it was suspicious but couldn't see me, an aristocrat, mixing with them," said von Dirlinger.

Lafarge looked at Mathilde and wondered whether she had indeed spun him a line because von Dirlinger was convincing him that there was nothing credible in her claim. But then why would she lie?

Was it another of their games? He could leave it aside for the moment and come back to it later, see if anything came up in other matters that von Dirlinger talked about which gave him away.

"Well on the matter of the jewellery burglary I am afraid you are firmly in the mix," said Lafarge.

Von Dirlinger looked relieved that the matter of him ordering the murder of Lafarge had been dropped, and he held up his hands.

"Well it was too good an opportunity to pass on. Marguerite told me about it, her incessant search for protection and self–assurance.

"I told her that of course it would not lead back to her and that we could resolve the problem of de Chastelain. We would also make enough money to be financially secure for the rest of our lives," he said.

Lafarge was astonished at the insouciance of von Dirlinger, who had just admitted to a crime which not only would bring disgrace and ruin on him but also a prison sentence.

"I would reflect on what you just said colonel as if you stick to that story I will have to charge you," said Lafarge.

Von Dirlinger didn't flinch.

"No you won't. You are not going to charge a high ranking officer of the Abwehr with complicity after the fact in a burglary. That may have worked with Bousquet, but it will not play with my superiors," he said.

"Besides my work is invaluable to the German war effort, in particular to preventing a successful invasion of France by the

THE TORTURED DETECTIVE

Allies. Sadly that moment, of an invasion at least, is getting nearer by the day."

Lafarge had expected this ploy from von Dirlinger and he agreed with him that arresting him on a charge of accomplice after the fact would be given short shrift by his superiors. He would have to drop it but he was still pleased he had got him to confess to his role in the conspiracy.

"Yes that may not be enough for your superiors. However, the fact you conspired to have the other members of the ring got rid of may be regarded as worthy of punishing you," said Lafarge.

"How so?" asked von Dirlinger.

"Well you set up de Chastelain, firstly by having Marguerite warn him not to turn up in court to defend the burglar Lescarboura. By orchestrating that you denied Lescarboura the one man who could give him a proper defence, even more so because de Chastelain was also involved.

"Then not content at just making him a fugitive from justice you falsely pinpointed him as the murderer of Marguerite. That could bring a charge of wasting police time as well as a more serious one of obstructing justice," said Lafarge.

"I take it that when you said the burglary would take care of de Chastelain that is what you meant? Ridding yourself for good of the one rival for Marguerite's affection. Something which was apparent when you asked her and she complied to warn him of his impending arrest.

"Then you knew that she still harboured strong feelings for him and that irritated the hell out of you," said Lafarge, warming to his task.

Von Dirlinger tried to interrupt but Lafarge waved him aside. Mathilde simply remained mute, fiddling with her necklace.

"Bousquet was the only one of the gang that you could not oust so blatantly, for his work was, how would you put it, invaluable to the SS and the Nazi ideological war.

"However, conveniently you knew very quickly that I was the perfect weapon to use because of my longstanding dislike for the man. Thus you could sit back and allow me to take care of him, or turning it on its head we would both rub each other out. Well you got your result there too.

"Mathilde also furnished me with information that makes it even harder to accuse de Chastelain of murdering Marguerite. She told me she accompanied him down the stairs and saw Bousquet leaving and saying goodbye in both German and French, which can only lead to one conclusion that you were still in the apartment.

"Now she tells me that you have always protested that when you eventually left she was still alive. I am asking you face to face whether that is true or you did indeed murder her.

"For according to Bousquet the conversation was a lively one. Even he, a man who prefers to murder people with the impersonal stroke of a pen and not pull the trigger himself, felt the compunction to strangle her as she was incapable of telling you both where the jewels were.

"So if he didn't then there remains only one person who could have done and that is you colonel, unless of course it was Mathilde and de Chastelain," said Lafarge staring at Mathilde.

Von Dirlinger too looked at Mathilde his expression one of surprise. She looked aghast and scowled yet again.

"That is ludicrous Inspector! I don't know where the border between reality and fantasy end with you but this theory is outrageous!" she yelled.

"Is it Mathilde? After all we only have your testimony and that of de Chastelain, who is no longer here, to support your version. He did tell me that he had come down here on his own. You say to the contrary that you accompanied him. But is this yet again another false trail to throw me off the scent?" asked Lafarge.

"You know it's not possible that we murdered her. You heard two versions all but similar save that perhaps to protect me de Chastelain said he came down here alone. Why on earth would I give you an account protecting a man who has disappeared, it doesn't make any sense," she protested.

"That is true but this case has been an interesting one for I have been dealing with criminals above the normal level of intelligence. Masters at role-playing and games and you and de Chastelain could be the best of the lot.

"What did he promise you? That he could find the jewels and if you helped him with Marguerite he would share the spoils. You saw your chance to lift yourself out of this miserable situation you had found yourself in after the death of your husband.

344

THE TORTURED DETECTIVE

"One where you could be independent and live it as you wanted, be free of the constraints of the colonel and being Suzy Solidor's pathetic down at heel lover," Lafarge said viciously.

Those remarks hit the target, for Mathilde launched herself out of the chair, anger blazing from her eyes but also tears too. She went for Lafarge, grabbing him by the lapels, which he easily extricated himself from.

"Go to hell Lafarge! You disgust me, how dare you insult me and my life. What the hell do you know about it! I am not going to sit here and be abused and accused by you. You are the nastiest type of man, allowing your prejudices to overcome your sense of justice and judgement.

"Just because I wouldn't sleep with you, let alone allow a drunken sot to fiddle with me. You should take a good look at yourself. You are no angel, going around with all this anger and bitterness inside you believing you are righting wrongs done by your compatriots when you are no better than they are," she screamed before walking towards the kitchen.

Lafarge and von Dirlinger exchanged glances. The latter looked completely stunned by the latest turn of events, the former had everything under control.

"Colonel you stay here, I better go and see if I can stop her from leaving or at least calm her down. You stand by just in case I need you," said Lafarge looking all apologetic.

Von Dirlinger held his hands up and laughed.

"Well it's your show inspector, not only is it very entertaining but I am also intrigued. A few minutes ago I was the suspect and all of a sudden I am the innocent spectator.

"I am not altogether convinced that you have the right person but please feel free to bring her back in here as I can't wait for the climax," he said still laughing.

Lafarge strode across the room into the kitchen where there was no sign of Mathilde. He exited and made his way along the corridor to the main bedroom where he saw that the door was slightly ajar. He pushed it open and saw Mathilde bending over the dressing table, pulling open a drawer.

He hoped it wasn't a gun, so he all but ran over and slammed the drawer shut catching the tips of her fingers in it. He put her hand over her mouth to stop her making any noise and put his finger to his mouth.

She nodded so he released his hand but only so he could take the capsule out of his pocket, force her mouth open and then with both hands force her jaw shut so that she bit right down on the cyanide.

Her eyes widened, Lafarge thought it was a mix of fear and surprise, but it was too late to fight back for the poison took hold and she slumped down onto the floor.

He felt for a pulse but there was none. He walked back purposefully to the drawing room where von Dirlinger was still sitting.

"Colonel, you better come I think she has taken something," said Lafarge feigning concern.

He jumped to his feet and ran with Lafarge to the bedroom, though, the detective stopped at the door. Von Dirlinger went over to see if he could do anything for Mathilde. He looked up shaking his head and mouthed 'cyanide' only to stop.

"Colonel you know you were correct when you said you thought I had the wrong person for the murder of Marguerite. It wasn't you and it wasn't Mathilde, it was me," and with that Lafarge shot von Dirlinger twice in the head.

THE TORTURED DETECTIVE

CHAPTER THIRTY ONE

Lafarge sat in his study in Nice preparing for their departure for Spain, then Portugal, and a boat to Argentina.

He had been kept in Paris for a week while Massu, and when his boss allowed it, von Dirlinger's Abwehr colleagues asked him questions about what had happened in the apartment that night.

It had been easy for him. The Abwehr generally weren't prone to violence in their interrogations, too ungentlemanly for them. Like the Wehrmacht they preferred to see themselves as the honourable partners in the German crusade, but they were no idiots either.

So Lafarge had stuck by his story of how he had confronted von Dirlinger and accused him of the murder of Marguerite, whereupon eventually he confessed. Unfortunately Lafarge had allowed him to go and get his coat while his accomplice Mathilde had excused herself saying she was going back to her room before going out.

That was when he heard the shots.

He had been too late to save the colonel and before he could subdue Mathilde – who had feared that von Dirlinger would persuade Lafarge to just hold her responsible for the murder – she had bitten down on the capsule, which she must have taken from the drawer and within seconds was dead.

The gun Lafarge had used was von Dirlinger's. He had taken it from his holster, which had been hanging up in the dressing room adjacent to the bedroom, and following the shooting he had wiped it clean and pressed it into the hand of Mathilde.

The Abwehr were appalled at the potential scandal if this news leaked out.

Thus with the willing complicity of Massu and Lafarge they released a version whereby Colonel Karl von Dirlinger had been murdered by an ungrateful woman, who had never got over the death of her husband at the hands of the Germans. Feigning friendship she had gained his confidence only to strike him down in brutal and cowardly fashion.

It was all typical German pomposity thought Lafarge, but it suited his ends whatever way they couched it in.

The important thing was that Massu believed him and his confidence seeped into the consciousness of the Abwehr officers, who were keen to put any other rumours to rest.

Besides when they learnt from Lafarge of all the links between von Dirlinger and the French Gestapo their sympathy for their former colleague ebbed away.

This was sheer hypocrisy for Lafarge knew full well some of von Dirlinger's superiors had links to them too or had done in the past. However, again it suited his cause that they outwardly at least were appalled by their subordinate's behaviour.

He had been congratulated on bringing the case to a close and sent on his way, Massu allowing him to keep his police ID card in case one day he felt his place belonged back with them.

That was to prove useful one last time. Other than that Lafarge was finished with the police, well a triple murderer investigating murders might be useful to the force for his insiders view but in truth he had had his fill of the job.

Thus he returned for a final time to his apartment to bid Madame Grondon farewell, give her a handsome tip, pack some things and to leave Aimee a note should she not be there.

In fact she had been and they had celebrated, for a final time, as any married couple would do his release. In the morning he had left telling her she could stay for as long as she felt it was safe to do so, that Madame Grondon would not betray any friend of his.

He didn't try and excuse himself again for having betrayed her. In a way she understood although he equally didn't reveal the whole truth behind his Machiavellian plan, but he felt sad as he bid her farewell for the final time.

For she unlike the others in the affair was a genuinely good person and he hoped she would see the war out. He also left content that he had erased his debt to her by offering her a safe house.

Madame Grondon assured him that she would be well looked after and they too had a tearful parting, the old lady telling him he was a good and decent man, which coming from her made him feel better than he should have done.

Thus it was that he found the police ID card useful on one last occasion. For before returning to Nice he passed by the farm belonging to Marguerite Suchet's parents and flashing the badge

THE TORTURED DETECTIVE

told them he was the man responsible for solving their daughter's murder.

Naturally they were extremely grateful and allowed him to search through the things in her room, which remained like a shrine to her.

Framed photographs of her, alone in studio promotional shots and at premieres surrounded by admirers and friends, were hung up or sat on the table and desk in the room. He gave them the briefest of glances because it was the chest of drawers he was most interested in.

It didn't take long for him to find at the bottom of the drawer, containing her lingerie, a neatly wrapped package which on unwrapping it before him lay the jewels.

Mathilde it was who had alerted him to the possible whereabouts of the missing jewels when she said that Marguerite had paid a visit to her parents after the burglary. To Lafarge it had made sense, it was the safest place to hide them. They were her life insurance and her nest egg for her childhood friend Lescarboura and whichever man she decided was to be hers.

He sighed and thought well they are mine now and wrapping them back up he put them in his briefcase. He had then had to go through the excruciating experience of lunch with her parents, who had laid out a fine spread for him as he discovered when he descended the stairs.

There he sat making polite conversation with the parents of the girl he had murdered and with the jewels that had sparked the whole sequence of events, or was it sequins he joked darkly to himself, beside him in his briefcase.

Now as he sat looking out the window into the garden where the children were playing with Isabella, he remembered the look of surprise in both Marguerite and von Dirlinger's faces as he killed them.

He of course would never reveal to his wife the truth. He would perhaps one day put it all on paper, for to him it wasn't murder in the strictest definition of the term.

It was him acting as a lone resistant. Far easier and safer too because there was nobody one had to rely on and trust, equally to be afraid that if the others were caught you could be the next to receive a call at the door.

Being a policeman of course had helped. A maverick is always going to be regarded with suspicion, but only from a political point of view and a man as arrogant as Bousquet would never have thought Lafarge was capable of concocting such a plan.

True it had all started on impulse. The pathetic Marguerite in her ceaseless search for protection and placing her trust in anyone that held any authority, had called him and asked him to come to her apartment.

He must have arrived only minutes after von Dirlinger had left and he had found her in a terrible state.

Although they had not seen each other since before the war, she said she had always held him in high regard and knew she could trust him.

Thus she had given him the whole story from the origins of the burglary to the enrolling of both von Dirlinger and Bousquet in the ring.

Lafarge had not thought much about it until she mentioned Bousquet's name. De Chastelain he didn't like but he was now a figure of the past as he was on the run and von Dirlinger well at the time he meant little to the detective except he was just another German colonel.

But Bousquet now there was a man he would love to bring down.

Quite aside from their personal animosity he was disgusted at how he had enthusiastically embraced collaborating with the enemy. Worse he had accepted a position that could only lead to authorizing dishonourable acts in the name of France, not because of his ideological beliefs but because of naked ambition.

Lafarge had witnessed firsthand on the front line how the Germans behaved.

Even the better regarded Wehrmacht had acted with such savagery towards civilians and prisoners of war that he had thought if they are seen to be the good bad guys what on earth are the SS and the Gestapo like?

Thus once Marguerite said Bousquet had been there that evening Lafarge knew he had been presented with a golden opportunity to harass the secretary–general. He would try and sew enough suspicion around him that it could not only destroy him but also undermine Vichy in both the Nazis and the French people's eyes.

THE TORTURED DETECTIVE

Lafarge had consoled Marguerite about the invidious position she found herself in, although he didn't really feel that way at all. In reality he regarded her with nothing but contempt, and the idea of killing her and then implicating Bousquet and the colonel, was too attractive a possibility to pass over.

Lafarge had played the role perfectly of the sympathetic listener as she recounted the quandary she found herself in, being bullied by her lover and threatened by the overbearing and glacial Bousquet over the stolen jewels and their whereabouts.

But she had said, smiling confidently, their hiding place was her security and she would never surrender that information. However, she wanted Lafarge to keep an eye out for her, to keep his ears open at work or better still to try and wean his way in to becoming a trusted lieutenant of Bousquet's.

Lafarge had thought then that she really was deluded if she thought he could be won over to playing a role he had no taste for by her charm and sweet smiles.

It had been easy to procure von Dirlinger's gun. He had excused himself to go to the bathroom and instead had walked into the dressingroom. Sure enough, just as would happen the evening he disposed of von Dirlinger and Mathilde, the colonel had left in his holster a charged pistol.

Lafarge had barely even reflected on the fact that he was about to commit murder, let alone that the victim was a woman.

The only thing he saw in front of him was the chance to destroy Bousquet and inflict a damaging wound on Vichy. People would see that Vichy for all its pompous declarations on purity and moral values had a head of police, their young turk, who was himself little better than the criminals that his police force sought to track down.

In any case he had justified the death of Marguerite as just another civilian victim. One more to lay alongside the hundreds of thousands that had already perished, mown down or blown up by a sociopathic regime intent on spreading its evil and hateful ideology all across Europe.

Armed with both the weapon and his sense of righteousness he had found it a simple task to execute his mission. He had felt nothing as he swivelled round when he reached the mantelpiece and shot her hitting her once.

Then luck had fallen his way, in avoiding de Chastelain and Mathilde when he left and even more so when Massu appointed him to the case. Bousquet had acquiesced in his nomination although he had told him later he had wanted him removed. But he knew it would be difficult to justify it as he was the best homicide detective on the force.

How he must have regretted that decision once Lafarge found his cigarette case and linked the murder with the burglary.

That had been a moment of genuine delight for Lafarge, for without any eye witness testimony Bousquet would have started to suspect that Lafarge appeared to know a lot about a crime. Even for a man of his talents.

Lafarge had been only too happy to play along with the de Chastelain angle and indeed his desire to catch him was as great as Bousquet and von Dirlinger's, only for different reasons.

For de Chastelain could provide first hand testimony implicating the good colonel and Bousquet. However, Lafarge was never going to allow those two to get their hands on the lawyer. It would have totally screwed up his plan for a scapegoat to take the blame.

De Chastelain too would never be around to seek vengeance on him, were he to commit pen to paper. This was the greatest irony. The man who he had entrusted the lawyer's safety and eventual escape from France, Dr Petiot, the caring and effective general practitioner, had just been exposed as a serial killer.

The address where Lafarge had left de Chastelain had been revealed as a charnel house, with bones and fragments of people's bodies lying in a pit, their belongings or some of them strewn round the uninhabited house. Massu had taken charge of the case, for this was of such magnitude only his calm assurance and powers of detection could be counted on to solve it.

Massu had called Lafarge in the early morning after the gruesome discovery to ask him if he would return for one last time, but he had declined. He thought it too much of a risk for if Petiot was arrested he could if he so wished identify him as having delivered de Chastelain to him.

Questions would be asked as to why he had aided a wanted man to escape justice which would have set Massu off thinking over the Suchet murder. Lafarge didn't think he would be capable to outwit the master detective, he would have slipped up somewhere.

THE TORTURED DETECTIVE

Thus he rejected Massu's request in the politest of terms saying that he was finished with police work and he wanted to look towards the future with his family.

That was what he stared out on now. His beautiful wife ordering their young children to come inside for bath time, and asking them for the umpteenth time that day had they packed everything they wanted to keep for they were leaving for a new life...

Lafarge knew it wouldn't be easy to leave behind the memories of the past two years but he could live with that, there were many like Bousquet who he prayed would find it not so simple.

EPILOGUE

Lafarge stood by the rail of the liner, Isabella and the children beside him, as they looked out on the Atlantic Ocean, which they had now been cutting through for the past three days.

They and hundreds of others had been fortunate enough to gain passage in Lisbon on an Argentinian registered vessel, the Simon Bolivar, bound for the Uruguayan capital of Montevideo. From there a ferry would transport them across to Buenos Aires and their new life.

It had taken them three weeks to make the journey from Nice to Lisbon. A hard trek across the Pyrenees had been the worst of it, but the children had borne it well and Lafarge had been justifiably proud of them for their resilience and lack of moaning and whining.

Once over the border into Spain their lives had been far more comfortable.

His father–in–law had organized with the Argentine embassy in Madrid for a car to come and pick them up. After a stopover for several days in the Spanish capital, where they were able to recuperate and relax, they set off in high spirits for Lisbon.

With Isabella's father, being held in high regard by the Peron regime in Argentina, they were allocated a large and comfortable cabin on the ship, with a bathroom to boot.

They were the fortunate ones. The passengers for the most part were either crammed into cabins which were only used to at the most four people, the sanitary facilities were negligible, and many preferred to sleep up on deck.

The food too, apart from for people like Lafarge and his family, was of poor quality, but the majority of the ship's human cargo put up with the privations. They were just happy to be leaving a continent devastated by war and setting out for a new life in a country, which while run by a dictator, at least offered peace and new opportunities.

Lafarge spent most of the time reading or walking with the children on deck. They tried to catch sight of the dolphins or other species of fish which rose to the surface and swam alongside the

THE TORTURED DETECTIVE

boat, hoping the remains from what meals were served would be thrown their way.

The children, especially, found this amusing and diverted them from other moments when squalls hit the ship and they would have to retire inside and lounge around while the boat rocked from the stormy weather.

They were now out on the deck, after one of those squalls had passed over, after emerging to see if there were new breeds of fish swimming alongside, when Pierre nudged Lafarge.

Lafarge turned to him slightly annoyed at his elbow having connected with his ribs.

"What do you do that for Pierre?" he asked tetchily.

Pierre smiled and pointed with his little hand.

"Look papa. Those two fish are swimming straight at the boat, normally they swim alongside it," he said.

Lafarge looked down and saw the two 'fish' that Pierre had pointed out and they were indeed going very fast below the surface. Lafarge put his hand protectively over his son's eyes, and with his other arm he held Isabella and his daughter tight, and then as the 'fish' hit the ship with two great bangs the sky went dark.

f

HISTORICAL NOTE

While the majority of the characters are fictional several are real and below is a short account of what happened to some of them:

René Bousquet

Following his resignation he and his family were taken to Bavaria by the Nazis and kept there till the end of the war. Brought back to France he remained in prison – he stayed faithful to Laval and passed the time with him in his cell throughout the night prior to the former Prime Minister's execution. He was put on trial in 1949, the last of the main protagonists of the Vichy Government, who hadn't escaped justice, to be tried. Extraordinary as it may seem at the time he was not charged over the deportation of the Jews, some say that the then French government preferred such unsavoury matters were not brought up four years after the end of the war, and thus received a light sentence. Shameless as ever he became an advisor to the bank of Indochina and supported Francois Mitterrand financially in his presidential election campaigns against General de Gaulle, all of them unsuccessful. Eventually most people including the judicial authorities came to disagree with Mitterrand, whose own role under Vichy was subject to debate though of far less importance than Bousquet's, and he was charged in 1991 with crimes against humanity. However, one of those lone gunmen, a French version of Jack Ruby, gained access to Bousquet's apartment block and shot him dead when he answered the door in 1993 – he was 84. A lot of people breathed a sigh of relief that Bousquet had been silenced before perhaps he exposed them in court. For others, though, it erased any chance of seeing one of the coldest, most callous and able characters of the Vichy regime finally answer for his true crimes.

Jean Leguay

He was made Prefect of the Orne department of France following his resignation from his post as deputy to Bousquet in December 1943. Persona non grata post the Liberation he managed to escape to the United States where he worked for a cosmetics company, they probably being unaware of his unsavoury war record which had seen him organise the trains to deport the Jews and other undesirables and execute Bousquet's orders on the ground. He eventually returned to France and worked for a research laboratory near Paris. His past finally and belatedly caught up with him when the former Vichy appointed Commissioner for the Jewish Question Louis Darquier de Pellepoix – who had escaped certain execution by making his way to Spain after the Liberation – revealed in an interview both Leguay's and Bousquet's integral role in the deportation of the Jews. Leguay was charged in 1978 with crimes against humanity but incredibly 11 years later on his death aged 80 he had yet to face trial. Many believe that like Bousquet, powerful political figures were nervous what Leguay might say were he to have his day in court.

Pierre Drieu La Rochelle

He was a much admired writer and remained close to several – including Andre Malraux – who disagreed with his virulent anti–Semitic views and blind devotion to the Nazis. However, this veteran of the Great War did not forget his friends either as he intervened to have the writer Jean Paulhan released in May 1941. He came to doubt his belief in Fascism being the future and that the Nazis would win the war. He went into hiding on the liberation of Paris but increasingly desperate as the authorities searched for him he succeeded in committing suicide, after two failed attempts, on March 15 1945. His phrase published posthumously sums up his rather cynical attitude by the time of his death: 'We played, I lost. I ask for death.'

Otto Abetz

The German ambassador was a cultivated man, who made much of his francophilia. However, that did not extend to those who were considered to be members of the countless organizations that the Nazis despised and outlawed and certainly not the Jews. He supported Laval through thick and thin – earning a reprimand from the Nazis in Berlin at one juncture – but remained at his post, a brief interlude apart, until the eve of the liberation of Paris. Arrested in October 1945 he was sentenced to 20 years hard labour in 1949, but was released in 1953. He died aged 55 as a result of injuries sustained in a car crash in 1958.

Doctor Marcel Petiot

On the exterior a well regarded general practitioner. However, in reality he was a highly intelligent but most probably certifiably mad ingenious moneymaking serial killer. Doubts had already arisen about several patients disappearing prior to the war but had been dismissed for want of concrete evidence. However, in the chaos of war he flourished inventing the story that he provided an escape route for the many people who wished to get away either from the Nazis or from the Bonny and Lafont French Gestapo. Some have alluded to the possibility that he received aid from the Germans, who were attracted by the riches he accrued from his victims, and also the French Gestapo. Whatever the truth he took it with him to the guillotine, after a farce of a trial helped no end by his mischief making. He was found guilty of 27 cases of murder, although he claimed he had only murdered collaborators. The morning of his execution, May 25 1946, he joked to one of the delegation that came to his cell that he looked deathly pale and if he wished he could give him an injection. His final words as he was strapped to the guillotine were: 'Look away. This will not be pretty to see.'

Pierre Bonny and Henri Lafont

Bonny and Lafont were arrested in the summer of 1944 while hiding out in a farm having declined to take flight with their German friends. At their trial Bonny divested himself of all blame laying it at Lafont's door. Lafont was defended by Petiot's lawyer René Floriot, but the latter like with Petiot later was unable to save his client. Bonny's pathetic efforts at trying to avoid all responsibility failed and he was executed by firing squad alongside his partner on December 26, 1944. Several of their gang were also executed but others succeeded in escaping to South America while others flourished in France thanks to powerful political godfathers, whose campaigns were no doubt funded from the French Gestapo's loot from the war.

George–Victor Massu

Despite his herculean efforts in tracking down Petiot and other criminals in Paris during the Occupation, after the Liberation, he was arrested and tried for collaborating with the enemy. He was so desperate that he tried to commit suicide while in prison but was saved and it was fortunate for him as he was to be cleared of all charges. He returned to the police force and he was the inspiration, though not 100 percent of it, of his friend Georges Simenon's legendary character Inspector Maigret.

THE TORTURED DETECTIVE

SUGGESTED FURTHER READING

Several historical books about this darkest of periods in French history proved educational in terms of background. They were primarily:

Death in the City of Light by David King

And The Show Went On – Cultural life in Nazi–Occupied Paris by Alan Riding

Americans in Paris by Charles Glass

*

Printed in Great Britain
by Amazon